RYMELLAN 4

SARAH ETTRITCH

DECISIONS

NORN PUBLISHING

KINGSTON, CANADA

Copyright © 2022 Sarah Ettritch

All rights reserved. No part of this book may be reproduced,
except for brief quotations in articles or reviews,
without written permission from the author.

This is a work of fiction. Names, characters, places, and incidents
are the product of the author's imagination or are used fictitiously,
and any resemblance to actual persons, living or dead, business
establishments, events, or locales is entirely coincidental.

ISBN 978-1-927369-66-1

Cover design by Boulevard Photografica/Patty G. Henderson

First Printing September 2022
v1

Published by Norn Publishing
www.NornPublishing.com

For Jennifer

CONTENTS

.....

LOVE DISMISSED

.....

RUTH CLOSED HER EYES AND FOCUSED on the hum generated by the energy cells, listening for the pulse that should occur every 1.25 seconds. Even though the maintenance bay was buzzing with activity, her trained ear was able to pick up the pulses over the voices of her colleagues and the hums of other fighters. There, and there, and there. She opened her eyes, read the figures on the panel in front of her, and shut down the fighter's energy cells.

Yesterday David had jogged over to her after finishing his shift, complaining his flyer didn't sound right. Mechanics and pilots developed an ear for such things, knew instantly when a fighter sounded off. It had taken Ruth less than five minutes to diagnose the problem. A faulty cell almost drained of energy. Healthy ones wouldn't drain so quickly and could be charged. The one she'd replaced had been on its deathbed.

"Lieutenant."

Ruth turned and pasted a smile on her face.

Her superior, Lieutenant Commander Addison, gestured at the fighter. "Leave that for now. I have to talk to you."

She'd finished anyway. A minute later, she stood at attention in Addison's office. Her previous two supervisors had never insisted on ceremony, but Addison was different. Unfortunately Ruth had taken an instant dislike to her, and the feeling was mutual. Neither of them had done anything to offend the other; it was just one of those things. Addison always seemed to be smirking and had a superior air about her that went beyond her rank and position. Her office walls were plastered with accolades going back to her Learning Academy days. The reward Ruth had received for tying her shoelaces had long since been recycled, but Addison apparently still cherished hers.

Addison plunked into her chair. Ruth had the feeling that if it wouldn't be entirely inappropriate, the woman would lean her chair back as far as it would go and put her feet on her desk.

"I have wonderful news for you, Lieutenant," Addison said. "You've heard about the *Harrier*?

Who hadn't? The *Harrier* was the Rymellan fleet's newest ship, though inaccurately named, in Ruth's opinion. It wasn't a warship, but a research ship, powered by the latest and greatest energy cells and carrying state-of-the-art equipment.

"It will be taking its maiden voyage five weeks after the *Falcon* docks," Addison said, not waiting for Ruth to answer. "Everyone wants a spot on board, of course. There are way more applicants than spaces." A smile played on her lips. "Our best people are already on tour, so every ship was asked to sacrifice a few, maintenance included. I put your name forward, and it was accepted. Congratulations. You'll report to the *Harrier* for its first voyage."

Excitement made her stiffen, but it was quickly replaced with concern. What about Shay?

"Your orders will be dispatched to you shortly. Our loss will be the *Harrier*'s gain, of course. We'll be sorry to see you go."

Her peers would be sorry to see her go. Addison would dance a jig when the *Falcon* departed on its next tour without Ruth on it. She'd never interfered with Ruth's career, though. Until now. To be fair, every mechanic would jump at this chance and would have felt the initial burst of excitement Ruth had experienced. But not every mechanic was in a long-term relationship with another Solitary. They wouldn't be standing here desperately hoping their beloved would receive new orders, too.

Addison frowned. "I thought you'd be pleased."

"I am." Ruth wouldn't ask if the orders were final until she talked to Shay. "Thank you for putting my name forward."

"It was my pleasure. You're an excellent mechanic, Lieutenant. The

Harrier will be lucky to have you." Addison flicked on her comm station. "You can return to your duties now."

Ruth whirled and marched from the office. She wouldn't meet Shay in the canteen for another two hours. Time would drag.

The moment she returned to her station to update the fighter's maintenance log, Ian came over to talk to her. They were around the same age and had worked together in maintenance since she'd come aboard the *Falcon*.

"What was that all about?" he asked.

Addison hadn't said she couldn't tell anyone. "I've been transferred off the *Falcon*," she said, loud enough so he would hear her over the ever-present hum of energy cells. Nobody whispered on the launch and maintenance deck. "I'll be going out on the *Harrier*."

His eyes widened. "Lucky you! Did she say if anyone else will be transferring?"

"No. But that doesn't mean nobody else will be."

"What about Sheila?"

That was the critical question. She did not want to be separated from Shay again. "I don't know yet. I hope so."

"I'd love to be on the *Harrier*. Next generation fighters, the new quad-yield cells." His voice was filled with awe.

Ruth didn't want to come across as ungrateful, and this could be fantastic news. It all depended on Shay. "They've been flying those fighters out of the stations for the past year." Mo had told her the last time they'd lunched together on 72. "New models are always flown closer to home first."

"Maybe I should transfer back to 68."

Ian had been stationed there before getting a tour. Ruth had spent her first few years on 72.

"Congrats are in order." Ian scratched his cheek. "I'd be lying if I said I'm not jealous. Put in a good word for me with your new supervisor."

She cocked her head. "I'll think about it."

He grinned and went back to his station.

For the rest of her shift, Ruth did her best to concentrate on her work but couldn't help wondering what she'd do if Shay didn't receive orders to report to the *Harrier* next tour. They'd survived their last separation, savouring the handful of weeks they had together whenever the *Falcon* was docked. Ruth hoped they'd survive another one, especially when the two ships' docking schedules didn't coincide. Unless one or both of them received a transfer, it could be years before they saw each other again. Even the strongest relationships would wither under those conditions. Including theirs.

WHEN RUTH ENTERED the canteen on Deck 9, Shay was already at their usual table tucked away in a corner away from the windows. Nobody ever wanted that table, but it suited them fine. They both had plenty of opportunity at other times to gaze into the almost perfect vacuum of space, especially Shay, who flew most days. When they ate here together, they preferred to be as alone as they could be in public.

Ruth pecked her on the cheek and sat down across from her. Within a minute, she knew Shay hadn't received orders. Shay wasn't one to hold anything back. Orders to transfer to the *Harrier* would have had her almost dancing on the table—once she knew Ruth had them too. But nothing. Just the normal "How was your day?" and all that.

She waited until they were almost finished eating to suggest a change of plan. "I know we said we'd hang out on the observation deck for a while and then see whether there's a game of cards going anywhere, but can we go back to our quarters instead?"

Shay waggled her brows. "Sure," she said, in a way that conveyed she expected a romantic evening in. "Sounds great."

Maybe they *would* spend a romantic evening together. It would depend on how Shay reacted when Ruth told her the news. She wished she'd had the presence of mind to go to their quarters first and put away anything breakable.

As soon as they entered their quarters and the door had slid shut behind them, Shay slipped her arms around Ruth's waist. "We haven't spent an entire evening together like this in a while," she said, moving in to nuzzle Ruth's neck.

Ruth pressed her hands against Shay's shoulders and gently pushed her back. "I need to talk to you first, the reason I wanted to come here. But," she said, when Shay's face fell, "after we've talked, I'm game for staying in."

Shay grinned. "Nothing bad, then."

"It depends." Ruth swallowed. "I received new orders today. I'm being transferred off the *Falcon*, onto the *Harrier*."

Shay stared at her. Her fists clenched.

"You didn't get new orders," Ruth said slowly.

"No, I flaming-well didn't." Shay stomped over to the sofa, grabbed a cushion, and flung it against the wall.

Ruth eyed the glass sculpture of 72 they both adored. It was sitting on the small round table next to the sofa. She darted over to it, in case she needed to save it from being shattered into pieces. "Maybe pilots will be getting their orders later."

"Or maybe I'm not being transferred," Shay snarled. Her eyes were wild. She marched to the door, then back to Ruth. "I'm going to see Baker."

"Now?"

"Yes, now. I want to find out what he knows." She stomped back to the door and punched the *Open* button.

Ruth reached for her, even though Shay was too far away to touch. "Shay don't—"

Shay disappeared through the doorway.

"—say anything stupid." Ruth blew out a long sigh. She wanted to go after her, but it would only aggravate Shay further, who would not see it as being supportive. Hopefully Baker would overlook any insubordination. He'd know what a blow it would be if they were separated again.

She sank onto the sofa. *Separated again.* She couldn't bear the thought, let alone the reality.

SHEILA WANTED TO roar with frustration as she rode the elevator up to Baker's deck and marched along the corridor to his quarters. How dare they? How dare they do it to them again? Four flaming years last time, four flaming years that had felt like an eternity, with dispatches the only thing keeping their relationship alive. Finally, finally, Ruth had been transferred to the *Falcon*, and now she was being transferred off again? Hadn't one person who'd handled the transfer orders—and there would be a few on the *Falcon*—stopped and thought, "You know, Sheila and Ruth have been in a serious relationship for years. Maybe we should keep them together."

No, probably not. Because they weren't flaming Chosens, so their relationship didn't count. She wanted to scream and knock the flaming stupid portrait of some former officer to the floor, which would be difficult because it was bolted to the corridor's wall.

She stopped outside Baker's door and took a moment to calm herself. Normally she wouldn't disturb him off-duty, but she needed to know, and she needed to know now. She pressed the door chime. The door slid open. Baker peered down at her.

Sheila clasped her hands behind her back. "I'm sorry for disturbing you, Commander, but I need to ask you something urgent."

Baker glanced over his shoulder, making Sheila wonder if someone was there. He stepped into the corridor and waited until the door had shut behind him. "What's on your mind?"

"The *Harrier*. I'm wondering if any pilots will be transferred over for its first tour."

"I doubt it. Why?"

"Because Ruth has received transfer orders. If I don't go over, we'll be separated." Her voice sounded shrill. She reminded herself it wasn't Baker's fault.

He made a calming motion with his hand. "When did this happen?"

"Today. If pilots from the *Falcon* aren't going over, why are mechanics?"

"Let me look into it." Baker grimaced. "But I'm fairly certain no pilots will be going. I'd be the first to know."

"I thought there was some unwritten rule about keeping long-term Solitary couples together."

He nodded, but his words dashed Sheila's hopes. "I've heard that rumour. I'm afraid it's not true."

Then Ruth's transfer to the *Falcon*, after they'd been separated for four years, had been luck. Dumb luck. They were at the whims of military bureaucrats.

"I'll look into why mechanics are going over." Baker smiled at her, a weak smile that didn't reach his eyes.

She couldn't muster one in return. "Thank you." She strode away, not wanting to keep him from whoever was waiting for him in his quarters.

When she entered her own quarters, Ruth was sitting on the sofa. Her eyes searched Sheila's face.

"He doesn't know anything." Sheila sat next to Ruth and took her hand. "He'll poke around tomorrow, try to find out why you're going over. But as far as he knows, no pilots are going." A lump rose in her throat at the sight of Ruth's glistening eyes. "That rule about not separating Solitary couples if they've lasted three years. It doesn't exist."

Anger yanked her hand from Ruth's and forced her to her feet. "Any idiot bureaucrat working in personnel deployment can separate us," she spat, placing her hands together and pulling them apart in one smooth motion.

"What can we do about it?" Ruth sounded tired.

"Nothing. That's the whole flaming point." She stared down at her. "Did you ask to be transferred?"

Ruth's eyes widened. "No."

"Are you sure? You weren't down there in mechanics talking about how wonderful the *Harrier* must be and how you'd love to see it. You didn't go on about how much you'd love to work on the new fighters."

"No, I did not," Ruth said evenly.

"Then why has this happened?" she shouted.

"I don't know, but I do know it's not my fault."

"You're the one going."

Ruth shot to her feet. "And you're staying. So what? Do you think I want to go without you?"

"I don't know. Maybe you asked for this transfer."

"Why would I do that? Why?"

"Maybe you wanted a little freedom, like the last time we were separated." The moment the words were out of her mouth, Sheila wanted to take them back.

Ruth's face tightened. "Don't do this."

"What?" she asked, knowing full well what Ruth meant.

"Take it out on me. I know you're angry. I get it. But it's not my fault."

Sheila walked away from her and took a moment to breathe. "I don't know if I can go back to seeing you a few weeks a year." She softly snorted. "No, I do know. I can't do it again. I can't." She turned back to Ruth. "I can't."

"I don't want to do it either, Shay. Let's sit down and come up with a plan."

"What plan? You're going, I'm not."

"I'll have to go on the one tour. I can ask for a transfer after that."

Her chest tightened. "Remember how long it took for you to get the *Falcon* last time? And transferring off the *Harrier*, back here? That won't look good."

"I don't care how it looks. And maybe I won't transfer to the *Falcon*. Maybe I'll ask for a space station. You can do the same. Or you could try for the *Harrier*."

Sheila vigorously shook her head. "The only way we'll guarantee that we'll see each other is if one of us doesn't go on tour. We'd have to stall our careers, limit ourselves, to stay together. It's not fair. If we were Chosens, we wouldn't even be having this discussion."

"But we're not."

When Ruth reached for her, Sheila willingly let herself be hugged, but her anger still simmered. It wasn't fair, wasn't fair that Chosens were never separated, but two Solitaries in a long-term relationship could be torn apart without any consideration for how it would affect them. She and Ruth had given years of their lives to the military, had endured a four-year near total separation for it. In return, nothing. Their sacrifice hadn't earned them a note in their personnel files, stating that every effort should be made to keep them together. To the military, they weren't connected in any way. They were Lieutenant Commander Sheila Dorrington and Lieutenant Ruth Simms, to be toyed with in any way the military saw fit.

She wrapped her arms around Ruth and held her tight. "I can't do this again, Ruthie. I can't."

"We'll figure something out," Ruth whispered.

Would they? How? Any plan they came up with would mean at least one of them asking for a transfer she didn't want. Fourteen years, and where had it got them? Sheila thought back to when they'd gotten together, wondering if they would have pursued a relationship if they'd known what a struggle it would be to stay together.

AFTER FINISHING OFF a lunch that always tasted better on the day everyone was leaving on break, Sheila returned her dirty dishes to the rack and left the Military Academy's mess hall, wondering how long she should wait for a dispatch that might never arrive. When she'd asked for a time slot for this afternoon, the attendant had said there weren't any available, but she could go on the waiting list in case one opened up. Ever the optimist, Sheila had agreed. But nothing yet. So while all her friends had already raced down the steps to the train station to head home for their break, she was still here, waiting and hoping.

She left the mess hall and wandered around aimlessly with the sun beating down on her, willing her comm unit to beep. Sweat beaded on her brow. She was itching to get out of her uniform, but it would have to wait until she got home. And she was not leaving for home until she'd given her flaming comm unit every chance to beep twice.

When it finally did, she wondered if she was imagining it. She quickly checked the dispatch and was about to whoop and pump her fist into the air, when she realized she needed a partner. The dispatch said two cadets.

Now, this was a problem. Most of the other cadets had left for home already. The entire reason Sheila had tried for simulator time today was because she'd figured her chances would be better. She'd done the same thing last break and whenever some event was happening that many cadets would attend. Her plan had worked, but so far, she'd only flown solo missions, so when she'd put her name on the waiting list this time, she'd specified two simulators, planning to link up with another cadet.

Then she'd forgotten to line up the other cadet. Nobody would ever accuse her of overplanning, okay?

If she showed up alone, whoever was working the counter at the sim centre wouldn't be pleased. Sheila did not want to annoy anyone connected to sims or pilots in any way, worried that doing so would jeopardize her chances of getting into the fighter pilot program.

She mentally ran through the list of cadets she knew were going for the program. David had gone home, she'd just said good-bye to Mo and Lesley before she'd sat down for lunch, and they always flew sims together anyway. Patrick was gone, Mike was gone, Janice was gone, and so was Ann.

She continued to run through names, only vaguely aware of where she was going. Then she stopped dead. Up ahead, a cadet sat on a bench, staring at her comm unit.

Ruth.

Sheila believed she was trying for the program, but she wasn't sure if Ruth had been in a simulator yet. Not ideal. Ruth kept to herself and had maybe said two words to Sheila the entire time she'd been at the academy. Also not ideal. But Sheila was desperate, and Ruth was there. She squared her shoulders and strode up to her.

"Hi," she said cheerfully.

Ruth didn't look up.

"Hello?"

Now Ruth's head came up. "You're blocking the sun."

"Sorry." Sheila plunked down next to her. "You're going to try out for the fighter pilot program, right?"

"Do you always bother people when they're obviously doing something else?" Ruth said, her attention still on her comm unit.

"Not always. But I have simulator time in fifteen minutes and I'd like to link with another cadet." She grinned when Ruth finally turned her way. "Have you ever flown in a sim before?"

"No. There never seems to be an open spot."

"You have to book off hours. Really off hours." Another tactic Sheila had used to get time in a simulator. "I booked time for 04:00 once."

"I'll have to try that." Ruth's eyes went back to her comm unit.

"You could go in a simulator right now. Link with me. I'll show you the ropes."

"I don't know," Ruth murmured.

"Look, if you're trying for the program, you need sim time. Seriously. And I'm offering it to you. Like I said, just about everyone else has been in one at least once. You're already behind."

Ruth huffed a sigh and tore her eyes away from her comm unit again. She gazed at Sheila for a few seconds. "Do you really have simulator time?"

"Yes!" She almost added, "Why the flaming else would I talk to you?"

but stopped herself just in time. She needed the woman. "I'm dropping an opportunity right in your lap. You do want to get into the fighter pilot program, right?"

Ruth slid her comm unit into its holder. "Okay, why not? I'm not leaving for another few hours, anyway."

"Great. Come on."

On the way to the pilot training complex, Sheila tried to engage her in conversation. "How come you're still here?"

"Why are *you* still here?" Ruth said, without looking at her.

"Because I put in a request for sim time for today and got put on the waiting list. I stayed in case a slot opened up. And guess what? One did."

"But you're going home later?"

Sheila nodded. "Are you?"

"Yes."

"But not for a few hours."

"Right."

Ruth didn't offer any details as to why she hadn't already left, and Sheila didn't care. She'd run her through the basics for ten or fifteen minutes, and then they'd have almost two glorious hours left to run missions requiring two pilots. The more sim time she had, the more likely she'd ace the fighter pilot program entrance evaluation and live her dream.

SHEILA STUMBLED FROM the simulator and waited for Ruth to emerge from hers. The moment Ruth did, Sheila doubled over with laughter. "I think you busted my ear drums," she said between gasps.

Ruth smiled sheepishly. "It was my first time doing that spiral. I almost lost my lunch."

"Shay," Sheila said, her voice pitched high. "Shaaaaay!"

"I was trying to say Sheila. My next words would have been, 'I think I'm dying.' But I couldn't get the words out. I felt like my body was being ripped apart."

Sheila wiped a tear from her eye. "The first time I did it, I remember almost throwing up. I was alone, though."

"How fortunate for you. I didn't need an audience." Ruth's cheeks were flushed and her eyes bright.

Sheila's breath quickened. A familiar warmth stirred within her. She swallowed, her throat tight. "I won't tell anyone."

"You'd better not."

They strode back to the equipment room and handed in their helmets. "Time to catch a train," Sheila said. "You going to the train station too?"

"I've got to pick up my bag."

"Perfect. Me too."

Ruth frowned, creating the cute little dimple in the middle of her forehead Sheila had only noticed on their way to the training complex. She hadn't really paid much attention to Ruth before. She remembered making small talk with her during orientation, but Ruth had sort of got lost in all the classes and groups after that. Sheila hadn't gone out of her way to ignore her, but Ruth never seemed to initiate a conversation. Now she realized Ruth wasn't anti-social, but shy, and rather private. All the time she spent on her own might not be by choice. Everyone had assumed Ruth hung back because she wasn't interested in making friends.

Sheila realized she'd like to fly sims with Ruth more often. Sure, Ruth had made a ton of mistakes, but it had been her first time. They'd still managed to complete an easy mission.

She plucked up her courage to ask her after they'd picked up their bags and were strolling to the train station. "You want to fly more sims together after the break?"

Ruth took her time answering. The sweat beading on Sheila's brow wasn't due to the sun.

"Sure," Ruth finally said.

"Great. I'll book a slot. Do you prefer dawn or middle of the night?"

"Aren't they pretty much the same thing, depending on the time?"

"Sometimes."

"Either one is okay for me. Actually, no. I'd prefer dawn."

"I'll book us in." Something to do on the train. "Where do you live?"

"B8."

Different trains, then. Too bad.

"You?" Ruth asked.

"B3."

"Opposite direction."

"Yeah."

They reached the top of the stairs leading down to the train platform. Ruth stopped and turned to Sheila. "Thanks for, you know, taking me along."

"No problem." Sheila couldn't resist. "Shaaaaay!"

Ruth chuckled. "That's what I'm going to call you from now on. Shay."

"You're giving me a nickname?" Sheila placed her hand on her heart. "I'm honoured."

"As you should be. I don't give many people nicknames. Not nice ones, anyway."

She barked a laugh. "You think Shay is nice?"

"It'll make me smile."

Ruth's eyes shone, and she smiled, a wide smile that coloured her cheeks and made Sheila's heart sing. She felt herself smiling in return. "Are you same-oriented?" she asked.

"Why?"

"Because I'm wondering if you'll have supper with me after the break."

Ruth's brows shot up. "I might be a Chosen."

Same-oriented, then. Otherwise she would have just said she was diff-oriented. "So what? Twenty-five is a long way off."

"That doesn't mean I want to get involved with anyone."

"Are you a Chosen?"

Ruth hesitated a beat. "I don't know yet."

"You're only seventeen?"

"For three more days."

"Your birthday's in three days?"

Ruth's eyes danced. "Not much gets past you, I see."

"Okay, how about this? If I guess correctly whether you're a Chosen or a Solitary, you have to have supper with me."

"You really want to do it that way?"

"Or you could just say you'll have supper with me."

"All right. Guess."

Sheila stared at her. "Fine. Solitary."

Ruth blinked. "You think I'm a Solitary."

"I'm hoping you are."

"Why?" Ruth asked, her face darkening.

"Because I'm a Solitary."

Ruth snorted. "Has anyone ever told you you're unhinged?"

"Explicitly, no. Implied it, yes. So we're on, then? If you're a Solitary, you'll have supper with me?"

"Okay." Ruth raised her finger. "But if I'm a Chosen, I don't. I wouldn't anyway."

"You're going to be one of those 'saving myself for my Chosen' Rymellans?"

"More like, 'no point getting involved with someone because it won't go anywhere' Rymellans'." She paused. "I'd be worried about falling in love. I'd rather avoid the whole thing."

"You're a Solitary, so you won't have to worry about it," Sheila said.

Ruth shook her head and swung up her comm unit. "I have to catch the next train. Enjoy your break, Shay."

"You, too."

Grinning so widely her cheeks ached, Sheila watched her descend the stairs.

TWO WEEKS LATER, Ruth disembarked from the train and climbed the steps to the Military Academy's courtyard. She couldn't help searching for her—Shay—and couldn't stop herself from smiling when she spotted her sitting on a bench, trying to appear relaxed. Or was she just hoping Shay was trying to appear relaxed?

Funny, she hadn't given Shay a second look since arriving for her first day here. She'd known of her. She'd sat in classes with her. But she'd dismissed her, and until two weeks ago, her eyes had always slid past her, barely registering her existence. She'd made up for it since then, unable to get Shay out of her mind. And now here Shay was, waiting for her.

Ruth laughed at herself. Shay didn't know what train she was arriving on. Surely she hadn't sat there all day—or maybe she had, because she was making a beeline for her right now.

"Welcome back!" Shay said. "So?"

"So, what?" Ruth said, even though she knew exactly what Shay was asking.

"Are you going to have supper with me?"

Sadness mixed with anticipation. Her eighteenth had been a small affair, exactly the way she'd wanted it. Only her family and a couple of close friends she'd kept in touch with from the Learning Academy. Like now, she'd felt mixed feelings when she'd woken up that day. She wanted to be a Chosen. Didn't everyone want to be a Chosen? But she hadn't stopped thinking about Shay since she'd left her at the top of the stairs, desperately wanting to glance back at her and determined not to do so.

Ruth had confided as much to Daisy, one of the friends, who'd assured her it wasn't unusual to fall for someone right before one's eighteenth. It was almost as if everyone wanted that one last free choice before they found out they were a Chosen, because Ruth would be a Chosen, Daisy was sure of it.

Ruth didn't know whose eyes had bulged the most when a Chosen Council courier had shown up at the house at two minutes before 15:00 and handed her an envelope everyone knew contained a Solitary Notification. Daisy had been beside herself. Mama had cried. Papa had put on a brave face. Her two brothers and her sister had all told her it didn't matter, which meant it did, otherwise they would have teased her about it.

She'd read the notification several times, to make it real. No Chosen. No Joining Ceremony. No children.

After everyone had forced down the wonderful supper Mama and Papa had laboured over, Ruth had snatched fifteen minutes to herself to weep in her room. She'd reminded herself that life wasn't over. She still had her family and friends, and she would return to the Military Academy, her first step to her chosen career. Still, the thought of going on a date with Shay had helped her get through her eighteenth and the days following it.

Being with her now had already made the day and her mood brighter. She met Shay's sparkling green eyes. "I'm having supper with you."

Shay's mouth dropped open. She whooped, then covered her mouth and appeared contrite. "I shouldn't celebrate, I guess. It means you're not a Chosen. Most Rymellans want to be Chosens."

Ruth was both miffed and amused. "Did you?"

"Yeah. But it didn't happen. Maybe because I'm unhinged."

"Maybe," Ruth said, chuckling. "When and where?"

"You free for supper today?"

She'd hoped Shay would say that. "I am."

"Southeast entrance, 18:00. I know a great eatery only five minutes from there. And might I suggest that if we enjoy ourselves, we go dancing afterwards. At the 'after the break' dance."

Ruth wanted to roll her eyes. There was always a dance going on for some reason. Normally she skipped them, but... "Let's see how it goes."

"I'll take it. What are you doing between now and supper?"

"Nothing, really."

"Let's hang out."

Ruth tried to glare but couldn't. She also seemed to have lost the ability to say no. Her plans to spend the afternoon reading in her room went out the window. "Why not?"

Shay whooped again. On the way to the residences, she chattered Ruth's ear off about what she'd done on her break and when she'd booked sim time for them, and peppered Ruth with questions about how the rest of her break had gone. Normally Ruth would have run out of patience five minutes in, but not with Shay.

Fortunate, since she enjoyed chatting with her over supper and ended up dancing the night away in Shay's arms.

The present day

AT THE END of her shift the next day, Ruth tapped on her superior's open office door and stepped into her office when invited to do so. Addison had looked up from her comm station and was gazing at Ruth, waiting for her to speak.

Ruth clasped her hands behind her back. "I was wondering whether my transfer to the *Harrier* is final," she said.

Addison's brows knit together. "Of course it's final. Why do you ask?"

It was done, then. She and Shay would be separated. A wave of sorrow and apprehension washed over her. Since there was nothing she could do, she thought about whirling and leaving, but an inner force rooted her to the spot.

"The tour is still four months away. Ian said he'd jump at the chance to transfer to the *Harrier*. Is there no way you can substitute his name for mine?"

Addison picked up a pencil and tapped it on her desk. She studied Ruth, then dropped the pencil and leaned back in her chair. "You should consider your transfer a great honour and a recognition of your work and your reputation. They asked me for one name." Addison held up her right index finger. "One. I submitted yours."

Ruth shifted her weight. "I'm very grateful, but a transfer is a big change. I would have appreciated it if you'd asked me about it first, before you submitted my name."

Addison's eyes grew so wide, they looked as if they might fall out. "I am not expected to consult with subordinates every time I make a decision," she snapped.

Normally Ruth would give up at this point. She hated confrontation. Right after she'd forced herself to say her piece, to speak up, she always felt sick and wondered if she'd done the right thing. This time, she didn't need to force herself. Indignation and a sense of unfairness were driving her forward.

"It's just that Sheila—Lieutenant Commander Dorrington—won't be receiving orders to transfer to the *Harrier*. It means we'll be separated for years at a time."

"What are you saying, Lieutenant? Your girlfriend is more important than your military career?"

Girlfriend. They could be together for fifty years and Shay would still be her girlfriend. Her eyes went to the Chosen ring on Addison's right ring finger. Last night, she'd worried Shay would say something stupid. Now she worried about herself, and took a moment to think before she spoke.

"I'm saying I value them both." And that usually transfers were discussed before they were submitted, either because they were requested by the person themselves, or their superior officer had the decency and courtesy to bring it up before filing the request. She could understand obligatory transfers if they were at war. But they weren't, and it would have been easy for Addison to send someone else, like Ian.

Ruth would never voice those thoughts. Addison wouldn't care. She'd never liked Ruth and so had abused her position, as far as Ruth was concerned. Maybe she'd file a grievance. She'd think about it.

"When you trained for your position and requested to go on tour, you should have understood you could be transferred to another tour or space station or planetside at any time. If you value your relationship so much, you should have remained planetside." Addison's tone turned sarcastic. "I am so sorry you aren't pleased you'll be aboard the *Harrier*'s inaugural tour, the tour that had many more applicants than it does spots. You are, of course, free to request a transfer to wherever your lieutenant commander is once you've completed your *Harrier* tour." Addison pushed back her chair and stood. "I hope your superior on the *Harrier* has better luck with your attitude than I have. Now, if you don't mind, I'm due to meet my Chosen."

Yes, meet your flaming Chosen, the one you never have to worry will be whisked away to another ship without any discussion or notice. Once again, Ruth reminded herself to keep her mouth firmly closed.

She'd tried. She'd be able to tell Shay she'd asked Addison to send someone else instead and received no sympathy whatsoever. That left them only a few ways they could avoid being separated again: either one or both of them resign from the military, or request a transfer to a space station or planetside. The only other way was if Shay got orders to report to the *Harrier*. Ruth didn't see any other options, and the latter option wasn't likely to happen.

Her heart sank. She knew what was coming. They would be torn apart. Again.

SHEILA STOMPED INTO her quarters and didn't wait for Ruth, who was anxiously looking up at her from the sofa, to ask. "I won't be transferred. The pilot positions are filled." She wanted to punch the wall, scream, go back to Baker and yell at him, even though it wasn't his fault. No, it was Addison's fault. That woman had hated Ruth from the start. Using her authority to split them up was beyond the pale. Ruth was great at what she did, but Addison could have submitted anyone's name. Anyone's.

"I spoke to Addison," Ruth said.

Hope stirred.

"She refuses to budge. Told me I should have understood serving in the military meant I could be sent anywhere at any time."

"Yeah? Well, Chosens don't have to understand it in the same way we do." She had better not run into Addison.

Sheila wanted to pace and rant and break everything she could get her hands on. But Ruth's tired and pale face stopped her. She flopped onto the sofa and took her hand.

"I might file a grievance against her," Ruth said. "I know the military doesn't have to keep us together, but I can't think of anyone else who would have done what she did. And she knew exactly what she was doing." She exhaled slowly and pressed her free hand against Sheila's cheek. "We need to talk about where we go from here."

Sheila wanted to murmur platitudes, to say, 'Don't worry, we'll get through it,' to talk about how their love would survive everything. Except she wasn't sure she believed it. Not this time. Not after they'd snatched pockets of time together over four years and almost broken up. They'd fought for their relationship, won it back. It was stronger than ever. But what was the point if they'd hardly see each other?

She wasn't ready to give up quite yet. "I've been thinking. I'm going to find out how to petition for an article to be added to the Chosen Tradition. About keeping Solitaries together."

Ruth gaped at her. "Are you out of your mind?"

She shot to her feet. "Why is it such a ludicrous idea? What do you want us to do, say, okay, I guess we'll be separated again for who knows how long? That's fine. It doesn't matter."

Now Ruth was on her feet. "Of course it matters! But we can limit it to one tour or avoid it altogether. We have options."

"What options?"

Ruth hesitated.

"What options?"

"Try to listen, okay?"

Sheila folded her arms. "I'm listening."

"One or both of us could resign from the military."

"No."

"Why no?"

"Because it wouldn't be fair. We're both good officers with excellent records."

"So we'd let a separation go on for years to prove a point?"

"We worked hard for our positions. And what would we do if we quit? What would our families say?"

"I think mine would understand."

Sheila's probably would too, but they shouldn't have to understand why their daughter, who'd always wanted to be a fighter pilot, had to give it up to stay with the woman she loved. It wasn't fair. "I'm not resigning."

"I'll resign."

"No. You shouldn't have to do that to keep us together."

"Shay." Ruth rubbed her forehead. "I agree. I shouldn't. But we need to deal with what's happening, not with how we think things should be."

"We're not resigning over this."

"We could both request transfers after the next tour." The moment Sheila opened her mouth, Ruth raised her hand to forestall her. "Yes, we'd be separated for six months."

"Almost seven," Sheila said. "The *Harrier* leaves two weeks after the *Falcon*."

"If we both transfer to a space station or planetside, we can limit our time apart to that."

Sheila wanted to shake her. "It won't be that simple. Remember how many times you requested a transfer to the *Falcon*." Tears of frustration blurred her vision. "Four years. Four flaming years."

"It will be easier to transfer off a tour. Most people want on a tour, not off."

"But there's no guarantee. What if it takes two years? Three years?" She shook her head. "Not again, Ruth. Not again. And why should we have to stick close to Rymel while others go on tour? We shouldn't have to limit ourselves like that."

"Shay, if we don't want to be separated for a long time, we're at the point where we have to choose our relationship or tours. Don't you see that?"

"Let's say we both transfer off tours. What's to say in a year, some other idiot doesn't decide to transfer one of us to a tour? Or halfway around the planet? I don't want us to be at the whim of any idiot with the authority to separate us."

"Then we resign."

"We went through that already."

"Then what?"

"Let me find out about petitioning for an article to be added to the Chosen Tradition," Sheila said evenly.

"Even if it's possible, it won't happen just like that. It will take time."

"Then I'd better get started. I'll need to engage an advocate."

Ruth stared at her. "Before you do, how about you ask someone what they think the chances are of getting an article added to the Tradition. Off the record."

"Nothing's off the record."

"I meant ask someone you know, rather than some advocate you don't."

"Like who?"

"I was thinking you could send a dispatch to Lesley."

Sheila waved the suggestion away. "You don't want me to talk to an advocate, but you want me to talk to a commander in Interior."

"She's a friend."

"I'm sure she's busy."

"Just send her a dispatch, Shay, please," Ruth said, her exasperation coming across loud and clear. "If she's busy, she'll tell you."

Given that Ruth obviously thought she was truly unhinged to even consider trying to get the Tradition to acknowledge the love between Solitaries was important too, Sheila agreed. "All right. I'll send her a dispatch. Want to help me write it?"

"Sure."

It didn't take them long to tell Lesley about Ruth's transfer to the *Harrier* and their—Ruth had agreed to go along with it—question about petitioning for an article to be added to the Tradition that would give some recognition, some protection, to Solitary couples who had been together for some minimum amount of time.

Sheila hit the *Send* button with satisfaction.

"She won't get it for at least an hour, and it might take her a while to respond," Ruth said. "Days, even."

"At least we're doing something." Because Sheila would not take this lying down. She wouldn't do anything to risk her or Ruth's lives or careers, but to meekly acquiesce to this latest insult to their relationship wouldn't feel right.

She felt Ruth's hand on her arm. "We should talk about what we'll do if she tells us not to bother," Ruth said.

Yes, make plans that would involve one or both of them giving up their careers, their dreams. Sheila wanted to bury her head in her hands and cry, because she didn't see any way of staying with Ruth that wouldn't stick in her throat and make her feel as if she wasn't in control of her life. Because she wasn't. Not anymore.

Lesley checked the time on her comm station's display and closed the file in front of her. Time to wrap up. Mo and Jayne had said they'd meet her in the reception area at noon rather than come to her office with Ellie and Kat. There was less of a chance of their daughters disturbing anyone. Lesley wasn't worried about them being naughty. Her children were well behaved. She was more worried about the adults stopping to talk to them in the corridor, right outside someone's open office door.

It was only 11:40, but she wanted to see Laura on her way to lunch. Laura looked up when Lesley stopped outside her open office door and cleared her throat. "Do you have a minute?"

"Sure." Laura motioned for her to enter.

"Question out of the blue. What do you think the chances would be of successfully petitioning to add an article about Solitary relationships to the Chosen Tradition?"

Laura's eyes brightened with curiosity. "What sort of article?"

"One recognizing their, uh, importance? Their validity? I'm not sure what the right word is. It's a couple of friends of mine. They're both Defence and have been together for a long time. One has received orders to report to another ship. The other hasn't, meaning they'll be separated for long periods."

"That's rough."

Lesley knew from experience how rough it would be. "They're wondering if it would be a waste of time to petition to add an article about not separating Solitaries in long-term relationships."

"Yes," Laura said flatly.

"I figured, but…"

"It's already been tried. Twice. No, three times. The last time wasn't long ago, in Chosen Tradition time. About ninety years." Laura lifted her hand and waved her finger. "It wasn't the exact article your friends want, about separation. But the gist was the same. Adding an article that would appear to elevate Solitary relationships to the same level as Chosen ones. To bestow them with the same status."

"Denied."

Laura smiled. "Gold star. I see the unfairness of it to long-term Solitary couples, but there isn't an overseer alive who'll add an article like that to the Tradition. Even if I thought there was the tiniest chance, it would take years to get one added. But I don't. There's zero chance." She paused. "Your friends could try taking another route, though."

"What do you mean?"

"They need to scale down their problem. The military is separating them, not the Chosen Tradition."

A light bulb went on in Lesley's head. "They should try to get something added to military regulations."

"Exactly. I don't think they'll succeed, but they'll at least have a chance."

"How would they go about doing that?" Lesley hadn't given much thought to who regulated the regulations.

"If they search for the regulations, they'll find a dispatch code they can send comments and suggestions to."

"Someone actually reads the dispatches?"

Laura chuckled. "They aren't automatically discarded, believe it or not. The regulations board considers anything that isn't undoable or unreasonable. I'd say this request would pass both tests. That doesn't mean it will be added. I doubt it will. But it's worth a try."

"How often does the board meet?"

"Twice a year."

Maybe Sheila and Ruth wouldn't have to be separated for long. But Lesley would be sure to downplay the possibility of success in her reply. She agreed with Laura. The chances of the military trying to keep Solitaries together was slim. It had enough problems keeping Chosen couples together. Doing so created a bunch of logistical headaches, especially when someone was notified or newly Joined and suddenly a place had to be found for a Chosen.

"Thanks. I'll let them know. Anyway, I should go. I'm meeting Mo and Jayne for lunch."

"With the twins?"

Lesley nodded.

"I'll come say hello." Laura opened her desk drawer and fished out some biscuits. The twins loved Auntie Laura because she always gave them treats when they visited her at Mama Lesley's work.

"Can you tell them to eat the biscuits after lunch?" Lesley said.

Laura chuckled again. "I'll leave that to their mama."

"Thanks," she said, her tone making Laura's smile widen.

"Not long now until they go to the Indoctrination Academy," Laura said as they strolled to the reception area.

"Six weeks."

"Where has the time gone?" Laura didn't wait for an answer. "You know, many Rymellans plan their next pregnancy for around the time their first child, or children, are at the Academy. Best to have the baby when they're home, so they're not blindsided when they get back and find a baby suddenly living with them, but it's nice to be pregnant when you don't have your firstborn to care for."

"It's under discussion." Lesley didn't want to say any more. The discussion about who would carry the baby had been going on for a while, with no end in sight.

RUTH COULD HEAR the excitement in Shay's voice as she read Lesley's response to their dispatch. She perched on the edge of the sofa in their quarters and continued to listen.

"...don't need to add an article to the Chosen Tradition to get what you want," Shay said. "An addition to military regulations would accomplish the same thing. The regulations board meets twice a year. You can use the comm code at the bottom of the military regulations document to send it your request. You'll have only a slim chance of getting a regulation added. But it's worth a try. I hope you don't mind, but I wrote a few arguments you can use, to get you started. Change the wording as you wish or write your own.

Lesley."

A grin split Shay's face. "This is better than I expected! Let's do it. Right now."

"She said the chances of success are slim," Ruth said, wanting to break Shay out of her orbit and bring her down to solid ground.

"So we don't try?"

"I didn't say that. But we need to temper our expectations, come up with a plan for what we'll do if the board denies our request."

"Why are you being so pessimistic? It's almost like you want us to be separated."

Ruth stood, tired of arguing, but unable to stop herself. "I don't! It's the last thing I want. But you read what she wrote. Only a slim chance. I want a Plan B, that's all. Why won't you even discuss what we should do? Every time I bring it up, you shut me down. We can't pretend it's not happening."

"I'm not pretending it's not happening," Shay shouted. "I am acutely aware it's happening. Believe me."

"Then why don't you sit down so we can talk about what we want to do?"

"We can't stop your transfer to the *Harrier*."

"I know that," Ruth said through clenched teeth. She slowly exhaled. She hated this, hated that they were shouting at each other, that ever since Addison had told her about the transfer, they hadn't relaxed for even a minute, hadn't talked about anything else.

She went to Shay, slipped her arms around Shay's neck. "Can we put this aside for tonight and pick it up again tomorrow?"

Shay frowned at her. "We need to send a dispatch to the board."

"I agree. Let's work on it tomorrow night. We'll get supper in and write the best flaming dispatch we can. Okay?" She willed Shay to relax, for the tenseness in Shay's body and face to soften.

"Okay," Shay breathed, but she still felt as stiff as a board.

"And we'll discuss what to do if the request is denied, okay?"

Shay's mouth pressed into a thin line. "If we have time."

Ruth's stomach clenched. She couldn't shake the feeling Shay was avoiding the issue because she'd already made up her mind about what they'd do. *I can't do this again, Ruthie. I can't.*

She pulled Shay close and buried her face in her shoulder. She'd always believed their love was unshakeable, that Shay loved her more than anything. Now she wondered if she was wrong.

SHEILA DREW BACK her racket and whacked the ball at the round green target on the front wall of the practice cube. The target turned red. She'd missed. A soft beep came from behind her. In one smooth motion, she whirled, found the target on the back wall, and hit the ball. Red again. A beep from above. She did a scoop swing. The ball contacted the angled ceiling—narrowly missing the target—and came racing back toward her. She took a step back and whacked it against the wall directly in front of her, so it would reach her just after the next target came up.

She avoided glancing at the scoreboard of hits and misses, because the hits would be a single-digit number and the misses a double-digit one. So much for booking a cube for an hour so she could blow off steam, instead of being surly with people. She should have realized missing the ball most of the time would only make her feel worse.

A beep to her right. She twisted, whacked the ball with her racket. The target turned green.

She was in an impossible situation. If the military board didn't accept her and Ruth's proposal—beep to her right again; an easy hit—she would have to choose between Ruth and her career. On the surface, it should be an easy choice. Ruth. No question.

The target was now on the front wall. She twisted, but not in time. Miss.

The thought of asking to be transferred to a space station made her want to scream. Target to her right again. She pivoted and hit the ball so hard it whizzed back toward her and past her, making it difficult to regain control of it before the next target came and went.

Why should she have to limit herself, why should Ruth, because they were Solitaries? They'd worked as hard as Chosens, and loved each other as much as Chosens did.

One of her uncles had—target behind her; she just managed to catch it—one of her uncles lived with a woman he'd met when he was doing his Level One at the Indoctrination Academy. They'd remained friends until they were both nineteen, when their feelings had blossomed into love. Both Solitaries. Sheila thought perhaps they'd have dated long before then, but hadn't wanted to let it happen until they knew if either of them had Chosens waiting in the wings.

She scooped the ball toward the ceiling. Miss.

At a family event, someone had said something that suggested her uncle and her aunt's—Sheila saw her that way, even though it wasn't strictly true—love for each other couldn't possibly be as deep as his love for his Chosen. Her uncle had said, "You're forgetting something important, Henry. The Chosen Council determines the best match that will produce children strong in the Way. They won't Join you with anyone you'll hate. They do try to match your personalities as best they can. But Chosens aren't necessarily the best love match for each other. A close match, sure. But not always the best."

When Sheila's Solitary Notification had arrived on her eighteenth, she'd remembered that remark. Back wall again. Hit.

She kept thinking about it now, when her relationship was under fire from Ruth's idiot supervisor who didn't like her and did what a lot of superior officers did. Transferred people they didn't like somewhere else. But this supervisor knew about their relationship and hadn't cared, hadn't even discussed the transfer with Ruth beforehand.

It was the casual dismissal of their love, their bond, that made Sheila want to rage and cry at the same time.

Front wall. She stumbled as she pivoted. Miss.

It was why what should be an obvious and easy choice was sticking in her throat. To ask to be transferred off the *Falcon* to domestic patrols would feel as if she was saying, yes, Solitary relationships deserved no consideration, that it was perfectly acceptable for the military to ignore them when issuing orders, that Solitaries would just have to deal with it because they didn't count. Choose, Solitary. Choose.

Your career or your girlfriend.

Your dreams or your relationship.

Happiness or respect.

Ruth or humiliation, failure, defeat.

Beep to her right. Sheila turned, whacked the ball. Miss.

She screamed, flung the racket with all her strength. Its frame buckled when it made contact with the wall.

A shrill tone reverberated around the cubical chamber, followed by an artificial but pleasantly cheerful voice. "You have received an automatic Level Two strike on your record for violating Article 694. That counts for two points toward the five-point disciplinary hearing limit."

"Sorry," Sheila mumbled as she retrieved the racket and winced at its condition.

She repeated her apology to the counter attendant, who merely raised a brow when she handed him her racket.

On her way back to her quarters to shower, she told herself if the board rejected their proposed regulation, she should choose Ruth. They'd have to endure an almost seven-month separation, but they'd keep in touch throughout that time, and both would ask for transfers. Ruth was right. They'd be granted. More personnel wanted on ships than off. After the separation, they'd be together again.

But it would feel like defeat. It shouldn't, but it would. Plus, how would she feel after flying a few years of domestic patrols? What if she was bored out of her skull? What if she desperately wanted to go back on tour? The last thing she wanted to do was resent Ruth, blame her for a situation that wasn't her fault. And what if they were separated again at the whim of someone who viewed their relationship as second rate?

Sheila couldn't see the Plan B Ruth wanted. Resigning, the only way they could guarantee never being parted again, was out of the question. There was no way she would ask Ruth to resign, and Sheila couldn't imagine herself doing it. Flying domestic would also rankle. It would be making a choice she shouldn't have to make. But the thought of breaking up with Ruth, of never seeing her again…

Today was a day off, for both of them. Ruth was at her normally scheduled session with her counsellor, the reason Sheila had booked the practice cube alone. She might have to get used to doing a lot of things alone. No, she couldn't break up with Ruth, but she couldn't resign from the military, and asking for a transfer to domestic would make her want to break another racket. She didn't want to feel this agony, this rage over the unfairness of it, for the rest of her life.

In her quarters, she peeled off her damp exercise clothing and hopped into the shower, where she could cry and rage and nobody would hear her, and she wouldn't receive any more strikes on her record and have to face a military disciplinary hearing filled with people who were quite happy to separate her from Ruth.

RUTH STOOD AND gazed out one of the windows into the vastness of space, weighing how she should respond to Counsellor Sherman's question. She hadn't been able to remain seated for more than a few minutes at a time, had been up and down like a yo-yo since the session had started.

"I'm not worried she doesn't love me," she said, considering each word carefully. "I know she does. But I always thought if she had to make a choice, she'd choose me, that we'd work together and come up with a plan. We always have before. We've always fought for us."

She thought back to when she hadn't made it into the fighter pilot program, but Shay had.

Twelve years ago

FEELING A BIT embarrassed even though they were alone, Ruth stopped jumping up and down and whooping. "Show me."

Shay handed Ruth her acceptance certificate. "Sheila Dorrington, up and coming ace fighter pilot."

Ruth grinned, despite her apprehension. She'd soon find out whether she was in too. Most of the hopefuls were gathered in the mess hall. She'd persuaded Shay to stay here, in their room, not wanting to feel as if she was on display when she found out whether she'd do what she'd hoped to do since she was about eight years old. Fly fighters. Glide among the stars. Years of dreaming about it had crystallized to this moment in time.

"I wonder how many have made it in already?" she mused aloud. Maybe they should have gone to the mess hall, so she could have counted the number of excited faces. It might have given her an idea of her chances.

"Just about everyone who came out when I was waiting looked like they'd found out someone died."

She shouldn't be pleased to hear that, but she was. "Do you know anyone who's in?"

"I might have peeked into the mess hall," Shay admitted. "But I didn't go in, and I didn't tell anyone I was accepted. I wanted you to hear it first."

Ruth had mixed feelings about Shay's detour. She wasn't surprised Shay had gone to the mess hall. Shay was social, making them an odd pair in that regard. On the other hand, she'd expected Shay to want to rush back here so they could share this moment together. Ruth's curiosity won the day, though. "How many have made it in, do you think?"

"Lesley's in. I passed David on the way back, so he's finding out now. Not sure about Mo. Either she doesn't know yet, or she didn't make it, because she looked a little tense. Ann's waiting. Patrick's waiting. Janice didn't make it."

"Oh, no," Ruth murmured. Janice had said if she didn't make it, she wasn't going to pursue a military career.

"Donald didn't make it. Neither did Andrea, or Jimmy. Uh, Terry, Jean, Jody came out while I was there. No go."

Ruth was feeling pretty good about her chances, but cautioned herself not to arrive at her appointment expecting to be accepted. Speaking of which... "I should go. I don't want to be late."

Shay drew her into a hug and squeezed her. "Good luck. Remember, if you don't get in, I won't think any less of you."

Ruth snorted. "Thank you, soon-to-be ace fighter pilot." She drew back from Shay, then hugged her again, her apprehension overwhelming her.

"I'll still love you," Shay said gently.

Tears sprang to Ruth's eyes. She blinked them away and forced herself from Shay's arms. "Be back soon."

Even less in the mood to talk than usual, she avoided anyone she knew on the way to the pilot training complex. Still arriving ten minutes early, she took a seat in the waiting room and tried not to appear too concerned, even though only one other cadet occupied a chair. Three offices shared this waiting room. The door to 22C swung open. Pete strode out, his head high, but his eyes red-rimmed. He didn't catch her eye as he blew past her.

An officer poked his head out 22C's doorway. "Cadet Appleton."

"Good luck, Tom," she mouthed to him as he passed her.

Ruth crossed her legs, uncrossed them, crossed them again. Time was crawling. Surely she'd been here for those early ten minutes and then some. A quick glance at her comm unit told her it was one minute before her appointment time.

She jumped when Natalie emerged from room 22A. She didn't appear crushed, but she met Ruth's eye and shook her head. Ruth gave her what she hoped was a sympathetic look, then drew a deep breath, slowly breathed out, breathed in, breathed out. She must be next.

A minute later, Lieutenant Commander Ross stepped into the waiting room. "Cadet Simms."

She stood. Fortunately her legs didn't feel as wobbly as she did. Inside the office, she accepted the offered chair and hoped she didn't look too eager.

Ross clasped her hands on the desk. "I want to congratulate you for undergoing the evaluation, Cadet Simms. As I told everyone on your first day, it's quite the accomplishment in itself to make it to this stage."

Ruth murmured a thank you.

"On that day, I also said forty-eight cadets would undergo the evaluation, but only twenty-one would be accepted. I'm sorry to tell you that you aren't one of the twenty-one who will be entering the program this year."

Ruth entered an alternate dimension. Ross was still talking—Ruth could see her mouth moving—but nothing was registering. She'd failed. Her dream had been just that. The life she'd planned for herself no longer existed.

"...on your performance and tests, we've suggested the programs you might..."

She'd return home today to expectant and excited faces. Mama might even have baked a cake. Ruth normally had both her feet planted firmly on the ground, usually tempered her expectations. She'd let herself get caught up in the excitement of the cadets she'd trained and undergone the evaluation with, had become infected with Shay's natural optimism.

"Again, you should be proud you underwent the evaluation. You will make a fine officer."

Someone rose and accepted the envelope Ross held out. Someone left the office, stumbled through the blur, found the lobby, made it outside. Who was that someone? It must be her, but Ruth felt like her mind and body were out of synch.

What to do now? Shay was waiting. Shay had made it in. Shay would say she wasn't disappointed, but how could she not be?

Ruth walked aimlessly, but the someone who was controlling her body didn't. That someone found an empty conference room in the recreation centre, shut the door, sank to the floor, and sobbed, loud, heaving sobs that echoed around the empty room. What had she done wrong? What had made the instructors recommend she not be accepted?

Had Ross said something about even good pilots being rejected because there weren't enough spots, or was Ruth only hoping she'd heard those words so she wouldn't feel like a complete failure. Neither herself nor that someone controlling her body had listened after the words, "You aren't one of the twenty-one."

By the time she'd wiped her eyes, picked herself up off the floor, rushed to the nearest bathroom and cringed at her blotchy face in the mirror, that someone had relinquished control of her body. She felt the pain now, her tense muscles, the throbbing headache, the agony.

Shay was waiting. Shay would be wondering where she was.

Ruth left the bathroom and tried to hold her head high, but her eyes kept finding the ground.

SHEILA CHECKED THE time on her comm unit and wondered if she should head over to the pilot training complex. Almost an hour had passed since Ruth had left. She would have been a bit early, but not that early, and from what Sheila had observed and her own experience, nobody spent more than five or ten minutes inside an office. Ruth should have been back at least half an hour ago. Sheila didn't want to beep her in case there had been a delay and Ruth was in an office right now.

Ten minutes later, she couldn't stand it anymore. She was about to head to the training complex when the door swung open and Ruth stepped inside.

Sheila didn't have to ask. One look at Ruth's face and the envelope in her hand told her. "You didn't get in," she whispered.

For a second, Ruth appeared as if she'd be her usual stoic self and make some type of crack, but the envelope slid from her hand and her face crumpled.

Sheila rushed to her and wrapped Ruth in her arms. "I'm so sorry," she said, stroking Ruth's hair. "I know how much you wanted it."

She held Ruth, aching for her, until Ruth's sobs subsided. Only then did she loosen her grip, worried Ruth would collapse. But her strong Ruthie was returning. With a groan, Ruth pulled away from Sheila and sank onto the bed.

"I'll make a fine officer, though," she murmured.

Sheila didn't know how to react. Anything she said would sound trite and make no difference, not for a while, anyway. She sat next to her, held both of Ruth's trembling hands. "Did they tell you why?"

"Maybe. I don't know. The moment she said I wasn't in, my brain shut down."

"Maybe you could try again next year."

"No. I can't go through this again, and I doubt they'd accept me anyway. Think about it. Nobody who underwent the evaluation was trying for the second time. They don't want you the first time, they won't want you the second time, right?" Bewildered and sad eyes met Sheila's. "I think she said something about other programs..."

Sheila remembered the envelope on the floor, but she didn't want to let go of Ruth's hands.

"I guess this is it, then," Ruth said.

"What?"

Ruth lifted Sheila's hands and let them fall. "This. Us."

Her heart sank. "Why? I'm not going anywhere."

"Come on, Shay. You've made it into the elite program, you'll make new friends."

"I'm sure I will, but what does that have to do with us? I'll still be here at the Military Academy."

"Until you train on 72."

"Maybe one of those other programs will have you training on 72. And even if that's not the case, we'll still find time to see each other."

"You say that now. What about when you go on tour?"

Sheila kissed Ruth's hands. "One step at a time, Ruthie. One step at a time."

One step at a time...

The present day

RUTH TURNED BACK to Counsellor Sherman. "When I wasn't accepted into the fighter pilot program, I wasn't sure what to do. If not for Sheila, I might have dropped out of the academy at that point. We looked at the programs the military thought were a good fit for me. I chose mechanics because we figured it would give us the best chance of serving together. It worked, until Sheila was assigned to a tour and my application was turned down." She never thought she'd smile at the memory, but now she did. "It didn't break us. We got through all the separations until we were finally together again. But now this."

"What's making you worry this separation will be different, that Sheila might not want to stay together?"

"She's not reacting the same way." Ruth plunked into the chair again. "I know, it's been years since then. But this time, she's angry. And she won't talk about it, which is completely not like her. Lesley said the chances the board will add our proposed regulation are slim. Sheila won't face it. She won't discuss what we'll do if the regulation isn't added." Ruth placed her hand against her heart. "I just want a plan. I want to know how we'll limit this separation to only one tour. I want to know—" Her voice choked off and her eyes moistened, something they rarely did during these sessions.

"You want to know if you'll stay together."

With a lump in her throat, she nodded.

Counsellor Sherman handed her a handkerchief.

Ruth dabbed at her eyes. "I want some reassurance. Last time we were separated for a bunch of tours, but I endured it because she hadn't been on tour before. I would never have asked her not to go. Now she has quite a few tours under her belt. I want to know if she'll be willing to request a transfer to domestic patrols. That's all I want to know."

"She could be avoiding the subject because it's painful for her. Perhaps she's not ready to talk about it yet."

"Sheila's not like that." Ruth stood and examined what should be a calming image of a forest trail hanging on the wall. It wasn't working for her. "Maybe she doesn't want to tell me it's over." Apprehension, worry, made her drag her eyes away from the image and turn to Sherman.

"You can't know what she's thinking." Sherman leaned forward. "Why don't you give the subject a rest for a while? We're still almost two months away from docking. You don't have to make a plan right now. You can wait until you're on your next tour. You'll have until the transfer request deadline, which is months away."

Ruth wanted to know now. She didn't want to wait months to find out if Shay would choose her.

"I know it's difficult," Sherman said, as if reading her mind. "But you've tried pushing her and it's causing tension. Give the subject a rest. Just be there for her."

"What if she never wants to talk about it?"

"She'll have to at some point."

Ruth hoped so. She'd hate for their relationship to fade away without so much of a, "We had fourteen great years together, but it's over." After all, if neither of them requested transfers for after their next tour of duties, when would they ever see each other again? The *Falcon* and *Harrier* docking schedules weren't in synch.

They spent the rest of the session talking about Ruth's own resentment over the situation, especially toward her superior officer.

Twenty minutes later, Ruth returned to her quarters. Shay came out of the bathroom, raking a comb through her wet hair.

"How did you do in the cube?" Not the question Ruth wanted to ask, but she was trying Sherman's suggestion and giving it a rest for now.

"Great. Your session went okay?"

"Fine."

"Good."

They stared at each other.

Ruth broke the silence. "Listen, why don't we have supper in tonight, instead of in the canteen? And then find a quiet place to sit and watch the stars. We haven't done that in a while. I want to lay my head on your shoulder and relax for a bit."

Shay brightened. "Sounds like a plan to me."

But not the plan Ruth desperately wanted them to work on.

Ten weeks later

RUTH LOUNGED IN a garden chair and watched Daniel cartwheel across the back garden of her parents' house. One cartwheel, two, three, four. And down he went, collapsing into a giggle. Wanting to be a supportive aunt, she clapped. "Wow, you did four. I don't think I could do four."

"You can't do four?" He raced over to her and plopped down at her feet. "How many can you do?"

"Now? I don't know. But when I was your age, I could do maybe two in a row."

"Only two? Do you want me to teach you?"

Her comm unit beeped twice. Wondering if it was a dispatch from Shay, she wanted to look at it. "Not right now. Why don't you show me again?"

Daniel didn't need any encouragement. He leaped to his feet and went right into a cartwheel, fortunately away from her. She clapped again, then shifted her attention to the dispatch. When she read the sender's name, she stood and beckoned Daniel over. "I have to go inside for a bit, okay?"

"Aw."

"Maybe you can show me again after supper." It all depended on the dispatch.

Inside the house, she went up to the guest room, which didn't feel like a guest room to her since it was her old bedroom. She opened the dispatch from the military regulations board.

We considered your proposed regulation carefully; however, we will not be adding it to the military book of regulations.

Even though Ruth had expected this result, it still felt as if someone had punched her.

While we understand the hardship that may be suffered by Solitaries in long-term relationships, it would be impractical for us to track every Solitary relationship, and it would add to the already sometimes difficult task of keeping Chosen couples together.

The rest of the dispatch was a canned thank you for trying to improve the regulations and good luck to you. Ruth wanted to weep. Why did the dispatch have to arrive on one of the days she and Shay weren't together during this break? Had Shay seen this yet? Ruth beeped her.

"Hey," Shay said.

"Hey. Did you get the dispatch from the military board?"

"I just read it."

Ruth waited. "And?"

Shay blew out a sigh. "We need to talk."

Finally! "Let's talk, then. I was thinking that—"

"Not now. I'd rather have this conversation in person."

Uneasiness snaked through Ruth. This was their last day of family visiting. They planned to spend the rest of Shay's leave—all four days of it—on 72, catching up with friends. Ruth wouldn't leave on the *Harrier* for another two weeks. "All right. We'll talk tomorrow, then?"

"Yes. But not on 72. Let's stay down here for an extra day. I'll come to you."

Now Ruth's throat was tight and her surroundings faded away. Why did Shay want to have this conversation in person, on the planet? Ruth could only think of one reason. She fought against it, chided herself. Don't jump to conclusions. Don't instantly go to the worst-case scenario, something Counsellor Sherman often cautioned her about. Shay might want to talk planetside because she'd decided she didn't want to go to 72 right away, or she wanted to be somewhere more private, where they wouldn't be interrupted by friends coming to Shay's temporary quarters to say hello. She might want to talk in person because it could be a difficult conversation, one that might alter the course of their military careers. This wasn't the time to get hysterical.

"What time?" she managed to squeak out.

"Around 14:00."

"Okay, see you then. And Shay."

"What?"

"I love you."

"I love you, too."

They disconnected. Trying to make herself feel better, Ruth forced a smile. Shay hadn't hesitated. There hadn't been an awkward silence before she'd said it back. There was nothing to worry about. Absolutely nothing. So why couldn't she shake the feeling that tomorrow would be one of the worst days of her life?

GRIPPING SHAY'S HAND, Ruth strolled through her parents' back garden, away from their house and into the trees. She waited until she was confident nobody could see them from a window before she stopped walking and turned to Shay. "It's safe to talk now. Okay, so I can put in a transfer to 72, or even planetside."

"What would you do planetside?"

"Shuttle maintenance. I'm trained for fighters, shuttles, aviacrafts, anything that flies, really."

"It would be a huge comedown from maintaining fighters."

Ruth didn't think so. Sure, fighters were sexy and everyone on the outside of the fighter clique envied those on the inside. Ruth couldn't care less about that. "I wouldn't mind. It would be a change, and the transfer would probably go through. Most people would think the same thing. What a comedown. They want out of shuttle maintenance, not in."

"So why do it, then?"

Ruth blinked at her. "So we can be together."

"It'll only work if I also transfer, unless you don't mind us being separated for months at a time."

"I do mind. I think we've done enough of that, and we have a seven-month separation coming up. I don't want another one after that. Do you?"

"You're proposing you transfer planetside, I transfer to 72, maybe on a three-four rotation, and that way we'll only be separated for four days at a time."

"Only if I never go up to 72. And the best thing about working on shuttles? When I come down from 72, I'll already be at work. What do you think?"

Shay scratched her cheek with her free hand. Ruth was still holding the other one. "I think it's unfair that we have to limit ourselves because we're Solitaries."

"I agree, but there's nothing we can do about it. We can only do what's best for us."

"And you think giving up our dreams is best for us?"

"How are we giving up our dreams? I'd be perfectly fine doing shuttle maintenance. You've been on quite a few tours now and you'd still be flying fighters."

"But we shouldn't have to do this, Ruthie. We should be able to be together and pursue whatever we want in the military."

"But we can't! We can't have both! You said you don't want more separations. I don't either. So we don't have much choice."

"No matter what we do, transfer, don't transfer, as long as we're in the military, our relationship isn't completely under our control," Shay said levelly. Her tone had been flat, unemotional, since she'd arrived. "There will always be a chance we'll be separated."

"We can reduce the chance."

"The only way we can make it impossible is if we both resign from the military."

"I'm not suggesting we do that."

"No, you're suggesting we stay in but limit ourselves."

Frustration made Ruth want to scream. She pulled her hand from Shay's. "So what are you saying? Do you want us to endure Argamon knows how long of a separation to prove some point? To who? Us? Military superiors who don't care?"

Shay moistened her lips. "I'm suggesting that maybe it's time for us to find out what it's like to not be with each other."

Ruth froze. Every brain cell, every fiber of her being, froze.

"I love you," Shay said. "I want to be with you. But I don't think…I can't…I'm raging inside. I wake up angry. I go to bed angry. I can't relax and enjoy myself anymore. Every time I think about this, about us being forced apart again, I feel like lashing out, hitting something. I'm afraid I'll say or do something stupid, something that could result in a serious strike. I can't live with this rage for the rest of my life, and both of us requesting transfers will only make things worse." She grimaced. "I'm sorry, but I can't live like this. I can't worry about some other superior turning our lives upside down in a decision that takes them five seconds to make. I can't do this anymore."

Ruth managed to find her voice. "So you'll let them win. The system, superiors, whoever. I don't get it. I really don't get it. You've been on tour, and not just once or twice. A lot."

"I don't want to feel like someone else is controlling my life."

"You don't think breaking up is letting someone else control it? You don't want anyone controlling your career, but you're perfectly fine with them controlling your relationship? It's the same thing, Shay. Can you really not see that? But I can see you've made up your mind. And you know what?" She jabbed her finger at Shay. "I don't need to find out what it will be like to not be with each other. I already know. Awful. Horrible. So painful that showing up for my shifts will be all I'll be able to manage. I guess you're hoping it won't hurt as much for you."

Shay reached for her. Ruth stepped back. She wanted to keep yelling at her, but she was shaking, and she knew her voice would shake, and everything around her was a blurry mess.

"I can't live with this rage. I can't live with the uncertainty," she heard Shay say through the haze.

Ruth clenched her hands, dug her fingernails into her palms, sucked down air, again and again and again. "It's not that," she said, the snarl in her voice surprising her. "It's that you want to fly on tours more than you want me. So go, then. If that's what you want, go fly. Good luck to you."

"Ruthie."

She pointed down the path. "Go!"

For a few seconds that felt like an eternity, Shay didn't move. Then she whirled and marched away.

Ruth hugged herself, watched Shay round the familiar curve and disappear from view. Surely this wasn't it. Surely they'd talk again, when Shay had come to her senses. Fourteen years of joy, tears, contentment, laughter, passion, couldn't be over, just like that.

Shay would reconsider. Shay would realize breaking up over this was worse, in every sense, than being proactive and making decisions that would keep them together. Shay would come back to her.

Right?

THAT NIGHT, RUTH still clung to her hope that Shay would want to talk, that her comm unit would beep and she'd hear Shay's voice. But it didn't.

She spent the days until Shay would leave on the *Falcon* lying to everyone except her sister about why she hadn't gone to 72 after all, why Shay wasn't with her. She wept when she could snatch time alone, argued with Shay in her head, went through the motions, forced herself to eat.

The morning the *Falcon* would undock, Ruth dragged herself out of bed and asked herself whether she could let Shay leave without at least trying to talk to her. She was eating another breakfast that tasted like cardboard when Evie walked into the kitchen and quirked a brow. "You're here."

"Where else would I be?" Ruth snapped.

Evie's expression didn't change. "I've been beeping you for the last hour."

Yeah, she knew.

"I decided to come over to see if you're all right, though to be honest,

I thought you'd have gone to 72, to see Sheila. What time does the *Falcon* undock?"

She shrugged. "17:00."

Evie checked her comm unit. "You still have time."

Ruth dropped her spoon into her cereal. The side of her arguing against rushing up to 72 now argued against Evie, too. "To do what? Beg?"

Her sister gave her a sympathetic look. "To not let her leave without trying one more time."

"Why would I do that?"

"Because you love her."

Ruth picked up her spoon and stabbed it into her cereal again and again.

"You don't want to leave things like this. Once she's gone, you won't be able to see her for six months."

"Seven months." Seven long, flaming months. "She probably doesn't want to see me."

She felt Evie's arm around her shoulders. "Of course she does. You at least have to try. Or you'll regret it. You will."

"She broke up with me because she's not willing to compromise. She chose her military career." Her lips trembled. "I'll just be a bother."

"Don't be silly," Evie said, squeezing her. "Get yourself dressed and go see her."

"What if she rejects me again?" Ruth whispered.

"You'll have tried. You won't forgive yourself if you don't try." Evie squeezed her again. "I know you're not one for begging, for admitting you need something, or someone. But this isn't the time to pretend it doesn't matter. You need to go see her."

She wouldn't admit to Evie that rushing up to 72 frightened her. What if Shay laughed, or turned her back, or wouldn't even agree to speak to her? But could she let the *Falcon* undock without at least trying? She wouldn't have another chance for seven months.

She pushed away her cereal. "Okay. I'll go. I'll do this."

By the time she made it to 72, the *Falcon* would be boarding. Shay might already be in their—her—quarters. She might refuse to come to the boarding area. But Evie was right. Ruth had to try, had to plead for their relationship one more time. Because she loved Shay and would do anything for her, and couldn't understand why Shay had stopped feeling the same way.

SHEILA LAY ON her bed in her usual quarters aboard the *Falcon*, her fingers laced behind her head. When the crew logistics officer had asked if she wanted to change quarters, she should have said yes. She'd thought remaining in the space she'd shared with Ruth would make things easier, especially since Ruth hadn't taken much except her uniforms and clothes, and her family images. "I'm not planning to stay on the *Harrier* long, Shay," she'd said. All of this had happened before their last conversation. That horrible last time they'd spoken.

Since then, Sheila had existed in a fog. She didn't remember the ride up to 72, walking up the boarding tunnel to the *Falcon*, and making her way to these quarters that felt empty and bleak. Everything between her last conversation with Ruth and right now was a blank. Well, not everything. The argument she'd been having in her head for months, the rage, and now the grief, were constant companions. She was so discombobulated, she didn't know what she was doing half the time. Fortunately she spent most of her patrols on autopilot, both literally and figuratively.

She'd made the right decision. She honestly believed a break from each other might bring some clarity. But so far, it hadn't brought any relief. All it had evoked was pain, a pain so deep she could see it hovering in her peripheral vision, taste it, almost touch it. One thing she couldn't do was sleep through it. Exhaustion weighed her down.

There was no way she could have gone along with Ruth's plan feeling like this. Her anger would have ripped her apart. But now, without Ruth... she hadn't gone a day without writing or speaking to Ruth since she'd met her coming off the train after the break at the Military Academy. And she had hurt Ruth, wounded her. She'd never forgive herself, even though she'd had no choice. Everything was a mess, including her.

On launch day, she'd normally be in the canteen, catching up with everyone and excited to be undocking again. A couple of people had already come to her quarters and rung the door chime, but she'd pretended she wasn't here, afraid of snapping at everyone. She had no idea how she'd make it through this tour. Maybe she shouldn't have been so stubborn. No, she'd meant every word she'd said to Ruth, but she wished she'd been gentler, and had let Ruth see her pain.

Her comm unit beeped. She picked it up, checked the display.

Ruth.

She should ignore it. She should let it beep and beep and beep until silence reverberated around the room. But she couldn't. "Ruthie?"

"Shay. Argamon. I'm here, on 72, in the boarding area. Will you come out and say goodbye? I won't try to convince you to change your mind, but I don't want us to leave things the way they are, not when we're both going on tour. Please come out and see me."

Sheila's eyes moistened. She should say no, but the bond they had, the bond that was weeping, wouldn't let her refuse. "All right."

Five minutes later, she searched for Ruth among the families say-ing goodbye to their loved ones. When she spotted her, she had to restrain herself from running to her, but she didn't try to stop herself from throwing her arms around her and holding her tight. The tears she'd tried to hold back fell. She clung to Ruth, fought to beat back her grief, but failed.

"I'm sorry it's come to this," Ruth said into her ear.

"I don't know what I'm doing right now," Sheila sniffled. "I don't know what I'm doing."

Ruth drew back. Her eyes reddened and her forehead creased. "Do you really think not talking to each other for a while will help?"

"I don't know. But I feel like I need some time, some space. Not because I don't love you. I do. I really do." Her chest heaved. She wanted to press her cheek against Ruth's again, but that wouldn't be fair.

Ruth couldn't keep her distress from her face. "I hate to see you like this. It's...I..." She let out a shuddering sigh. "If you think it will help you figure it all out, then let's not talk to each other for a while. But you can send me a dispatch any time, okay? If you want to start talking again tomorrow, we can. In three months, we can. I'll always be there for you. Okay?"

Sheila's throat was so thick, she couldn't speak. She loved the woman in front of her. She had no doubt whatsoever about her feelings. But something deep inside was telling her, begging her, to put space between them, to the point they shouldn't beep while she was still in range and shouldn't send dispatches afterwards. Not until her rage subsided and her head cleared. "Okay.

She took Ruth's face in her hands. "I'm not doing this because I don't want to be with you. I love you."

"I love you, too." Ruth squeezed Sheila's hands and gently removed them from her face. She wiped away Sheila's tears with her thumbs. "You should go."

"Good luck on the *Harrier*." Sheila wanted to say, tell me all about it, but she couldn't.

"I'll miss you every second, but I'll be fine," Ruth said, in her usual stoic way Sheila knew didn't reflect how she felt. She needed Ruth's strength right now, but she had no right to it. No right at all.

They gave each other another quick hug. Sheila wanted more and had to tear herself away. She turned at the entrance to the boarding tunnel, knowing Ruth would still be there, watching. They waved to each other.

She walked up the tunnel, increasing the distance between them on every possible level. When she got back to their—her—quarters, she threw herself onto the bed again. This time she wouldn't go to one of the observation decks with everyone and watch as 72 receded from view. She wasn't sure when she'd show her face. She had to eat. She had to report for duty. If she didn't check in with her friends, people would worry. She was social Sheila, after all.

So she'd try, go through the motions, hope the rage, the monster inside her, didn't make her hands shake, didn't have her arguing with everyone, didn't earn her another strike for breaking equipment. Those two points she'd received for damaging a racquet hadn't expired yet.

She wasn't sure what she was hoping would happen by not talking to Ruth. She just knew she needed to keep her at a distance while she figured it out.

RUTH WATCHED THE *Falcon* undock and grow smaller and smaller. *Have a good tour, Shay.* But could she? Ruth didn't get it, she honestly didn't get it. Shay loved her. She was certain Shay wanted to be with her. What would not talking to each other change? They'd still be on different ships unless they requested transfers. They'd still not see each other for years at a time. So what would avoiding the issue accomplish?

     RYMELLAN 4

She did agree with Shay about one thing, though. If Shay wasn't willing to ask for a transfer, their relationship, for all practical purposes, would be over.

I'm not doing this because I don't want to be with you.

Then why? What was she missing? Ruth usually had some inkling of what was going on inside Shay's head. Not this time.

Was it the kiss? To give her the strength to break up, had Shay internally dragged up everything they'd argued about over the past fourteen years, and now she couldn't let go of it all? The kiss hadn't meant anything, as Ruth had explained to her at the time. Shay had been on tour, Ruth had been at the Dance Hall. She'd danced with a friend, a friend she hadn't expected to lean in and kiss her. Ruth had immediately stepped back and left the dance floor, and had dropped that friend without a second thought for presuming. For knowing about Shay and doing it anyway.

She'd thought about going to Interior, but the line was different for Solitaries. If she were a Chosen, the mere act would have been enough for Interior to jump into action. But she wasn't, so Interior would have had to believe, beyond a doubt, that the kiss had been unwelcome and uninvited. There was no way Interior or Ruth could have proven that. If the friend had persisted and chased her around the Dance Hall, different story. But she hadn't.

She'd only told Shay because it had happened publicly, and she hadn't wanted Shay to hear about it from someone else. Shay had pouted. She'd stamped her feet. For the couple of years following, she'd occasionally brought it up when they were having an argument. She'd eventually gotten over it, not that there had been anything to get over. But Ruth had given her the time to work through her jealousy.

No, it wasn't the kiss, which was history now. Was it because Ruth had reeled off a plan to her, and Shay hadn't felt consulted? No, Shay had come to the house intending to tell her she wanted space. And not consulted? How many times had Ruth asked her, begged her, to sit down so they could discuss their options?

Shay kept saying she was angry, and Ruth understood why. It was unfair they were being separated, while a couple that had been Joined for two weeks would be kept together. But what was the point of being angry about it? They'd tried to have a military regulation added, had been advised by someone they both trusted that petitioning for an article to be added to the Chosen Tradition would be a waste of time and effort. They'd done everything they could. Being angry about it would only hurt themselves. It *was* hurting them.

So what was it? What wasn't Ruth seeing? Did Shay even know what was tying her in knots?

All Ruth could do was trust their love, trust that Shay would work through whatever was gripping her, enraging her. It was only a question of when Ruth would hear from her. And she would hear from her. She had to believe that, because the alternative was unthinkable.

A month later

SHEILA WANTED TO mute her flying partner so she wouldn't have to listen to his incessant babbling about his Chosen and having another child and isn't it mind boggling their second son was due to enter the Indoctrination Academy and how time flew, just like they did, and—

"Sheila?"

Huh? "What?"

"Just wondering if you'd nodded off."

If only. She was lucky if she managed three hours of sleep a night. She'd grown used to the fatigue, the weariness.

"How's Ruth?"

Her jaw tightened. "Fine."

"She's on the *Harrier* now. Getting to know a brand new ship, working on the newest fighters. Wonder when the *Falcon* will get them?" David didn't wait for Sheila to answer. "Must be exciting for her."

Sheila wanted to punch the flight control panel. "Yes, I'm sure it's really exciting, being separated again. I know it's been really exciting for me."

Silence. She would not apologize.

"It must be rough," David said.

She struggled to bite her tongue. If she uttered even a single word, she'd never stop. She'd bury him, set him alight, unleash every word she'd imagined herself saying to Ruth's former supervisor, the members of the military regulations board, everyone wearing a Chosen ring. She couldn't stand seeing Chosen rings anymore. Every time she saw one, she felt as if someone had stabbed her. She was trying not to feel the same about Chosens themselves, but she didn't always succeed, especially when they sounded inane and stated the obvious.

"Can we, maybe, not talk?" she said. "You know, remain silent. Keep our mouths closed."

"Are you sure you don't want to talk? You've been a little…tense ever since you came on board."

"I'm sure."

"If you ever need to—"

"Be quiet! Please." Tears welled in her eyes, hot tears of frustration. "How about we listen to music?" He could break in any time if he needed to talk to her, and it had better be a flaming emergency.

Without waiting for an answer, she muted herself and tapped the panel. She selected serene music that would usually have her fighting sleep, then tried to do what Counsellor Evans had suggested and consciously relaxed each muscle in turn, from her toes to her head. It wasn't working. It never worked.

Her hands clenched. Maybe she shouldn't have thought of Counsellor Evans, because it made her think of their useless sessions. Evans always parroted the same questions. Why are you angry? Why did you push Ruth away? Can you tell me why you refuse to entertain a transfer? Can you tell me why, why, why?

She screamed, knowing David couldn't hear her. She was alone, in this fighter, in the vastness of space. A flea. A nothing. No, not a nothing. A ball of rage, of frustration, of worry. Ruth didn't make friends easily. Ruth was alone on a strange ship.

Why did you push Ruth away? Why won't you entertain a transfer? Why are you so flaming angry all the time? So angry you're afraid you'll say the wrong thing to the wrong person, break another piece of equipment, end up in front of the military disciplinary committee or worse. Why, Sheila? Why?

RUTH FINISHED HER shift for the day and did what she always did as she walked to the nearest elevator. Flipped up her comm unit to see if there was a dispatch from Shay. She sighed. She'd expected a couple of weeks, or maybe a month, tops. Not two months. Two months of silence, of wondering, of hoping, of trusting their love. Two months of misery. And not only because of Shay, though their separation was the main reason for Ruth's inability to enjoy anything.

She was homesick. Years on 72, several tours, and she'd never felt this way before. She wished she was at home, in her former bedroom, at family suppers, in the garden watching Daniel do his cartwheels. She wanted to be on Rymel, with the wind at her back and the rain dancing on the windows and the sun warming her skin. She longed to be there, wished she wasn't stuck on this ship everyone else was clamouring to be on.

"Hi," a feminine voice said. She glanced over her shoulder. Lieutenant Kimberly Aston smiled at her. "You heading to the canteen?"

"Uh, yeah."

"Want to have supper together?"

Ruth's mind raced. Kim was a fellow mechanic who was trying to be friendly. So far, Ruth had turned down her invitations to grab a tziva on their break or eat a meal together. She hadn't been in the mood to socialize. Okay, when was she ever in the mood to socialize? If not for Shay, she'd have spent the last fourteen years reading a lot and forcing herself out for the occasional social engagement, just so nobody thought she was too weird. Just weird.

"I don't feel like eating alone again," Kim said.

Maybe not eating alone would help both of them. "Sure, why not?" One meal wouldn't hurt.

They made small talk over supper. Ruth didn't mention Shay, but she thought about her. Shay was always there, lurking.

It happened right after Ruth had finished her piece of strawberry pie.

"So, what are you going to do now?" Kim asked.

"Read. I'm halfway through a good book. A patrol is missing and everyone's frantic to find them."

Kim sipped her water. "Would you consider going to the dance on Deck 14? I thought maybe we could go together?"

The way Kim's voice climbed way too high when she finished her question, her slightly trembling hands she hadn't hidden under the table quickly enough, her too bright eyes... Ruth knew what she was asking. In the past, on the odd occasion someone had asked her out, she'd declined with no explanation, mainly because she didn't owe them one, but also because she'd wondered whether they knew about Shay and had asked anyway. Some Rymellans thought Solitaries were always up for grabs.

This time she knew Kim had no idea, and Ruth liked her—as a friend. Even if she'd felt attracted to her, she would not betray Shay. Until she heard from her, they were together, and if she never heard from her, it would be a long time before she'd feel like going out with someone, if ever.

"I appreciate the invitation." Ruth grimaced sympathetically. "But I'm with someone, have been with them for many years." She quickly continued, to answer the question that must be on Kim's mind. "I haven't mentioned her because, well, we've hit a rough patch. We're trying to figure things out."

"I'm sorry to hear that." Kim sounded sincere, and to her credit, she didn't suggest they go anyway as friends, or that going together wouldn't do any harm because "the someone" wasn't there and their relationship was on shaky ground. She simply said, "I hope you work things out. And I hope we can still have supper together sometimes." She managed a smile. "I'm not into wrecking relationships."

"It would be nice to not eat alone all the time," Ruth said, meaning it. She sensed Kim enjoyed socializing as much as she did. The occasional supper wouldn't do any harm.

She hadn't considered for a second accepting Kim's invitation, but as she strolled back to her quarters, she felt lonelier than ever. Someone reaching out to her had brought into sharp focus how isolated and alone she felt.

Ruth came to a decision, a life-changing one she'd normally discuss with Shay. But Shay wasn't here and wasn't interested in talking. And honestly, there wasn't anything she could say that would change Ruth's mind.

_* * *_

THE NEXT MORNING, Ruth arrived for her shift ten minutes early and went straight to her supervisor's office.

Lieutenant Commander Carter barely glanced at her as he shuffled through the paper file on his desk. "Good morning, Lieutenant."

"Good morning." She liked Carter. He was good-natured, pragmatic, and fair, a vast improvement over Addison. He had nothing to do with her decision. "I have what might sound like a strange request."

Now she had his full attention. "What is it?"

Ruth swallowed. "I enjoy my work here, enjoy working on the new fighters." She hesitated, faltering, but found the strength to force herself to continue, to be honest. "But I'm homesick. Desperately homesick. I've been away from the planet more than I've been on it for years now. I feel like I'm losing my connection to my family. Last time I saw one of my nephews, my brother had to remind him about who I am. I want more time at home." She squared her shoulders. "So I'd like to request that I be transferred after this tour to shuttle duty. Planetside."

His brows shot together. "Shuttle duty?"

"I know. Not very exciting compared to a tour here. But it's what I need right now. I know an excellent mechanic who can fill my spot next tour. Lieutenant Ian Williams on the _Falcon_."

He studied her face. "Are you sure about this, Lieutenant?"

"I am. I know it probably sounds strange to you, but it's what I want."

"It doesn't sound strange. Everyone has to do what's best for them."

If only Shay agreed.

"I just want to be sure you're sure. If I put through the request, it will be accepted. A mechanic of your calibre and experience will be snapped up. It will be next to impossible to return to the _Harrier_ if you change your mind, not until it's no longer seen as the exciting new ship."

"I'm sure," Ruth said firmly. Nothing within her protested, but she couldn't help but think of Shay. She'd fretted over whether this would sink their relationship, if they still had one. It still worried her, but she had to start doing what was best for her.

"Very well. I'll submit the request today. Any preference as to which shuttle base you're assigned to?"

"Anything from A5 to B10 would be fine."

"I'll be sorry to lose you, but I understand, and I commend you for making this request. Much better than suffering for appearance's sake."

Could she put him in touch with Shay? Maybe he could talk some sense into her. "Thank you. Well, I'd better go get started on the fighter that blew a cell yesterday."

Carter nodded. "Dismissed."

Three days later she received her new orders. Report to shuttle base B7 six weeks after the *Harrier* docked. She silently thanked Carter. He'd told her he'd asked for a date that would give her some extra time to enjoy being planetside again. Too bad he hadn't been her supervisor on the *Falcon*.

If—when Shay got in touch, Ruth would let her know. Then it would be up to Shay. Ideally, she'd request a transfer to a space station. If she didn't, they'd be back to seeing each other six weeks a year, but at least they'd have those six weeks, and Ruth would have her family. Friends to reacquaint herself with, if they were still interested. Activities to enjoy that she'd cast aside because they weren't practical on a space station or on a ship. Sailing came to mind, something she'd always enjoyed but hadn't had the time to do since she'd graduated. Every visit planetside was always about catching up with family, with no time for recreation.

In the past, she hadn't minded always living in quarters, either on 72 or on a ship. But she didn't want to do that anymore. Quarters always felt temporary, even ones she and Shay had shared for years. Her latest transfer had justified that feeling. Now she wanted roots, somewhere to call home seven days a week, a place her two feet were planted on solid ground. Most of all, she wanted Shay to share that home and hoped Shay would want the same.

If Ruth ever heard from her again.

SHEILA STORMED INTO her quarters and threw herself onto the sofa. Every shift she resolved not to snap, not to be rude, not to wish she was flying alone, and every shift she failed. Every flaming shift. Worse, the sight of Chosen rings was still making her jaw clench. Chosen rings! How was she supposed to live when she couldn't bear the sight of Chosen rings? She felt as if she was going mad.

Ten minutes later, she rallied herself, forced herself to get up from the sofa. She needed to eat. She didn't feel like it, just like she didn't feel like playing cards or booking a cube or going to see the military quartet's concert in two days or hanging out with her fellow pilots in the canteen.

The door chime sounded. Sheila's nails dug into her palms. She ignored it, but it sounded again. With a sigh, she pressed the *Open* button.

Angie stood outside, and she did not look happy. "Do you mind if I come in?" she said, her voice low. "I want to talk to you."

Sheila stood aside and motioned for her to enter.

Angie strode in and whirled to face her. "Look, I don't know what's going on with you. I wish I did. I wish you'd tell us instead of insisting you're fine. But the way you're treating David has to stop. You know him, he's laid back. He doesn't confront. He tries to get along. I know him really well, and I can see how hurt he is every time he comes home from a shift."

She wanted to tell Angie to mind her own business, but when her mouth wouldn't move, she just stared at her.

"I know it's about Ruth," Angie said, folding her arms.

"Why?" Sheila croaked.

"Because nothing else would make you behave the way you're behaving. Have you split up?"

"No."

"Then what's going on?"

She slumped back onto the sofa, biting back the frustration that made her want to break something. Did she have to spell it out? Apparently, she did. Angie was a Chosen. Of course she would never think about how unfairly the military treated Solitaries.

Angie took Sheila's sitting down as an invitation to sink into the chair across from her. "You'll feel better if you talk about it."

"I'm talking about it with my counsellor," Sheila snapped. She'd told Evans why she was angry. Because she and Ruth had been forced apart. Why wouldn't Evans accept her answer? All she did was ask more questions that were too nitpicky. Yes, Sheila was angry. Yes, she was angry all the time. She needed help, not a flaming interrogation.

"It doesn't seem to be helping," Angie said.

Sheila leaped to her feet. "I'm sorry I'm not behaving the way you want me to. Do you know what it feels like to be ripped apart from the one you love? No, of course you don't, because it'll never happen to you."

Angie's face tightened. "You're upset because you've been separated again."

"No, I'm upset because the canteen's not serving sandwiches today."

"I was making a statement, not guessing. Why haven't you talked to anyone about it? It's not like you."

"Because it's my problem."

Angie gave her an indulgent look. "Since when have you kept your problems to yourself?"

Sheila wanted to hang her head. She didn't like this, being surly to her friends. She understood Angie was trying to help, was concerned, cared about her, but she couldn't help herself from lashing out at everyone, and that frightened her. It had frightened her since setting foot back on the *Falcon*.

She forced herself to meet Angie's eyes. "I'm too angry to talk about it. You've seen what happens every time I open my mouth. Ask David."

"Then talk about it. Get it off your chest."

"I can't."

"Why not?"

How would Angie react if she told her? Would she listen? Would she understand? Would she beep the Interior officer on board?

Drained, Sheila returned to the sofa, forced herself to sit, and held her head in her hands. She had to trust someone. She'd thought about telling David, but whatever she said would be recorded.

Asking Angie to keep it between them would be unfair, so she'd have to hope Angie didn't recoil. Because she was right. If Sheila didn't get it off her chest, her anger, frustration, her resentment, was going to rip her apart. It already had her pushing away everyone she cared about. It already kept her up at night. She hadn't had a solid night's sleep since leaving Ruth's parents' house.

Her fingers dug into the cushion next to her. Say it! Otherwise she could be stuck like this forever. Angry at everything, everyone, every Chosen. She couldn't live like this for the rest of her life. She'd rather have a commander put her out of her misery.

"I think I'm falling from the Way," she whispered.

Angie didn't flinch. "Why?"

"Because I shouldn't be so angry."

"About what? I know you're angry about the separation, but it's got to be more than that."

Sheila couldn't speak, couldn't breathe. Her eyes filled with tears. She forced out the words, fear making her heart race. "The Chosen Tradition. For separating us. For not caring. I know that sounds ridiculous. It's not alive. It doesn't care about anything. But you know what I mean."

"I do," Angie said quietly.

"How can I be mad at the Chosen Tradition? It's not going to change. But it's not fair. Not fair that Ruth and I don't count." Her anger flared. With it came humiliation. Helplessness. "You'll never be separated from your Chosen," she growled, the harshness of her voice shocking even her. Everything she'd said in her head to Chosens tumbled out. "You'll never have to make a choice between the person you love and your career. Nobody will ever look down their nose at your relationship, upend it on a whim, dismiss it as not important. As not important."

Tears came fast and furious now, and the sobs she couldn't hold in were making it difficult to speak. "As...if...all the sacrifices you've made...made for each other...for fourteen years...not important. Meaningless. Dismissed...just like that. No regard...for our lives. Our...life together."

She surrendered, cried hot, angry tears, and held herself until she was spent.

"I'm angry at the Chosen Tradition," she said, when she could speak again. Avoiding Angie's gaze, she dug a handkerchief out of her pocket and blew her nose. "So now you understand why I'm falling from the Way."

"I don't, actually. I'd be angry too. I'd be beside myself." Angie's forehead creased. "I'd also talk to my friends. Honestly, Sheila, I'd be more worried about you falling from the Way if you weren't resentful. Because you're right. It's not fair. But it exists for a reason."

"I know. I'm angry at it. I don't want to abolish it."

"Which is why you're not falling."

"You really believe that?"

"If being angry at the Tradition meant you were falling, I'd be falling too. So would a lot of other Rymellans."

Sheila stared at her. "But you're a Chosen."

Angie barked a laugh. "You think that means I never shake my fist at the Tradition? True, I'll never be separated from David. And if he wasn't military, maybe that would be okay." Her face scrunched up. "Or maybe it would still be a problem. I guess I can think of other scenarios where the Chosen isn't military—anyway, he goes on tour, I go on tour. I don't hate being here, far from it. But it means I'm not doing the research I really want to be doing, and a ship isn't my first choice for where I want my children to grow up."

Angie smiled sheepishly. "I know, small problems compared to yours. At least David and I are together, and I'm grateful for that. But it's not ideal. And I feel resentful sometimes too." She leaned forward. "Not at him. Whenever I'm having a moment, I remind myself that I do enjoy the research I'm doing, and the children will be fine, and I do not want to limit him by insisting he fly domestic. And honestly, I wouldn't want to be separated from him for months on end. Still, though, I sometimes feel resentful at the Tradition. It can limit our choices."

"You're not angry at it, though. The sight of a Chosen ring doesn't make you want to hit something."

"Because I don't sit alone and let it fester. I talk to David. He talks to me. If we weren't doing that, I'd be talking to my family, my friends, being honest with my counsellor." Angie gave her a pointed look, then her eyes narrowed. "How's Ruth doing? She must be struggling too."

"I don't know," Sheila mumbled.

"You said you haven't split—"

"I asked her for some space. To think."

Angie gaped. "You haven't talked to her since we undocked?"

"That's how I thought you'd look at me when I told you I thought I was falling from the Way."

"You should be talking to her. She wouldn't want you in this state. She'd want to help."

Sheila shook her head. "I didn't want her near me. I don't want her talking to me."

"Why not?"

"Because I'm so angry. I didn't want her near me when it boiled over. I—" Her voice choked off when the realization hit her full in the face.

"I had to make sure she wasn't near me, or talking to me, or associated with me in any way."

Understanding dawned in Angie's eyes. "You're protecting her."

Sheila nodded. "So when it happens, she'll be able to say to Interior, I had no idea she was falling." Her voice dropped to a whisper. "She can say, 'I haven't seen or spoken to her at all.'" At all. *I'm so sorry, Ruthie. I'm so sorry. If I was going to throw away my military career, blow up at the wrong person, fall from the Way, I didn't want you caught up in it. I wanted you to live, to love again, to not be tainted because of me. I wanted you to be able to say, "Sheila Dorrington? Ancient history."*

She forced herself to meet Angie's eyes. "It could still happen. I'm still mad at the Chosen Tradition and your Chosen ring." She groaned. "Argamon, I can't believe I'm saying these things out loud."

Angie smiled. "You need to tell your counsellor everything. You can't keep it bottled up. Life must be unbearable if the sight of a Chosen ring brings up all the hurt, and the unfairness of you two being separated."

"Life *has* been unbearable."

"Then work through it so you can get back to Ruth. Tell your counsellor."

Her eyes moistened again. For the first time, she felt understood. Someone was listening, rather than dismissing. Now she realized Ruth would have listened too. Would have taken her seriously too. If only Sheila's fear of taking Ruth down with her hadn't made her drive Ruth away. "Evans might beep Interior."

"She won't. You're not falling. You're not even violating an article. Thoughts aren't actions, remember? How many times did we repeat that at the Indoctrination Academy?"

Hundreds. No, thousands.

"My grandpapa told me something once I've never forgotten. I can't remember how it came up, but I remember him saying, 'Rymellans who are falling from the Way never think they are, and Rymellans who are worried they might be rarely are'. That's always brought me some comfort when I feel like I'm pushing an article in my mind."

Now Sheila would remember it too. "I'll talk to my counsellor, but it won't change what's most unfair. To be with Ruth, I might have to stop going on tours."

Angie tutted. "What's a tour, anyway? Flying, but farther away. I honestly don't understand why military see them as better than being closer to home. But David feels the same way. That's why I'll never insist he transfer to domestic."

"I guess it's how everyone talks about it and sees those who go. Pilots who fly domestic are seen as second rate."

"You think Mo's a second-rate pilot?"

"No. But she's been on tour."

"So have you." Angie paused. "Don't focus on what you'll lose. Focus on what you'll keep. Who you'll keep. You'll still be able to fly."

Busy absorbing Angie's advice, Sheila grunted.

"I came to ask you to stop taking out whatever's bothering you on David."

"Tell him I'm sorry."

"No, no. You tell him. You have to come back with me for supper."

Sheila shook her head and twisted the damp handkerchief in her hands. "I don't know."

"You have to! I want to see the look on his face when you walk in with me. I told him I'd get you to come, and let's say he was quite skeptical about it. I need to win the bet."

"What will you win?"

A smile played on Angie's lips. "That's between me and David."

Sheila felt herself grin. "Well, we can't let you lose that bet." Her mind still buzzing, she went into the bathroom to splash some water onto her face, then left her quarters with Angie, determined to tell her counsellor the truth, despite how bad it would sound. Angie had convinced her she wasn't falling from the Way, and she understood thoughts weren't actions, but she couldn't help but feel as if she were doing something wrong. It would still feel embarrassing to be honest with Evans, but she'd do it for Ruth. For herself.

The rage within her still burned, but for the first time, Sheila believed there would be a day when it would no longer consume her.

RUTH LEFT THE maintenance bay with Kim, something she'd gotten into the habit of doing three or four times a week. They'd become friends. Strictly platonic.

As they strolled to the elevator, she swung up her comm unit, something she did every day without thinking about it. When she glanced at the display, shock made her abruptly stop walking. She did a double take.

Shay.

After that initial supper together, Kim had asked a few times whether Ruth had worked things out with her "special someone," and eventually dropped the subject when Ruth had said she didn't want to talk about it. She'd never told Kim she and Shay weren't even speaking, because she hadn't wanted to suffer the humiliation of telling her she'd been permanently dumped, or have Kim wondering why this wonderful woman Ruth loved still hadn't contacted her.

She hadn't wanted an audience for her grief and loneliness and sorrow, hadn't wanted someone else counting the days and wondering. She didn't like sharing her pain, as Shay had pointed out to her many times. She especially didn't like sharing it with a work colleague like Kim, even though they were friendly.

"Do you mind if we have supper together tomorrow instead of tonight?" she said to Kim. "A dispatch came in while I was on shift. I want to read and reply to it ASAP. Family drama."

"I hope everything's okay," Kim said.

So did Ruth. "I'm sure it is. I'll see you tomorrow, okay?"

She strode away, not stopping at the elevator, even though taking it would have been the shortest route to her quarters. The last thing she wanted was to be trapped inside with Kim and her questions. She hoped Kim would think she was heading to one of the observation lounges.

As she strode to another elevator, her heart pounded in her ears. The worst-case scenario ran through her mind. Had she been a fool to wait for Shay, to trust in their love?

As soon as she stepped into her quarters and the door swooshed shut behind her, she slid her comm unit from its holder. She stood still for a second, wondering if she was experiencing the last few seconds of her life before her world was blown apart. Deep breath.

She opened the dispatch.

Dear Ruth,

I'm sorry it's taken me this long to figure things out. You know how stubborn I can be. But I have indeed figured it out. I understand a few things better now. I've been seeing my counsellor almost every day for the past week, after I realized what was going on with me, and it's helped me a lot. I'll still be seeing her most days. I'll tell you all about it when I see you.

Ruth let out her pent breath. They'd see each other. And had Shay not wanted to waste time typing or dictating what she'd figured out, or was it more that she hadn't wanted to put it in writing?

I hope you still want to see me. I know I've tested your patience and your love and I hope I haven't ruined us. I'll tell you the main thing Counsellor Evans has helped me with. Focusing on what I can control and to accept, or let go, of what I can't. I know you were way ahead of me on that, but you've always been the smarter, more pragmatic one. Don't think I don't realize it.

Ruth chuckled. Shay was just as smart. Pragmatic? Most of the time. She was definitely the dreamer in the relationship.

If you still want to put your plan into action, I'll put in a transfer for domestic patrols. I would have done it already, but if you've decided you've had enough of me, I'd rather stay on the Falcon. And if you have decided you've had enough, I'll be crushed. I hope you haven't had enough, though. Please say you still want us to be together.

I have no right to say this, but write back soon!

Love,
Shay.

Ruth read the dispatch through again twice. She sank into a chair and typed her reply.

Dear Shay,

I haven't had enough of you. Not even close. And, as usual, I'm way ahead of you. I requested a transfer off the Harrier. I'll be doing shuttle maintenance. I'm staying planetside. Obviously I can still go up to whatever space station you get (Request 72. We have friends there), and like I said, I'll already be at work when I reach the planet.

I would have talked it over with you, but I couldn't wait. I had to put in the request. I've been terribly homesick this tour, ever since we undocked. I figured if you wanted to stay together but weren't willing to put in a transfer, at least we'd see each other sometimes. And if you'd decided you were done with us, I wanted to be home, with my family, not up on a space station most days. Because it would have been devastating, because I love you so much. If you'd decided you weren't coming back to me, I would have needed everyone around me to hold me for a long time.

When we're together again, I want to hear about everything you figured out. I can't wait to see you.

Argamon, the time was already crawling, but now it's crawling even more. I dock two weeks after you do. Get your family visiting out of the way before I come back, okay? Because I'll want you to myself for a while.

Life is already brighter because we're talking again. I've missed you so much. I thought I understood how much, but now that we're back in each other's orbit, I realize how big a chunk of me has been missing.

Love you to bits.
Ruth.

She deliberately hadn't kept track of the *Falcon*'s route. A few of her and Shay's mutual friends—all pilots—had written to her, and so had a few of her former co-workers. She'd answered them all, simply saying she missed Shay. Either Shay hadn't told them about their separation, or they'd pretended they didn't know, and Ruth had been happy to go along with it.

Now she went to her comm station to look up the *Falcon*'s current location. Okay. Shay wouldn't receive the dispatch for at least fifteen minutes.

Her stomach grumbled. It hadn't done that for a while. Ruth hadn't forced food down, but even her favourite desserts hadn't tasted as delicious as usual. She'd go to the canteen on Deck 5 so she wouldn't run into Kim, who'd still be eating. She wanted to grab supper, come back here, read Shay's dispatch again, and hope to receive another one from her before she went to bed.

It arrived a couple of hours later. Ruth curled up on the sofa and read it.

My dearest Ruthie,

I love you, and I can't wait to see you. I wish you were with me already. I've already put in my transfer request. I did it right after reading your dispatch. Baker was very understanding. He pretty much knew why I was asking and said he'd make sure it happens. Just a few more months to get through and we'll be together again. I'm dancing here. Doing that wavy arm thing that drives you crazy in a bad way.

It drove her crazy because when Shay had done it at Ruth's parents' house, she'd knocked over Mama's favourite vase and broken it. Since then, Ruth always tensed up when Shay did that wavy arm thing, even though it did look ridiculous, and because it was Shay, adorable.

About coming up to 72 (or wherever I'm posted) a few times a week. That'll be great. What about when you're on the planet? You're not going to live on 72, right? I mean, you could. I'd love it. But I was thinking maybe it's time we had a home, you and me. Not quarters the military assigned to us, and not your parents' guest room. A home. Where we keep most of our stuff. So when I'm on 72, I'm away from home. What do you think?

Ruth thought it was lovely. She wiped her eyes and continued reading the rest of the dispatch, which was quite emotional, even for Shay. What a difference from the angry woman who'd refused to even consider what they'd do after their current tours, and had insisted on no contact and stuck to it for months. Ruth was curious about the breakthrough Shay had mentioned and wanted to hear about it. But right now, she wanted Shay in her arms, and in her bed.

A week before the Falcon docks

SHEILA CUT THE music David had played soon after their fighters had cleared the *Falcon*'s launch bay. After that day when Angie had come to see her, the tension had eased between them, but despite apologizing, she still felt guilty every time they flew a patrol. She wanted to make sure everything was all right between them before she left the *Falcon*. They'd studied and flown together for too many years.

She cut into the channel and raised her voice. "David."

The music volume lowered. "What?"

"Can we cut the music? I want to talk to you."

He barked a laugh. "Are you sure?"

Ah, so he was still a bit miffed. She couldn't blame him. "Yeah, I'm sure." She cut the music herself. The silence hung between them. "Okay, so I know I was horrible to fly with and pretty rude to you. I can't say sorry enough, but I'll say it again anyway. I'm sorry."

"Did you and Ruth make up?"

"We didn't break up," she insisted. When she'd told him over supper that night in his and Angie's quarters about not having spoken to Ruth since she'd boarded the ship, he'd said it sounded like a breakup to him. "We were figuring out what we wanted to do."

"I see." He paused. "When she was transferred and you weren't, I knew something had to give. Not because you don't belong together. Because you were being separated again."

"The last separation, if we can help it. I'm not going out again. I have new orders to report to 72."

"And you're only telling me now? We have to give you a send-off. We can throw something together quickly, but—"

"Don't do anything. Let's all meet in one of the observation lounges one night."

"But—"

"I don't deserve anything. I know I was horrible to everyone."

"But we're your friends. We knew you were going through a bad time. It was hard for us to see you struggle, but every time we tried to talk to you about it, you shut us down."

Tears prickled at her eyelashes. "I'm sorry," she whispered.

"No. No need. I should say I'm sorry. I should have tried harder. I should have cut the music and tried. It shouldn't have been Angie."

"No, this is on me."

"Well, you're forgiven."

Now she smiled.

His voice lifted. "You'll be back one day."

"I don't think so. We don't want to be separated again. Ruth has new orders too. Shuttle maintenance planetside."

David's voice conveyed his surprise. "That's quite a change."

"One she wants."

He grunted. "And you? You love it out here."

"I love being in a fighter. I can do that out of 72." She'd miss the camaraderie, the closeness, of belonging to a tour crew, but it was a sacrifice she would willingly make. She did love being in a cockpit. But not as much as she loved Ruth. When she'd burst from the train and bounded up the stairs to the Military Academy that first day many years ago, she never would have imagined saying that. She'd always dreamt of flying fighters and going on tours. Then Ruth had happened, changing her priorities and her dreams. She'd wobbled. She'd lost sight of what was true and would never change: life without Ruth would be unbearable.

"There's a slim chance we'll be separated again," she said to David, "but we'll deal with that if it happens."

"I wouldn't worry about it. There are always more pilots wanting tours than there are slots. Sure, pilots transfer off, like you're doing, but only a handful across tours every year. And hey, if you never go out again, you'll be in good company. Think about the pilots we trained with. Lesley's definitely planetbound, which means Mo is too, unless she asks for a tour. I doubt they'll offer her one otherwise, and what are the chances she'll ask. She has her hands full. With Chosens and children. They're pregnant again."

"I hadn't heard." Her tour mates weren't the only ones she'd neglected. "I shouldn't ask this, but do you know, uh, whose it is?"

"You're right, you shouldn't ask. Does it matter?"

"Not really."

David continued on as if she hadn't asked an inappropriate question. "Look at Ann. She's so confident she won't be ordered on tour that she built a house with Andrew."

Sheila chuckled. "Never would have seen that coming in a million years."

"She's happy. You'll probably fly with her. And Mo."

"It'll be like old times."

"For you, yeah."

"When you're planetside, we'll have to hang out," Sheila said.

"We'd like that."

They lapsed into silence. The conversation had run its course. "You want music again?"

"Sure."

Sheila resumed the piece she'd interrupted. For the first time since the tour had started, she relaxed and let herself take in the experience of being out here in the vast expanse of space. Flying out of 72 would be no different. If she ever wanted to pretend she wasn't a stone throw's away from a space station, she'd just have to close her eyes for a minute. Except instead of heading to her quarters or the canteen when the flying part of her rotation was over, she'd head to the shuttle launch area, fly down to the planet, and go home. To Ruth.

RUTH TURNED TO Kim when they were almost three quarters down the tunnel leading to the waiting area. She could hear the excited and chattering voices of family members greeting those returning from tour. Her family wouldn't be there. She'd told them a few years ago not to come, relishing the hours of silence on the train before all the visiting began, most of the journey with Shay, the other reason she wanted to say goodbye to Kim now. Shay was waiting for her, which was why Ruth's heart was pounding and what she really wanted to do was race into the waiting area and into Shay's arms.

"I'm glad we got to know each other," she said to Kim.

"Me, too. It'll be strange eating alone next time."

"I hope you find someone else." Ruth paused. "Let's keep in touch." An invitation she rarely extended, but she liked Kim and wouldn't mind seeing her occasionally. "Next time you dock, come over for supper."

"I'd like that. I want to meet Sheila."

She'd finally told Kim more details about what had happened between her and Shay. "I'd invite you this time, but we don't have our own place yet."

Kim smirked. "No need to explain. I'm sure you want to catch up with her too. And don't worry. I won't insist you introduce me to her today."

Ruth smiled gratefully. "Anyway, I won't keep you. We both have people we want to see. Just wanted to say I don't want to lose touch."

"Me, either."

The voices at the end of the tunnel grew louder. Kim rushed off to her left the moment she stepped into the waiting area. Ruth gazed in that direction and grinned when Kim fell into her mama's arms.

Then she searched for Shay.

"Ruth!"

Ruth whirled in the direction of the familiar voice that tightened her throat and made everything around her fade away. "Shay," she breathed.

Then she was in Shay's arms, pressing into her, holding her and being held. "I missed you so much," she murmured when she felt she could speak again.

They shared a kiss, one that lingered and wanted to be more, but they were in a crowded waiting area.

Another hug and squeeze and Ruth reluctantly pulled back. She knew her eyes were as moist as Shay's. "I really, really missed you!"

"I really, really, really missed you too."

Ruth blinked at Shay's face, the most precious face on the planet, and took that precious face in her hands. She touched her forehead to Shay's. "Got all your family visits out of the way?"

Shay nodded.

"We're stuck in my parents' guest room until we find our own place."

"Not quite. I mean, we can head to your parents, but we don't have to go right away."

Ruth shot her a quizzical look.

Shay unhooked the bag from Ruth's shoulder and slung it over her own. "I already have assigned quarters here. We can properly reunite at your parents', or we can spend a few hours in my quarters, and then go."

Warmth, desire, flooded through Ruth. "Lead the way."

"I was hoping you'd say that." Shay slipped her arm around Ruth's shoulders. "I said my quarters, but they're not home. We'll look for a place."

"We'd better hurry, because…" Ruth trailed off.

They didn't have to hurry. They weren't going anywhere. They were staying here, for weeks, months, years. No more separations. No more packing their bags with keepsakes and clothes and unpacking them in whatever quarters they were assigned. From now on, they would always be here.

Together.

In a place they called home.

THE KILLING OF LIEUTENANT CHRISTINE LEEDS

.....

SHACKLED

CHRISTINE LEEDS CHECKED THE TIME ON HER comm unit for the tenth time, then switched direction and paced to the other side of her office. Five minutes until Cadet Thompson arrived, and the cadet would be on time, probably a few minutes early. Christine should sit at her desk, but she was too wound up.

Footsteps rang in the corridor, approaching her office. She quickly returned to the chair behind her desk and composed herself, but it wasn't the cadet. She let out her pent breath and tried to adopt a casual posture, relaxing her shoulders and gazing at her comm station's blank monitor. She must do whatever she could to get Thompson to agree to see her socially, use every tool at her disposal. A young life would be damaged, otherwise.

Another set of footsteps. Christine stared at the door. Her shoulders tensed when Cadet Thompson—Lesley—hovered for a moment in the doorway, then stepped inside the office.

"Right on time." Christine gestured at the chair in front of her desk.

Lesley sat. Her eyes darted around the office and settled on Christine's face. She looked like she could bolt from her chair at any moment. Christine wanted to shake her. If the cadet understood the peril she was in, she'd punch through her resistance and grab the lifeline Christine was throwing to her.

"The replay looked good." She met Lesley's eyes, held her gaze. "As I mentioned the other night. So there isn't anything to discuss as far as your last session goes. But we have other things to discuss, don't we?" And this time, for her own good, Lesley had better agree.

Christine rolled back her chair. She strode past Lesley and closed the door. "Have you given any more thought to what I said?" she asked as she lowered herself back into her chair.

"I told you, I don't need to think about it."

"And I told you that I think you do," Christine said, frustration clenching her jaw. "Do you want people whispering about you? What will it take to get through to you, Lesley?"

She wanted to thump her fists on her desk when Lesley sat silently, her expression giving nothing away.

"Being seen out with someone else will be good for you. I'll be good for you." Argamon, anyone would be good for her, anyone new. Why was she being so obtuse? "I don't understand why you can't see that."

Nothing.

"Are you just going to sit there?"

"I've told you several times that I'm not interested in having any type of personal relationship with you. Can we go to the simulators now?"

Use every tool. She must do everything she could. "Tell me you'll give some thought to seeing me on 72 and we'll go to the simulators."

She studied Lesley's taut face, but the acquiescence she'd hoped for didn't happen. Once again, she wanted to shake her. Lesley had to get away from Middleton, or at least lessen her emotional attachment to her by seeing others as well. Could she not see that? Christine wanted to weep. Was she the only one who saw the inevitable tragedy approaching?

Someone knocked at the door, startling her. "Yes?"

The door opened. Lieutenant Commander Brixton stood in the doorway. "I'd like to see you, Lieutenant. In my office."

"Yes, Lieutenant Commander." Leeds stood. "Wait here," she murmured to Lesley as she passed her.

In the corridor, she fell into step with Brixton, curious about why he wanted to see her. What could be so urgent that he'd interrupt a session with a student?

When they reached his closed office door, he swung it open and motioned for her to go inside. She entered and stopped short. Two commanders stood inside, behind Brixton's desk: Commander Morton, and a commander she'd seen around the Military Academy a few times. Her mind searched for a name.

Finney. Interior. Christine's temples throbbed, even though she couldn't think of any articles she'd recently violated.

"Do you want me to stay?" Brixton asked from behind her.

"No," Morton said. "Thank you for your help."

The door closed. The two commanders stared at her. "Sit down," Morton ordered.

Christine's limbs felt heavy. She plunked into one of the guest chairs and clasped her clammy hands on her lap.

"Do you know why you're here?" Morton asked.

"No."

The two commanders exchanged a glance. Morton sank into Brixton's chair and stared at her. Finney rounded the desk and perched on its edge. "I'm Commander Finney. I oversee Sector C3, Cadet Thompson's sector."

Somewhere deep within Christine, panic stretched out its talons and squeezed her. But it felt so far away, almost as if she were hearing a distant echo, or feeling the aftershocks of a quake that had happened on the other side of the planet.

"Today, I am striking you under Articles 998 and 662," Finney said.

Christine gaped at her. She wasn't falling from the Way! "What for?"

"For your behaviour in relation to Cadet Thompson."

"What behaviour?"

"Your persistent and unwanted personal attention toward her."

Fools. "Perhaps if you were doing what you're supposed to do, I wouldn't be sitting here."

Finney's brows raised slightly. "What do you think I'm supposed to be doing?"

"Honouring the Law and the Chosen Tradition, which includes looking out for the Rymellans in your sector."

"You don't believe I'm doing that."

"Obviously not."

Once again, the two commanders exchanged a look.

"Why exactly am I here?" Christine asked, despite a voice she could barely hear begging her to remain silent, to listen, to be respectful, to thank them. "What behaviour are you referring to?"

"You've asked the cadet to meet you personally, on what could be called a date."

Christine snorted. "You're going to be very busy if asking someone out is a violation."

Morton slammed his fist onto Brixton's desk. The sudden loud crack made Christine and Finney jump. "You will speak to the commander with respect," he shouted. "Do you understand what's happening here, Lieutenant? You are being struck under Articles 998 and 662. Combined, that's a hair's width away from execution. So wipe that smirk off your face and address the commander respectfully."

The voice that had been barely a murmur grew louder. Be quiet. Choose your words carefully. Don't provoke them.

Finney shifted her weight. "When the cadet refused your invitation to go on a date with you, you persisted. You showed up at her room in the residence, uninvited. You pushed your way inside. You insinuated that you would use your position as the future supervisor of domestic patrols on 72 to—"

"A position you will no longer be occupying," Morton spat.

Finney glanced at him and raised her finger. "You used your position to try to coerce her to go out with you. She refused. Rather than letting it go, you just did it again, telling her you would only go to the simulators if she agreed to meet with you on 72."

So they'd watched. They'd planted surveillance equipment in her office and watched, listened, spied. She hadn't forced herself on Lesley. She would never do that. She was trying to help her, and yet here she sat, accused of being a potential threat to the Way unless Interior intervened. It made no sense.

"I was trying to help her," she said to Finney.

"You were trying to help Cadet Thompson?"

"Yes."

"How?"

"I shouldn't have to explain it to you."

"Explain it anyway."

"I was trying to get her away from Middleton."

"Why?"

"You should know why."

"I'd like you to tell me why."

Finney's expression was dispassionate. For a second, Christine wondered what Finney would do if she reached up and tweaked her nose. "I shouldn't have to tell you why."

"This is a waste of time," Morton bellowed. "I'm not going to stand here anymore while she plays games with us. Strike her and be done with it."

Finney opened her mouth, then shrugged. She pulled out her data collector. "Lieutenant Christine Leeds, I am striking you under Article 998, which is a Level Four strike, and Article 662, which is a Level Three strike. You will be confined to the adult wing of Sector B7's Indoctrination Academy until you are released by Interior."

Christine shot to her feet. "What? I don't understand. Can't you see I was trying to help her?"

"Sit down, Lieutenant," Finney's voice cracked.

The harshness of it pierced through Christine's shock. She almost fell back into the chair.

Finney slipped her data collector back into its holder and focused on Christine. "This is what will happen now. I'll escort you to an avia-craft. We'll fly to the B7 Indoctrination Academy. When we get there, I'll explain a bit more about what will take place during your stay." She slid off the desk. "If you'll come with—"

"No," Morton said.

Finney turned to him.

"After the way she's spoken to us, she doesn't get to slip out the back. She'll be escorted out the front."

"I believe the lieutenant might be experiencing a mental health crisis. I think some sensitivity is warranted."

Oh, so that was how Finney was going to play it. She figured everyone who disagreed with her, who saw what she couldn't, was experiencing a "mental health crisis." Christine bit back a laugh.

Morton rolled his eyes. "C3 is making you soft. Even if what you say is true, it was her responsibility to deal with whatever difficulties she's experiencing with her counsellor."

"That's why I still struck her under 998 and 662."

"And it's why she'll leave through the front entrance." Morton's attention shifted to Christine. His cold eyes sent a shiver down her spine. "I run a tight ship here. She'll serve as an example to others."

"I'm not escorting her out the front."

"Fine, have other Interior officers do it. I've cooperated with you on this. I'm asking for this in return."

Christine didn't care who escorted her where or how or why or what or when. No matter what they did, the treatment would be unjust. Article 998? When the strike was reviewed, as all serious strikes were, Finney would be called in front of her superior and asked what in the Argamon she'd thought she was doing, striking Lieutenant Christine Leeds, who'd only been trying to help a cadet, with Article 998.

"...disagree, but I won't insist," Finney said.

"Wise choice."

Finney pulled out her comm unit and spoke to someone about needing Interior officers at Commander Brixton's office.

They sat in silence for who knew how long until four officers arrived. "You are to escort the lieutenant to the aviacraft waiting on Pad 46C," Finney said to one of them.

"Escort her across the lobby and out the front entrance," Morton added. He scowled when the officers looked to Finney, who nodded.

"Come with us, please," one of the officers said to Christine.

She stood, not wanting to cause trouble. They had it wrong. She didn't need their intervention. She'd been trying to help. Once she could explain it to someone who wasn't determined to see her as a threat, everything would be fine.

The officers closed in on her, one in front, one behind, and two flanking her. When they reached the lobby, she could feel the attention, the gaping, the stares, the whispers, the only sound the ringing of boots on the hard floor.

She held her head high. The apologies would roll in when everyone realized Finney had overreached. Christine would soon be back in her office, preparing for her new role on 72, perhaps with a shiny new commendation pinned to her uniform.

THREE DAYS LATER, she wanted to scream. Apart from a couple of role-playing sessions with Indoctrinator Madison and a discussion of Article 662, nothing had happened. Nobody had spoken to her or listened to her side of the story.

They were treating her well. She had a bright, cozy bedroom, access to an entire wing of the academy—apparently she was the only adult here—could exercise outside and stroll in the pretty garden and courtyard, and the food was adequate. But she was already itching to get back to the other academy and her students. She still needed to help Lesley, and any other cadets who found themselves in a similar situation.

She did not belong here and was already wondering what to do with herself. None of the books in the library interested her, it didn't take long for her to keep up with the daily announcements, the crafts room had held her attention for all of two seconds, and the same went for the music room. Since lunch, she'd lain on her bed as the seconds, minutes, and hours crawled by. She'd asked how long she'd be here, but nobody had answered her.

Footsteps.

She sat up, swung her legs off the bed, tried not to appear bored. Indoctrinator Madison stood in the doorway. "Would you come with me, please. You have visitors."

Visitors? As she followed him down the corridor, she wondered who'd come to see her. Interior would only release information about her whereabouts to—her heart sank.

Madison stopped outside an open doorway and swept his arm toward it. "Take your time," he said.

She stepped into the room and wanted to hide. Her parents sat on the sofa in the visiting room furnished like a living room, with its sofa, two comfortable armchairs, and plush carpet. Mama's eyes were red-rimmed and Papa's avoided her.

The door clicked shut behind her. Mama stood and held out her arms. Christine hugged her, felt her damp cheeks. Anger clenched her jaw. It was one thing to put her through this, quite another to upset her parents. Her siblings must also be upset, perhaps ashamed of her. They'd only know what Interior had told them.

Mama drew back, her face bewildered. "What's it all about? Article 998? 662? What happened, Chris?"

Christine waved away her question. "It's a misunderstanding, that's all. Once I have a chance to speak to someone in Interior, they'll let me go."

"Interior doesn't have misunderstandings," Papa said softly. The disappointment in his eyes cut her to her core.

"I was trying to help someone. They misinterpreted my intent."

He looked doubtful. Why wouldn't anyone listen to her?

"We just met with someone for almost two hours," Mama said. "A counsellor. She asked us all sorts of questions about you."

"I'm surprised they didn't come to the house and search every nook and cranny." Papa's voice sounded reproachful.

Mama gripped Christine's shoulders. "We asked what you'd done, but she wouldn't tell us. When we asked how long you'd be here, she said until they were certain you weren't a threat to the Way."

Papa shot to his feet. He moved to a nearby window and gazed out at the courtyard.

"Do I look like a threat to the Way, Mama?"

"No."

"I'm sure the Adamses didn't either," Papa said. "If you could tell by just looking, there would never be any capital violations."

"This is our daughter we're talking about," Mama snapped.

"I'm aware of that, believe me," he snapped in return.

"What did you do, Chris?" Mama asked.

A sense of futility washed over her. If she told them, would they believe her? "I was trying to help a student, that's all. She must have misinterpreted my actions and reported me."

"What would she report you for?"

"I don't know, Mama. If I knew, I'd understand why I'm here."

"You really don't understand why?"

"No, I don't."

Was that doubt in Mama's eyes. Sympathy? Pity?

"I'm sure this will all be cleared up soon and I'll be back at the Military Academy."

Papa snorted.

"Why do you assume I've done something wrong?" she asked him.

He turned away from the window. "Interior wouldn't strike anyone with 998 unless they were sure they could support it. The same goes for 662."

"We told the counsellor you haven't been yourself for a while," Mama said.

What did Mama mean?

"If we'd known you weren't well, we would have done something."

Not well? "I'm fine."

"Chris." Mama's eyes moistened. A lump rose in Christine's throat when Mama cupped her face. "We don't understand what's happened, but we love you. We're glad you'll get the help you need here."

She knocked Mama's hands off her face and backed away from her. "I don't need help, Mama. I wish everyone would stop telling me I do. I'm fine. This whole thing is a huge misunderstanding."

Her hands clenched when tears ran down Mama's cheeks. Had everyone lost their minds? She was fine! Once she had the chance to talk to someone about Lesley, they'd all understand. It hadn't gotten past Christine that so far, nobody had discussed the cadet with her. Maybe they were covering up Interior's mistake. Maybe they knew that once someone with a brain sat down with her and listened, it would be obvious she shouldn't be here.

"Let's sit down." Papa sounded tired. "Let's talk about something else. Anything else."

Mama plunked down onto the sofa right after he did. Christine chose to sit across from them. She wanted to leave, burst out of this stuffy room and leave her parents behind, the parents who'd betrayed her. They claimed to love her, but they'd quickly accepted she was a threat to the Way. People who loved her wouldn't do that. But she'd be polite. She'd talk about trivialities, while Lesley hurtled toward inevitable disaster.

TWO DAYS LATER, she was escorted from her bedroom to see a counsellor. Something Finney had said on the aviacraft on the way to the Indoctrination Academy came back to her. A counsellor would get to the bottom of her difficulties. A counsellor would decide when she could leave the academy. This was the person she had to make understand. This was the person who would decide her fate.

She entered the counsellor's office, sat in one of the comfy wing armchairs, and crossed her legs. She met the woman's eyes, and didn't avert them when the counsellor gazed back at her from where she sat several metres away. Christine had done nothing wrong. She had nothing to be ashamed of, nothing to hide.

"I'm glad to finally meet you," the counsellor said. "My name is Counsellor Miller. I work with Rymellans who have wobbled off the path."

Christine didn't return her small smile.

"Is it all right if I call you Christine?"

"Go ahead." What did she care?

"Thank you. How's your room?"

"Fine."

"Is there anything that's making you uncomfortable, or anything you don't have that you feel you need?"

She needed to be released, but she had to be careful not to antagonize this woman. "No."

"That's good." Miller glanced at the notepad on her lap. "Let's begin, then. Do you understand that you've been struck under Articles 998 and 662?"

"Yes."

"Can you tell me what those articles are about?"

She wanted to roll her eyes. "Article 998 is used when Interior deems someone a potential threat to the Way unless they intervene."

"And Article 662?"

"Article 662 is used for cases of sexual harassment."

"Very good. Do you understand why you've been struck under those two articles?"

"No." Good, Miller didn't flinch. Maybe someone would finally listen to her.

"Can you tell me why Interior thinks you violated Article 662?"

"It's all a misunderstanding."

"In what way?"

"I was trying to help someone."

"Who were you trying to help?"

Christine folded her arms. "One of my students."

"Which student?"

"I'm sure you know the details already."

"You said it's all a misunderstanding, so I'd like to hear it from you."

She unfolded her arms and leaned forward. "Cadet Thompson."

"Why does Cadet Thompson need help?"

"You must have read her file."

"I'd like you to explain why you think she needs help."

Frustrated, Christine folded her arms again. Miller was just like everyone else who couldn't see it.

"You don't want to explain why you think she needs help?" Miller said.

"I shouldn't have to."

"I'd like to hear it in your own words."

"I don't want to talk about that right now." She was tired of explaining herself to people who never understood.

"All right. Let's talk about what happened, then. What do you think you did that made Interior strike you under 662?" Miller's forehead creased. "You said you were trying to help Cadet Thompson? What did you do?"

She blew out a sigh. "I asked her out."

"What did she say?"

"She said no."

"How did you react?"

"I asked her again, and I'll save you from asking the next question. She said no again. So I asked her again."

"Why did you keep asking her?"

Because she'd been trying to help her. This whole session was a waste of time!

"Do you want me to tell you what I've been told about it?" Miller asked.

"Please do." If she knew how they saw it, she could point out what they'd misunderstood.

"You initiated physical contact with Cadet Thompson during a simulation. You accessed her military file quite a number of times, much more than expected or reasonable. You invited her to call you by your first name, rather than your last name and rank. All this occurred before you asked her out. When you did ask her out, to supper, she said no. Most people would have left it there. Why didn't you?"

Now she was officially having a conversation with a dullard. "Sometimes you have to ask more than once. She didn't say she didn't want a relationship with me. In fact, it sounded like she didn't realize I was asking her to supper on a date."

"You didn't consider that she might have been trying to be polite, to not blatantly reject you."

"It didn't seem that way to me."

"Okay. Let's continue. You later showed up at her room, when you knew her roommate would be away, and—"

Christine's shoulders stiffened. "Not her roommate."

"No?"

"Her...girlfriend."

"All right, her girlfriend. You pushed your way into her room when her girlfriend was away, chased away another cadet who happened to drop by when you were there, asked Cadet Thompson if she wanted to spend time with you. When she clearly stated she was not interested in pursuing a personal relationship with you, you became angry. You made unwelcome and unkind comments about the cadet's personal life. You then returned to her room and threatened to use your position to schedule the cadet and her girlfriend on different rotations on Space Station 72." Miller met Christine's eyes. "How am I doing so far?"

Miller made her sound like a mad woman. "I wasn't angry. I was passionate. I was trying to give her advice."

"You were trying to give her advice when you threatened to use your position to influence the rotation schedule?"

"Sometimes you have to take matters into your own hands when someone isn't listening, When they're not doing what would be best for them."

"You thought keeping Cadet Thompson and her girlfriend apart would be best for her."

Christine nodded. Maybe Miller wasn't such a dullard.

"You saw the cadet next when she came to your office prior to a scheduled simulation session. Once again, you urged her to consider having a personal relationship with you. Once again, the cadet made it clear she wasn't interested in such a relationship. When she expressed a desire to go to the simulator, you told her to agree to seeing you on Space Station 72 first."

"When someone needs help, you do what you have to do."

"How does she need help?"

"The answer should be clear to you now."

"Does it have anything to do with her relationship with Cadet Middleton? You seem angry about it."

"Not angry. Concerned."

"Why?"

Christine snorted. "If you can't see it, you shouldn't be sitting in that chair."

Miller's expression didn't change. "I'll tell you what I do see that I find surprising. You were quite aggressive and forward with the cadet. You boldly asked her out several times, and when she refused, you were aggressive with her, including using threats, to the point that you violated Article 662 and your behaviour was serious enough to warrant striking you under Article 998. You say you did what you had to do to help her."

"Yes."

"You've been here almost a week now, but we're only meeting for the first time because I wanted to talk to people who know you. Your parents, your siblings, your friends, your colleagues. Do you want to know how they described you?"

"Does it matter what I want? You're going to tell me anyway."

Miller read from the pad on her lap. "They describe you as kind, considerate, quiet, a bit shy at times, a wonderful and effective instructor who takes time with her students and gives extra help to those who need it, patient, sensitive. That doesn't sound like the woman who was aggressive and insensitive with Cadet Thompson."

"I've already explained why I needed to push."

"To help her."

"Yes."

"Those closest to you said you haven't quite been yourself for a while. You've been terse, sometimes angry, broody, you haven't pursued your hobbies as much."

Christine uncrossed her legs, then crossed them again. "How would they know? They don't see me very often. I'm at the Military Academy or on 72 most of the time."

"But they *have* seen you over the past year, some of them quite often. You have supper with your parents every two weeks."

She conceded the point with her silence.

"And even though you're not particularly close to any of your work colleagues, they also see you frequently, and they noticed that you've been tenser than usual and have seemed preoccupied." Miller paused to take a breath. "What else has been going on for you? Are you happy with your position at the Military Academy?"

"Yes."

"Has anything been bothering you?"

"No."

"What about Cadet Thompson and her relationship with Cadet Middleton?"

"Apart from that, no."

"Has anything unusual or noteworthy happened to you during the past year?"

Her temples pulsed. She resisted the urge to grip the arms of the chair. "No."

"Nothing at all?"

"No, nothing."

Miller stared at her. "We're going to stop for now. We'll meet again tomorrow. I'd like you to think about the past year and let me know if you remember anything."

"I won't."

"I'd also like you to think about why the relationship between Cadet Thompson and Cadet Middleton bothers you."

"I'd think it would be obvious."

"I'd like you to explain it to me."

Idiot.

Christine rose when Miller did and returned to her room with a sigh of relief. She'd think about Miller's questions all right, and formulate answers that would hopefully satisfy her, so she could get back to her office and her students. As for helping Lesley, she'd have to bide her time, let a few months go by, then approach her on 72. Nobody else was going to step in. It was up to her to save her student.

AFTER SUPPER, CHRISTINE went into the library to use the comm station. They'd restricted her access to everything except the daily announcements and personal dispatches, which she suspected they were reading. They were reading her replies too. She always chose her words carefully.

Mama wrote to her every day, and so did her older sister Hannah. Her two brothers had written to her once, to say they were thinking of her. She hadn't heard from Nancy, the baby in the family. She considered writing her a dispatch, then decided against it. If Nancy couldn't be bothered to write a dispatch, Christine wouldn't write one either.

She wrote back to Mama and Hannah, saying the usual things. She was fine, the food was fine, they were treating her well. She didn't mention her counsellor was slow. Her family must have spoken to her. They'd know. Christine simply said she'd met Miller and they'd had a good conversation.

Miller had mentioned friends. Christine wondered who she'd meant. She played on the instructor volleyball team when the season was underway, and when she had the time, she participated in the various staff card games taking place around the academy and on 72. She rarely had the time, though. She was busy teaching and conducting practicums. In fact, she'd taken on extra work a few months ago, agreed to cover for an instructor who was away having a baby. That was why she'd lost interest in her models and had been thinking of dropping out of volleyball. Any time she thought about trading for a new model kit or attending a volleyball practice or game, she just felt tired.

The counsellor had gotten one thing right, though. Christine loved her position and immersed herself in military life, rarely leaving the Military Academy. Those biweekly suppers with her parents and the odd visit with her siblings were the only times she left the academy to go anywhere other than 72. She had to admit, she'd been distracted lately, but that was because she cared about her students. How could she not have stepped in, not tried to help, when she'd understood the danger Lesley was in?

Christine could try to make Miller understand, but the counsellor would only twist her words and throw them back at her in the form of a question. However, she needed Miller on her side to get out of here, so perhaps she would answer as honestly as she could. If she could get Miller to understand, the counsellor would recommend the strikes against her be removed and release her immediately. Christine was sure of it.

"I WAS REVIEWING our conversation from yesterday," Miller said, from her chair in the room with the walls painted in soothing tones. "You said you were concerned about Cadet Thompson's relationship with Cadet Middleton. Can you explain why?"

Christine wanted to retort for the millionth time that she shouldn't have to, but what good would that do? She needed Miller on her side. "They've been together for a while. Some people say they treat each other like Chosens."

"What does that mean, treat each other like Chosens?"

"They see each other exclusively, they live together at the academy, they've been together for years, from what I understand."

"You don't know any other young couples who are exclusive and room together at the academy?"

She thought about it. "A few, I suppose. But they haven't been together long. And most of them are Solitaries, so they won't have to break up."

"If Cadet Thompson and Cadet Middleton were Solitaries, would their relationship bother you?"

Christine shifted in her seat. "No, it wouldn't."

"It bothers you because they're both Chosens."

"They're not each other's Chosen."

"The cadets are both twenty-one. They won't receive Chosen Papers for at least four years."

"But they've been together for a long time. And they have Chosens out there, waiting for them. Does it matter that their Papers are at least four years away? They'll have to break up, and there's no reason for them to be so attached, not when it will all be for nothing in the end." Her voice sounded shrill. She gulped down air.

Miller grunted. "So their relationship bothers you because they have Chosens."

"They're not being very smart."

"You think it would be good for them to see others."

Christine nodded.

"Like you, for example?"

"Anyone who doesn't want to get serious."

"How many casual relationships have you had?"

The question took her by surprise. "What do you mean?"

"How many relationships have you had where it was understood that the basis for the relationship was purely or mainly physical. Or where exclusivity wasn't expected or committed to, or where you knew there was no significant emotional attachment between you and the other party?"

She swallowed. "None."

"So when you told Cadet Thompson you weren't looking for anything serious, that you would be satisfied with her as a bed partner, if she had entered into a casual relationship with you, that would have been unusual for you."

"I needed to help her."

"By weakening her relationship with Cadet Middleton, or by breaking them up entirely, you would have been helping her."

"They need to stop acting like they're each other's Chosen."

"And you were willing to enter into a casual relationship with Cadet Thompson to make that happen."

"Yes."

"What danger was Cadet Thompson in if she continued to treat Cadet Middleton like she would treat her Chosen?"

Christine wanted to get up and march from the office. If the idiot across from her wasn't responsible for deciding when she could go back to her life, she would do exactly that. "Cadet Middleton isn't her Chosen," she said slowly, "so eventually they will have to break up. That will be difficult for them. Don't you see? I wanted to help her. The longer she stays with Middleton, the more difficult it will be when her Papers arrive. She might even fall from the Way."

Miller's lips pursed. "Let me tell you what I think you're saying. Cadet Thompson and Cadet Middleton aren't Chosens, but their relationship is exclusive and they've been together for a long time. Even though their

Papers are at least four years away, you're worried that when they arrive, the cadets will have trouble breaking up. Is that fair?"

"Even if they do break up, it will be a horrible time for them. Why would anyone set themselves up for something they know will cause them so much pain?"

"I gather, then, that you don't think Rymellans who know they have Chosens should be in long-term exclusive relationships, meaning that Cadet Thompson, for example, should not have entered into any long-term exclusive relationship after her eighteenth birthday."

"Well, I don't know. I'm not saying...they were already in a relationship. From what I've heard, they got together while they were still at the Learning Academy."

"Do you think that if a Rymellan is in a relationship and does not receive a Solitary Notification on their eighteenth birthday, they should leave that relationship?"

She shifted in her chair again. "I suppose it depends. If it's not serious..."

"Your position is that Rymellans who have Chosens should stay away from relationships, or only have casual ones, until they receive their Chosen Papers."

Christine balled her pants in her hands. She did not like the way this conversation had shifted. "My position is that it depends," she snapped.

"In Cadet Thompson's case, you believe her relationship isn't healthy, mainly because she and Cadet Middleton have been together for a while."

"And they treat each other like Chosens. It's a recipe for disaster. They'll have to break up at some point." How many times would she have to explain it before Miller understood?

"Is that how you were helping Cadet Thompson? You wanted to prepare her for the day when she'd have to break up? Or you wanted her feelings, her attachment, to Cadet Middleton to lessen?"

She nodded.

"You decided to give the cadet the opportunity to experience a relationship with someone else, namely you."

"She would see that it's possible for her to be with other people, that Cadet Middleton isn't the only one for her. She has to see that, doesn't she? She's a Chosen."

"When she refused your advances, you persisted because you believe she could fall from the Way if she's too emotionally attached to Cadet Middleton. What did you say to her?" Miller checked her notes. "You said her relationship with Cadet Middleton is inappropriate and the way they cling to each other is unhealthy."

"Yes."

Miller studied her. The sudden silence felt awkward. "Are you sure that's why you behaved the way you did?" the counsellor finally asked.

Christine froze. For a moment, she could only stare back at Miller. Then anger flared. "It's the truth! If Interior had done its flaming job, I wouldn't have needed to do anything. Those colleagues you spoke to were right. I care about my students. I help when I see one flailing."

"Why didn't you try to help Cadet Middleton?"

The question momentarily gave her pause. "Cadet Thompson is in a special mentoring program. More is expected of her."

"Why didn't you go to Interior and express your concerns about her relationship?"

Christine lifted her hands from her lap, wanting to shake Miller. She quickly clenched them on her lap again. "Like that would have done anything. Look at what's happened. I try to help someone who's only going to run into trouble in the future and I end up here, back at the Indoctrination Academy, role-playing articles I know like the back of my hand and sitting in a counsellor's office answering inane questions."

Miller didn't react in any way. Christine wanted to throw something at her, to see if she'd try to dodge it. The woman must be made of stone. No matter what Christine said, Miller sat calmly.

"All right." The counsellor rubbed her lower lip with her forefinger. "The primary reason you're worried about Cadet Thompson's relationship with Cadet Middleton is because they treat each other like Chosens, as you put it, which will lead to problems in the future. Cadet Thompson could fall from the Way. No matter what happens, it will be a deeply painful time for her."

"Yes. When her Chosen Papers arrive."

Miller gazed at her. "Would it be fair to say you believe nobody should treat anyone like a Chosen unless they're actually Chosens to each other?"

"Yes."

"Being a Chosen means something."

"Yes."

"It's special."

Inane statement number 599. "Yes."

Miller nodded. "Let's talk about something else. Yesterday, I asked if anything unusual or noteworthy happened to you over the past year. I asked you to think about it. Did you remember anything?"

"No."

"Nothing at all."

"Nothing."

"You are," the counsellor's forehead crinkled, "thirty years old, correct?"

"Correct."

Miller pointed at Christine and swept her index finger through the air, from left to right. "You're not wearing a Chosen ring. You're not Joined."

Heat crept up Christine's back and spread to her neck and face. "I'm sure this is all in my file."

"You're a Solitary."

"Yes."

"You received a Solitary Notification on your eighteenth birthday."

Her breath quickened. She clenched her hands tighter. "No."

"You did not receive a Solitary Notification on your eighteenth birthday."

"No."

"When you were eighteen, you found out you're a Chosen."

"Yes."

"But you're thirty and you're not Joined. What happened?"

She blinked at the counsellor, willed her to disappear, to go away, to leave her alone. "You know what must have happened."

"I'd like you to tell me."

"Why?" she snarled.

"I'd like to hear it from you."

"Just read my file."

"I've read your file," Miller said, her tone annoyingly level. "I'd like to hear it from you."

"It didn't matter."

"Then you won't mind telling me about it."

She unfurled her aching fingers to stretch them, then clenched her hands again. "I received a Death Notification."

"When?"

"Seven months ago."

"Can you tell me about it? Where were you when the courier arrived?"

In her office at the Military Academy. When the knock at the door had come and she'd looked up and seen the courier in his gold cloak… "At work."

"At the Military Academy?"

"Yes."

"Where exactly? Were you alone?"

"Yes. In my office." She'd grinned, greeted him, stretched out her hand to receive the Papers she was beginning to think would never arrive, even though she knew she was a Chosen. Only three months until she turned thirty and they still hadn't come. Then he'd reached into his bag and offered her an envelope. She'd stopped smiling. "The envelope he gave me had a black border and a black band across it."

Something pushed against her, deep inside, struggling to be released, searching for a crack, a weakness, that would allow it to burst forth and overwhelm her. She fought it, pushed back with all her strength, forced it to retreat, to go back into that place deep inside her where it couldn't touch her. "The envelopes shouldn't look like that. It's nobody's business."

"I think Death Notifications have the banding because when some Rymellans receive their Papers, they want to open them with their families and friends," Miller said, in her annoyingly level tone. "My understanding is that when Chosen Council couriers deliver a Death Notification, they do everything they can to deliver it privately, to give the recipient time alone before they tell anyone."

She hadn't told anyone for several weeks. She'd bowed out of her next usual supper with her parents, but had known she could only do that once without worrying them. She'd shown up for the next one, and when Mama had asked the question she'd asked for more than four years at that point—"When are your Papers going to arrive? You turn thirty in fill-in-the-blank months"—she'd had to tell them.

"Did you read the notification right away?" Miller asked.

She wasn't sure. She thought so. She'd read it in her office, but she couldn't remember if the courier had caught her just before a practicum or class. She might have slipped the envelope into a desk drawer and read it later. After she'd seen the envelope, all she remembered of that day was reading the notification. Short, to the point, sympathetic. "I'm not sure. I don't remember. It wasn't a big deal."

"No?"

"No."

"How did you feel?"

She felt herself relax. This was familiar territory. She'd talked about this with her own counsellor, who'd also been notified that Christine Leeds's Chosen had died, and therefore said Christine Leeds was now a Solitary. "Surprised," she said to Miller. "Shocked. A little upset, but I'd never met her so..." She shrugged. "I was more upset about not being able to have children."

"You wanted children."

"Yes. But I thought, I'll just focus on my career, and at some point I'll meet someone. We won't be Chosens, but we'll still love each other."

"But you didn't feel any grief over your Chosen's death."

"I'd never met her. You can't grieve someone you don't know."

"Did you have any relationships after you turned eighteen and knew you were a Chosen?"

The sudden change of topic threw her for a second. "Sure. They weren't casual, but I was young, and I knew I was a Chosen. I never saw them as long-term."

"What about after you turned twenty-five?"

"No."

"You wanted to be ready for when your Papers arrived."

Christine nodded.

"As the years went by, you must have wondered how long it would be before they came."

"Of course." With each passing month, her anticipation had grown. When she'd turned twenty-nine, she remembered feeling extra happy. Less than a year, and all the waiting would be over. She'd receive her Papers, meet the woman the Chosen Council had selected for her, and they'd begin their life together, love and support each other, have daughters. By the time that day in her office had arrived, when the Chosen Council courier had knocked at her open door, she'd woken every morning wondering, "Will this be the day?" She'd been content, even happy. And so hopeful. Her life had been full of wonderful possibilities.

"Do you ever wonder about who your Chosen was?" Miller asked.

"No."

"You've never asked yourself how she died, what her vocation was, which sector she lived in?"

"No. I never knew her. She was a concept to me. Nothing more."

Something hit her top lip. She felt the spot with her tongue, tasted salt, then licked away the tear.

"Let's stop for today," Miller said. "Like yesterday, I'm going to leave you with something to think about."

More homework from a counsellor. Christine wanted to roll her eyes.

"I want you to think more about how you felt when you received the Death Notification. How did your expectations for your life change? Did you see yourself differently? I'll ask you those two questions tomorrow."

She could hardly wait.

After leaving the stifling room, she strode to the one unlocked door to the outside world, burst into the cooler air, and jogged around the fenced exercise space, an acceptable way to burn off the anger coursing through her. How long would she have every detail of her life thrown in her face by a counsellor who didn't seem all that interested in why she'd done what she did? Maybe this was how they punished those who violated 998 and 662. Torturing them with questions about minutiae, trivia, events that didn't matter. Well, she'd play their game. She had no choice, not if she wanted to go back to her life.

THE NEXT AFTERNOON SHE WAS BACK in that same room, in the same chair, wondering what idiotic questions Miller would ask her today. The counsellor started off with one of the two homework questions. Christine hadn't given them much thought. She'd already told the woman how she'd felt about the Death Notification, but Miller was determined to go over everything hundreds of times.

"You didn't feel anything," Miller said, her voice even.

"I was shocked. Surprised. I've already told you that." Christine couldn't keep the edge out of her voice.

"Your expectations for your life must have changed."

"Of course. Five minutes earlier I'd been a Chosen, expecting Chosen Papers. Now I was a Solitary with a dead Chosen." Were all the counsellors who worked with those who'd "wobbled" this obtuse?

"You were also upset that you won't be able to have children."

"I'm sure every Solitary feels that way. Being a Solitary doesn't mean I can't live a happy life."

"Still, you were upset."

"I'm not the only one who's found out I can't have children. Rymellans adjust."

"That can take time."

"Not for everyone. Every Solitary manages it."

"Most Solitaries find out when they turn eighteen. Until that moment, they temper their expectations around children, and then release them completely. You didn't have to do that. You expected to have children, and to Join, until you were almost thirty."

That something inside her, the unmentionable thing she'd bound and caged, struggled once again to break free, to seize control, choke her, push her head underwater and drown her. "I don't know how many times I have to tell you that receiving the Death Notification wasn't the huge event you think it should have been. I couldn't grieve for someone I didn't know, or for a life I never had. Was I shocked? Yes. Was I disappointed? Yes." She thumped the arms of her chair. "What do you want from me? What do I have to say to make you believe me?"

As usual, Miller didn't react. Her tone remained calm. "Did you cry when you received your notification?"

She rolled her eyes. "No."

"Did you take any time off?"

"No."

"Did you tell your superior about it?"

"No. Why would I?"

"Let's go back to Cadet Thompson. She refused your advances."

"Yes." Otherwise she wouldn't be here answering inane questions thrown at her by a slow counsellor.

"What would you have done if she hadn't refused?"

The question surprised her. "What do you mean?"

"What were you planning to do? I assume you were hoping she'd say yes. You must have had some idea of what you'd do, where you'd go, what you'd talk about. Tell me about it."

Christine stared at her. "I—I thought, I mean..." She seized on the thought that entered her mind. "I asked her to have supper with me."

"What were your plans? What were you going to talk about? Were you going to ask her somewhere afterwards, like the Dance Hall, or maybe back to your room?"

Her mind drew a blank. Her mouth moved, but nothing came out. Panic shallowed her breath and made the counsellor's face appear distorted. She hadn't thought about it. At all. She'd just known she needed to ask Lesley, touch Lesley, persist with her until she—

Said yes?

"How long have you had a crush on her?" Miller asked.

Christine swallowed.

"I know you were trying to help the cadet, but I assume you wouldn't ask someone out unless you were interested in them."

"Of course not."

"You'd try to help in some other way."

"Yes."

"But you asked Cadet Thompson out and were very persistent about it, so you must have had a crush on her."

"Yes," Christine whispered.

"When did you first notice her?"

"She's difficult not to notice. She's quite tall, she's pretty. I heard her name quite a lot because a commander at the Military Academy had taken an interest in her. Not that type of interest." She wasn't sure if Morton was capable of liking anyone other than himself. "He felt she was one of the students who could make admiral. He offers those students extra support."

"When did you realize that your interest in her was more personal, that you were attracted to her?"

She hadn't. No, that couldn't be right. When they were in the simulator, she'd felt compelled to be close to her. "When we were flying a sim together. Her practicum."

Miller glanced down at her notes. "You moved into the cadet's personal space during the first sim you flew with her. During the second sim, you touched the cadet's leg, correct?"

"Yes."

"So the moment you realized you were attracted to the cadet, you immediately acted on it. That's quite bold."

Blood pounded in Christine's ears.

"How often had you interacted with the cadet before the first sim?"

"I taught a few of her classes."

"Are you sure you didn't develop a crush on her during one of those classes?"

No, she had not. But she must have. She must have had a crush on her before that first sim, because Miller was right. Christine wouldn't have reacted the first time she'd felt physically attracted to Lesley. She wasn't that brave. "I must have."

"You're not sure."

"I don't remember. I…"

"Before the first sim, did you fantasize about the cadet?"

"No!"

"Were you working up the courage to ask her out, and being physically closer to her in the simulator was your way of trying to gauge how she might react?"

"No. I mean, I don't think so."

"Why did you touch her leg in the simulator?"

"I wanted to."

"Why did you want to?"

"I don't know," she shouted.

Her words reverberated around the room.

"I just wanted to, okay? I didn't think about it. I didn't plan it. The first time we were inside the simulator I just...crowded her. I don't...I must have been attracted to her. I must have been trying to suppress it and it just came out."

"You don't know when you developed a crush on the cadet, you didn't fantasize about having a relationship with her, you don't know why you crowded her physical space or touched her in the simulator."

"I didn't say that. I said I don't remember when my crush started."

"You still have a crush on her."

"No—I mean..." What did she mean?

"You've been here for a week now. You must miss seeing Cadet Thompson."

Christine could hardly breathe. She'd thought about Lesley since arriving here, but not in that way, not once. Maybe not ever. No, that couldn't be right.

"I've been waiting for you to ask about her, or to express concern for her, but you haven't, to me or anyone else here. Apart from worrying that she might fall from the Way in the future. You've expressed concern about that, but otherwise you haven't been concerned about her at all."

"I'm so used to suppressing it..."

"You violated the Way for her and find yourself in the adult wing of the Indoctrination Academy. That doesn't sound like you were suppressing it."

Miller's tone was mild and her expression sympathetic, but her words pummelled Christine, made her want to cringe and raise her hands to protect her head.

"If you're able to suppress your feelings for the cadet so effectively, why weren't you able to stop yourself from making unwelcome advances toward her?"

"I think suppressing my feelings to that extent wasn't healthy. They came out in ways they shouldn't have."

"Let me say what I think you're saying, to make sure I understand it.

You're saying you developed a crush on Cadet Thompson, but you suppressed those feelings, so effectively that you don't remember when you developed the crush, and you never thought about being in a relationship with the cadet. But those feelings you weren't feeling had to come out somehow, and they came out in the simulator, and when you asked her out."

"Yes."

"You were making your feelings clear then, weren't you? You weren't suppressing them."

"No, I suppose not."

"When she said no, why did you keep going back? Why did you threaten to use your influence to keep Cadet Thompson and Cadet Middleton from flying with each other on 72? Why didn't you accept she wasn't interested?"

"I don't know."

"I thought you were trying to help her."

"Yes! Yes, I was."

"And you had a crush on her, which is why you decided to help her by asking her out."

"Yes."

Miller fell silent for a moment, then drew breath. "When we first met, you didn't talk about your feelings for the cadet. You didn't say you miss her, or express any concern for her, or ask how she's doing. Since then, you haven't expressed any feelings about her, about how she makes you smile, or how you'd like to dance with her or hold her hand, or how you'd like to spend time with her." She paused. "You've talked about how you needed to help her, but you've shown very little interest or concern for the cadet, apart from saying you think she behaves inappropriately with her girlfriend. Today, you're saying you had feelings you were suppressing and they came out the wrong way."

"You said I must have a crush on her."

"You don't have a crush on her."

No. But that didn't make sense.

Miller interpreted Christine's silence as agreement. "Then why did you say you must be suppressing your feelings?"

She wanted Miller to shut up, to stop confusing her.

"You've made it clear that you believed she was behaving inappropriately. Rather than offering her some advice, as her instructor, you decided to handle the situation by making advances toward her in the hope she'd stop behaving inappropriately with her girlfriend."

Christine moistened her lips. "That doesn't sound right."

"I'm repeating what you've told me. Your reason for persisting with Cadet Thompson. You say you wanted to help her, and that's why you persisted in pursuing her, even though she made it clear she wasn't interested in having a relationship with you. At the same time, you weren't interested in having a relationship with her."

"That doesn't make sense."

"I agree. Do you think it's possible you've been telling yourself a story to explain why you behaved the way you did? A story about how you're interested in Cadet Thompson, and because of that, planned to help her avoid future grief by dating her, and that's why you were so persistent? A story that's not true?"

Her heart felt as if it were leaping from her chest. She wanted to bolt from the room. "I don't know," she mumbled.

"Why have you stopped participating in activities and hobbies you enjoy?"

"I've been busy."

"You've been busy before."

"I guess I just haven't felt like doing the same old things."

"What have you been doing instead?"

"I took on an extra class and agreed to supervise a few more practicums. I'm covering for an instructor having a baby."

"You must have some free time. What do you do when you aren't working?"

"Sometimes I'm tired. I nap." Christine shrugged. "I don't know."

"When did Cadet Thompson's relationship with Cadet Middleton start bothering you?"

"I don't know. I don't remember."

"You don't remember when her relationship started bothering you. You don't know why you asked her out. You said you were helping her, but you could have simply offered her advice."

She met the counsellor's eyes, then looked away. She *had* been helping

Lesley, and she must have been interested in her. She'd felt such a compulsion to ask her out, to keep asking, to not let up.

Miller leaned forward. "Let me throw something out and you can tell me what you think. The Death Notification you received was a huge shock and deeply affected you, but you didn't deal with it. You soldiered on, repressed your grief. You lost interest in life and felt adrift. You're a private person, quiet, you have few friends, by choice, I've been told. You don't like to appear weak or to ask for help. But deep down, you knew something was wrong. You knew you needed help. The part of you that knew drove you to behave the way you did with Cadet Thompson. You wanted to be struck, so you would be sitting where you are right now, getting help."

She snorted. "That doesn't make sense. Who would want to be struck and end up here?" And be marched out of the pilot training complex, humiliated, in front of their peers. "If I needed help, I would have seen my counsellor. I *was* seeing my counsellor."

"Acting out when there's a problem, unconsciously wanting Interior to step in and help before it's too late, is more common than you'd think. You viewed the cadet's file quite a few times before you first approached her. She's being groomed for admiral for a reason. You knew she would refuse your advances. And that she'd report you before things went too far."

Christine shook her head. "It's a nice theory, but the Death Notification didn't affect me that deeply. Like I keep trying to make you understand, I can't grieve an abstract person. I never knew her. Yes, my expectations for my life have changed. My future has changed."

"Have you thought about your future, now that you won't be Joined?"

"Not really," she mumbled.

"Have you dated since you received the Death Notification?"

"No."

"You received it seven months ago and you haven't dated anyone since you turned twenty-five. Since the notification didn't affect you at all, why haven't you dated anyone?"

She wished Miller would shut up and leave her alone. "I don't know."

"Have you danced with anyone at a dance or at the Dance Hall? Or had a meal with a woman you're attracted to? Perhaps not a date, but the beginnings of a friendship that could develop into more."

"I'm not interested in dating right now."

"If that's true, why did you ask Cadet Thompson out?"

"I—I had to."

"If she'd said yes, what would you have done? Would you have told her you didn't mean it? That you weren't actually going to spend any time with each other socially?"

She was really beginning to dislike Miller. Counsellors were supposed to listen, not twist words and ask ridiculous questions.

"We've covered a lot today," Miller said. "We're going to take a break. I'll see you in a few days. Take the time to relax and think about what we've talked about."

Christine couldn't stop herself from scowling, even though she knew it was rude. A few days. She'd hang around twiddling her thumbs, when she could be teaching or training pilots. But she bit her tongue. Miller's input would be critical when it came to deciding when she could leave and get back to her life.

TWO DAYS LATER, Christine sat in front of the comm station in the library. She'd started to read the daily announcements, but the last session she'd had with Miller kept intruding into her thoughts. Despite trying to avoid dwelling on what had transpired, she kept going back to it. She could admit the way Miller told "the story of what had happened with Lesley" didn't make sense. Christine had thought back, tried to pinpoint when Lesley had first caught her interest, when seeing her and Middleton together had annoyed her.

She could recall the latter incident. She'd seen them walking across the courtyard, hand in hand, talking, acting, as if they were the only two there, that the courtyard wasn't packed with cadets and officers and instructors. About six months ago. That was when she'd stopped to watch them, then carried on to her office, her jaw tight and her afternoon ruined.

But she couldn't remember when she'd first felt an attraction to Lesley, a meaningful attraction, not just a passing "isn't she pretty" attraction.

"Christine," a familiar voice said from behind her.

She pasted a fake smile on her face and twisted in her chair. Miller. "Reading announcements?"

She nodded.

"I'd like to talk to you for a minute. I won't keep you long."

Her heart thumped. Maybe she was getting out. Maybe Miller had said they wouldn't be seeing each other for a few days because she'd decided to meet with the indoctrinators and whoever else held the key to her cage.

She walked with Miller, sank into her usual chair in Miller's office, and waited with bated breath.

Miller sat in her usual spot, but she didn't have a notepad on her lap this time. "I wanted us to break for a bit so I could speak to the Chosen Council about your situation. Normally, Chosens who receive Death Notifications don't receive any information about their deceased Chosen. Since you weren't affected by your Death Notification, you were shocked, yes, but otherwise you moved on with your life, I didn't see any harm in approaching the Council and asking if it would be possible for them to approach your Chosen's family and ask if some information could be released. The family agreed to release an image of your Chosen."

Christine's throat tightened. She couldn't breathe. She clawed at her neck, choking, trying to pry off whatever invisible force was squeezing her life away. Why wasn't Miller helping? She was just sitting there.

Her fingers ached. She realized she was digging them into the chair, that she was breathing, that the light in the room appeared hazy, and everything she could see—Miller, her chair, the framed images on the wall—was shimmering.

"I thought you'd be interested in the image, but I won't force you to view it. I've dispatched it to you. You can view it at your leisure, or you can delete it. It's up to you."

She didn't want it. The moment she left this room, she'd go to her bedroom, find the dispatch on her comm unit, and delete it. She did not want to deal with this at the comm station in the library.

"That's all I wanted to say. Enjoy the rest of your day." Miller rose. "I'll be here if you need me, and you can beep me any time as well. You have my code."

Christine stood. Her limbs felt jerky as she left the room. In her designated bedroom, she reached for her comm unit. Her hand stopped a few centimetres away from it.

She went back to the library and picked up the announcements where she'd left off, but she couldn't get her comm unit out of her head, could see Miller's dispatch in her mind, Miller's name, the image attachment indicator. What point would there be to viewing an image of her dead Chosen? The woman was dead. Gone. Lying in some crypt somewhere. Dwelling on it, thinking about what could have been—that vice tightened around her throat again.

She shot up from the chair, hurried to the kitchen, poured herself a glass of water and gulped it down. Flaming incompetent counsellor. Christine felt worse than when she'd arrived. Was that what they did here? Was that the punishment for pushing the Way? Being poked, prodded, interrogated.

Intending to return to the library, she left the kitchen, but found herself drawn back to her bedroom. To her comm unit, sitting on the nightside table, daring her to pick it up, to open the dispatch. To look. She could grab it and delete the dispatch, end any compulsion right now. But she felt paralyzed.

She wanted to look.

She didn't want to look.

She wanted to look.

She snatched up the comm unit, opened the list of dispatches, found the one from Miller. Her grip tightened around her unit as her throat closed again, her heart raced, she couldn't catch her breath. She sank to her knees, struggled for air, willed herself to breathe in, breathe out, breathe in, breathe out.

She stood, put the unit back on the nightside table, stared at it. Fear snaked through her, angering her. She wanted to look! But she didn't want to die.

Now she sounded insane. It was a dispatch. An image. It couldn't kill her. But when she reached out again, wind rushed in her ears and her breath grew shallow and she sank onto her bed, afraid she would faint.

The comm unit sat silently, taunting her, beckoning to her.

She snatched it up again, almost ran from her bedroom and down the corridor, knocked on Miller's open office door. "Can I come in?"

"Of course."

She stepped inside, forced the words out. "I'd like to view the image of my Chosen here, right now." She could feel her chest rising and falling and knew her face was red. If Miller thought she'd lost her mind, she didn't show it.

"Sit down and take your time," Miller said.

She sat in her usual chair, stared at the comm unit in her hand, forced herself to focus on the list of dispatches, on the one that leaped out at her.

She opened it, read the short dispatch from Miller. "This is the image I told you about." All she had to do now was bring up the image, but something inside her didn't want to do it, pummelled against her, screeched in panic, urged her not to look, not to see, to run, hide, hurl the comm unit out the window, shattering glass.

She'd beaten down that thing inside her before, and she did it again, regained control. The Death Notification hadn't affected her. She couldn't mourn a dead Chosen. The image was of someone she didn't know, couldn't possibly care about. An abstract person, she'd told Miller. The image would make the woman less abstract, but only as much as viewing an image in an announcement made a person less abstract.

She went to open the image. Her body rebelled, squeezed her eyes shut, closed her throat, accelerated her heart, distorted her senses. Gasping for air, she forced her eyes open.

Miller was in motion. She rolled her chair next to Christine's, sat down, and gazed at her with sympathetic eyes. "I'll be right here, okay?"

She managed a nod.

"Do you want me to open the image for you?"

"No," she rasped, shocked at how weak her voice sounded. "I'll do it."

"Take your time."

She forced her eyes back to the dispatch, battled the force trying to keep her finger from opening the image, and pressed the indicator.

The image of a woman filled the unit's screen, a woman with thick curly brown hair framing an oval face, lively and curious bright green eyes, a pert nose, a toothy smile that warmed Christine. She touched the image, traced the hair, the eyes, the lips. This was her Chosen, the woman she would have met, Joined with, had children with, laughed with, danced with, made love to, shared everything with. This was the woman the Chosen Council had chosen for her, the one she couldn't have helped but love with all her heart and mind.

It was also the face of a dead woman, a cold woman rotting away in a crypt, who'd never heard the name Christine Leeds, had never known about the pilot and instructor, the volleyball player, the model builder, the woman who would have loved her and cherished her and protected her.

The woman who'd been Christine Leeds, a Chosen, one second, and Christine Leeds, a Solitary, the next, who hadn't known the moment her life had changed, hadn't been there to hold her Chosen's hand, would never know the woman who would have shared her life, shared everything.

That thing inside her broke free of its chains, burst forth, gushed from her, drowning her. The comm unit thudded to the floor. She hugged herself, rocked, couldn't stop the wrenching, ragged, despairing sobs that tore from her.

Her Chosen was dead. Her Chosen was dead.

Three weeks later

"...HELPED BY REPORTING me. I understand it now, can see in hindsight how I couldn't face it. I'm ashamed by my behaviour. I wish I could go back and do it differently. I wished I'd taken time off, told my counsellor how wrong I felt, realized losing interest in everything wasn't normal. I told myself I wanted to dedicate more time to teaching and helping my students, but I'd always believed I would serve my students best by taking care of myself first. I'll keep that in mind from now on."

Her eyes moist, Christine looked up from the journal on her lap and waited for Miller's reaction.

"I'm proud of you. I know it's difficult to write about it so honestly, and share what you've written with me. You're doing so well." Miller paused. "I only have one concern. Your shame. I know it's natural for you to feel that way, but you have no reason to feel ashamed. You weren't yourself. You were in crisis."

"My behaviour affected someone else, made her feel uncomfortable. I realize now I never expected her to enter into any type of relationship with me, but at the time, the compulsion was real. To her, it was all real. And unwelcome. I wish I could erase it all for her."

"Would it help if I arranged for you to meet with her here, so you can apologize to her, and perhaps explain, to the extent you feel comfortable, what was really going on?"

"No," she quickly said. The cadet deserved an apology, but Christine was horrified at the thought of having to explain the reason behind her inexcusable behaviour. She would never again let any personal shock, any devastation, turn her into the insensitive, horrible creature that had almost forced herself onto a young cadet. She'd scream, cry, for help. She'd learned her lesson and understood herself better, could see now how suppressing pain and anguish had been a pattern for her. Throw herself into her work, carry on, that was her motto. It had worked okay until the pain had been so great, she'd had to almost lose herself, lose who she was, to control it.

Fortunately her true self had survived, had screamed to be released, had desperately wanted help. A dire need that had surfaced in the most inappropriate and shameful way Christine could imagine.

"I can't face her," she said to Miller. "That sounds cowardly, but I can't."

"It doesn't sound cowardly. It sounds honest."

"I'd thank her, if I could. Though I'm sure she would have preferred that I'd just asked her for help."

Miller's mouth turned up at the corners. "The story you told yourself was she needed your help, but the reality was you wanted her to help you."

"Yes." She'd subconsciously chosen the one cadet she'd been sure would turn her down and report her. Most cadets would have reacted the same way, but with Cadet Thompson, that part of herself that was still thinking, still strong in the Way, had been sure.

"I want you to keep journaling."

"I will."

"Your parents will be visiting later today. Do you think you can tell them what you've learned about yourself, about the reason for your behaviour?"

Tears blurred her vision again. "Yes," she whispered. They deserved to know. Despite their obvious disappointment and fear, her parents had stood behind her and regularly visited. They hadn't asked, pried,

shouted, or berated. Neither had her siblings. She had a strong family. If only she'd leaned on them, instead of always wanting to appear
strong for them.

"It will be okay. They love you."

Her chin trembled. Miller should have said they still loved her. She
didn't deserve their love, not after what she'd done.

A month later

CHRISTINE SLUNG HER bag over her shoulder and strode to the adult
wing's main entrance. The indoctrinators she'd worked with were waiting for her and wished her luck. She thanked them and watched them
stroll away, on their way to their scheduled classes with the children
she'd heard during her stay, but never seen. Only one person stood
waiting now.

She turned to Counsellor Miller. She'd wondered what to say, how
to express how grateful she was, and realized there weren't adequate
words. "You gave me my life back. Thank you."

Miller smiled. "I helped you to see what you needed to see, that's all."

That was everything.

"I've told Counsellor Irving about what we discussed. She'll continue
working with you, but you have my comm code too. Don't hesitate to
use it if you need to."

"Thank you."

"I wish you all the best, Christine. You're going to do fine."

There was nothing left to say. She'd miss this counsellor and wanted
to say that, but it would be inappropriate, even though she'd mean it
in the most innocent way possible. "Goodbye."

"Goodbye, Christine."

She pushed the exit door open, headed toward the two people waiting for her, and fell into her mama's arms, into freedom.

CHRISTINE STOOD AT ATTENTION IN COMMANDER Morton's office, her muscles taut and aching from the tension, and her hands clasped behind her back so tightly, she wondered if she'd be able to unclasp them.

"I've read the report from the Indoctrination Academy," Morton said from behind his desk, "and I've considered the recommendations from the indoctrinators, the counsellor, and Commander Finney, who also received the report. I disagree with those recommendations." He stood and leaned over his desk. "We've grown too soft in recent years. Mental health issues. In crisis. Unresolved grief. What does any of that really mean? Do you know what I think when I read phrases like that?"

Christine murmured a no, even though she could tell he didn't want an answer.

"Convenient excuses. Telling people what they want to hear."

He rounded his desk and stood a respectful distance from her. "You may have fooled everyone else, but you don't fool me. When you need help, you tell your flaming counsellor. You don't violate the Way and mouth off to two commanders when you're caught. You were this close to execution." Morton held the thumb and forefinger of his right hand several centimetres apart. "Now you waltz in here as if it never happened."

His eyes raked her from head to toe. "You're not fit to wear that uniform. If it was up to me, you'd be dishonourably discharged from the military. Unfortunately it's not." He raised his finger. "But I'll tell you what is up to me. What goes on at this academy. The report says no more one-on-one sessions and supervising others for a while, but teaching classes is fine." He snorted. "They still think it would be okay for you to be in a position to teach others, to infect them with your ideas, with your weakness. I don't.

"You've already been informed your practicum duties are over and you won't be supervising domestic patrols on 72 after all. We don't need someone who'll use their power to get dates," he spat. "But that's not enough."

He plucked his comm unit from his belt, tapped away on it. "Your position here is terminated. I've just forwarded you your new orders."

She shouldn't be shocked, but she was. A wave of sadness threatened to wash over her, to bring tears to her eyes and slump her shoulders. She fought it, kept her back perfectly straight and her eyes forward, but not because she'd already forgotten what she'd learned at the Indoctrination Academy. She would not soldier on this time, pretending everything was fine, but she would not give Morton the satisfaction of seeing her break down here. She would return to her parents' home and weep on Mama's shoulder. She had no right, because she deserved this. Morton was right. She'd brought it on herself.

"You will leave this office, collect the personal items we packed for you from the room next door, and get off these grounds. You are no longer welcome here. If I learn you've been spotted anywhere at this academy, you had better have a flaming good reason. Get out of my sight!"

She whirled and left his office, collected the box that contained the few models and images she'd kept in her room at the faculty residence, and headed for the train station, keeping her eyes forward the entire time. If anyone stopped to stare, she didn't see them. If anyone called out to her, she didn't hear them. When she'd arrived, she'd gone straight to Morton's office. If he'd thought having someone else pack her things, that denying her one last look around her home for the past seven years would hurt her, he was wrong. He'd done her a favour.

She didn't read her new orders until she'd left the train station closest to her parent's home and reached a quiet spot on the path leading to the residential area known as C-7-Oak, where her childhood home stood amongst many other houses served by a variety of local businesses.

Before her breakdown, she'd always felt herself relax when she stepped off the train here and rode her bike along the familiar paths. Not anymore. Now she always rode with her head raised just enough to see the path in front of her, feeling the eyes on her as she breezed past homes, sensing the curtains twitching. Neighbours greeted her politely but didn't stop to chat. She was no longer the upstanding Defence officer training pilots who would defend the Way. She was disgraced. She'd almost fallen.

She forced her mind back to her orders. Not knowing what to expect, she read Morton's dispatch, her heart sinking with every word. Administrative work, stuck away on Space Station 65, a military research station. No patrols flew out of 65.

She'd expected them to bar her from one-on-one teaching and to give the position on 72 to someone else. She hadn't expected to lose her teaching job, and she'd still expected to fly. The dispatch said she could apply for other positions in two years. Two years of mindless paper pushing.

She couldn't complain, though. She was grateful she was still allowed to wear this uniform, albeit in disgrace.

Five years later

CHRISTINE CARRIED HER tray to her usual table in the canteen and set it down across from Joshua. Five years ago, she'd arrived on 65 not knowing what to expect or how much they knew. The details of her violations and the Indoctrination Academy's report were private, and officers like Morton would know not to divulge them. But Interior couldn't stop innuendo and sly suggestive wording during private conversations.

She'd quickly gathered her immediate supervisor knew something, or at least suspected something, and she must have whispered it to everyone else. Christine could still remember the stares on her first day, and the way everyone always had somewhere to be or something to do when she tried to engage them in conversation.

Over time, she'd managed to make a few friends, all men. Her female colleagues were professional and polite, but gave her a wide berth otherwise. Not that she minded. Despite feeling like herself again, she worried about saying the wrong thing, accidentally brushing someone's shoulder, and being summoned to an office where a commander waited, even though she'd done nothing wrong. A taint clung to her now. Those around her viewed her differently and would interpret her actions, however innocent, in the worst possible light.

She'd accepted that her friends and acquaintances would be male, that she'd spend most of her off-duty hours alone, that she'd never go on a date again. Building and painting her models, playing the odd game of volleyball and cards—with men—and reading books reminding her of what camaraderie felt like, occupied her time.

Filling in applications also kept her busy. Since her two-year anniversary on 65 had passed, she'd tried to find a patrol position on another space station. The replies explaining that no positions were available never took long to arrive. Someone, probably Morton, had done their job well. She knew from her time at the Military Academy that filling the night patrol spots on 72 was sometimes difficult and assumed it was the same at the other space stations.

Recent graduates always flew at night because nobody else wanted to—not that "night" meant anything. It was an artificial construct on a space station. But meetings, parties, and activities all took place during the station's designated daytime hours. Flying nights meant you were green and biding your time until you flew days, where there were always one or two experienced pilots who had declined to go on tour.

Christine had accepted that they just didn't want her, a trained pilot who'd almost graduated at the top of her class and had taught many of the pilots who now flew domestic patrols or undocked on ships. When resentment clenched her hands and jaw, she always reminded herself that she was lucky to be sitting here, in uniform. The administrative job wasn't so bad. She did have to use her brain occasionally. A couple of times, in a good month.

Joshua picked up his fork and stabbed a piece of lettuce. "Who do you think will win the hunt?"

He didn't have to elaborate. The annual 65 scavenger hunt was coming up. Christine had considered throwing her name into the ring, but the slim possibility of her winning, of having her name up on the scavenger hunt board and so many eyes on her as she accepted the prize, had been enough to keep her from signing up for the competition. "Did you sign up?"

He shook his head. "I'm terrible at deciphering puzzles and riddles."

"We could have put our heads together behind the scenes. Most of the names on the board have a team behind them." Another reason she hadn't entered.

"I'd feel as if I was cheating if I didn't solve the clues myself."

She wasn't surprised. Joshua followed every department rule to the letter, even the ones everyone else bent because they hindered getting work done. She wouldn't have predicted he'd be someone who didn't mind hanging out with her.

"You didn't say who you think will win," he said.

She thought it over. "Allan's in again this year, right? He's won two of the last three years. He'll probably do it again."

Joshua scowled. "I think there should be a rule about how many times someone can enter—"

His comm unit chimed, her comm unit chimed, the chiming of comm units drowned out the various conversations taking place in the canteen.

"Mandatory announcement. Right in the middle of lunch." Joshua pushed his tray away and rose.

Christine walked with him to the nearest public monitor and waited, her foot tapping to the rhythmic sound of the chimes sounding all around her. The insignia of the Interior Division appeared on the monitor. The chimes cut off, leaving an eery silence behind. The insignia faded. An Interior officer materialized on the screen. "My fellow Rymellans. I have grave news."

Christine's throat closed. Her heart pounded, pounded, pounded. A vice closed around her chest. She tried to say something, but there was no air. She clutched her chest, yelled for help, her mouth wide, but nothing came out.

Her vision swam. She sank to her knees.

Joshua's voice, sounding far away.

What was happening to her?

She reached toward the voice with trembling hands, her heart roaring away in her ears. Now she was sucking down air, but she couldn't catch her breath.

"...team to the public monitor in the canteen on Deck 17."

"...hyperventilating?"

"Look at me, Christine. Try to slow your breathing."

A burst of fresh air. New faces, in medical uniforms. Something hit her face, a spray. Her breathing slowed. She clutched at her chest. "I think something's wrong with my heart," she gasped, as her hands jerked up and down with its every beat.

"Negative," a clipped voice said from the other side of her.

"We're going to take you to the infirmary," one of the men attending to her said. "Can you walk?"

With his help, she stood upright, swayed for a moment, then fell into step with him. Those who'd crowded around parted, their faces a blur.

Able to breathe normally now, her head had cleared by the time they reached the canteen's exit. They were just passing through it when someone shouted something from the monitor's direction, making her wonder if she'd heard him right, or if her senses were still distorted.

"It's a Chosen Violation!"

"THERE'S NOTHING WRONG with your heart," the physician said with a kind smile.

Sitting on a medical bench, Christine wanted to believe him. "Are you sure? I couldn't breathe. My chest was so tight, and my heart was beating so fast."

"I'm sure. You had what's called a panic attack, which isn't unusual given what's happened. A Chosen Violation." He grimaced. "You won't be the only one experiencing such a strong reaction today."

No, it wasn't that. She hadn't heard a word that came out of the officer's mouth. The moment she'd seen her...oh, no. Her hands felt clammy. Her breathing quickened.

The physician's brows lifted. He gripped her arms. "Slow down, Lieutenant. Slow down. Breathe with me." He made a great show of breathing in, breathing out. Breathing in, breathing out.

She matched his pace, breathed in, breathed out, felt herself relax.

"Clearly the next few days are going to be difficult for you. There are bound to be more announcements." He picked up a medical unit from a nearby table and tapped on it. "I've just dispatched a medical dispensation to you. It states that you do not have to view mandatory announcements at a monitor until Article 553 has been lifted."

"Article 553?"

"It's now in effect. Terrible business." He shook his head. "Now, if you're challenged by Interior for not being at a monitor for a mandatory announcement, show them the dispensation. But remember, it will no longer be in effect when 553 is lifted."

"Thank you."

"You do have to read the mandatory announcements however, and be prepared to answer any questions about them if asked. We've found that reading about material that's distressing to you will be much less likely to evoke a strong physical reaction than viewing the material. Something about multiple senses being engaged, and if viewing at a public monitor, there can be a group type of effect. If you feel yourself experiencing the same symptoms while reading the announcements, stop and beep medical. Understood?"

"Yes." She wouldn't need to beep medical. News of a Chosen Violation was shocking and horrible, but not what had evoked this panic attack.

"I'm also ordering you off duty for the next two days. Relax. Do what you enjoy."

"I will."

"That's all, then. Return to your quarters and take it easy."

She did as he'd suggested, then checked the text of the announcement she'd missed. Fortunately, reading the name of the officer who'd made the announcement and participated in the investigation didn't have her gasping for air again.

It wasn't as if she hadn't seen the officer on the monitors before. Whenever Christine had seen her, she'd always experienced a physical reaction, but never this strong. She'd learned to quickly move away. The announcements hadn't been mandatory. Perhaps she'd experienced a panic attack because the officer hadn't appeared on the monitors for a while now. Christine had assumed her schedule hadn't permitted it and hadn't expected to see her again. Out of the blue like that...

To distract and calm herself, she sent a dispatch to Joshua, wanting to put her version of events out there before he and everyone else came up with their own.

"The physician told me I had a panic attack because of the Chosen Violation," she wrote, hoping it would make sense. Would Joshua remember she was in distress before the officer had spoken of the Chosen Violation? If so, she could always say she'd guessed what was coming. "I have a dispensation to read the mandatory announcements rather than view them, and I'll be off duty for the next couple of days, resting. Thanks for being there for me. I feel a bit silly about it."

His reply was kind. "News of a Chosen Violation is shocking to everyone. Peterson gave us the rest of the day off. Glad you're okay."

She would be, now she knew she could handle reading the name, abstracting it, pretending she didn't know the officer. She couldn't do that when the officer's face was right in front of her, in full colour, and she could hear her speaking.

But she could read the name.

She could read the name Lieutenant Commander Thompson.

PEOPLE WERE CONSIDERATE to her for once. When she arrived for her shift after taking the prescribed days off, almost everyone in her department asked if she was all right. One woman who hardly spoke to her told her about someone else who'd fainted during the announcement, on Deck 5.

Christine thanked everyone for their concern, made small talk, told them she hadn't watched the procession because she hadn't wanted to risk another panic attack, making sure they knew she had a dispensation. Things would soon be back to normal, meaning most of them would politely ignore her.

She was right. By that afternoon, she was back to being the person to avoid. But when she showed up for her shift a few days later, those already in the administrative office were clustered together, whispering. Christine wondered if they were talking about her, until Joshua spotted her and beckoned her over.

"Have you read the Chosen Notifications yet?" he asked, as she hovered on the periphery of the group, trying to make out what two of her co-workers were saying in hushed tones.

"Not yet."

"I don't think it will upset you as much as the announcement the other day, but you never know. Maybe you should find an empty conference room and read them there, because everyone's talking about it."

"I'll do that now. Thanks."

At this time of the morning, most rooms were empty, so she didn't have trouble finding one. Her curiosity around what "it" was ran high as she sat at the comm station in the corner of the room and brought up the announcements. Wondering if a colleague had been notified and ended up with someone everyone knew they hated, she skimmed the notifications, hoping "it" would jump out at her.

It did, with a force that would have knocked her out of her chair if it had possessed corporeal form.

Thompson. Middleton. And a third name, followed by a short notation about triads. *Adams.*

Now she understood what everyone was gossiping about. And wow. Adams.

But a triad, and seeing the name Adams, wasn't what was making her hands tremble. It wasn't making her feel as if she were sitting in a freezer. She was alive, sitting here in this chair breathing, because of a technicality. She had tried to come between *Chosens.* Yes, she hadn't known. Yes, they hadn't been notified at the time. But if she'd behaved in the same way now, rather than all those years ago, there would be a procession for her, and her name would go up on the Wall of Offenders.

Obviously her cry for help back then had not crossed into capital violation territory. She'd come to understand that she'd wanted to live, to feel again, to find her way out of the darkness and into the light, not commit suicide. The part of her that had fought to save herself had known how much it could push the Law. Still. She was here on a technicality.

In the quiet of the conference room, she closed her eyes and did one of the breathing exercises Counsellor Miller had taught her. What would Miller think when she read the notifications? Would the same thoughts run through her mind? That she'd sat in the same room with someone who had tried to break up Chosens?

Christine swallowed, forced herself to focus on her breathing. She had not violated the Chosen Tradition. At the time, Thompson and Middleton could have dated anyone, and those other partners would not have been violating the Tradition. The past was the past. She was not weak in the Way. She was strong in the Way. Since that terrible time, she hadn't been struck once, hadn't so much as told a woman her hair looked nice, or asked anyone on a date.

Her equilibrium slowly returned. She tried not to think about what Thompson must be thinking and feeling, but she couldn't help it. Unless they'd gone through a fiery breakup, something Christine doubted, Thompson would be happy about Middleton. But Adams? And a triad?

Even the strongest of Rymellans would be tried. Christine felt sympathy for her. She certainly would not participate in all the breathless gossip.

A knock at the open door made her jump. "Are you all right?" Joshua asked.

She opened her eyes and twisted toward him. "I'm fine."

"You sure? You look a little pale. Peterson would probably give you the day off."

"I'm fine, really." She pushed back the chair and gave him a reassuring smile.

"Can you believe it?" Joshua said. "Did you even know they had children?"

"I didn't know. And if you don't mind, I don't want to talk about it."

His forehead creased with concern. "You sure you're okay?"

"I'm okay. I just don't want to gossip."

"Okay."

They went to their respective desks. Christine had just sat down when her comm unit beeped. Her counsellor.

"I thought I'd beep and see how you're feeling," Counsellor Irving said.

"I'm okay."

"Do you want to move up our next appointment?"

She was about to say no when she changed her mind. She didn't want to gossip, but she wouldn't mind talking about it with her counsellor. Miller's work with her had stuck. She didn't keep things bottled up anymore, didn't pretend nothing was wrong. She talked to the few people she could trust, and her counsellor. "Sure."

They set something up for the next time Christine would be on the planet. After that, she focused on her work, deliberately ate lunch alone, and spent the evening in her quarters, working on a model of a vintage fighter.

A FEW DAYS later she was in her quarters, getting dressed for another riveting day of proofing research reports and distributing them to the appropriate personnel, when her comm unit beeped. The name on the display both excited and frightened her.

Archer.

"Leeds."

"Good morning, Lieutenant. I don't know if you remember me. I help with scheduling patrols on 72."

She wanted to snort. Of course she remembered him.

"We have a shortage of pilots for night patrols. Most of the latest batch of graduates went straight to day patrols because of the *Kite*."

Oh, yes, the latest and greatest warship in the Rymellan fleet. Another one was also being built. The *Harrier*. It would be ready for its maiden voyage in a few years.

"I was wondering if you'd be willing to transfer to 72 and fly nights."

She almost gasped. This was it. The door was opening a crack. She'd be back in a cockpit. She didn't care that she'd be flying with green pilots on a shift seasoned pilots didn't want. First it would be nights, then days, then she might be able to go on a tour. No more boring research reports. No more correcting spelling and grammar and word choices. And it was 72. She knew people there, and they'd known her. Surely they'd be more welcoming than 65 had ever been.

"I would like that very much," she said. "But I'll need simulator time. I haven't flown for a while."

"Understood. I'll reserve you time on our simulators here and issue your new orders later today."

"Thank you."

"Archer out."

She stared at her comm unit, wondering if she was dreaming or had imagined the conversation.

When her new orders came through after lunch, she could still hardly believe it. In under a week, she'd report to 72, spend a few days in the simulator, and join the domestic patrol night shift.

For almost six long years, she'd told herself that one day they'd forgive her. Now, that day had arrived. She was returning to the cockpit, to what she was meant to do.

A month later

IT DIDN'T TAKE Christine long to realize that transferring to 72 had been a terrible mistake. She'd thought the reputation she'd been proud of before her breakdown would serve her well here, but it was as if her life had begun the moment the Interior officers had escorted her from the Military Academy.

Stares, whispers, polite masks...it didn't matter whether the personnel or visitor keeping their distance had witnessed her disgraced exit from the academy or not. The story of the officer who'd done something terrible enough to warrant a public display was common knowledge, a tale told to everyone who entered the C6 Military Academy or stepped foot on this station. Christine wondered what was said, given only a few knew the details.

Her former colleagues, some of whom must have met with Miller and recounted what a wonderful instructor Lieutenant Leeds was, wanted nothing to do with her. If she was lucky, she received a curt nod as she passed them in a corridor. Others looked right through her. Nobody asked how she was doing. Nobody suggested they meet and catch up.

The green pilots who flew the night shift treated her as if she didn't know what she was doing, sometimes barking orders to her when they flew, even though she outranked them. To her shame, she kept her mouth shut. She didn't fight back, didn't put them in their place. Didn't point out when they performed a maneuver wrong. She needed this position, needed to prove herself, to show them she was the Lieutenant Christine Leeds they'd respected. It had taken six years to finally climb into a cockpit again. It would take time here too, but eventually, her stellar behaviour and performance would win them over.

If only she wasn't so lonely. Even the men didn't want to associate with her. She played solitaire in her quarters, watched ships dock and undock, built and painted her models, showed up for mandatory social events, stayed half an hour, and heard the collective sigh of relief when she left.

Archer must have been desperate for pilots.

At least she was flying, soaring through space again, where she could forget the station and the contemptuous stares and just be, especially when she and her flying partner listened to music for the entire shift.

Some night shift pilots liked to get up, have breakfast when everyone else was going to bed, fly, then enjoy the rest of their day until it was time for bed around mid-afternoon. Christine didn't follow that routine. Flying relaxed her. After finishing her shift, she always returned to her quarters, fell into bed, and went right to sleep. She ate breakfast when everyone else was eating lunch, lunch when everyone else was eating supper, and supper just before she flew.

A couple of months after arriving on 72, she waited in line at the eatery on Deck 10, two decks below her quarters. She'd forced herself to not order her meals to go. Even though she ate alone, the chatter of those at other tables was a welcome respite from the silence of her quarters. She'd developed an immunity to any surreptitious looks aimed in her direction.

She reached the front of the line and ordered her usual eggs, hash browns, and toast for breakfast. As she waited for it, she sensed someone's eyes on her. As usual, she didn't turn to look, but the watcher spoke.

"Do you always eat breakfast for lunch?"

Now she twisted in the direction of the voice. A lieutenant she didn't recognize gave her a sheepish smile. "I couldn't help overhearing your order," he said.

"I fly nights."

"Oh. You're a pilot?"

She nodded.

"I just arrived on the station last night. David Noonan. I work in the infirmary. Physician's assistant."

Just arrived, and he was chatting with her. He hadn't heard yet. "Christine Leeds."

He didn't flinch. "I wouldn't mind some company while I eat. Want to share a table?"

Maybe he had heard but he'd decided to give her a chance, to judge for himself. "Sure."

Her breakfast arrived. "I'll grab a table," she said to him. Usually she sat in a corner, out of the way. She considered choosing another table in the thick of it, but went to her habitual table and set her tray down. Another reason she always sat here was because she could observe the entire eatery from this position.

She could see Lieutenant Noonan waiting for his order. She noticed a man eating near the order counter rise from his table, approach Noonan, and talk to him. They both glanced in her direction. Her face flushed.

 RYMELLAN 4

She could guess what they were talking about. She picked up a piece of toast, took a bite, watched the man sit back down again.

Noonan collected his tray. He headed in her direction, but placed his tray at the table occupied by the man who'd spoken to him. He hesitated, then he strolled toward her. She braced herself.

"Sorry, but someone from the infirmary asked me to join them, and I don't want to say no. I'll be working with them and they're trying to be friendly. I hope you understand."

She understood perfectly.

"Another time, perhaps?"

"Sure," she said, knowing there wouldn't be another time.

He hurried away.

With a sigh, she continued eating her breakfast. She'd barely been out of bed an hour and the day already felt ruined. No, she couldn't let herself get down. She'd do what she always did. Carry on. Think about her parents, her siblings, her love of flying. Remind herself of how fortunate she was to still be in this uniform.

After returning her dirty dishes to one of the racks, she left the eatery and headed for the nearest elevator. She turned a corner and— her breath caught in her throat. Middleton, up the corridor, talking to another pilot. Her heart racing, Christine pivoted, headed back toward the eatery, passed by it, and carried on to one of the other elevators on the deck.

She willed the elevator to arrive while continuously glancing down the corridor, expecting Middleton to suddenly appear and wondering how Middleton would react when they came face to face. She must know the details of what had happened, and she was a hot shot pilot with a stellar reputation soon to be Joined to an Interior commander on her way to admiral, the Interior commander who used to be a cadet and had reported her instructor for harassing her. She could whisper a word into the right ear and Christine would be right back on 65, pushing paper. Did Middleton know she was here, on 72? She must.

The elevator arrived. Christine rode up to Deck 12 and took sanctuary in her quarters. Forget any plans she had for today. This day was determined to tweak its nose at her. She'd stay inside.

CHRISTINE LEFT THE eatery on Deck 10 and headed to a lounge that was usually quiet at this time of day. The end of the quarter was approaching. New flying orders would be issued. Some pilots on the night shift would be moved to days, and other pilots, usually green ones, would replace them. She'd flown the night shift for over a year, swallowed her humiliation and disappointment as everyone she'd started with, except those who explicitly requested to stay, had moved from nights to days. Some had even departed on tours. But not Christine Leeds, who was now almost old enough to be the mama of the pilots she flew with. She tried not to wonder what they thought of her, but she couldn't help it.

She could read her new orders in her quarters, but she always forced herself to read them in a lounge, or observation deck, or strolling through the corridor. That way she couldn't cry, couldn't scream, couldn't sit and wallow in it. She took it on the chin, reminded herself of how fortunate she was to be here—on a technicality, no less. Though she was beginning to ask herself if her life, her days, would always be the same, and always spent alone, a subject—worry—she was discussing with her counsellor. She'd learned her lesson.

When she arrived at the lounge, she found a quiet corner and pulled out her comm unit. Her new orders lived up to her expectations. Lieutenant Christine Leeds, still on nights. Three other pilots had moved up. To her horror, she could feel her chin trembling. She choked down her disappointment and beeped her mama, a quick way to force herself to move on.

"I'll be down for supper in a couple of days, as usual," she said to Mama.

"How are things going?"

She hesitated. "Fine."

"It's just that you don't usually beep me about your visit until you're about to leave for the shuttle."

"I just felt like—" Miller's face flashed through her mind, Miller reminding her to not keep it bottled up. Christine's current counsellor was easy to talk to and more astute than others she'd had, but Miller had seen her at her worst, not flinched, and helped her crawl out of the abyss. "My new orders for the next quarter arrived today. I'm still on nights."

"I'm sorry," Mama said, her tone conveying her sincerity.

She swallowed. "At least I'm flying."

"You deserve to fly. You're a good pilot."

That didn't seem to matter.

"We're looking forward to seeing you. We always love it when you come home."

"Thanks, Mama." Her voice sounded raspy. "I should go."

"You know you can beep me anytime."

She knew, but she tried not to. Her mama was always encouraging, and so was Papa, but they must be terribly disappointed with her and how her life had turned out. Gone were the days when Christine would discuss her students with them around the supper table, regaling them with stories about how a student she'd thought would never make it through the program had managed it, or how proud she'd been when a group of cadets she'd tutored had successfully flown a tough simulator mission and passed a class.

She no longer discussed her future plans with them, because there weren't any. No new positions to look forward to, no promotions, nothing. She used to imagine her parents telling their friends about how well their daughter was doing. Now what did they say? What had they told their friends about their daughter's unfortunate breakdown? Did they say to their friends, "Oh, guess what? Our daughter is flying nights with your grandson?"

Mentally battering herself wouldn't help. She could see if a cube was available, but maybe she'd run around one of the gyms instead. She wasn't a runner, or a jogger, or anything like that. But the thought of spending time alone, in the silence of her quarters, made her want to weep, which frightened her. She usually didn't react this way. She'd thought she'd grown immune to the disappointment, the insult. She wanted to tire herself out. After the run, maybe she'd nap until it was time to eat again.

With a sigh, she forced herself to stand and go to her quarters to change. After shedding her uniform and resisting the urge to fling the trousers to the floor, she decided to skip the run. Instead, she crawled into bed and slept the day away.

CHRISTINE LISTENED TO THE HUM OF the conversations around her as she waited for the shuttle back to 72 to launch. The supper with her parents had gone as expected. She was always pleased to see them, always felt safe and loved the moment she stepped over the threshold of their home. She needed them right now. Mama had seen it, had said she'd beep every day. Christine had cringed at the worry on Mama's face and in her voice. She felt terrible, making them anxious again. She'd caused them enough trouble already. So she was talking. Talking, talking, talking, to them, to her siblings, to her counsellor. Doing so kept her lethargy, her depression, at bay, but it was there, lurking, wanting to slither out and take over her life.

To get out of her own head, she forced herself to focus on her surroundings. The shuttle was packed tonight. There must have been an event on the planet. A cadet paused by the empty seat next to her, then moved on. She wondered what would happen when the seat next to her was the only one left. Would the last person they let onto the shuttle choose to stand?

She gazed out the window. It was a clear night, not that it would matter where the shuttle was going. When she got back to 72, she'd read for a while and—

Someone sat down next to her and sighed loudly. Christine gave them a sidelong glance. A woman, non-military, early forties maybe.

"Just made it," the woman said, smoothing her long skirt. Her eyes darted around, taking in the shuttle's interior. "When I said I'd visit him regularly, I didn't think about how I'd get there. I don't even like flying on aviacrafts, but here I am, about to blast off to some station, when I'd rather have both my feet firmly on the ground."

Christine stared at her, unsure of what to say. "This is your first time on a shuttle," she said, brilliantly.

"Sorry, I babble when I'm nervous."

She was about to say there hadn't been a shuttle accident in many years, but thought better of it. "You don't have anything to worry about."

"I'll try not to hyperventilate." The woman smiled at her. "I'm Lynn. Lynn Porter."

"Christine. Leeds."

"Pleased to meet you, Christine."

She'd change her mind when whoever she was going to visit found out the Christine she'd sat next to was *that* Christine. "Who are you going to visit?"

"My brother." Lynn rolled her eyes. "He turned fifty a few months ago and told everyone he wanted to do something different, or rather, work somewhere different."

The announcement system crackled to life. They were about to launch. "You need to fasten your seatbelt," Christine said. "Otherwise the shuttle won't launch."

"Right, right." Lynn did so.

"Just before we launch, a shoulder guard will drop onto you. When we're through the atmosphere, it'll automatically lift."

"Glad you warned me." Lynn closed her eyes.

Christine felt herself smile. She was relieved and disappointed that Lynn was no longer interested in conversing, too wrapped up in not hyperventilating.

She settled down for the ride, but kept an eye on the woman next to her, ready to offer a reassuring word if necessary. But Lynn sat quietly until the shoulder guards lifted. Her eyes snapped open and she grinned.

"That wasn't so bad." She turned to Christine. "What was I saying? Oh yes, my brother. He's a researcher. Been a scientist all his life, but in a lab on the planet. He decided he wanted to transfer to a space station, and that's how he ended up on 72. We're close, so I'm used to seeing him often, so I said, sure, I'll come visit you every few weeks. Anyway, I'm not nervous anymore, so I'll shut up now. I just wanted to finish what I started. I don't usually talk this much. Especially to someone I don't know. Honest."

"I don't mind." This conversation was already the longest one she'd had in recent memory with anyone connected to 72.

"That's kind of you to say. Do you mind if I ask you a question?"

She tensed. "No."

"I can see you're military. Are you posted to 72?"

"Yes."

"What do you do?"

"I'm a pilot."

Lynn's mouth turned up at the corners. "No wonder you're so calm. This must be routine for you, being on a shuttle." She gazed past Christine, at the beauty of space, then quickly faced forward. "Maybe one day I'll feel comfortable sitting where you're sitting. But not today."

Christine wanted to keep the conversation going, but didn't want it focused on herself. "What type of research does your brother do?"

Lynn explained a bit about her brother Derek's area of expertise. Christine asked lots of questions, wanting to avoid questions in return, though when Lynn asked what type of ships she flew, Christine did tell her she flew fighters on night patrol, which prompted more questions and answers about how she structured her days. Before she knew it, the approach to 72 was announced.

"You don't need to fasten your seatbelt for this," Christine said, when Lynn reached for hers.

"Thanks for telling me. You know, I'll be on my own tomorrow until Derek finishes for the day. Maybe we can meet for, I was going to say lunch, but for you it would be breakfast, right? And then you could show me some of the station. If you're not busy."

Christine swallowed. She'd like that, she really would. For some reason, she'd felt instantly comfortable with Lynn, who didn't strike her as same-oriented, so she could be a safe friend. But that was the problem. It would only be a matter of time before someone helpfully told Lynn that perhaps Christine Leeds wasn't the best person to hang out with. The last thing she wanted was for Lynn to be shunned for having the wrong friend.

"Sorry, I didn't mean to put you on the spot."

"No, no, you didn't." Christine thought quickly. "I'd be happy to meet you for lunch and show you around, but your brother might have other plans for you. Maybe he's already arranged for someone to give you a tour. So how about this? Beep me tomorrow if you'd still like to meet.

I'm usually up by 11:30. If you make other plans, that's fine. If I don't hear from you by 11:45, I'll assume you've made other arrangements."

"Sure. Sounds good."

The shuttle docked. Lynn grabbed the bag Christine hadn't seen her place in the overhead baggage compartment. She hovered next to the seat for a few seconds, making Christine feel terrible, but it would be better for Lynn if they weren't seen walking off the shuttle together. "See you tomorrow maybe, then," Lynn finally said.

"Bye."

She waited until Lynn had moved down the aisle before leaving her seat, wondering how long it would take for someone, probably her brother, to tell her all about Lieutenant Christine Leeds. She didn't expect to see or speak to her again, but it had been nice to sit and chat with someone for a while.

THE NEXT MORNING, Christine rolled out of bed at 11:28 and drank a glass of water to chase away the morning cobwebs in her throat. By the time she'd finished checking the early announcements, it was 11:38. She headed for the shower, but her comm station beeped.

"Leeds," she said, assuming it was Archer, her mama, or her counsellor.

"Christine? It's Lynn."

Surprise stilled her voice.

"Lynn Porter. I sat next to you on the shuttle last night."

"Good morning. Uh, afternoon. Almost afternoon."

Lynn chuckled. "You said if I hadn't made other plans, to beep you."

But she hadn't expected… "I did, yes."

"You still want to meet for lunch?"

"Uh, okay. Sure. I usually eat breakfast in the eatery on Deck 10. What deck are you on?"

"Twenty."

"Do you think you can find your way to the elevator in section 5?"

"I think so."

"Take the elevator down to Deck 10 and when you get off, turn left. Keep walking and you'll see the eatery."

"I'll meet you outside."

She cringed, for Lynn. But it would be odd to insist Lynn enter the eatery by herself, and walking in together would hasten the inevitable. The sooner someone enlightened Lynn, the sooner Christine could deal with the humiliation and move past it. She thought about changing her mind, telling Lynn she'd just remembered she had a meeting. But she didn't want to lie to her, this woman who had been kind so far. "Is 12:15 all right?"

"Perfect. I'll see you then."

They said goodbye and disconnected. Christine stared at her comm station for a few seconds, then shook herself and hustled into the shower. As the water streamed over her, she played a game with herself. How long would it take for a helpful Rymellan in the eatery to warn Lynn about her? And who would it be? Another pilot, maybe. The Rymellan who took the meal orders? Christine would try to order first, so she could get to her usual table and watch what happened. Plus, it would be easier if Lynn came over and said she'd decided to sit elsewhere. Christine did not want to have to approach a table filled with others and ask Lynn if she'd changed her mind about lunch. In fact, she wouldn't do that. She'd just assume, slink to her usual table, eat at lightning speed, and retreat to her quarters.

Hadn't her brother said anything? Maybe Lynn hadn't told him about the pilot she'd chatted with on the shuttle. Maybe her brother hadn't heard anything. No, Lynn had said he'd arrived at the station a few weeks ago. He must have heard something about the disgraced Christine Leeds.

By the time she left the elevator on Deck 10, she expected to be publicly humiliated. She'd briefly considered not showing up, but why spread her misery to other people? It would be unkind and unfair to Lynn, even if the woman quickly ditched her.

She forced a smile when she spotted Lynn waiting outside the eatery. Lynn was wearing a long-sleeved blouse and an ankle-length skirt. The woman clearly liked her long skirts.

Lynn returned her smile. "I'm glad you agreed to be my tour guide."

Wondering how long Lynn's sentiment would last, Christine flashed her a frozen grin. When they entered the eatery, she maneuvered herself so she'd give her order before Lynn. When her usual eggs, hash browns, and toast arrived, she turned to her. "I usually sit at the table over in that corner," she said, jutting her chin in that direction. "I'll grab it before someone else does."

Lynn murmured her agreement.

Christine hurried away. She set down her tray, sat where she could see the entire eatery, and watched. Lynn collected her order, strolled toward her—here we go. A female military on her way out of the eatery slowed as she neared Lynn, then stopped in front of her. They exchanged a few words. When the military and Lynn glanced in her direction, tears prickled at Christine's eyes, disappointing her. She should be used to this by now.

The military continued toward the eatery's exit. Wanting to appear casual and disinterested when Lynn arrived to say she'd made other plans, Christine picked up her fork and focused on the eggs sitting on her plate, the ones she really didn't feel like eating now, but she'd force them down.

She tensed when Lynn arrived, then tried not to gape when Lynn set her tray down and sat in the chair across from her. Lynn plucked the napkin from her tray, unrolled it, and placed it on her lap. "Those eggs look good," she murmured.

For a second, Christine wondered if Lynn was playing some type of game, and if everyone else in the eatery was in on the joke. "You made a good choice," she said, relieved her voice sounded normal. "I order that sandwich a lot for lunch."

"At supper."

"Yes."

"When you eat your supper, do you eat it here? Do they still serve meals at 10:00 or whenever you eat?"

"The station's alive twenty-four hours a day, and so are the eateries. Most night pilots go to an eatery right after their shift. I'm an exception."

"Because you sleep right afterwards?"

She nodded and started in on her eggs and hash browns, but a minute later, she set her fork down. Lynn's back was to everyone. She couldn't see the surreptitious glances being thrown in their direction, didn't notice when two Rymellans on their way to a nearby table slowed to peer at them. As much as Christine would like to continue eating with her and show her some of the station's highlights, it wouldn't be fair to Lynn.

Lynn swallowed a bit of her grilled cheese sandwich. "Something wrong with your breakfast?"

"No, it's fine. But there's something you need to know." She clenched her hands on her lap. "I'm not the most popular person on the station. I usually eat here alone. People have noticed I'm not alone today. It would be better for you if you found someone else to show you around. You said you'd be coming to the station often to see your brother. I don't want...I don't want you to be put in the same category as me."

Lynn blinked at her, then picked up her tziva and took a long sip. She set down her mug. "That's three times I've been warned off you. Well, two. Derek didn't really warn me off. The officer I spoke to a minute ago did. And now you. I have to admit, I didn't expect you to warn me off yourself."

Christine was momentarily nonplussed. She hadn't thought about it that way. "I was thinking of you."

"I know. I didn't mean to be facetious, but that's essentially what you were doing. Warning me off yourself. Now, I don't mind having lunch... breakfast...whatever with you, unless you mind."

"I don't."

"Then you don't want your breakfast to get cold."

She unclenched her aching hands and picked up her fork.

"When I came to 72, I didn't expect to feel like I'm back at the Learning Academy." Lynn took another bite of her grilled cheese, and after swallowing it, stuck a couple of fries into her mouth. "So what exactly happened? I'll tell you what I've been told. You've had some trouble with Interior. You were marched out of the Military Academy by a bunch of officers. That I might want to choose my friends more carefully."

Lynn's bluntness surprised Christine, in a good way. Most people accepted whatever they were told about her. She forked some hash browns into her mouth, to give her time to figure out how much she wanted to divulge.

"If you don't want to tell me, that's okay. You hardly know me and I'm asking you a terribly personal question. But I figure if we're going to hang out together and be stared at and whispered about, let's talk about it and get the elephant out of the way."

"What else have you been told?"

"That's it."

Christine supposed that made sense. The details of her violations weren't public knowledge, though she suspected the gist of what had happened, the broad strokes, were known, and she suspected Morton had been the one to communicate them, albeit carefully. "Suggest you not have the lieutenant work closely with other women." Nudge, nudge, wink, wink. She'd certainly felt some people on 65 knew more than they should. She wasn't sure what had made it to 72 beyond her humiliating departure with an Interior escort. It was possible Middleton had told her peers what had happened, but Christine doubted it. It all went back to Morton.

She'd worked hard not to blame him for the way her career had nosedived since that day, but she couldn't help but be angry at him. If Interior hadn't escorted her from the pilot training complex, nobody would have known what had happened to her. They would have wondered whether her sudden extended absence from the Military Academy was due to an illness, or a sabbatical, or perhaps a confidential assignment. They wouldn't have assumed Interior had struck her and moved her to the adult wing of the Indoctrination Academy. And if not for Morton, she'd be teaching right now, not eating breakfast after flying a domestic night patrol with a green pilot.

But that didn't mean he was responsible for her predicament. She was. She'd handled the Death Notification badly. She hadn't been honest with her counsellor and her family. She'd harassed Thompson. If she hadn't been so weak in the Way, he wouldn't have been in a position to make an example of her.

She could feel Lynn's eyes on her. "It's not easy for me to talk about. But I'll try." And she'd be brutally honest. Lynn deserved that for sitting with her after being warned off. "I was struck under 998 and 662."

Lynn's brows lifted slightly. "That's pretty serious. Let's see, 998 is sort of a general, 'there's a serious problem with someone and we need to step in before it gets worse' article. And 662 would cover whatever you did to make Interior worry about you. You harassed someone. Sexually."

"Yes. And so I need to tell you something else, something that could change your mind about spending any time with me."

"What?"

"I'm same-oriented."

"Okay." Lynn was silent for a minute. Christine could tell she was thinking. "Who did you harass?" she asked.

"A cadet. When I was an instructor at the Military Academy. I behaved horribly. Threatened to use my power over her to influence her flying schedule. She reported me, rightly so." Her voice dipped. "Saved my life."

Lynn had stopped eating. "I don't know you, but it's difficult for me to believe you would do that, maybe because it's difficult to believe anyone would."

"I was going through something at the time, something I didn't even realize I was going through. The counsellor I worked with at the Indoctrination Academy concluded my behaviour was a cry for help. She said it's not uncommon. I chose—unconsciously—a cadet I knew would report me." She held up her hand. "Not that I'm saying I wasn't responsible for what I did. I was, one hundred percent. I deserved to be struck and everything that's happened to me since then. I'm just telling you what I learned at the Indoctrination Academy. I know that sounds weird, what I learned. But that's how it happened."

"You must be okay now. You're here."

On a technicality. But she nodded.

Lynn picked up the remaining half of her grilled cheese. "It's unusual for Interior to make such a big show of a violation, especially when someone might be in distress."

"Two commanders were involved in striking me," she said, making sure to keep her tone level, her anger out of her voice. "One was the commander for the cadet's sector of residence. The other was a commander at the Military Academy, the one who oversees the instructors. Still is. The sector commander realized pretty quickly I might not be myself. But I mouthed off to them. I really, really wasn't myself. And the commander at the Military Academy is an idiot." She'd never liked him, and her feelings had been shared by many of her fellow instructors. She'd wondered how he remained in his post, then realized that like her, he'd been stuck at the same rank for years. Nobody else wanted to deal with him.

"Over the sector commander's objections, he insisted I be walked out. Made an example of. If he hadn't done that, I might have kept my teaching position. Actually, no. The commander at the Military Academy still would have dismissed me, even though the report from the Indoctrination Academy stated I could be permitted to teach, but not one-on-one." She looked down at her hardly eaten last egg and cut off a piece. "I'm not blaming him. I accept full responsibility for what I did."

"It does sound unfair, though."

"It was my responsibility to get help before I behaved badly."

"When did this happen, exactly?"

"Almost seven years ago."

Lynn's eyes bulged. "Seven years ago? Seven? That woman, and Derek, made it sound like it was last week. Not really, but you know what I mean. Have you been struck since then?" She grimaced. "Sorry, not my business."

"It's a perfectly natural question, given what I've just told you. No, I haven't."

"I'm so sorry. You're being treated very unfairly."

She snatched her napkin from the table and dabbed at her mouth, when she really wanted to wipe her moist eyes. Lynn politely pretended not to notice.

"You should eat your egg before it gets cold," Lynn said, pointing at it with her fork. "And thank you. For being so honest. Really, I had no right to ask, but I thought you'd be more comfortable if we got it out in the open, whatever it was."

"More comfortable?"

"Not as tense. I hope you can relax now. And while I appreciate that you were trying to protect me by warning me away, there's no need. I can handle looks and whispers, especially when I know the ones doing the looking and whispering think they know something, but they really don't. I still want that tour."

"That's kind of you," Christine said, surprised and grateful. "People *will* talk."

"I get to leave, go back to my life on the planet." Lynn paused. "You don't," she said softly.

No, she did not. This was her life, here on this station. Not much of one, but it was hers.

They ate in silence for a few minutes, but it didn't feel awkward.

Christine made quick work of the rest of her breakfast and laid down her utensils. "Is there anywhere in particular you'd like to see on the station?"

"I know what I don't want to see. Anywhere with large windows. I'm not ready for that yet."

She chuckled. "The observation decks are out, then."

"Observation deck? No, no, no. Definitely out. Just thinking about it…" Lynn shuddered.

"We can start with the arboretum."

"That's a brilliant idea. Let's start there."

They continued to discuss where they'd go until Lynn had finished off her fries. After returning their trays to the rack, they left the eatery. Christine could feel everyone's eyes on them and wondered if Lynn felt it too. If she did, she didn't show it. She was the picture of poise.

FOUR HOURS LATER, Christine strolled with Lynn to the research laboratory on Deck 15. The afternoon had flown by. They'd spent almost an hour in the arboretum, where Christine had learned how much Lynn loved trees and nature in general. "I spend a lot of time walking," she'd explained. "I also garden as much as I can."

After the arboretum, they'd explored the recreation facilities on Decks 20 and 21. Christine talked about how she sometimes played cubeorb by herself, and showed Lynn the equipment and cube. "I've never played," Lynn had said. "Maybe we could have a game next time I'm here, if you don't mind playing with someone who'll miss all the time."

Christine had smiled. "I'm sure you'll hit the ball most of the time." She'd been about to say, "I'll show you how to hold the racket," but stopped herself. She'd imagined herself grasping Lynn's wrist and gently pulling her arm back into a swing. But even though it would be a completely innocent gesture, she'd never touch her. She'd have to demonstrate it herself, coach Lynn from afar.

Afterwards, they'd stopped at a canteen for tziva and dessert, where they'd discussed their families. It turned out Lynn was the baby in her family, with six years separating herself and her closest sibling in age: Derek. Christine did the math. Forty-four. Her guess on the shuttle had been close. Lynn's siblings were all involved in research in some way, had all followed in their mama's footsteps. Lynn didn't strike Christine as a scientist. "What do you do?" she asked her.

"My official title is Slot Article Creative."

It took Christine several seconds to parse her response. "You mean you create the articles Rymellans slot at crypts?"

"I do."

"How did you get into doing that?"

Lynn laughed. "As opposed to something less morbid, you mean? I love what I do. I don't sit around thinking about death all day."

She certainly didn't come across that way. Christine had learned Lynn was super curious and laughed easily.

"I was the odd one out," Lynn said. "My brothers and sisters pretty much knew from birth they wanted to do research. I knew I didn't, but not much beyond that. When I was due to graduate from the Learning Academy, I still didn't know. All my friends were off to college or the Military Academy or some apprenticeship, and I was still trying to figure it out." She forked a piece of strawberry cake into her mouth. "Mmm. This is great. Anyway, my parents said I had to do something. I would have been fine working the counter at a Trading Centre for a while, but they said I should at least apprentice somewhere. By then, most positions were taken for that year. Except the ones nobody wanted."

"Like, uh, Slot Article Creative."

"Exactly. Can't say I was thrilled when the attendant at the Vocation Centre suggested it to me. One of the two open apprenticeships, he said. The other one involved cleaning businesses. Definitely didn't want that one," she said with a chuckle. "So I took the creative one, figuring I'd do it until I knew what I really wanted to do with my life. And here I am. Still doing it."

"But you like it."

"Love it. I feel like I'm really serving Rymellans, and I do more than create the articles now. I do administrative work too, help run the business. I've always gotten along well with Sally, the owner. She's in her late sixties now and only comes in a few days a week. I pretty much run the place when she isn't there. We're one of only four companies on the planet that create articles, if you can believe it. We supply all the

Trading Centres from A1 to D16, and Rymellans can come right into the shop too, and order directly from us."

"Sounds busy."

"It is. And we have our crazy periods, like around the Festival of the Way. We always have to hire extra hands for that and call in the retirees." Lynn ate another bite of cake. "I can't believe I'm talking so much. When I said on the shuttle I usually don't babble, I meant it."

"I don't mind." It was nice to listen to someone talking as if they were friends. Christine had forgotten what it was like.

"You, on the other hand, are a quiet one."

"My life isn't as interesting as yours."

Lynn snorted. "Never thought I'd hear that from a fighter pilot."

They'd finished their desserts in silence, and that was when Lynn had checked her comm unit and exclaimed at the time, and now here they were, outside the research laboratory where Derek worked. Lynn would be having supper with him and a few of his colleagues, then she was going to a play with them at one of the station's theatres. She'd head back to the planet the next morning.

"Thank you so much for the tour," Lynn said. "I enjoyed it. I should be up again in a few weeks. Perhaps we can continue it then?"

Christine readily agreed. "There are still lots of places you haven't seen."

"I'll beep you."

"Great. Enjoy your evening and have a good trip home."

"Thanks. Have a good shift."

Christine headed for the nearest elevator, still surprised and a little shocked at how her day had turned out. She'd learned a couple of other things about Lynn: the woman was courageous and independent minded. Christine looked forward to seeing her again.

Her good mood lasted until she arrived at the fighter launch area and met the pilot she'd fly with at the launch deck elevator.

"Lieutenant," the other pilot said.

"Sub-lieutenant."

They rode the elevator in silence and turned to the music channel the moment they'd launched. The next conversation Christine expected to have that would last more than three sentences would be with her parents, when she had supper with them in a couple of weeks.

FIVE WEEKS LATER, Christine had given up on seeing Lynn again. There hadn't been a peep from her. No beep, no dispatch, no chance encounter in a corridor. If Lynn had visited her brother again, it would have been easy to avoid the lieutenant she'd spent an afternoon with.

She'd seemed so sincere. Christine wondered why she'd changed her mind about getting together again. Had the whispers and looks gotten to her? Had she decided she'd rather find an uncomplicated space station tour guide? Maybe she hadn't been sincere. Maybe she'd shown up out of curiosity and left satisfied, with no desire to share air again with the woman who'd been struck under 998 and 662. At least the details Christine had shared with her weren't circulating on the station. Whatever Lynn's reason for not contacting her, she'd kept Christine's confidences to herself.

Still, as Christine went to the eatery to eat lunch alone at her usual table, she couldn't help but think about Lynn and feel both disconcerted and sad about it. She'd believed her, expected her to beep and for them to see each other again. Was she that desperate, that easily fooled? How many more meals would she eat alone before someone took a chance on her and became an acquaintance, even a friend? How many years would it be before they transferred her to days?

She was just finishing off her chocolate pudding dessert when a dispatch arrived. She'd stopped hoping it was Lynn, so disappointment didn't stab through her when she saw it was from Lieutenant Commander Ross.

She skimmed the contents. Fighters on 72 were being phased out for the latest and greatest model. Christine had seen a couple of the new fighters in the launch bay and had wondered who was flying them. Patrols weren't. She'd figured it was instructors and the two new fighters she'd seen were training fighters, and she was right. The dispatch was all about an upcoming class and practicum for all 72 pilots. Day pilots would be trained first. In a couple of weeks, night pilots would get their chance to fly one of the new fighters.

There would be one classroom session lasting about 90 minutes, one simulator session, then an actual flight. After that, each pilot would be evaluated by the instructor. If they passed, they would fly the new models from then on.

Excitement chased away her sadness over Lynn. This would be a short interruption to her routine life. She was going to sit in the cockpit of a new fighter! She'd have to think for a while, learn, pay attention for her first few patrols.

She read the instructor's name, the instructor who would give the class and conduct everyone's practicum.

Lieutenant Commander R. Thompson.

She could no longer read the dispatch because the comm unit was shaking. She plunked it on the table, sat on her hands, tried to process what she'd just read.

How could it be her? Didn't she know the pilot roster? She must, so why would she agree to train Lieutenant Christine Leeds, get into a simulator with her, share a training fighter, conduct her evaluation? Surely she must know what had happened back at the Military Academy. Had she been ordered to do it? Or had she seized her chance to get back at the lieutenant who'd harassed her Chosen?

Christine wasn't under any illusions about what would happen to her if she failed the evaluation. Forget about day patrols. Forget about ever being accepted among her former colleagues again. She'd be back on 65, pushing paper.

Lieutenant Commander R. Thompson now held Christine's career and future in her hands.

TEN DAYS LATER, Christine was grateful she could fly night patrol blindfolded. Since receiving the dispatch about the upcoming training, she hadn't thought about much else, still upset and confused about the instructor's identity. Maybe it was one big joke they were all having on her. Maybe Thompson had asked to do it. Christine had assumed she'd be appalled by the idea, but if she wanted revenge, making Christine worry, making her lie awake at nights imagining herself back on 65 and feeling sick about it, would do nicely.

Well, Christine wouldn't make it easy for her. If Thompson wanted to fail her, she'd have to lie about her performance. Christine had spent most of her free time studying the new model's specifications and watching all the simulator recordings she could find. She probably already knew whatever Thompson was going to teach in the class, but it didn't matter. She planned to sit in the back and keep her mouth shut, but if Thompson called on her to answer a difficult question, hoping to humiliate her in front of the class, Christine would be up to the challenge.

The practicum session would be different. She dreaded it and knew she wouldn't sleep the night before, which worried her. She would need to be sharp, not have dull reflexes and a foggy mind. But that wasn't what made her shake when she was alone and her mind was going around in circles, and her heart raced, and her breath came in quick gasps.

What if Thompson accused her of harassment? What if that was her intention, to leave the simulator and beep Interior. Who would they believe? Christine knew the answer to that one.

She had to keep reminding herself that all she could control was her own behaviour and performance. At least the classroom part would be over soon. She'd get past the seeing Thompson part. Maybe it wouldn't rattle her as much as she imagined. Maybe it would rattle her more.

For the rest of the patrol, she forced herself to focus on the music playing in her earpiece and did some of the breathing exercises Miller had taught her all those years ago. After her shift, she returned to her quarters and spent hours staring into the dark before she finally nodded off.

THE NEXT MORNING, she took a longer than usual shower, trying to clear her grogginess. Despite falling asleep so late, she stubbornly woke up every morning at her usual time. This afternoon, she'd try to take a nap, even though they eluded her too.

She was buttoning her uniform when her comm station beeped. "Leeds."

"I didn't wake you, did I?"

Hannah. "No."

"Good." A pause. "Carl is interested in visiting 72. He—"

"No." She did not want her nephew on the station.

Hannah huffed an exasperated sigh. "Can you at least let me finish?"

She didn't wait for an answer. "He's interested in flying, Chris. He wants to see what you do, see a fighter. Can't you do that for him?"

She'd love to do it for him, share her love of flying, give him a tour of the controls in a fighter cockpit, tell him how wonderful it felt to zip through space. "Now isn't a good time."

"When will be a good time? Because you've known for a while he wants to visit, and you pretend you don't know."

She sank onto her bed. "I'm busy."

"You don't fly every single day."

"I—"

"What's the real reason you don't want him up there? Tell me, so I can understand." Hannah's words were clipped.

Christine swallowed. She could tell Hannah was in a mood and would not accept any lame reason she came up with, that her sister would keep asking, and why shouldn't she? She wanted to encourage her son's enthusiasm. Flaming Argamon, he was interested in flying, and his aunt was a fighter pilot. If Christine were anyone else, he would have been up on 72 for at least one visit by now.

She squared her shoulders, forced out the words. "I'm not popular up here, Han. I get talked about. I don't want him to see that." The familiar shame flooded through her, filled her eyes with tears and made her want to curl up into a ball.

"Is it really that bad?" Hannah's voice had softened.

Christine nodded, even though Hannah couldn't see her. "I'm the cautionary tale." She winced at her trembling voice. Usually she could ride out the shame, let it run its course, but this was Hannah, her sister. Family. She'd never forgiven herself for disappointing them, frightening them. She did not want Carl to see the looks and hear the whispers. If he did, she'd never want to get out of bed again. "I can't bear for him to be here," she whispered.

"I didn't realize." Hannah paused. "Have you ever thought of living off the station?"

That wouldn't make a difference; in fact, it might make things worse. They'd all be able to speculate about what she was doing. And live off the station? Where? The cadet residence at the Military Academy, her rooms there when she was an instructor, and her quarters here and on

65, were the only homes she'd known since leaving her childhood one behind. At least here she ate her meals in the same area as other people, sat in lounges with them, and passed them in the corridors. She existed, albeit on the fringes.

"Maybe it's something you should think about," Hannah said into the silence.

"Maybe." Christine wanted this conversation to be over. She cleared her throat, collected herself. "Anyway, that's why I don't want Carl here. Not because I don't want to…" Argamon, she could feel her composure slipping again. She inhaled deeply, exhaled slowly. "To give him a tour or encourage him. I would if I felt it would help him. I'm not sure having him here would help. It might put him off."

"Okay. I get it. Thanks for telling me."

Hannah hadn't given her much choice.

"I'll try to explain it to him."

A burst of panic momentarily drowned out her shame. "What are you going to tell him?"

"The truth, Chris. In the best way I can. Trust me."

"Okay." But would she ever be able to look Carl in the eye again?

"Are you going to be at Mama and Papa's for your usual supper soon?"

"Yes."

"Mind if we come?"

"I don't mind at all."

"Then I'll see you soon. You know you can beep me, right? Any time."

"I know." But she wouldn't. She'd caused them enough trouble already.

"Okay. I'll let you get back to whatever you were doing."

They said their goodbyes. Christine sat quietly for a minute, then resolutely continued to button her uniform.

AFTER BREAKFAST, SHE took her time returning to her quarters, stopping by the observation decks closest to the docking ports. Carl would love it here. If only he could be next to her, excitedly chattering away as she pointed out docked ships. What would he think of her after Hannah explained why his aunt didn't want him to visit? Christine didn't want to think about it, and now she understood why Hannah had said they'd all be at the next supper.

To get her mind onto other things, she thought about checking her dispatches, but she was still feeling vulnerable from her conversation with Hannah and was worried she'd break down right here if an upsetting dispatch had arrived. She waited until she was in her quarters to have a look.

There were only two, one from her mama, making her wonder if Hannah had filled her in on their earlier conversation. The other was from L. Porter.

Lynn.

Christine opened it.

Christine,

I'm sorry I haven't been in touch. I thought I'd be visiting again in a few weeks, but one of my nieces received her Chosen Papers and you know how busy everything gets and all plans go out the window. And because of the Papers, I saw Derek here instead of up there. If that wasn't enough, something came up at work. I'll tell you about it when I see you, assuming you're available to meet again on Thursday. We can do the same thing – meet for breakfast/lunch, then continue our tour. Let me know if that works for you.

Lynn

Christine read it again. Thursday was the day before the classroom training for the new fighter model. She could tell Lynn she wasn't available and study more, but she was prepared, when she didn't even need to be. Middleton—Thompson—was going to teach the class what Christine had already taught herself. Though she suspected Thompson would cover more, since she'd actually flown the new model. It wouldn't be all dry textbook theory. Plus, if Christine met Lynn, she wouldn't spend Thursday hanging around in her quarters, fretting about seeing Thompson.

Lynn,

I'd be happy to continue our tour. Why don't we meet at the same eatery, at noon?

Christine

Lynn's reply arrived twenty minutes later. Thursday, the same eatery, at noon. That probably meant Lynn would be arriving on 72 the night before. Christine wouldn't see her, but it would be nice to remind herself that a friendly acquaintance was nearby when she lay awake in bed after her shift, worrying about the upcoming class.

CHRISTINE ATE HER last bit of egg—Lynn had asked if she always ate eggs, hash browns, and toast for breakfast, and her brows had risen when Christine had said yes—and continued to listen to Lynn's news about work.

"It didn't come out of the blue, but I was still surprised," Lynn was saying. "I knew she'd retire at some point. I guess 'some point' was always sometime in the future for me."

"Were you surprised when she asked if you wanted to own the business?"

"Yes and no. I've been running it when she isn't around, and I've been her right-hand woman for a while. I'm the natural choice. At the same time, I thought maybe she'd pass it down to one of her children."

"Do any of them work with you?"

"No, which is probably why she's not passing it down," Lynn said with a wry smile. "Maybe there were conversations about whether any of them wanted to take it over, or maybe she came straight to me. I didn't ask."

Out of the corner of her eye, Christine noticed an officer giving them a look, but for once, she didn't care. "What did you say? You're keeping me in suspense."

Lynn chuckled. "I said I'd think about it."

"You mean you haven't answered her yet?"

"It's a big decision, and a lot of credits."

Christine wanted to ask if Lynn had the credits, but it would be rude. They weren't close friends. Not even friends, really. "Do you want to do it?"

"Yes! I'd be crazy not to do it. I love the work. I can't see myself doing anything else. If I don't do it, someone else will take it over, someone I might not like or who might not like me or who might be overbearing or take away a lot of the control I have now."

Maybe she didn't have the credits. "What's stopping you, then?"

Lynn sipped her water. "This might sound silly, but I feel like I have to take some time because it will affect my life quite a bit. Well, not quite a bit. Like I said, Sally hasn't been around as much for a while. But she was always there, in the background. She was my failsafe, I suppose. I always thought, 'If this situation gets too tough, or this client continues to be annoying, Sally will have to handle it.' I won't have that anymore. It'll be me. All me."

"Have you ever needed Sally to step in?"

Lynn thought for a moment. "No. I've consulted her, but usually to make sure she was okay with whatever I planned to do."

"Could you still do that, if you wanted a second opinion?" Christine absently forked more hash browns into her mouth.

"I'm sure I could. She said to call her in for our really busy periods. She's not going anywhere." Lynn's eyes met Christine's. "You're right."

"The more years go by, the less you'll need her as a mental safety net."

Lynn smiled. "That's what she is. A mental safety net. One I don't like using. I've sometimes said to myself, 'Don't worry about it. You can always throw it to Sally.' But then I try doubly hard not to involve her." She straightened. "I'm going to do it. When I get back to the planet, I'm going to beep her. I just needed that one little push."

"You were going to do it anyway."

"Probably. Yes," Lynn said with a grin. "But talking it out always helps."

"That's true."

"I get the feeling you need to talk something out."

Christine felt her shoulders stiffen. "Why?"

"You're not sleeping."

"Why do you say that?"

"You look tired."

She wasn't sure whether she admired or resented Lynn's blunt observation.

"Sorry, Chris. I'm too nosey for my own good, sometimes. Well, I like to think of it as curious, but there's a fine line." She frowned. "I just called you Chris, didn't I? I don't know why, but I think of you as Chris. Do you mind?"

Christine shook her head. "Everyone called me Chris when I was younger. Until I entered the Military Academy and it was all 'Cadet Christine Leeds'. My family still calls me Chris."

"Maybe I shouldn't, then."

"No, go ahead. I don't mind."

"All right, Chris, what's on your mind?"

Lynn was right. She really was nosey. Christine swallowed the last bit of toast and laid down her fork. She sort of wanted to talk to Lynn about the upcoming class with Thompson. She hadn't wanted to burden her parents with it, and she didn't feel as if she was spiralling into a depression or needed extra help from a counsellor. Of course, she'd discussed it with her counsellor, but discussing it with Lynn, an acquaintance she trusted, would be different. She might get a new perspective.

At the same time, they were sitting in a crowded eatery. Christine glanced around. The table to their left wasn't occupied, but the table to their right was, and its occupants were eating their lunch in silence. They might be able to overhear anything she said.

"We can talk about it somewhere else," Lynn said.

Christine focused on her. The woman was as sharp as a tack.

"How about we take our tzivas and go to my quarters?"

The suggestion took her off guard, even though she knew it was innocent. She preferred to remain in public when she was having any type of interaction with a woman. Less chance of being accused of something she hadn't done. "Uh, I'm not sure that's a good idea."

Lynn studied her. "Why?"

Christine was about to explain how she preferred to be in public, then realized what a complete lack of trust it showed in Lynn. "Never mind. Okay. Let's go to your quarters."

"You sure?"

"Yes," she said, even though fear snaked through her, fear she knew was unjustified but she couldn't quash. Lynn wasn't luring her to her quarters so she could falsely accuse her of harassment.

They ordered and collected their tzivas, then went to Deck 20. Christine followed Lynn into her quarters, took in the typical layout with all the essentials in the sitting room. Lynn plunked onto the sofa. Christine sat in the chair across from her and set her tziva on an end table.

"So what's going on?" Lynn said

She chuckled. "You *are* curious."

"That's a nice way of putting it."

She chuckled again, and wondered how much to tell her. "We'll be flying a new model of fighter soon, so we all—the pilots—have to attend a class and do what's called a practicum."

"What's a practicum?"

"We'll fly the new model in a simulator with an instructor, and then we'll fly for real, in a training model. If we pass, we're certified to fly that model." Christine clenched her hands on her lap. "I have to pass. Otherwise I won't be able to fly. It won't be long before all our current fighters are replaced by the new model."

"Are you're worried you'll fail?"

"No. Well, yes, but not because I can't pass." She anticipated Lynn's next question. "It's the instructor. It's someone who might be motivated to fail me."

"Why?"

Christine drew a deep breath and slowly exhaled. "I told you I harassed a cadet." When Lynn nodded, she continued. "The instructor is that cadet's Chosen."

Lynn's brows shot up.

"It gets worse. The instructor and the cadet were involved when I harassed her."

"You mean, they were dating before they were notified?"

A burst of panic forced Christine to her feet. She rounded the chair, gripped its back for support. "A few years later and what I did would have been a Chosen Violation."

"But it wasn't," Lynn said emphatically. "It wasn't."

Too busy trying to control her breathing, she couldn't respond for a few seconds.

"They hadn't been notified yet," Lynn said. "Before Papers come, everyone's dating someone else's Chosen, sleeping with someone else's Chosen. Well, unless someone's a Solitary, but you know what I mean."

"I do," she managed to croak. "But that doesn't...still—" Her voice choked off.

"Look, I'm not going to excuse the harassment, and I know you don't, either. But don't take on more than you should. What you did wasn't a Chosen Violation. It wasn't even a little bit of a Chosen Violation."

She blew out some air, swallowed, continued gripping the chair.

"So you've ended up with this cadet's Chosen as an instructor," Lynn said.

Christine nodded, grateful to her. "I'm sure she knows what happened back then."

"I'm sure she does."

"She must know the pilot roster. She must know I'll be one of the students, that we'll have to be in a simulator together..." She dropped into the chair, buried her head in her hands.

"You okay?"

She forced herself to meet Lynn's eyes. "Why would she agree to teach me?"

"Who is she?" Lynn lifted her hand. "I don't mean her name. I don't expect you to tell me that. Does she usually teach? What's her reputation?"

"She teaches. She flies domestic supply, meaning she fills in for other pilots. But her main role is teaching."

"Then it's not unusual she'd teach you."

"I'm sure she could have backed out or declined to do it. It's a one-off type of thing."

"Is she the sort of person who'd agree to do it just to get some type of revenge on you?"

"I don't know. She has a great reputation. Probably the best pilot on the station."

"But would she fail you by default?"

Christine honestly didn't know. "I could appeal if she did. Most of the practicum will be recorded." But not the interior of the simulator and the two pilots in it. "I guess I'm more worried about her accusing me of harassment. I'll be in a simulator and fighter with her. There won't be a lot of room."

Lynn eyed her over her mug of tziva. "Making a false accusation to Interior is a severe violation. Do you think she'd do that?"

"She's Joined to an Interior officer. A commander."

She watched Lynn connect the dots. "The cadet you harassed is now a commander in Interior?"

"Yes." She wouldn't tell Lynn that Thompson was originally a pilot. She didn't want her figuring out who they were talking about.

"Is she a by-the-book Interior officer or one who throws her power around in ways she shouldn't."

Christine smiled, surprising herself. "By the book. Absolutely by the book."

"Then you don't have anything to worry about. In my opinion."

"She must know too. About her Chosen teaching me. Unless her Chosen hasn't told her and is going to make life difficult for me on her own."

Lynn's forehead creased. "Now you're being paranoid. Look, I suppose there's a teeny-tiny chance this instructor will have it out for you and make a false accusation. But it's more likely she thought about doing this class and discussed it with her Chosen, and decided teaching you would be fine. Her Chosen would be able to check your record and see that you haven't been struck since what happened back then."

Christine hadn't thought of that. Would Thompson be able to see her entire record, including the Indoctrination Academy report and the reason for her mental health crisis? Would she have read it? Christine felt exposed. And for the thousandth time, she wished she could turn back the clock to when she'd received the Death Notification and do it all over again. If she'd known the dire impact that repressing it, forcing herself to appear strong, would have on her life for years, she would have let it drown her. Fear had stopped her. A crippling, controlling fear, the fear that had won and destroyed her dreams, and to some extent, her life.

"It's possible your instructor is as apprehensive about teaching you as you are about being taught by her," Lynn said.

"You think so?"

"Well, perhaps not as apprehensive as you, but I'm sure she's not going to be comfortable getting into that simulator, at least not for the first few minutes, anyway."

Lynn was right. Few would even eat at a table with her, but that wasn't because they were uncomfortable. They were protecting their reputations, though in Christine's eyes, they were less worthy of respect because of it. She hated to admit it, but she would have been like them, treated someone like her in the same way.

Not anymore. She was acutely aware of how unfair it was. Which was why when she'd glimpsed Thompson's other Chosen, the Adams one, sitting in an observation deck sketching, or wandering the station alone, she would have liked to have said hello. But she couldn't. She was sure the Adams Chosen knew all about the terrible Christine Leeds too, and she had more reason to be wary than everyone else who shunned the fallen pilot.

"You're right," she said to Lynn. "Everything you've said makes sense. It won't stop me from worrying, but maybe I won't hyperventilate."

Lynn smiled. "Good." She eyed Christine's mug.

She grabbed it, drank some tziva, savoured the liquid warming her tongue and throat. Talking to someone really did help. Alone, going around in circles in her head, she could hear only her own perspective and fears. They were echoed back to her, amplified.

"When do you start this class?" Lynn asked.

"The classroom part is tomorrow. Just an hour and a half. My simulator session is scheduled for next Thursday." At 13:30. She'd be a wreck that day, and probably running on little sleep.

Lynn pulled out her comm unit and tapped away at it. "What time's the class tomorrow?"

"Uh, 14:00."

"Two o'clock." She tapped again. "I'll send you a dispatch tomorrow at around four. If I don't hear from you, I'll assume you've been dragged off by Interior."

Christine couldn't help but laugh.

Lynn grinned in return. "Ha! See, deep down, you know it's not going to happen. But I know you'll still worry."

She gulped down her tziva, feeling more energized and optimistic than she had since she'd received the dispatch about the training. She wanted to tell Lynn how much she'd helped, how wonderful it was to be able to discuss her fears with her, to share the burden with someone supportive. But she was super cautious now, especially when speaking to women. It was unfair to Lynn, but the part of Christine that protected her would not budge. Since leaving the adult wing of the Indoctrination Academy, she'd never said anything to a woman—or a man, for that matter—that could be even slightly interpreted the wrong way.

"Should we continue our tour?" she said instead, wanting to give something back, however inadequate.

"Sure. Just let me finish my tziva."

"Do you want to start in the workshop area?"

"What's there?"

"Any indoor hobby you can think of, you can do in the workshop area. Woodworking, knitting, calligraphy—"

Lynn shook her head. "I love calligraphy, but I get enough of it on the job."

"Are you a collector? There are some collections on display, and a place where people can trade items."

"I'm not, but the workshop area sounds great. Though I have to warn you, we might spend all our time there if something catches my fancy."

"That's okay."

Five minutes later, they were on their way to the workshops. Christine felt lighter. The apprehension was still there, but she could see herself sitting in the classroom, listening to Thompson, without checking the door for Interior officers every five minutes, and without the need for anyone to call for a medical team.

THE NEXT DAY, she managed to force down a tasteless breakfast and a mug of tziva. Afterwards, she roamed the corridors, rather than returning to her quarters. She needed distractions, something to stop her brain from reminding her every second that the class would begin at 14:00, the class with Thompson as an instructor. She'd done the homework nobody had given her. She'd read everything she could get her hands on about the new fighter model. If Thompson tried to show her up in front of the other pilots, she'd have to come up with an obscure question.

Christine's legs were wobblier than jelly when she strode into the classroom at 13:50, not wanting to arrive too early, but early enough that she figured there would still be empty seats at the back. It turned out she was the first person there. Not wanting to risk being alone with Thompson, she whirled and left, and positioned herself where she'd see anyone else enter. When two chatting pilots went into the classroom, she quickly followed them and grabbed a seat in the back row.

By 13:58, she was clenching her hands on her lap, wondering where Thompson was. Had she just realized she'd be teaching Christine Leeds and had bowed out? Did she like showing up right on time? Christine dreaded seeing her, but now she wanted her to show up, so this torture would end. She counted heads. The classroom was about two-thirds full, but all the regular night patrol pilots were here.

At 13:59, she finally strode in. Thompson, formerly Middleton. She stood and surveyed the classroom. If she spotted Christine, she didn't show it.

Christine had occasionally glimpsed Thompson on the station but had never stayed around to have a good look at her. The woman hadn't changed much. Sure, she no longer looked twenty. But otherwise she hadn't changed. Christine quickly thought of something else, not wanting to be taken back to the Military Academy, to the time she wished she could do over. But it was impossible to avoid thinking about it with Thompson right there, in her face.

Her eyes went to the Chosen ring on Thompson's right hand. A frisson of surprise ran through her when she glanced at Thompson's left hand and didn't see a ring. Only one, then. One that must have both names on it.

"Okay, let's get started," Thompson said, motioning for everyone to settle down.

A couple of pilots clearing their throats and the rustle of others shifting in their chairs punctuated the ensuing silence. Christine clenched her hands tighter. The thought that the student had become the teacher surfaced, then quickly disappeared.

"I'm Lieutenant Commander Thompson, and I'll be conducting your class today, and your practicums." Thompson paced in front of the class as she spoke. Not too fast, not too slow. Christine would have done the same thing.

"We'll start with going over the technical specifications you need to know, but we won't spend too long on them, because you just want to know how to fly Model 3459-B. Am I right?"

A chorus of yesses rose, along with a smattering of applause.

Thompson grinned. "I've been flying the new model for a while now. You'll love it. After we go over the specs, we'll study flight footage. I'll focus on the differences between 3459-B and 3328-C. But before any of that, you know each other, and I know some of you, but not all of you. Please introduce yourselves, starting with…" Thompson's eyes went to the pilot sitting at the other end of the back row. "I used to sit in the back all the time, too," Thompson said, to chuckles. "Name and rank please. No need to stand."

"Sub-lieutenant Rick Evans."

"Thank you. Next."

There were only two pilots between Evans and Christine. She wanted to slink down in her chair. What if Thompson didn't know she was here? What if there would be a scene, right here, right now?

"Sub-lieutenant Lisa Munroe."

Oh no, she was next.

"Thank you. Next." Thompson's attention shifted to Christine.

Somehow she found her voice and the strength to meet Thompson's eyes. "Lieutenant Christine Leeds."

"Thank you." Thompson pointed to the pilot in front of Christine. "Next."

Christine almost felt dizzy with relief. Now she was sure Thompson had known she'd be here, because her expression hadn't changed. No slight widening of the eyes, no frown, no shift in her tone when she'd pointed to the next pilot. Christine wondered about her own voice. Had it sounded normal? She'd been too worried to pay attention, just wanting to get her words out without fainting.

She slowed her breathing, and quietly did one of Miller's exercises while the remaining pilots introduced themselves. Thompson went to the comm station at the front of the classroom. "All right, everyone, switch on your monitors. You'll see a diagram of…"

Christine managed to calm down and focus. She didn't speak again, but she could have. She knew the answers to every single question

Thompson posed about the technical specifications, and when Thompson had asked a question while the class was viewing flight footage, Christine had wanted to raise her hand. But she couldn't. It just wouldn't go up. So Thompson had waited a few seconds, then said, "That's okay. I didn't expect anyone to know that. You haven't flown the model yet." And Christine's shoulders had slumped.

But the hour and a half passed quickly. "That's it for classroom training," Thompson said. "Next will be your practicums. If you haven't received a dispatch with your scheduled sessions, let me know. Have a good rest of the day."

Christine wanted to bolt from the classroom. She fell into step behind another pilot and let him set the pace. In the corridor, she let out her pent breath, grateful she'd received her session dates and times. A couple of pilots had been moving to the front of the class when Christine had left, probably to ask questions. Even if she hadn't understood a word Thompson had said, there was no way she'd approach her. She still didn't know how she was going to show up to the simulators and climb into one with her. It would be just the two of them. The class had been the easiest part of the training.

She'd just entered her quarters when her comm station and unit beeped twice. A dispatch, from Lynn: *How did your class go?*

She wrote back: *I survived. Actually, it wasn't bad at all. The only tense moment was when we had to introduce ourselves. I appreciate you asking. Thank you.*

Lynn replied: *I'm glad you weren't dragged away by you-know-who. We still haven't finished our tour. It would be a real pain to have to find someone else.*

Christine chuckled and felt the knot between her shoulders loosen.

Speaking of our tour, I'll be up on 72 again next week. Thursday. How about supper this time? And if it's all right with you, Derek will join us. If you don't want him to, just say. I won't be offended. We can meet for tziva around 3:30 and continue our tour afterwards, and meet Derek at 6:00.

She wouldn't mind at all if Derek joined them. Lynn had mentioned him enough times, and he was her brother. Christine was curious about him. But Thursday...

It suddenly hit her. That was the day of her simulator session with

Thompson. It was at 13:30, something Lynn knew because Christine had told her yesterday. Was that why Lynn was coming and had suggested an afternoon tour and supper? Or was it coincidence? After all, her brother wouldn't have as much time if he joined them for lunch. At the same time, Lynn had only just been on 72 yesterday. Christine hadn't expected to see her again for a few weeks.

Whatever Lynn's reason, Christine would welcome her visit.

She replied to Lynn: *Sounds great. I'll see you then.* She'd wanted to write, "I'll look forward to it," but she didn't want to scare Lynn off.

But she *was* looking forward to it. And she did want to see her again.

THE TIME BETWEEN the class and Christine's simulator practicum raced and crawled. Some days she wanted it to hurry up and be here so she could get it over with and stop worrying. Other days she couldn't imagine herself greeting Thompson, climbing into the simulator, and flying a sim with a functioning brain. Time didn't care about such concerns and wishes. It marched on at its steady pace.

When the day finally arrived, Christine woke up bleary eyed and with a slight headache. She swung her legs off the bed and perched on its edge, fretting. Three and a half hours of sleep. She'd lain awake with all sorts of terrifying scenarios taunting her: accidentally brushing against Thompson's arm or leg, leaving the simulator to find Interior officers waiting for her, crashing the new model repeatedly because she couldn't concentrate, Thompson telling her the entire practicum was a sham because she was going to fail her and there was nothing Christine could do about it.

Lynn not showing up.

She'd thought about Lynn more than she should since their dispatch exchange after the class. She told herself it was natural to be worried about losing her as a friend, given the grandiose number of friends she'd had since leaving the adult wing of the Indoctrination Academy. She'd told herself that talking to Lynn about her strikes, about her worries over the new model training, about her life as a tainted Rymellan, had created an intimacy—she hated to use that word, even though she meant emotional intimacy—between them that normally wouldn't exist with someone after spending only two meals and two afternoons with them. Then Miller's face would flash through her mind, and all the hours she'd spent in Miller's office, sitting in that chair, made her tell herself the truth.

Christine wasn't sure, honestly wasn't sure, if Lynn was often intruding on her thoughts because she was attracted to her, or because of the other reasons she'd told herself. She reminded herself that if it was attraction, it might not be real. Lynn was the first woman she wasn't related to or working with that she'd had a real conversation with in years. She was also, Christine believed, diff-oriented, though they'd never discussed relationships and Lynn hadn't mentioned a boyfriend or partner. Christine was certain she was single, or at least not seeing anyone seriously. It didn't matter either way. Christine would never act on any attraction she might have for Lynn. If it was real, she expected it would quickly burn out. She hoped it would, anyway.

Now she roused herself again. She couldn't sit on the edge of her bed forever. She needed to calm this headache and have breakfast, though she wouldn't be able to manage her usual eggs, toast, and hash browns. Something lighter would make more sense. She did not want to throw up in the simulator. It wouldn't be the maneuvers making her nauseous, but her nerves.

TEN MINUTES BEFORE her sim session was scheduled to begin, Christine stood waiting in the launch area, where the elevator would take her and Thompson up to the simulator wing. She'd waffled between showing up at 13:29 or early, and had settled on early. With her luck, if she'd tried to show up almost right on time, the elevator would have had a problem, or a superior would have stopped her in the corridor to speak to her.

She'd first stood at attention, then relaxed her stance. But her hands were still clasped behind her back, and she was reconsidering her decision not to eat her usual breakfast. Maybe her stomach felt upset because of nerves, or because it hadn't received what it usually got, or a combination of both.

The door to the launch area swooshed open. Christine hadn't thought it possible, but she tensed even further when Thompson walked in. She strode over to Christine. "Ready for your session, Lieutenant?"

Not trusting her voice, Christine nodded.

"Let's get to it, then."

Christine desperately hoped someone else would show up, and the more someone elses, the better, so they wouldn't be in the elevator alone. But luck hated her. The elevator arrived, and it was just her and Thompson. The silence was deafening. Christine watched the deck number indicator change.

"Do you have any questions about the new model?" Thompson asked, not sounding the least bit stressed.

She was trying to make conversation. Not wanting to sound disinterested or come across as rude, Christine cleared her throat. "During the class, when you showed the footage, I noticed you corrected for starboard drift after launch, but only during one flight. Port, too. You didn't have to do it for the other flights. I was wondering if there was a problem with the fighter or if the 3459-B has a tendency to drift."

Silence, then, "No, that was me. That footage was from my second flight." Thompson chuckled. She actually chuckled. "I was still getting used to the fighter. You didn't see it in the later clips because I had more experience flying it."

Christine opened her mouth to apologize, but Thompson continued talking. "You might do the same in the simulator at first. I figured out it's because the 3328-C actually has the tendency to drift to starboard immediately after launch, and we've become so used to correcting for it that when we first fly the new model, we correct for something that's not happening and end up off-centre port. So during that flight, I was correcting for starboard which I didn't have to do, which led to me correcting for port." She paused. "Drifting—we're talking nanometres here. And the 3328-C always stabilizes pretty quickly after launch. But I hate drift. I want my craft exactly where it should be." She glanced at Christine. "Good catch."

Christine felt herself relax a smidgen. Maybe she'd get through this in one piece and with her freedom.

The only other awkward moment was climbing into the simulator and waiting for Thompson to do the same, then belting up with mere inches separating them. They weren't suited up for this because it was more a "getting used to the controls" session and she wasn't a green pilot, meaning this training didn't involve getting used to all the gear.

　　　　　RYMELLAN 4

She was more than used to it. She spent a considerable amount of her time in a flight suit.

The awkwardness quickly subsided as they flew. They were both pilots, after all, pilots who enjoyed flying. Except now Thompson was the instructor and Christine the student. How things could change! But she didn't resent her. It wasn't her fault Christine had harassed her Chosen, and the fact that Thompson was sitting next to her in a simulator, and wasn't treating her any differently as far as Christine could tell, earned respect. Especially since she'd crossed the line with the other Thompson doing exactly what they were doing right now.

Before she knew it, the session was over. Somehow she'd managed to lose track of the time. Yes, she loved flying, and yes, she was flying a new model, but she still hadn't expected to relax enough to forget the past and her instructor's place in it.

"The only comment I have is you can do the Catargon Loop with four energy cells," Thompson said in the simulator wing's reception area. "You don't need eight with this model. Eight still works, but…"

Christine finished the sentence along with her. "Always use the least amount of energy. I'll keep that in mind when we actually fly. Thank you."

"See you next week."

Thompson moved over to the counter, maybe to avoid the awkwardness of them having to leave the wing together and ride the elevator again. Christine didn't begrudge her that, and she might have a legitimate reason for going to the counter.

As she rode the elevator back to the launch area entrance, the tension drained from her body. She'd made it. And she wasn't as concerned about the test flight next week. If Interior officers showed up at her quarters and told her Thompson had reported her, she'd be flabbergasted. She'd still be nervous when she flew the new model, though. She still had to pass.

She had half an hour until she would meet Lynn. In her quarters, she splashed some water on her face, then just sat and decompressed. They'd arranged to meet at the canteen where they'd stopped for tziva and a dessert the first time they'd hung out together. While there, Christine would have a snack to tide her over until they met Derek for supper.

She'd eat supper with two people who weren't family or work colleagues. She hadn't done that since she'd left 65.

CHRISTINE POPPED ANOTHER bite of blueberry muffin into her mouth and waited for someone passing by their table to move out of earshot before continuing to tell Lynn about the practicum. "If she was nervous or uncomfortable, I couldn't tell."

"You know what I think it means."

"What?"

"That she considers it in the past, and so does her Chosen. If that wasn't the case, I doubt she would have agreed to instruct you."

"You think so?"

Lynn sipped her tziva and nodded. "It was a long time ago, and you said her Chosen is a by-the-book officer. She's not going to hold it against you. Plus, look at who—" Lynn cut herself off.

"Look at who..."

Lynn set down her tziva and sighed. "I was going to tell you, honest. In this conversation."

"Tell me what?"

"Don't be upset with me."

Curious and a bit apprehensive, Christine forgot about her muffin. "Why would I be upset?"

Lynn glanced around, then leaned forward. "I found out who your instructor is. And when I say found out, I don't mean accidentally. I was curious. Okay, nosey. I couldn't resist. So I asked around."

"Asked around? Did you mention me?"

"No. I wouldn't do that."

"Who'd you ask?"

"A couple of pilots. I was kind of keeping my eye out for someone who'd know."

Christine wasn't sure how she felt about Lynn's revelation. On the one hand, she could understand her curiosity. On the other hand... "I would have preferred to tell you myself."

"I know," Lynn said, grimacing. "I'm sorry. I did tell you I was curious, right? I wanted to know. We were talking about your training a lot and I couldn't help but wonder who we were really talking about. But

I should have just come out and asked you." She moistened her lips. "Would you have told me?"

Christine took a moment to think about it. "Probably. Yes. I think I would have."

Lynn groaned. "Then I'm sorry I didn't ask. Lesson learned. The worst you can ever say is to mind my own business, right?" She met Christine's eyes. "Are we still having supper together or should I slink off now?"

Christine couldn't help but smile. "I should have told you. It's always irritating when someone's worried about something but is coy when talking about it, leaving out the juicy details everyone wants to know. I wasn't hiding it because I didn't want you to know, but because I…" Her throat tightened. She blinked rapidly and grasped at her muffin, for something to hold on to.

"It's okay," Lynn said softly. "I wasn't irritated, or upset. I was curious. I should have asked you, or waited until you felt comfortable telling me. You have the right to your privacy."

"But I was worried about the training and talking to you about it. I don't know why I didn't want to reveal that one detail. Actually, I do." The shame she'd never been able to shake, but she wasn't ready to say that out loud. "Now you know who I harassed."

"You did tell me it was a cry for help. If you were hoping to be reported, you chose well."

"I did." Now she understood what Lynn had intended to say when she cut herself off. "She's Joined to an Adams, but that's different. As far as I know, her Chosen, her Adams Chosen, hasn't been struck with anything, or at least not with anything as serious as 998 and 662."

"Still, she—the one you harassed—is probably more open to giving someone a chance when they deserve one, and less likely to judge until she has all the facts, especially since she's a trained Interior officer now. I'm not saying she wouldn't report you today. I'm sure she would. But she's by the book and Joined to someone many people would be uncomfortable to be in the same room with." Lynn shrugged. "I don't know what conversation took place between her and her Chosen about teaching you, but I think it was probably an, 'It was a while ago and she hasn't been struck since,' type of conversation. Speculation, but that's my guess."

"Whatever the conversation, her instructor Chosen agreed to do the training and is treating me like everyone else." Christine chewed another bite of muffin while she considered whether she wanted to ask the question that had popped into her mind. She swallowed and forged ahead. "Is that why you're okay hanging out with me? It was a while ago and I haven't been struck?" She wanted to duck her head, look anywhere but at Lynn, but she forced her gaze in her direction.

"No. I stuck to having breakfast-lunch with you that first time before I knew any of that."

That was true.

Lynn rested her elbows on the round table. "I'm not twelve. I don't let a committee choose my friends for me. I'm old enough to know that some people with stellar reputations make lousy friends, and some people with not-so-stellar reputations make great friends. Having said that, I would not be friends with someone who is clearly weak in the Way and is only going to be trouble. With you, sure, Derek told me the 'being escorted out of the Military Academy by Interior' story. But that's all I knew. Which is nothing, really. Certainly not enough for me to blow off someone who'd been kind to me on the shuttle."

Christine slowly exhaled. "Sorry."

"For what?"

"Asking."

"No need to be sorry. In your position, I'd be wondering about me too. I'm the odd one out when it comes to you." Lynn lifted a finger. "Which shouldn't be the case, I hasten to add." She drank more tziva and set her empty mug down. "So what are you going to show me in the," she glanced at her comm unit, "hour and a half we have before we meet Derek?"

"I thought maybe the parts of the fighter launch and maintenance area open to the public. But that means pilots will see us together."

"And whisper? I don't care, but if you will, we can go somewhere else."

"I'm more concerned about you."

"Then let's go. I'd like to see where you take off? Launch? Fly?"

"Any of those work."

As they strode to the elevator, rode it to the launch deck, and approached the public viewing area, Christine could feel the tension in her body growing. She hadn't expected to be nervous about showing

Lynn an important part of her life. She glanced at Lynn and couldn't deny she felt a closeness to her that was unusual with someone she hardly knew. This was only the third time they were seeing each other, but it felt as if they'd known each other for ages. Lynn was easy to talk to and had given her a chance.

Careful, she warned herself. *Don't get carried away.* Lynn was the first female friend she'd had in years. This closeness she felt was filled with gratitude and surprise and admiration, for Lynn not listening to the whispers, or at least ignoring them and making up her own mind. It was natural she'd feel close to her, but Lynn, who Christine was sure must have many friends, wouldn't feel the same way. While Christine couldn't deny she felt drawn to her, she expected how she felt with Lynn to settle down over time. Walking with a friend through the station, not eating alone in the eatery, discussing her fears with someone other than her counsellor, was all new. And wonderful.

Her tension was natural. For her, this friendship with Lynn was already important and something she'd hate to lose.

DISCONCERTED

THEY SPENT ALMOST AN HOUR ON the launch deck. Christine was sure she must have pointed out things Lynn had no interest in, but Lynn had gamely asked questions.

"I don't know how you do it," Lynn said, when they headed to the elevator.

"What?"

"Get into one of those fighters and launch. Into space." Lynn shuddered. "Have you noticed I still haven't suggested an observation deck? It doesn't help that I don't like heights."

"You're afraid of heights?"

"Afraid is too strong a word." Lynn cocked her head. "Or maybe not. I do avoid them."

"Do you fly in aviacrafts?"

"I've done it twice. With my eyes closed."

Christine thought back to when she'd met Lynn on the shuttle. She'd appeared nervous, yes, but not petrified.

"Anyway, let's change the subject before I keep reminding myself we're suspended in space right now. I can fool myself most of the time, imagine I'm in some weird building at home, though no building at home would have decks, and not as many as 72 does." Lynn checked her comm unit. "We have about half an hour until we meet Derek."

They decided to visit the music wing on Deck 31, where Christine learned Lynn played the piano and guitar, and Christine admitted she didn't really play anything, that she'd taken piano as a child but given it up. "I regret it now."

"Nothing's stopping you from picking it up again," Lynn said, peering up at her from where she sat on the piano bench.

"True." But she wouldn't do it here, and she wasn't motivated enough to find a tutor on the planet.

Lynn sprang to her feet. "We should go."

They headed down to Deck 10 and the eatery, where Derek was

waiting for them. When Lynn introduced them to each other, Derek was polite, a politeness which continued through their supper. It wasn't a cold politeness, or an uncomfortable politeness. They talked about the things people who have just been introduced to each other talk about. Christine didn't get the sense he'd rather be anywhere but having supper with her. If he was worried about being seen with Lieutenant Leeds, he didn't show it.

He and Lynn shared the same nose, laughed at the same things, and had the same way of cocking their heads when they were thinking.

While Lynn had previously told Christine she had four siblings who were all researchers, she'd never mentioned their names, except for Derek. When she said something about one of her other brothers and Christine asked his name, Lynn reeled off the names of all her siblings. "John is the oldest, then Matthew, then Peter, then Derek, then me. And Derek will say no, but I think I exist because they kept trying for a girl." Lynn raised her finger. "And almost gave up. There's two years separating each of my brothers, and then I'm born almost six years later, and then they stop."

"Papa obviously hadn't been re-reversed," Derek said, then he grimaced. "Sorry, Christine. I'm sure you don't care about the state of my papa's, uh..."

"What, Derek?" Lynn said mischievously. "What were you going to say?"

"I'm sure Christine can figure it out."

Christine rescued him. "I can. No need to spell it out." She met Lynn's eyes and chuckled along with her.

"Do you have siblings?" Derek asked. An ultra-polite question because one-child families were rare.

"I'm from a five-child family too. Hannah's the eldest, then Brian, then Nicholas, then Nancy."

"And where are you in there?" Lynn asked.

"I'm smack dab in the middle, between Brian and Nicholas. Girl, boy, girl, boy, girl."

"Are they Chosens or Solitaries?" Derek asked.

Another polite and perfectly acceptable question, but Christine felt her shoulders stiffen and hoped they hadn't noticed. Her mouth felt dry. She sipped her water. "They're all Chosens."

"So you're the only Solitary," Lynn said.

She swallowed. "Yes. How about your family?" she quickly asked.

"Um, three Chosens, two Solitaries."

"After the oldest three were Chosens, our parents were probably expecting all of us to be," Derek said. "Then I was a Solitary, and then Lynn too." He turned to his sister. "I think they were more upset about you than they were about me."

Lynn dabbed at her mouth with a napkin. "I don't know why. Okay, I'm the only girl. But I don't know why that would have made a difference to them."

"I think they thought it would hit you harder. No children."

"That's hard for everyone, men and women. It depends on the person."

Christine wanted to ask how Lynn had reacted when she'd received her Solitary Notification. If she'd been upset, disappointed, angry, or relieved. Some Rymellans, when pushed, would admit to feeling relieved. But she really, really wanted to get off this topic of conversation.

"Were your parents upset?" Lynn asked.

Christine blinked at her.

"When you received your Solitary Notification. It would have been the first time for them, with your two older siblings being Chosens."

She didn't know what to say. She didn't want to lie, but she didn't want to tell the truth.

She settled on something that was true, but not an answer to Lynn's question. "No, they weren't upset." Nothing about her eighteenth birthday had upset them. At midnight, they'd celebrated with her. No Solitary Notification. Like Hannah and Brian, she was a Chosen. Someone special was waiting for her, and she for them. Their distress had come later, when their daughter hadn't faced her grief and disgraced herself.

Fortunately she'd finished most of her sandwich. She no longer wanted the rest of it.

"Now it's nieces and nephews going through it," Derek said.

Christine looked at him, then stole a glance at Lynn. Neither were looking at her strangely, and they'd have no reason to do anything but take what she'd said at face value. But she knew. She knew she'd twisted the truth, translated Lynn's question from, "Were your parents upset that you were a Solitary?" to "Were your parents upset on your eighteenth birthday?" Shame made her want to hide. She was repaying Lynn's kindness and courage with lies.

THE REST OF the supper passed without Christine facing more what-shouldn't-be-uncomfortable questions. When Lynn suggested they visit the arboretum, Christine readily agreed. She expected Derek to go with them, but he bowed out, saying he'd arranged to meet a friend in one of the gyms. They said goodbye to him and headed to the arboretum. Christine had learned Lynn loved trees, flowers, bushes, anything with leaves or petals, really.

"He's nice," she said, when Lynn asked what she thought of Derek. "You have the same nose."

Lynn touched her nose, rubbed it. "Everyone says that."

"I didn't really understand everything he said when he told me what he's researching. I got that he's working on fighter shielding, but that's about it."

"Don't worry about it. We all tune out when Derek gets going talking about his research. I'm glad he found something he loves, though."

Lynn's words reminded Christine of something she'd meant to bring up when she saw her. "I've been meaning to ask whether you went through with buying the business."

"And I've been meaning to tell you." When Lynn pointed to a bench near an evergreen tree, Christine lowered herself onto it next to her.

"Last time, I was so busy worrying about my training that we sort of got off the topic, and I meant to ask you in my last dispatch but thought of it right after I sent it. I'm sorry about that."

"There's nothing to be sorry about." Lynn smoothed her long skirt and grinned. "I beeped Sally, just like I said I would. I would have been crazy not to. She'd groomed me to take over the business. I couldn't quite afford it, so my parents helped because they thought it was a great idea. I love the work. And I couldn't see myself working for anyone other than Sally. So it's done. I'm the proud owner of my own business."

"Congratulations."

"Thank you. The only thing I didn't like about the deal was when I'm taking it over. Next week, only a month before the Festival of the Way, right when things will get super busy. I know that's why Sally wanted me to take it over then, and she's going to come in and help out, but still. I would have preferred the Festival to be over and done with before I took over. That wasn't enough for me to say no though, or to argue about it. She traded it to me at a really fair price. She said she wanted me to take it over, someone who loves it as much as she does."

Lynn twisted toward Christine. "I've pretty much been running the place for the last few years, but it'll feel different now. I won't have that mental safety net anymore. I'll want to be on site as much as possible, at least until I feel more comfortable being really, truly, in charge." Her face scrunched up. "It means I won't be coming up to 72 for a while."

Christine's heart sank as a wave of sorrow washed over her. It had been nice while it lasted. "Now that it's yours, you'll want to be there to make sure everything's running smoothly," she said, for something to say. She wanted to sound encouraging and supportive, not selfish.

"I'm going to do what Sally did. Groom someone, someone I trust. Someone I can leave in charge and not worry—too much. I have a couple of people in mind, people like me who love the work and I can see staying with me long term. I guess that's what Sally saw in me. It'll take time, and I'm not saying I'll be tied to the business until I have a right-hand woman or man. I might have two, for good measure. But for the next while, I'll feel more comfortable being ten minutes away, rather than hours away."

Christine forced a smile. "If there's some type of crisis and you're up here, it would take a while for you to get back."

"Exactly."

"Well. Congratulations again."

"Thank you. And how about you? You mentioned your training. You have another practicum, don't you?"

"Next week. I'll fly in a trainer fighter with my instructor." She was only a little bit worried this time, and more about her performance than the instructor. While she supposed there was a chance Thompson could fail her for no good reason, Christine doubted it. Still, it would be difficult to see her. Every time she laid eyes on her, Thompson's Chosen flashed through Christine's mind. She'd thought about telling Thompson, instructor Thompson, to thank her Chosen for reporting her all those years ago. There were times she regretted turning down Miller's offer to set up a meeting with the cadet she'd harassed. But using her Chosen as a proxy wouldn't be appropriate, so Christine would keep her mouth shut. But it had crossed her mind.

"I'm not worried," she said to Lynn, who had her business to worry about now and didn't need to be fretting about a pilot she hardly knew.

"When is it, exactly?"

"Next Thursday, same time."

"I'll think of you."

Christine's throat tightened. "Thanks." She wondered if Lynn would. Even though Lynn would only take over the business next week, she was already running the place and was busy. Next week would just make it official.

It had been nice to have a friendly face on the station for a short time. Maybe Lynn would come up to 72 again at some point and look her up, or maybe Derek would transfer back to the planet or be the one to visit.

She spent another hour with Lynn, chatting on the bench and strolling with her in the arboretum, but all she could think about was whether she'd ever see her again.

CHRISTINE ARRIVED EARLY for her training flight. Her legs didn't turn to jelly when Thompson arrived, and though the elevator ride wasn't as awkward as the first one, it wasn't completely comfortable, either. But they were both pilots. Any awkwardness disappeared soon after they'd suited up and climbed into the new model's cockpit. Thompson took a few minutes to review the controls from her instructor seat located behind Christine. Then they launched.

An hour later, Christine touched down in the launch bay. As she unsuited, she wondered what Thompson would say. She thought it had gone well. Thompson hadn't said much. Just a comment here and there. Nothing critical, and she hadn't screamed in terror once.

As instructed, she joined Thompson in a small meeting room outside the flight preparation area.

"I don't have anything to say except great job," Thompson said. "You handled the fighter well and executed all your maneuvers as if you'd been flying this model for years. Your experience in the cockpit shows. I always tell my students whether they've passed or failed immediately after the training flight. You passed. You'll receive a written evaluation in about a week or so."

"Thank you."

They walked to the elevator. The entire time, Christine wanted to turn to her and say, "Can you tell your Chosen she did the right thing all those years ago and I'm very sorry about what happened?" But she didn't. It would be awkward and feel inappropriate. Thompson, the Chosen of the woman she'd harassed, had just passed her, meaning she could still fly. Best to leave it there.

They rode the elevator down to Deck 22, said polite goodbyes, and went their separate ways. They could go back to avoiding each other on the station now, but Christine's muscles wouldn't clench as tightly when she glimpsed Thompson in a corridor, and the thought of accidentally coming face to face with her wasn't as horrifying.

Her comm unit beeped twice as she was entering her quarters. A dispatch, from Lynn.

How did your training go?

Lynn had thought about her. Christine felt herself smile.

I passed. Thanks for checking in.

Good. I knew you'd pass. Now I have a question. You don't fly all the time, do you? You must have time off.

I fly what's called a 5-3-4-2 rotation.

What in the flaming Argamon is a 5-3-4-2 rotation?

Christine chuckled. *It means I fly five days, have three off, fly four, have two off, then it repeats.*

You said you have supper with your parents, so you must come down to the planet sometimes.

I always see them during the 3 part of the rotation. Which means I see them around every two weeks.

Would you have time to come have supper with me down here sometime? There's a great eatery not far from where I work.

Christine didn't have to think about it. *Sure. I'd like that.*

Let's figure out when, then.

They set up a time for the following week, during the 2 part of

Christine's rotation. Lynn warned Christine she might talk her ear off about her business, given it was all hers now. As far as Christine was concerned, Lynn could talk all night, if she wanted to. She was thrilled, and surprised, that Lynn had invited her down for a meal. She let herself hope, just for a second, that it meant Lynn saw her as a friend.

She spent the rest of her afternoon working on a model, then went to her usual eatery to eat lunch, with a bounce in her step. She was waiting in line to place her order when the conversation of two day-shift pilots a couple of people in front of her caught her attention, because they were speaking loudly.

"Not sure what she'd want with a washed-up pilot," one of them said.

The other one nodded. "I wonder if she knows about what happened at the Military Academy."

"She must. So she's either stupid, or desperate."

Both pilots looked Christine's way. They turned to each other and snickered.

Christine's face felt as if it was on fire. Her hands clenched in anger. These idiots could say whatever they wanted about her, but not Lynn. She willed herself to stay in line, order her lunch, carry it to her usual table and force it down. On the way out, she didn't stop to order the tziva she always took back to her quarters.

The moment she was in her sitting room and the door had swooshed shut behind her, she pulled out her comm unit, intending to send a dispatch to Lynn, cancelling their supper plans. But she couldn't do it. She didn't want to do it. Why should she let two idiot pilots who knew nothing stop her from having a friend? If Lynn was coming up to 72, it would be different. But they'd eat down on the planet.

Still, she wondered if she was being selfish. She deserved, had earned, whatever scorn was directed her way. Lynn hadn't, and Christine wanted to protect her.

THE EATERY LYNN had raved about seated around thirty people and half of those seats were empty. But it was early. Christine had followed Lynn's directions, taken the right train, walked the right paths, and arrived at 17:10, ten minutes before they were due to meet. She'd only waited five minutes for Lynn, who was always prompt.

"We're meeting outside an eatery I'm really familiar with for a change," Lynn had said with a smile. "Though I know your favourite eatery on 72 quite well now."

They'd been seated next to a window. While they waited for their meals—a sandwich and salad for Christine and a pasta dish for Lynn— Lynn pointed out people she knew as they passed by outside.

"I've been working here for over twenty years," Lynn said. "And I live fifteen minutes in that direction." She pointed off to her left. "Though I've only lived so close to work for the last five years. I didn't trade for a house until I was sure I'd never leave Sally's, and I didn't have the credits for a house until then."

Lynn must be a good saver. So was Christine, especially when she didn't have to spend many credits. Her quarters and meals on 72 were free, and she didn't go out at all. Model kits, personal items like soap, combs, and the few civilian clothes she owned didn't cost much. She could trade for a house, but it wouldn't make sense to force herself to leave 72 on her off days to pass time alone in a house that would feel empty. She wasn't a social butterfly on 72, but she did see people and exchange a few words here and there.

Their meals arrived. "How's it going at work, now that you're the owner?" Christine asked, after they'd unfurled their napkins and taken a few bites of their meals.

"So far, so good. I've already decided on who I'll groom to replace me when the time comes. Steven. I see myself in him, when I started all those years ago. But I'm also training Jeannie on everything I do. We've worked together for a long time, so she's already very experienced. She'll step in when I'm on holiday, or ill. Whenever I'm not there, really. Steven is more for later, when he has more experience and I'm thinking about taking a step back. Jeannie and I are too close in age for her to eventually take over from me."

Lynn gulped down some water. "Other than that, nothing's changed, not really. We haven't had a crisis yet, though. But the Festival of the Way isn't far off. Something will happen. We'll have too many orders and not enough calligraphers, or it will feel that way. We'll run out of paper, or a client will request a specific type of paper we special order and it doesn't arrive on time. We'll run out of paint, ink, whatever.

     RYMELLAN 4

Because no matter how much I'll order, it won't be enough. A client will complain because they'll say we did the wrong article, even though we didn't. That's something we double, triple, quadruple check. They change their minds, they know it's too late, but they show up hoping we have spares of the article they now want lying around, even though they asked for one with their name included." Lynn grinned sheepishly. "I'm making it sound worse than it is. Maybe one of those things will happen, but not all during the same year. But we'll be busy. I'll call in every retired calligrapher who's on my supply list, and we'll all work longer hours."

"What about the Festival of the Way itself? You don't work on that day, do you?"

Lynn shook her head. "Everyone wants their articles for Festival Day or before. The only good thing about the Festival—from the business point of view, not from the holiday point of view—is that the week after is quiet. Very quiet," she whispered, making Christine have to strain to hear her over the voices of the other diners. "I spend the Festival with my family, even though what I usually want to do is go home right after the morning program and sleep. Well, that's not entirely true. I do enjoy seeing everyone. I always wake up that morning convinced I'll doze off during the morning performances and not have enough energy to make it through the afternoon, but I always do." Her eyes met Christine's. "What about you? What do you do that day?"

Christine wished she hadn't asked. "Pilots still have to patrol. That's what I do. Pilots on patrol get an exemption. We don't have to attend the mandatory activities at the Festival."

"You do that every year?"

"I've done it since arriving on 72. When I was on 65, I spent it with my family." Some years she'd enjoyed herself, other years she'd felt like a failure. It had depended on who had joined them and what questions they'd asked her, and on the follow up questions when they found out she was working on 65 and not at the Military Academy, and was no longer flying. The first couple of years had been the worst, but even after that, she'd felt as if everyone was pitying her, or talking about her and wondering why she'd been moved to an administrative post. She'd jumped at the chance to skip it and stay on 72. She still flew nights, but she dragged herself out of bed and attended the morning program, even though she didn't have to.

"Is that what you're going to do this year?"

She nodded. "I've already submitted my name and received confirmation."

Lynn eyed her thoughtfully, but sort of changed the subject. "One of my nephews has his birthday a week after the Festival. Sometimes I go to his party, sometimes I don't. It depends on how much extra sleep I need after our busiest week of the year. This year, I'll have to go. He's turning eighteen."

"Oh." Christine focused on eating her sandwich, hoping Lynn would change the subject.

"He's Matthew's boy. Matthew hasn't talked about anything else for weeks. Their other three children are all Chosens. One is already Joined."

As Lynn continued to talk about her brother's hopes for his son and what would be an over the top party because her Chosen sister pampered her kids—in her opinion—and how she really hoped he was a Chosen because her brother would be devastated if he wasn't, Christine threw in the occasional nod and grunt and wondered how she could subtly change the subject.

"I'm talking too much, aren't I?" Lynn said.

It took Christine a second to realize she was waiting for an answer. "What?"

"I'm talking too much. Sorry. When there's a vacuum in a conversation, I have this compelling need to fill it. You got quieter than usual, and your uh-huhs and nods didn't have their usual oomph."

Christine chuckled. No matter how uncomfortable or awkward she felt, Lynn always managed to put her at ease by making her chuckle.

"I know it must be boring to listen to me ramble on about my family."

"No, it's not, really." She set her sandwich down. "The Festival of the Way, family stuff." And anything that might lead to her talking about the Death Notification she'd received. "They're not my favourite topics of conversation. My parents and siblings are great. They're all support-ive. But I've never felt the same about the Festival and family events since my..." She searched for how to describe the shameful period in her life. "Troubles with Interior. But I'm listening, and I do like to hear about you and your family."

"You sure?"

"Yes, absolutely."

"I'm also babbling because I don't really want to go to the party."

Christine blinked at her. Lynn wanting to miss her nephew's eighteenth? That didn't sound like her. "Why?"

"Someone will be there I don't like to see. I actively avoid her. But she's one of my brother's closest friends. They've known each other for years. That's how I met her." Her voice dropped. "I knew I was making a mistake when I started dating her."

Christine almost dropped her sandwich. Lynn was same-oriented? She hoped her shock, the shock making her body feel as if it were vibrating, even though she knew it wasn't, didn't show on her face.

"We were together for almost five years. Almost moved in together. Well, I kept asking her, and she kept saying not yet. I found out why when I was having supper with a couple of co-workers and she walked in with someone else, and they were clearly more than friends. I'm not sure who was more mortified. Me, or my co-workers. They didn't know where to look or what to say. I don't remember if I finished my meal or how we left the eatery."

She could hardly believe her ears. "That's terrible."

"I confronted her about it. She claimed we'd never agreed to see only each other." Lynn shook her head. "There are two types of Solitaries, right? Those who want as close to a Chosen relationship as they can get, and those who think being a Solitary means they can be with as many people at a time as they want, or go from person to person to person to person. One sign of trouble and they're moving on."

"You're the first type and your former girlfriend was the second?" she asked, even though she wasn't really comfortable talking to Lynn about her past relationship. To her surprise, and horror, she felt jealous. She did not want to have feelings for Lynn beyond the platonic. She valued their friendship too much, and Lynn would not want someone struck under 998 and 662, nor a washed-up pilot. Not as a partner, a lover, the one she came home to, the one she felt safe with.

Who was she kidding? She already had feelings for her, but she would never, ever act on them. She'd be a great friend, nothing more, and she was okay with that. It was more than she'd had for years.

"You got it," Lynn said, bringing Christine back to their conversation. "I'm definitely the first type of Solitary. I thought we were going to grow old together. Meanwhile, she was already moving on. And she wasn't kind when she made it clear I was out and this new person was in." Lynn picked up her water and drained her glass. "She listed the reasons I'd lost the competition I didn't even know I was in. It was a long list." Her face tightened at the memory. "Anyway, we broke up seven years ago, and I've managed to only cross paths with her once or twice. But she'll be at the party. It's his eighteenth." She shook her head. "When she asked me out, I ignored the little voice saying, 'But she's Matthew's close friend. It'll be really awkward if we break up.' Silly me."

"Do you still have feelings for her?"

"No! I just don't like to be reminded of that time."

"I can understand that. It's the same reason I'll be flying on Festival Day."

"Exactly." Lynn paused. "I bet you're the first type too."

"First type..."

"Of Solitary. You want to find that one person for life."

Her breath caught in her throat. She'd expected that one person for life. "You're half right," she managed to say.

Lynn gave her a quizzical look.

"I used to want to find that one person for life. Now I know there won't be anyone."

"Why do you say that?"

She wasn't a great catch, something Lynn already knew. "For obvious reasons. My troubles with Interior. And I'd never, you know, ask someone out. Tell her I have feelings for her." Argamon, her cheeks felt hot. She hoped Lynn would assume it was the subject they were discussing, and not due to her specifically.

"I guess if someone was interested in you, they'd have to be the one to say it."

"They'd have to spell it out, make it crystal clear. There's no way I'd risk misinterpreting anything or making the first move. I can't afford for someone to take offense and report me, even if that report turned out to be dismissed."

"You really think someone would report you because you told them you're interested? Even if they're not, they'd just say so, or suddenly not be available. They're not going to report you to Interior." Lynn's eyes brightened. "Interior would be run off its feet."

Christine vigorously shook her head. "I couldn't risk it. I just couldn't. I trust myself. I'll never cross those lines again. But my judgement was really impaired once. If I was interested in someone and decided to tell her, there would be a part of me that would wonder if my judgement was impaired again, if it would be inappropriate to say or do something, even if the rest of me knew it wouldn't be." She lifted her hands and let them fall to her lap, feeling the shame all over again, the shame Miller had told her to let go, but that had remained with her all these years. "I'd never say anything."

She couldn't risk ever making another woman feel uncomfortable, would be mortified if she asked someone on a date, or worse, misread someone's interest, danced with her too closely or touched her arm and let her fingers linger, and the woman recoiled. It wouldn't be inappropriate. People did it all the time to gauge interest and quickly backed off if the feedback was negative. But she'd never do it. She'd never make a woman feel uncomfortable because of her advances again, even for a second.

"That means the other person would have to put herself into a vulnerable position, though." Lynn pushed her pasta around her plate. "Even someone who's confident and outgoing might find that hard. To be so blunt. To risk a blunt rejection in return. No 'someone not returning your beeps'. No 'someone being busy all the time'. Just blasted with rejection, right in the face. That would be difficult for even the most confident person to take."

"I hadn't thought of it that way." Because she knew it would never happen. Nobody was going to make a move on her. She was the washed-up pilot who'd been marched from the Military Academy in disgrace. "You've been on 72, and it was the same on 65. I'm not dating material."

"And you're okay with that?"

"I don't have much choice, so..." She shrugged. "I keep busy."

Lynn forked a piece of pasta into her mouth, then another one.

Christine took another bite of her sandwich and tried to resist asking the question that kept running through her mind. She lost the battle. "Have you seen anyone since your bad breakup?"

"I've been out on a few dates with good people, but all of them were 'not for me' people. Not recently, though. I'd like to think there will be someone. Someone who can look past everything on Claire's list."

She was dying to ask, but then she realized she didn't care what was on the list. She liked Lynn, quite a bit. Claire's opinion of her didn't matter.

"Someone who can appreciate me, warts and all." Lynn grinned and waved her hands under her chin with a flourish. Her face relaxed and she met Christine's eyes. "Do you see yourself being on 72 for a long time?"

The change of subject threw her. "Right now I do. I expect to eventually be switched to days. It took years for them to let me fly again. I haven't been flying nights very long."

"What about tours? I hear military on 72 talking about them."

"I'm not sure I'd want to go on one." She'd always wanted to stay close to home so she could teach, but when she'd been on 65, she'd sometimes imagined herself undocking and leaving space stations and Rymel far behind. She was mature enough to realize she didn't really want to go on tour, but wanted to get away from the disapproval, the disdain, that surrounded her. Going on tour would be the worst thing she could do. She did not want to be trapped on a ship with colleagues who despised her. At least now she could go down to the planet. "I'm actually flying as much now as I would on a tour."

"But you want days."

"Nights are for green pilots, those who've just graduated. I'm there because, well, I'm lucky to be flying again. I'm grateful for that. But I'd like days better. There's a mix of pilots on days, mainly more experienced pilots who don't want to go on tour or can't for whatever reason. Pilots like me."

"You'd be happy flying days for the rest of your career?"

"I enjoy flying," Christine said indignantly.

"Sorry, that sounded wrong. I wasn't implying anything, just asking."

"Sorry," Christine mumbled in return. "I wouldn't mind teaching again. It's something I really enjoyed. That's never going to happen, though."

"You told me the report from the Indoctrination Academy said you could teach classes. How far does that commander's influence reach?"

"Far enough to prevent me from teaching again."

Lynn frowned. The atmosphere at the table felt heavy, oppressive.

"Can we talk about something else?" Christine said. "Something positive."

Lynn straightened. "Yes! Of course."

"Tell me more about your business. What happens when someone wants an article to slot and you get the order?"

Lynn launched into an enthusiastic explanation of the steps involved and which ones her business handled, which led to questions from Christine and more detailed answers from Lynn. By the time they'd finished their meals and taken a stroll in a public garden near the eatery, Christine knew the names of all Lynn's workers, their positions, who was fantastic, who was good, and who Lynn expected would move on at some point, either willingly or because they were pushed. She'd also learned more about what Lynn herself did (skilled calligrapher, administration, planning, hiring, firing, and everything in between) and her plans for the future of the business.

They said their goodbyes outside the garden, since they were heading in different directions, Lynn home, and Christine to get the train that would take her to the nearest shuttle launch complex. On the train, Christine gazed out the window at the lights whipping by. The next time they'd see each other was sometime after the Festival of the Way, which was about three weeks away. Lynn would be too busy for socializing before then.

Lynn, same-oriented. Christine had assumed incorrectly. Things hadn't felt more awkward between them, and Christine was determined to keep it that way. She valued their friendship, and everything she'd told Lynn about dating was true. She'd never confess feelings to anyone, never make the first move. She would enjoy Lynn's company and try to be a good friend to her. Someday Lynn would find that person, the 'for me' person, and she'd have less time for her friends.

But that was okay. Christine was used to being alone.

* * *

TWO WEEKS LATER, Christine sat on the carpeted floor of her quarters and opened up the new model kit she'd traded for last time she was on the planet. She examined the instructions. This vintage model of an aviacraft was a complex one that would take her at least six months to do. Other modellers could do it in three or four, but her perfectionist nature wouldn't be satisfied with what she'd build and paint in that time, and there wasn't a deadline. She'd get a good start on it today, one of her days off, especially since it was only just after breakfast.

As she verified that all the model pieces were in the box, she thought about Lynn. They'd exchanged a few dispatches since having supper together, short ones asking how things were going. Christine hadn't initiated the exchange, but had quickly replied when Lynn's first dispatch had arrived. Lynn would be in the thick of it now at work, with the Festival so close.

Her comm unit beeped twice. Another dispatch from Lynn, probably asking how she was doing. Christine had wondered if Lynn was using these dispatches to keep herself grounded in the midst of the work madness. No time to talk, but enough time to write a short dispatch during her snatched lunch or between tasks.

This newest dispatch was short but made Christine's brow furrow with concern.

Maybe I shouldn't have bought the business. Dealing with my first disaster and I'm at a loss.

Christine moved the model box from her lap to the floor and pushed herself upright. *What's going on?* she replied.

I ordered one stock of paper, our most popular stock, months ago. Got half the order on schedule last week. The other half is due tomorrow and I just received a dispatch from the supplier saying it will be late. Five days late! I'm going to have a lot of irate families on my hands.

Did they say why it will be late?

Unforeseen absences in their delivery department. I'm guessing that means illness or notifications. Which I understand. But it leaves me in a terrible position.

So the paper is there. They just can't deliver it?

Just reading that frustrates me even more. It's never happened before. I've never had any type of problem with this supplier. At any other time, the delay wouldn't matter, but it does now. I've tried to engage a delivery company to pick it up, but everyone's booked.

Christine's mind raced. *How much does the paper weigh?*

Why?

No promises, but if there's a craft available that can carry the weight, I could pick up the delivery and fly it to you.

You'd do that?

I'm off today. But it will depend on the weight and whether I can get my hands on a craft.

Let me get back to you.

While she waited, Christine checked the military booking system, hoping there would be an aviacraft or cargo craft available. She found two, an aviacraft at the shuttle complex in A7 and a cargo craft at C6. She booked the C6 one, not wanting someone to snatch it from under her, and specified "personal" under the reason for the booking, which was perfectly acceptable. Pilots booked crafts all the time, a perk they enjoyed. If it turned out the paper would be too heavy for the craft, she'd release it.

Ten minutes later, Lynn replied with the weight. Christine sighed with relief. The craft could handle it.

Send me the location, and tell them they'll need to load the craft. I'll let you know when I've picked up the delivery.

I don't know how to thank you for this.

I'm not doing anything else today.

Still. I owe you big.

Christine wanted to say she didn't, that hanging out with her was payment enough, meaning Lynn's willingness to ignore the whispers, to be seen with the washed-up pilot, to be talked about, though Christine hadn't told Lynn she was now a target too. She also wanted to say friends did this sort of thing for each other, but she didn't want to presume.

I'd better get going. It would take a few hours to descend to the planet, fly to the supplier, wait for them to load the craft, and fly to Lynn's workplace.

She quickly changed into her uniform and headed for the shuttle launch area.

IT WAS ALMOST suppertime when she landed the craft in the cargo area behind Lynn's business. A man in overalls strode over to her. "You must be Chris. I'm Jack. Let me beep my crew and we'll unload the paper. Lynn said to go right in." He pointed. "Through that door, turn left, then you should see the floor. She'll be there somewhere."

"Thank you."

Christine entered through the door he'd indicated, expecting to hear the sounds of a busy workplace: voices, rustling, comm units beeping. But it was quiet. Not deathly so. There was a low murmur of voices, but this wasn't the bustling workplace Christine had expected.

When she reached the floor, she understood why. At least forty people sat hunched over calligraphy desks, concentrating on their work. Others moved silently between the rows of calligraphers, collecting completed articles and taking them through a doorway into another area of the business.

"That's where we package the articles for delivery to the appropriate Trading Centres," Lynn said from next to her, making her jump. "Sorry, didn't mean to frighten you." Even though her tone was quieter than usual, she'd sounded loud. "And through there," she jutted her chin toward another door, "is the public reception area, where Rymellans can order articles directly."

"I didn't know what to expect when I came in."

"I'd love to give you a tour, but I'll have to do it next time because I have to get back to my stack of articles. That sounds terribly ungrateful, doesn't it?" Lynn said sheepishly.

Christine shook her head. "I know you're busy."

"We'll be at it for a few hours yet, then I always take everyone for a late supper. That's how I work it in the two weeks leading up to the Festival, because we all pretty much live here, only going home to sleep. Say you'll come to supper with us. I know it means you'll have to hang around for a while."

The thought of having supper with a group of strangers intimidated her, but at the same time, if she left now, she'd return to her empty quarters on 72 and eat alone. "I'd like to." She watched a woman carry a stack of paper to one of the calligraphy desks. "I met Jack. He's unloading the paper."

"Usually the delivery company would do it. I hire Jack for the occasional odd job. Fortunately he was available when I beeped him today."

"Is there anything else I can do to help while I'm here?" Christine asked.

Lynn's brows shot up. "You've already done enough, and I'm so grateful to you. I don't even know how to thank you. You've saved me so much stress and explaining and headaches, and a bunch of families won't have their plans ruined. Thank you so much. That's all I can say."

Seeing Lynn smile was thanks enough. "I won't be doing anything except waiting, so if there is something I can do, put me to work."

"Well, Pam hasn't had a break for a while. One of the calligraphers usually fills in for her, but maybe you can do it. She makes sure our inkwells don't run dry, tops up paper at each desk, brings us tziva. Basically makes sure we have everything we need to keep doing what we do."

"If you think I can do it, sure."

"The worst thing you'll do is spill some ink. We know to protect what we're working on because spills happen."

"Okay."

"I'll go get her. She can show you what to do."

Lynn returned with Pam, a short woman in her mid-thirties, Christine guessed, who got right down to business and quickly showed her where to get the ink, how to carry it, how to refill the inkwell without making a mess. Carrying paper to desks didn't require any instruction, and Pam said not to worry about tziva or anything else.

Christine stood at the vantage point Pam had designated and watched for a calligrapher to raise his or her hand. In the half hour Pam was on break, Christine only had to fill one inkwell and carry paper to two desks. She found refilling the inkwell more nerve-wracking than flying a fighter, and was quite proud of herself when she managed it without spilling any.

When Pam returned, she said they were running low on tziva and a few other comfort supplies, as she called them. Would Chris mind going to the Trading Centre? The next thing she knew, she was pedalling the delivery bike along a wide path, nodding to Rymellans she passed and enjoying the breeze tickling her face.

She helped out with a few other odd jobs anyone could do until the calligraphers laid down their brushes together and stretched.

Lynn came over to where Christine had sat since she'd topped up everyone's tziva mugs. "I hope Pam didn't boss you around too much. I told her to find you stuff to do, but only if you wanted to do it."

"I enjoyed myself. It was a great change of pace. I can sit and work on a model any time."

"Is that what you were doing when I beeped to cry on your shoulder?" Lynn didn't wait for an answer. "You'll have to show me your models sometime."

That would mean Lynn visiting her quarters. Christine didn't have time to fret over the prospect. A group had assembled nearby, one that included the calligraphers, Jack and his crew, and Pam.

Lynn turned to them. "If you haven't met her, this is Chris. She picked up the paper we wouldn't have otherwise." Everyone clapped and cheered.

Christine's face felt hot. She wasn't used to this but didn't have time to feel embarrassed. Lynn was introducing everyone. Christine tried to remember as many names as she could using the memory tricks she'd used in the classroom.

They all left through a side entrance and headed down a nearby path. Christine trailed behind the group with Lynn, listening to the chattering taking place in front of her. She couldn't make out any single voice.

She turned to Lynn. "If you hadn't told me, I wouldn't have expected you to be so busy at this time. My family doesn't slot articles on Festival Day."

"Not all families do, but it's a tradition for some, and not just Festival Day. Some do it in the days leading up to the Festival. That's why our busy period starts well before it." She clasped her hands behind her back. "My family always slots articles. We go after the afternoon program."

"I bet they get their articles from you."

"Of course they do. I do them myself, and that goes for all the calligraphers. If it's a relative, I know who'll do the order."

They chatted about nothing important until they reached the eatery, where a room was reserved for them. Christine was surprised to see some seats at the tables already occupied.

"Chosens," Lynn said. "And partners, for Solitaries. Keeps everyone happy. I don't want people at home grumbling. I need everyone."

The wait staff knew everyone's names and what a few at the table would order. They must be like Christine, who always ordered the same thing for breakfast. She'd wondered why the staff at the 72 eatery didn't just cook up her eggs, hash browns, and toast around the same time every day, or when she arrived. Maybe they secretly hoped she'd surprise them one day, like she had the day of her sim session with Thompson.

Christine sat next to Lynn but didn't talk to her much. Her military uniform and the knowledge she was a pilot meant she was peppered with questions from the other four people sitting near them. At one point, she had to ask them to give her a break so she could eat her supper. "Yes, let her eat," Lynn had said, an amused glint in her eye.

Halfway through her meal, Christine asked if the Steven at the end of another table was the one Lynn planned to groom to take over from her someday.

"That's him," Lynn said, nodding. "I'd point out Jeannie, but she's not here today. She's been working non-stop for the past couple of weeks, so I told her to take today off. She'll be upset she missed all the paper drama and the pilot who helped us out. I'll have to fill her in tomorrow."

Before Christine knew it, everyone had eaten their meals and desserts and drunk their tziva, and people were filtering away. Assuming Lynn would be the last to go, she was contemplating whether to say her goodbyes to those remaining and leave Lynn to it, when Lynn stood. "All right. I'm going to escort our pilot back to her ship. Great work today, everyone. Only another week and we'll be able to sleep again. See you tomorrow."

A chorus of "good night" and "see you tomorrow" rose. Outside, they strolled back to Lynn's business. The sun was setting, but the lights lining the wide path were still dark.

"Did you enjoy your meal?" Lynn asked.

"Very much, thank you." She couldn't remember when she'd last eaten with so many people who didn't mind her presence.

"I've been taking everyone to that eatery for a few years now. Sally didn't like the idea when I suggested it. Credits out the window and all. But I believe in keeping everyone sane. The credits I spend on it will result in more satisfied workers and clients, or at least that's what I believe."

Christine wasn't a businesswoman, but she could see the logic.

"Sorry I took you away from your model to answer my distress call."

She chuckled. "Don't be. I had the time of my life today. It was a nice change."

"I assume all these models are in your quarters." Lynn's mouth turned up at the corners. "Is there room to move around in there?"

Christine barked a laugh. "There aren't that many. It can take me months to put one together."

"Maybe you can show me next time I'm on 72."

Christine didn't know what to say. She trusted Lynn. She knew Lynn wouldn't bring false accusations to Interior, wouldn't say Christine Leeds had crossed the line when they were alone and nobody was there to see. She'd gotten past that fear with Lynn. But she hadn't forgotten about the two pilots in the eatery.

"Or maybe you won't show me," Lynn said, her voice casual but her mouth pinched. "I shouldn't have assumed."

Mortification chilled her. Christine's usual caution around everything she verbalized fled. "No, I'd love to show you my models. It's just..." She blew out a sigh. "I think people on the station are talking about you." She lifted her hands, dropped them to her sides. "I don't think, I know. A couple of pilots said things about you when they knew I could hear them."

"Like what?"

She had to tell her now. "Like you're desperate to be hanging out with me, a washed-up pilot."

Lynn groaned. "I'm going to be forty-five soon. I don't care what a couple of pilots are saying about me. Or you."

"There could be more."

"I don't care. I don't know them, and they don't know me."

"It's just that if anyone sees you entering or leaving my quarters..."

"Let them talk. Really. I don't know about you, but I left the Learning Academy a long time ago and I hang out with adults. Let the children chatter all they want. I'd be fine being seen entering your quarters, or leaving, or hanging around in front of them, or dancing a jig in the corridor outside." She turned to Christine. "Unless it would bother you."

"I guess it would depend on what I thought of the jig," she blurted.

Lynn laughed.

Christine felt lighter. "If you don't care, neither do I. Sure, next time you're up on the station, you can see my models. Don't expect works of art."

"Honestly, I don't know what to expect. That's why I'm curious. You mention models a lot. I want to see one." Her eyes grew distant for a moment. "I should be able to come up in a couple of weeks. The Festival will be over. I'll have my nephew's eighteenth to go to, but I'll be rested enough. I'll come up a couple of days after that."

"That sounds good." Christine was already looking forward to it.

They lapsed into a comfortable silence, one that remained until they reached the craft and stopped to face each other.

"I really do appreciate what you did today," Lynn said. "I owe you."

The last thing she wanted was for Lynn to feel indebted to her. "You don't owe me a thing. It was fun. And I hope I'm not being presumptuous, but I think of us as friends." There, she'd said it, but part of her wanted to take it back and hide it away.

Lynn's brows slightly lifted. "Of course we're friends."

Warmth flooded through her. "I was just doing what a friend does."

Lynn straightened and nodded. "Well, this friend appreciates it very much."

Their eyes met. Christine scrambled for something to say, but nothing came. All she could do was see Lynn, fight the force pulling her toward her, hope Lynn wouldn't notice, though Lynn wasn't saying anything either. She was staring right back, intently, unblinkingly. For a moment, Christine thought they were going to hug.

Then it was as if someone had snapped her fingers and the pull, the draw, the force Christine could palpably feel, died as suddenly as it had arrived.

They both exhaled slowly and stepped back from each other, or maybe Christine only imagined them doing it. She didn't trust her senses right now. "I should let you get home," she heard herself say. "You have another long day tomorrow."

"I promise you won't have to rescue me again."

Christine wouldn't mind rescuing her again. Not at all. "Good night."

"Good night, Chris," Lynn said softly.

She climbed into the cargo craft, fussed with tapping the navigation panel in ways that wouldn't do anything while she watched Lynn walk away. Her breath caught in her throat when Lynn turned and waved and stayed where she was.

Christine waved back, fired up the craft, and ascended, a sense of loss, of longing, rising with her. It was still there when she was halfway to the shuttle launch complex, but so were her doubts, her disgust with herself, her shame. Lynn was not interested in her. She'd imagined it all, played something in her head that wasn't actually happening. She wished Lynn was diff-oriented, but she wasn't, and the fact that she wasn't didn't mean she was interested in every woman who crossed her path, and certainly not in a washed-up pilot who'd never make lieutenant commander, or would be completely gray and about to retire when she did. When Lynn chose the woman she'd spend her life with, she'd want someone as successful as herself.

Christine reminded herself she needed to be careful. She'd lost her way once, and she would not do it again, or lie to herself. Lynn was a friend. Just a friend. Christine hadn't had a friend for a while, and Lynn had been the first person to show any interest in her life for years, plus she was so kind and brave. That was why Christine felt so drawn to her.

Lynn had awakened a side of Christine that had lain dormant since that shameful period in her life. She wouldn't mind their friendship turning into more. But she valued their friendship. She needed it. And so she would have to be doubly careful never to reveal her feelings for Lynn. She'd be there for her, like today. She'd be a great friend to her, and nothing more.

THE COUPLE OF weeks until the next time Lynn would be up on the station turned into a month. Christine missed her, but they kept in touch through dispatches.

My nephew received a Solitary Notification at his eighteenth and didn't take it well. Neither did my brother. That's why I can't come up to 72 just yet, Lynn had explained. *I'll tell you more when I see you.*

Christine hoped he was okay. Maybe Lynn coming up today was a good sign, and Lynn arriving today was the reason Christine was straightening the cushion on her sofa and having one last look around her quarters, to make sure she hadn't missed any obvious dust. Her quarters had never been cleaner. Now she just had to wait. A quick check of her comm unit told her Lynn could arrive any moment.

As if on cue, the door chime sounded. Christine squared her shoulders and pressed the *Open* button. Lynn stood outside. She raised the two tzivas she carried. "Here I am."

"Come in." She moved aside so Lynn could step into her quarters.

"Here." Lynn handed her a tziva, then glanced around. "Are your quarters always this neat?"

"No."

Lynn chuckled.

"Not messy, though."

"I'm afraid to touch anything. I might leave microscopic particles behind."

Christine smiled. "Sit down."

"I want to see a model first," Lynn said. "Well, I can see one." She stared up at the model suspended from the ceiling. "It's a fighter, right."

"A vintage fighter. Model 459-A. We flew them two centuries ago."

"Do you know all the models?"

"Pretty much." She set her tziva on the oval table next to the sofa. After Lynn had followed suit, Christine motioned for her to come over to the small worktable in the corner of the sitting room. The model she was currently building sat on it. "If you look through this," she touched the large magnifier attached to the table, "you can see more detail."

Lynn perched on the rolling stool and peered through the magnifier. Christine could visualize what she was seeing: the point where an energy booster was attached to the chassis of the 875-F. "For some reason, I tend to use a tad too much glue," she felt compelled to say. "I don't know why. I guess I want to make sure nothing will fall off."

"That's your signature," Lynn said brightly, still focused on the magnifier. "If this was in some model gallery—do they have those?—the guide would say, 'And here we have an original Chris Leeds fighter, model, um, 123. You can tell this model was assembled by Leeds by the copious amount of glue holding every piece together, ensuring no piece ever falls off, and that has held true over the past one-hundred years. Every piece is still attached."

Grinning, Christine clapped.

Lynn stood and bowed. "Thank you." She gazed at another model on the worktable, one waiting to be painted. "These are exquisite," she murmured, leaning in for a closer look. "Do you paint the real colours, or whatever you want."

Christine understood what she meant. "Usually the actual colours the fighter had, but not all the time."

"When don't you?" Lynn asked, her eyes alight with curiosity.

She hadn't really thought about it. "I don't know. Sometimes I go with what appeals to me. But when I do that, I always build a duplicate model and paint it with the actual colours."

"Huh. Maybe one represents what's expected of you, and the other one, the one you paint with whatever colours strike you, represents what you really want to do."

"I'm not sure there's anything deep behind it."

Lynn cocked her head. "When you have a duplicate like that, which one do you display and which one do you hide?"

She was about to say she didn't hide any of her models, when she realized that wasn't true. There were those she displayed where people could see them, like the one hanging from the sitting room ceiling. And then there were those she placed where only herself, or someone she trusted, like a relative, could glimpse them. "I display the one with the actual colours," she admitted to Lynn.

"There you go."

Did it mean anything? Something to think about later. "There are more over here." She led Lynn to the display case partially hidden by the chair across from the sofa.

"Ah," Lynn said. "The collection."

Christine pointed to each model and named its call sign, even though she figured Lynn didn't care.

"You said it takes you months to do one?"

"I like to take my time."

"You do one or two a year?"

"Yes."

"When did you start?"

"When I was around twelve. Someone gave one of my brothers a model as a gift. He wasn't interested in doing it, and my other siblings were at the Indoctrination Academy, so I figured I'd give it a try."

"And you loved it."

"I was surprised. I only tried it because there wasn't much else to do that day and the box was right there, and he said I could have it. And he only said that because he figured I'd hate it," she added, making Lynn chuckle. "You know what brothers are like."

"I do."

Lynn's interest in how she'd gotten started warmed Christine, but it was time to let her off the hook. Lynn had shown the appropriate amount of interest in her models and must be wondering when it would be polite to talk about other things. "We should drink our tziva before it gets cold."

"Just a second." Lynn was shifting position, trying to get a better look at a model on the bottom shelf. "What's this? It's not a fighter."

Blood rushed to Christine's face. She'd forgotten to remove that item. "It's a dog."

"I can see that," Lynn said dryly. "You do animals too?"

She cleared her throat. "Not usually. We had a dog, Charlie. He died when I was fourteen and it hit me hard. Making that helped me work through it. I saw it as a sort of tribute to him."

"That's so sweet. And this is a sculpture, not a model."

"It's the only one I've done."

Lynn's eyes widened. "Really? You should do more. You have a talent for it."

"Thanks," she mumbled, wondering how much was real praise and how much politeness. She moved over to the chair she rarely used and sat down.

Lynn plunked onto the sofa and sipped her tziva. "Thanks for showing me your models. I'll be interested in how the one you're working on comes along."

Christine wanted to say she'd show it to her every time she visited, but that would be presumptuous.

After taking another sip of her tziva, Lynn leaned back and briefly closed her eyes. "Ah, it's nice to just sit and sip tziva like this. It's been crazy at home. I told you about my nephew."

She nodded and braced herself. She'd expected Lynn to talk about the Solitary Notification, but it would still be uncomfortable.

"Poor boy," Lynn said, still holding her tziva. "Well, I guess he's a man now. He was so upset when the Chosen Council courier arrived. My brother and Chosen sister were beside themselves. They rallied all the Solitaries to go talk to him and tell him his life isn't over, essentially. It didn't help much, so my Chosen sister wanted us to keep seeing him, to talk to him, in my case, to tell him how Aunt Lynn still managed to be content with her life even though she didn't have a Chosen or children. Which when you think about it, is pretty patronizing, but I didn't mind doing it because he's a decent kid and he was clearly suffering."

"How is he now?"

"Still upset, but the shock is subsiding. It's not the first time I've had to comfort someone at their eighteenth, using myself as an example that life isn't over. I'm sure you've done the same."

She tensed. Her siblings would never ask her to comfort their children under those circumstances. They didn't see her as a Solitary in the same way as Solitaries who'd never had Chosens, and she was the last person they'd want offering advice on how to handle a shocking notification. Though at this point in her life, having gone through that shameful time and with some distance from it, she would have some heartfelt and sage advice to give them, if they were willing to listen.

"How did you feel on your eighteenth?" she asked Lynn. It would be rude to abruptly change the subject, and she was curious.

"Not good. But I was mainly upset over not having a Chosen. Just between you and me, the 'no children' aspect didn't bother me."

"Really?"

Lynn frowned. "Yes, and the way you're looking at me is why I don't share that very often."

"No, no, I'm surprised, that's all. Because even though I'm sure there are Solitaries who feel that way, nobody ever says it."

"Since we're talking just between you and me, there are Chosens who feel that way too." Lynn leaned forward so she could set her tziva on the table. "When Rymellans order articles directly from us, we always take them into a private room, because for some the grief is fresh. Their loved one has only just died. And they tell us all sorts of things in those rooms. Even if they're slotting for someone who's been dead for years, they'll tell stories, and they'll admit things about themselves to us they wouldn't admit to anyone else. Not violation type things. We'd report those to Interior. Socially unacceptable type things." She raised her right index finger. "We have a strict privacy rule. We would never divulge specifics along with names. But we—me and my co-workers—we talk about generalities, and I wouldn't say it's common, but it's not rare for people to admit they didn't want children, or they're relieved because they won't have to have them, or to tell us the same thing about their loved one."

Christine had wanted children. But that desire, that expectation, felt like such a long time ago.

"This will make me sound horrible, but I didn't want the distraction and the responsibility. Don't get me wrong. If I'd turned out to be a Chosen, I would have had children and I wouldn't have resented them or anything. And if you'd asked me before I turned eighteen if I wanted children, I would have said yes. It was only when I got my notification that I realized I was disappointed, terribly disappointed, that I wasn't a Chosen, and that was it. Everyone else was assuring me I could live a fulfilled life without children, and I realized I didn't mind that part. I was free to do what I wanted, when I wanted. I wouldn't have to worry about anyone else but myself. I wouldn't have minded worrying about a Chosen, but that's a different type of worry, because she would have been an adult and needed me in a different way. But that didn't happen, and I came to understand there could still be someone special. Just not 'sanctioned by the Chosen Council' special."

"You don't sound horrible. You sound like someone who knew herself, even at eighteen."

"That's very kind. I assume you wanted children."

"I did." And she knew what was coming before Lynn asked, and couldn't see a way to head it off.

"How did you feel when you got your Solitary Notification?"

For a moment, she thought of lying, of telling Lynn she was disappointed, of course, and moped around, and got over it. But that would be a rather big lie, one she might tell to someone she didn't expect to see again or ever be close to. Not a lie she would ever tell to Lynn. She gulped down some tziva and carefully set her mug down. "I didn't receive a Solitary Notification."

Lynn peered at her, confused. She glanced at Christine's left hand, then at her right, to confirm what she already knew. That Christine wasn't Joined. Of course Lynn knew that. But Christine had shocked her, made her doubt herself for a second.

"But you're not—" Lynn's face froze. "I'm so sorry. Were you Joined?"

Christine swallowed. Time distorted, but she focused on her breathing, kept her eyes on Lynn's concerned face. "No. I received a Death Notification. I was twenty-nine."

"Twenty-nine," Lynn breathed. "You must have been expecting Papers to arrive at any time. I'm so sorry, Chris. That must have been so awful for you." Her eyes grew distant. Christine knew she was doing the math. "That would have been around the time..." She trailed off.

"Around the time I had my troubles with Interior. I didn't handle the Death Notification well." She shook her head. "That's an understatement."

"Can I ask you about it, or would you rather talk about something else?"

She'd rather talk about something else, and if it had been anyone else, she would have said that. But Lynn had just spoken honestly about herself, and Christine wanted to be open and honest in return. She didn't want any unanswered questions hanging between them. "I don't mind talking to you about it."

"If I ask something you don't want to answer, just say. You said you didn't handle it well. I know you were struck under 998 and 662, so I understand the consequences of you not handling it. But how didn't you handle it well?"

"I didn't process it. Didn't let myself feel it." Looking back, Christine couldn't understand why she'd wanted to appear as if nothing was wrong. Had she worried about what her colleagues would think? About the effect on her career if she had asked for time off? If so, she'd chosen to handle it in the worst possible way. "I brushed it off. Carried on as if nothing had happened. It didn't make sense for me to grieve over someone I'd never met, after all."

She lifted her hand when Lynn drew breath. "I don't believe that now. It's what I told myself back then. I didn't ask for time off, didn't tell anyone for a while, refused to acknowledge any sadness or shock. I just carried on, as if it had never happened. Well, I thought I'd done that." She motioned to the model hanging from the ceiling. "I stopped working on my models, stopped socializing, spent a lot of time in bed and told myself I was just tired. I stopped feeling. I couldn't risk feeling anything because those other feelings I was repressing might overwhelm me. I didn't consciously know that at the time, though."

"What about your counsellor? Didn't they think something was wrong?"

"I was good at saying the right things and leaving out the wrong things. Counsellors only know what we tell them."

"They can only help us if we tell them the truth."

She nodded. "I didn't. But eventually I started to feel again. Nothing good. Anger. Resentment. Bitterness. Fortunately I had a great counsellor at the Indoctrination Academy. We worked out that my inexcusable behaviour was a cry for help, that I chose the cadet I chose because somewhere, deep inside, I knew she'd report me. But I also chose her because she was in a relationship, and happy, with someone who I believed at the time wasn't her Chosen. The unfairness of it got to me. The combination of those two things—my anger and resentment, and the part of me that knew I was drowning—led to me being struck under 662 and 998, and I was fully responsible for that."

"Yes, but you also weren't well." Lynn held the tips of the index finger and thumb on her right hand a centimetre apart. "You have to give yourself a teeny tiny little break, don't you think?"

"I should have handled it differently."

"But you didn't. And you were hurting, a lot. I'm not excusing it. I'm just saying you're not a terrible person because of what happened. You were a decent person who ended up in a situation you couldn't emotionally handle."

"Rymellans get Death Notifications all the time."

"Everyone's different, especially when it comes to grief."

"I wasn't facing up to my grief. The report said my actions were due to unresolved grief."

Lynn rolled her eyes. "I hate that term. Is grief ever resolved? I mean, you're not crying every day for years, and I understand what they mean by it. I just wish they'd call it something else."

"Whatever they call it, that's what it was."

"So your time at the Indoctrination Academy…you spent it processing it all. The loss of your Chosen. Finding out you wouldn't be Joined and have children. And at twenty-nine. That would have been tough for anyone."

"It was three months before my thirtieth. I'd wake up every day thinking, 'Today could be the day, and if it isn't, I won't have to wait longer than however many days were left. I could count the days, Lynn. I could count them." She grabbed her mug, hung on to it.

"I'm so sorry." Lynn's eyes glistened, making a lump rise in Christine's throat.

They sipped their tzivas. Lynn broke the silence. "You know what's happened to you since then isn't fair, right?"

"What do you mean?"

"The way the military has treated you. It's not fair. You don't deserve it."

Christine struggled to hide her surprise. "I can understand why they didn't want me teaching one-on-one and needed some time to trust me again."

"I get the one-on-one thing. But not everything else. You told me your report said you can teach classes. Okay, some idiot of a commander who needs the Military Academy to feel important made a public example of you and prevented you from teaching. But you did what you needed to do at the Indoctrination Academy, you were released because you were no longer considered a threat to the Way, and you're an experienced pilot. You should have been assigned to fly right away, not stuck behind a desk. And the way people talk about you here, on this station, is inexcusable. I wish there was an article they could all be struck under, but there's nothing in the Law for malicious petty dimwits."

She quickly set her tziva down. "I did something terrible."

"Years ago. Years. And you were struck, and you did what was required of you, which I'm sure wasn't easy, given the circumstances, but you did it. You returned to your usual, upstanding, strong in the Way self. That should have been enough for everyone. They should have welcomed you back, pleased that you'd dealt with whatever it was. But instead they won't let you forget it and treat you as if you've fallen from the Way. It's not fair."

Christine didn't know what to say.

Lynn filled the silence. "Why is everyone so afraid that if they're seen with someone who's been struck under a serious article, they'll be seen as weak in the Way? Interior doesn't strike people for being friends with someone who violates the Way. And if it's something that happened years ago and it's never happened again, then obviously the person has handled it. We should forgive them. There has to be forgiveness at some point, right? But no, we keep punishing and punishing them, forgetting that if we're treating them as if they can't grow beyond it, then it means we can't and wouldn't be able to, either. Do you know what I mean?"

She nodded. She *had* returned to her strong in the Way self by the time she'd left the Indoctrination Academy. She would never, ever cross any lines again. But Morton had refused to let her return to the classroom, she'd laboured years behind a desk until she could sit in a cockpit, and she endured the looks and whispers, wondering if she'd ever see lieutenant commander or fly days. Her life was in a holding pattern, and she'd been lonely. Then she'd met Lynn, and she wasn't as lonely, but Lynn would eventually meet someone and would rightly focus her time and attention on her beloved.

Christine would like to build a better life for herself, make more social connections. But she couldn't see how. So yes, what Lynn said made sense. Her life would be very different if her former colleagues had welcomed her back.

"You sound passionate about this," she said to Lynn.

"I've seen it happen too many times. Someone's struggling. They're struck. They do whatever they have to do so it won't happen again. But they lose friends, and even the ones they keep sometimes don't trust them as much." She met Christine's eyes. "Honestly, I've never seen it so bad as it is with you, where so much time has passed and it's people who don't even know you."

"If I hadn't been marched out, I doubt—"

"But you were. And that commander who insisted on it should be struck. And if it was up to me, removed from his position. But again, there's nothing in the Law for someone who's been deliberately cruel." She grimaced. "But you don't want to hear me rant about this. It's something that happened to you. I didn't even know you then." She sighed. "Sorry."

"There's no need to be sorry. I wish that one part had happened differently. Me being marched out," she clarified. "Sometimes I, well, I do feel resentful about that. Maybe even bitter. I wonder, if he hadn't insisted on that, if only a few people had known I was in trouble with Interior, and not on sabbatical or away on some confidential mission, would I have been able to go back to my old life? Which I know isn't good. I need to let go of it."

Lynn snorted. "Uh, you know what? If he'd done the same thing to me, I'd hate him. I think it's perfectly natural for you to be bitter. In fact, I'd go so far as to say you're repressing again if the thought of him doesn't make you angry. At the same time, you do have to let it go in the sense that it's done, so you don't want to dwell on it. And if you hadn't been marched out, I don't think you would have been able to go back to your old life."

"Why?"

"Because he would have told everyone anyway. Not the details. Innuendo."

That was true, because he'd done it already. He'd somehow conveyed the details of her harassment to the supervisor on 65, and Christine knew he'd done the same with anyone who mattered on 72, and then some.

"You're right." She looked down at her lap. "It's just me wishing it hadn't happened, that I could turn back the clock and do it all over, starting with when the Chosen Council courier showed up at my office with the Death Notification."

"What would you do in your do over?"

Christine didn't have to think about it. She'd gone over this so many times in her mind and with Counsellor Miller. "I wouldn't carry on as if nothing had happened and go teach my next class or practicum." She still couldn't remember what she'd done for the rest of the day, just that she'd done it. "I'd let myself cry. Go see my superior, ask him for time off, and tell him why. Tell my parents right away. Let myself rail at the unfairness of it all." She gazed at Lynn. "Why didn't I let myself do that?"

"I don't know," Lynn said gently. "I didn't know you then, so I can only speculate. I don't think that would be helpful."

She smiled wanly. "I guess if I don't understand why, I can't expect you to. I understand I repressed it. That I became depressed, despondent. But I don't understand *why* I repressed it. Why didn't I let myself feel it?"

"All right, I'll speculate." Lynn tapped at her chin with her right index finger. "You're a stoic person. You don't like to ask for help or inconvenience anyone. You would have put your students first, perhaps felt that if you didn't just carry on, you'd be letting them down. That's based on what I know of you today. And it could be completely wrong, so I'd ignore it if I were you. Focus on yourself today, because you can't go back and do it again."

Christine knew that, but she had her moments when she wished it was possible to go back in time.

"Well, this certainly turned into a heavy conversation." Lynn drained her tziva mug. "How did we get here? Oh yes, my nephew."

"I hope he'll be okay."

"He will be, in time."

Christine drank the rest of her lukewarm tziva, met Lynn's eyes, and in the ensuing silence, felt an intimacy, an emotional intimacy, that she hadn't felt with anyone for a long time. Maybe that was why she was revealing things to Lynn she hadn't told anyone else, not even Miller. Things she'd thought about since leaving the Indoctrination Academy.

"I know we've been to the arboretum before, but I just love the trees," Lynn said, her voice sounding loud. "Want to stroll around there for a bit?"

"Sure."

They rose. "I'm kind of surprised you're in uniform," Lynn said. "I thought maybe you wouldn't be. Day off. In your quarters."

"I feel comfortable in uniform. It's easy to choose what to wear. And I knew you were coming and we'd be leaving. You like long skirts." She inwardly winced. She wished she hadn't said that.

Lynn didn't seem to mind. "I do wear pants, when I'm working in my garden or anywhere else a skirt would get in the way or wouldn't make sense. I usually walk everywhere, but on the odd occasion I ride my bike, I wear pants. But I do prefer skirts, usually long. I only wear below the knee when I'm somewhere really warm. Been that way since I was twelve."

Lynn would be forty-five soon. Christine wondered what to get for her birthday. Lynn had agreed they were friends, so it wouldn't be inappropriate to give her a gift. Hopefully she'd see her around that time.

"There's something else about long skirts." Lynn grabbed the sides of her skirt and swished them as she did a few dance steps. "You can do this while dancing, not the traditional dances, obviously. But when they do parallel dances at the Dance Hall, I can do this when I'm approaching and leaving my partner."

Swishing her skirt, Lynn sashayed toward Christine.

Her heart pounded. She wanted to step back. She did not want to step back. Her nails dug into her palms.

When Lynn was about a metre away from her, she whirled and sashayed back to the sofa.

Christine let out her pent breath, hoping Lynn wouldn't notice her respiration rate had shot up. If Lynn hadn't turned around, Christine didn't know what she would have done. Ran behind the chair? Reached out and caught her and danced with her around the sitting room? Her temples pulsed.

"Should we go?" she managed to say.

"Sure." Lynn went to pick up her mug.

"Leave it. I'll return them later." Right now, she wanted to leave the quarters that felt small and dangerous.

A WEEK LATER, CHRISTINE ROLLED OUT OF BED at her usual time and checked her comm unit. She had two dispatches from Porters waiting for her, one from Lynn and one from Derek. She wasn't used to seeing a dispatch from Derek, so curiosity compelled her to read that one first.

Christine,

As I'm sure you know, Lynn's birthday is coming up, and the family will be holding a surprise supper party for her. Can you send me your flying schedule for the next few weeks? I know Lynn will want you to be there, and I'm trying to find a time when everyone will be free.

Thanks,

Derek.

A party. The prospect of attending Lynn's birthday party both thrilled and intimidated her. She'd meet Lynn's entire family and others who were important to her. But there was no way she'd turn down this invitation. Derek seemed to believe Lynn would want her there, and Christine wouldn't miss it.

She typed a quick reply to Derek and attached her schedule for the next month. Then she read Lynn's dispatch and laughed.

Has anyone contacted you about my surprise supper yet? If they haven't, let me know and I'll drop more hints. They've held one every five years since my twentieth and there's more whispering and surreptitious looks than usual lately, so I assume they're doing it again for my forty-fifth, which is wonderful! I'll appear suitably shocked, of course. I'm quite good at it.

She composed another reply, saying Lynn didn't have to drop any more hints, without confirming the existence of a surprise supper. She added that she hoped Lynn's day would go well. They'd gotten into this routine of saying that to each other every day now, to the point Christine wouldn't have to pretend to be shocked if she woke up one morning and there wasn't a dispatch from Lynn waiting for her.

Almost an hour later, she was in a good mood when she ordered her usual breakfast in the eatery. As she waited for it, two pilots who flew afternoons walked in to place their orders. They nodded to her but kept their distance, not so far away that Christine couldn't hear what they were saying. For once, when pilots remained within earshot, they weren't talking about her.

"...the entire night roster," one was saying. "All of them, over to days."

"That's how they're going to do it?" the other one said.

"That's what I've heard. Almost the entire day roster will go on tour to fill the gaps of those being assigned to the *Raptor*."

"Who won't be going?"

"Ann. Uh, James. I think that's it."

"That's, what, the second reconditioned ship now? No wonder they're starting to run short. Who's going to fly nights?"

"Supply will be doing overtime, and any cadets they think are ready."

"Your breakfast, Lieutenant."

Wishing her order had taken longer, Christine jerked toward the voice and collected her tray. She went to her usual table, lost in thought. The entire night roster was moving to days. Would that include her? Or would she be left behind, as usual?

A few days later, she believed she had her answer. This time it was a group of officers that included someone from personnel deployment, discussing the changes as they waited for an elevator, one conveniently located near a corridor intersection. Christine took a left and stopped to listen.

"...in about five months, but there are so many moving parts we're planning it all now. Pilots being moved here and there, pilots going on tour earlier than they usually would, cadets still in their final year possibly flying some nights."

"It would be nice if they stopped improving the fleet and gave us a break," one said, chuckling.

"I think this will be it until the *Harrier* is ready."

"So the entire night roster will be new?"

"Yes. Everyone is moving."

"And only two remaining on days."

"Doesn't that mean you can hold two night pilots back?" the third one asked.

"No, because four of the night pilots are going on tour."

Christine wondered who they were. Not that she envied them. Serving on a ship where everyone was talking about her would be worse than it was here. Space stations were so much larger. There were plenty of places to escape to, and more personnel. On a ship, it would be the same people ignoring her and nowhere to hide in the small mess halls.

"That means we'll still be short on days, but—"

The voices cut off. The elevator must have arrived. She continued on to the next elevator and rode to Deck 12. Unless she'd totally misunderstood them, in five months, she'd finally—finally!—be assigned to days. See, she'd known if she was patient, it would eventually happen.

Days. She'd be satisfied with days, where she wouldn't be dealing with green pilots who'd been cadets mere months earlier. Her name would be on the same roster as pilots like Hawkins, an experienced fighter pilot who'd gone on tours. She hoped she wouldn't be partnered with Hawkins, who'd witnessed her shameful behaviour firsthand. Thompson, who flew the occasional day shift as supply, she wouldn't mind so much. They'd sort of cleared the air, though she suspected she'd never be paired with her or Hawkins, at their request.

She entered her quarters feeling lighter on her feet than usual. She was still smiling to herself the next day, and her mood soared when she checked her dispatches and read the one from Derek. The details for Lynn's party. It was on one of her nights off.

This time last year, she'd hoped to be transferred to days and had wondered when it would happen. Now she knew. She'd also been invited to a friend's birthday party, something she never would have expected to happen at all. She'd violated the Way almost eight years ago now. Perhaps her punishment was finally coming to an end.

THREE WEEKS LATER, Christine gathered her courage and strode up the path to the Porters' family home, with a long gift box tucked under her arm. Two wooden benches sat on the wide porch that ran the length of the front of the house, and a colourful welcome mat greeted arrivals.

The door swung open before Christine knocked on it. "Noticed you coming," Derek said, beckoning her inside. "How was the trip down from the station?"

"Fine."

"Here." He held out his hands for the gift box. "I'll tuck it away and bring it out after supper, when I think you'll be able to snatch a quiet moment."

She handed it to him with a murmured thanks and added her cloak to the many already hanging from the hallway cloak rack. He knew what was inside the box. She'd needed his help to arrange for Lynn's gift to be made.

Chattering voices finally penetrated her consciousness. Derek led her from the entranceway into the living room, where at least twenty people were gathered. She recognized a few from the day she'd spent at Lynn's business, and she saw Lynn's features in a man standing talking to his Chosen. She wondered which brother he was.

"I can introduce you around, or you can meet people as you, uh, meet them," Derek said.

"If you introduce me to everyone at once, I won't remember their names," she said, lying.

"I'll put this gift away and get you something to drink. What would you like?" He rattled off the choices.

She settled on an apple juice, grateful to him for taking her under his wing, though the moment he left her side, Pam came over, the woman Christine had taken orders from when helping out Lynn on that busy day.

"Good turnout," Pam said, surveying those gathered. "There are more in the dining room."

"How large is it?" Christine asked, wondering where they'd seat everyone.

"Not big enough to hold us all. We must be eating outside."

The weather had cooperated, in that case. Not too hot, not too cold, a clear blue sky with just a hint of a breeze.

"I wonder what time Jeannie will be bringing Lynn back."

"Jeannie?"

"She works closely with Lynn. That's right, you didn't meet her. She was off the day you were there." Pam leaned closer to Christine and lowered her voice. "I think she has a crush on Lynn. Wonder if she'll do anything about it today. Do you think it's good to tell someone you want to date them on their birthday, or bad, in case they don't feel the same way?"

"Uh, I don't know. I haven't really thought about it." Jeannie...Christine remembered Lynn mentioning her once, which in hindsight, seemed strange, because Lynn talked about her work quite a bit.

"I heard she gave Lynn a really nice bracelet for her birthday, and she jumped at the chance to be the one to keep her busy until suppertime. Wonder what they're doing."

Christine absently mumbled a response, her mind on Lynn, and Jeannie, and crushes, and nice bracelets, bracelets that would make her gift terribly boring in comparison.

"If they get together, things could be awkward at work. Nobody will want to get on Jeannie's bad side, and honestly, she can be a bit of a pain sometimes." Pam sipped her juice.

"How does Lynn feel about her?" Christine heard herself ask.

"No idea. She wouldn't give anything away at work. Too professional. For all I know, they're already dating."

Christine didn't think so, but maybe she was labouring under a misconception and Lynn didn't share all the important stuff with her. But to hardly mention this Jeannie at all, even in passing? That was strange, wasn't it?

Her mind was in a whirl now, but not enough to prevent the knowledge that Lynn being with Jeannie was bothering her. She didn't have to ask herself why. She'd known for a while, known that at some point, Lynn would get involved with someone, and the washed-up pilot on 72 would either be relegated to a friend Lynn saw when she had time, or dropped. Christine almost wished she'd be dropped, because it would be excruciating to listen to Lynn talk about Jeannie, how wonderful she was, their plans, how much they loved each other.

Maybe you should tell Lynn how you feel, a voice whispered to her. The thought clenched her stomach and filled her mind with images of Lynn's horrified face, Lynn running away from her, orange cloaks, Interior officers. She was sure Lynn wouldn't report her to Interior just for being honest about her feelings, but making any type of move on a woman, even verbally, terrified Christine.

What if her judgement was impaired again? What if she thought she was being reasonable and appropriate, but she wasn't? Verbalizing her feelings would not be a violation, but what if she lost control and said or did something that was? It had happened before. She'd clawed her way back and didn't believe she was repressing anything, but that didn't mean she couldn't slide again, no matter how much she believed it would never happen.

Then there was their friendship to consider. Christine's only friendship. She didn't want to risk it, unless it became too painful to remain friends when Lynn dated someone else.

"You must be Christine," a cheerful voice said, breaking her out of her thoughts. "The uniform," he added with a smile.

She didn't have to be told the man standing in front of her was one of Lynn's brothers. "You must be Matthew, or Peter." He didn't look old enough to be John.

"It's the eyes and nose, right?"

Christine nodded.

"I'm Peter. Pleased to meet you."

"And you."

"Is someone getting you a drink?"

"Me." Derek pressed a glass into Christine's hand. Pam had drifted away while Christine's mind was racing. Hopefully she hadn't ignored something Pam had said.

She chatted with Derek and Peter for a while. Then Derek delighted her by taking her over to the framed family images sitting on the fireplace mantel and pointing out with glee Lynn when she was fourteen, eighteen, twenty-five, thirty-five, and forty. She hadn't changed much. Her hair was shorter in each successive image, and she'd put on a few pounds, which Christine found attractive. She preferred curves. Lynn had been a little too slim until she'd hit her mid-thirties.

"They're coming," an excited voice said.

"Shush!" someone else ordered.

Everyone's attention shifted to the living room archway.

A minute later, the front door thumped shut. Lynn stood in the archway, with Jeannie, Christine presumed, at her side. She couldn't help but notice that Jeannie was lightly touching Lynn's elbow. Christine wanted to run, jostle her way through those blocking her path to the front door, burst from the house, run to the train station and never look back. But she would not ruin Lynn's party.

Lynn's brows shot up and her mouth formed an 'o'. "Argamon, what's going on?" she said.

"Surprise!" several people shouted.

Lynn's hands went to her mouth. Christine gave her top marks for her acting. Then everyone clapped. After quickly setting her glass on a coaster on the mantel, Christine joined in.

An older woman, clearly Lynn's mama, embraced her daughter. Her father hugged her next. Lynn waded into the group clustered close to the archway.

Christine hung back near the mantel and watched, her eyes on the petite woman who entered the living room after Lynn. Jeannie. Christine didn't know her and the woman could be the nicest Rymellan on the planet, but Jeannie already set her teeth on edge. When she met her, she'd have to remind herself to be polite, to smile, to chat amiably. After all, this could be the woman Lynn's heart was set on, a thought that soured Christine's mood further. Well, she would be a gracious guest and do her best to enjoy herself, then retreat to the station as soon as was politely possible.

She picked up her juice again, sipped it as her gaze flitted between Lynn, Jeannie, who was talking to Pam and another worker, and anyone else, just so she wouldn't appear to be watching only those two.

Her mood couldn't stop her from smiling when Lynn approached her. "You're here," Lynn said, grinning. "Welcome to my surprise supper."

"Thank you."

"Did I look surprised?"

"You looked very surprised."

"I'll be fifty next time. Fifty. But I'm getting ahead of myself. Glad you could make it."

"Me too." She twisted toward the images. "Derek showed me these."

"I bet he did. Not fair. I haven't seen any childhood images of you." She pointed at the one when she was eighteen. "That was taken on my birthday, just before my notification arrived."

Christine peered at it, but her mind was filled with the image of the bracelet she'd just seen on Lynn's wrist. She couldn't recall Lynn wearing jewelry before. It must be Jeannie's gift. She mustered a smile. "I can tell it's you."

"I haven't changed that much. In my opinion."

"I agree," she said, focusing on Lynn again. "You—"

She was suddenly there. Jeannie. At Lynn's shoulder, patting her arm. "We have a question for you," she said, tipping her head toward Pam and the other person Christine had recognized as a worker.

"What, now?" Lynn said. "Can it wait until we're at work?"

"It's not work related."

Lynn stared at Jeannie. "I don't think you two have met. Chris, this is Jeannie. She's my right-hand woman at work. Jeannie, Chris. Chris is a fighter pilot."

They both politely pretended to care.

"You helped out that day I wasn't there, didn't you?" Jeannie said.

"Saved us from a lot of irate clients, for which I was very grateful." Lynn flashed Christine a grin. "I'll go answer that question. Talk to you later." She joined Pam and the other worker.

Derek came over. "Just met Jeannie, I see."

She nodded.

He looked like he was about to say something but then thought better of it. She wanted to say, "What?" but didn't want to appear interested, even though she was dying to know. "How's the research going?" she asked him instead, and did her best to pay attention to his reply and not glance too many times in Lynn's direction.

When Lynn returned to her, she brought her parents along. "My parents tell me Derek didn't introduce you."

Derek tutted. "We, Chris and I, decided she'd meet people naturally, so she'd have a better chance of remembering their names."

"It's true." Christine hoped Lynn wouldn't pick up on the lie. She hadn't told her about the memory tricks she'd used when she was an instructor.

"If you wanted it that way, that's okay, then," Lynn said to her. "Mama, Papa, this is Chris." Lynn turned to her mama. "This is Donna, my mama, and Robert, my papa."

"Pleased to meet you," Christine said, studying their faces and seeing their daughter in them, especially in Donna's.

"And you," Donna said. "Lynn has told us quite a lot about you."

"Mama," Lynn said sharply.

Christine's smile remained frozen on her face. Had she told them about her troubles with Interior?

"Is it all right if I tell her that it's nice to finally put a face to a name, or will you snap at me for saying that?" Donna said lightly to Lynn.

Lynn looked like she wanted to strangle her. Christine felt her shoulders relax and stifled a chuckle.

"What do you fly?" Robert asked.

"Right now I'm flying the new 3459-B."

His eyes lit up. "Ah. I knew a pilot when I was younger. He was flying the," his face scrunched up, "the 3074-C."

"That was before my time,' Christine said.

"Have you built a model of it?" Lynn asked.

"Model?" Robert's voice lifted. "You build models?"

"Of vintage fighters, mainly. I wouldn't call 3074-C vintage." Not only because it wasn't, but she didn't want to offend Lynn's parents. Implying they were vintage would hardly endear her to them.

"I don't build models, but I collect images of vehicles, everything from fighters to trains to shuttles to aviacrafts. Vintage ones, too. The best ones are hanging in my study. Want to see them?"

He'd piqued Christine's interest. "Sure."

Lynn and Donna exchanged a glance. "Don't let him talk your ear off," Donna said.

"Actually, I think it will have to wait." Derek was looking past Lynn and their parents. "I think we're about to sit for supper."

Christine spotted the caterer Derek must have seen. The man in the apron announced it was time for everyone to be seated.

"Another time, then," Robert said, sounding disappointed.

"I'll look forward to it." Christine wondered if she'd ever be in this house again.

Three long tables had been set up in the spacious back garden. Each place setting had a nameplate next to it. Christine scanned for hers and was surprised to find it next to Lynn's. Lynn was thoughtful like that, would have known that Christine wouldn't know anyone else here very well. Then she realized this was a surprise supper. Yes, Lynn had expected it, but she wouldn't have had any say in where people would sit. Maybe Derek had suggested the arrangement.

She stood behind her chair, in case they were going to say the Words. Some Rymellans did so at party suppers like this. Plus, nobody else was sitting. When in doubt, follow along.

Lynn clapped her hands together twice. The murmuring of voices faded into silence. "Thank you all for surprising me with this lovely supper," she said. "I can't think of anything I'd rather do than spend this time with you all."

A chorus of "Aw" and "We're happy to be here," rose.

"I don't want to keep everyone from supper, so that's all. That's my grand forty-fifth speech. Let's say the Words."

Christine took Derek's hand and then took Lynn's, not wanting to hold it too tightly, but not wanting to give the impression she didn't want to hold it. She did. Too much.

"Disobedience means death. Death to those who commit a Chosen Violation. Death to those who disobey. Death to those who violate the Way. Death to those who violate the Way. Death to those who violate the Way!" She reluctantly let go of Lynn's hand and clapped with everyone else.

Supper passed quickly. The food was excellent; those serving the tables equally so. Everyone around her discussed recent announcements, the upcoming weather, what they'd done the day before. Safe and polite topics. Lynn occasionally turned to her and asked if she liked what she was eating, but otherwise they didn't converse much.

After supper, everyone took tziva back in the house. Christine had just accepted hers from one of the servers when Derek approached her. "Why don't you go sit on the porch with that? I'll bring you your gift and then Lynn."

She'd almost forgotten about her gift. "I'll do that." Outside, she lowered herself onto a cushion on one of the wooden benches and gazed out at the trees stretching into the dusk sky. She set her tziva on the bench's wide arm when Derek popped out and handed her the gift.

A minute later, he returned with Lynn. "There you are," Lynn said. "I was wondering what had happened to you." Her eyes went to the gift box. "Is that for me?"

"You know it's for you," Christine said, then grinned along with her.

Lynn plunked down next to her and accepted the box. She rested it on her lap, untied the red ribbon, lifted the lid and moved the protective paper aside. She lifted out the skirt and held it up. "It's beautiful," she breathed. Her brows drew together. "What's this?" She spread the skirt across her lap, peered at the embroidery and traced it with her fingers. "Trees!" She squealed. "Argamon, trees." Her eyes met Christine's. "This is so thoughtful. Thank you. I mean that, dearly."

Despite Christine's wide smile at Lynn's delight, a lump rose in her throat. "You're welcome. Derek helped." She glanced to her left, but he was gone. "He gave me the name of your seamstress."

"Della did this? I was just speaking to her the other day, and all the time she was keeping this secret." Lynn shook her head and lifted the skirt again. "I love it. I'll wear it next time we see each other."

Like she was wearing Jeannie's bracelet now. Christine wished the thought hadn't intruded.

"I'm going to carefully put this back together," Lynn said, placing the skirt back in the box, covering it with the protective paper, and replacing the lid. "Such a wonderful gift." She rested her arms across the box and gazed at Christine.

Something in Lynn's eyes gave Christine pause. Had the gift been inappropriate? Maybe she shouldn't have given her clothing, especially a skirt. Maybe an accessory for her bike, or something even more impersonal.

"I do a little reflection around every birthday, and this one's no exception." Lynn stared down at her hands. "I wasn't going to talk to you about this today because I don't know how you'll react and just in case you don't react well, I don't want a bad association with my birthday. But I've been wanting to tell you something for a while now, and I don't want to wait any longer."

Christine swallowed and clenched her hands on her lap.

"I'm usually not this timid, but this particular…subject. This is hard for me. I—"

The front screen door banged opened. Jeannie stepped onto the porch. "Ha! Found you. A bunch of us are going to the Dance Hall. You have to come, of course."

Christine knew she meant Lynn, who was scowling at Jeannie. She didn't think she'd ever seen Lynn scowl before.

"Did I interrupt something?" Jeannie said. "Sorry." She gazed at the box on Lynn's lap. "What did you get?"

"A skirt," Lynn said tersely. "Who's going to the Dance Hall?"

"Pretty much everyone except your parents."

"I'll persuade them. Nobody can say no to me today." Her attention shifted to Christine. "Including you. You're coming too, right?"

Christine wanted to say no. The Dance Hall? She hadn't stepped into one of those since…since she'd turned twenty-five. Actually, that wasn't true. She'd gone to private parties there. She hadn't gone there to dance, to meet anyone. She'd wanted to wait for her Chosen, and then, well, there hadn't been much point.

But going to the Dance Hall was the least of her worries right now. She wished flaming Jeannie hadn't come onto the porch, because something was bothering Lynn, something about her, and Christine wanted to put whatever it was right. At least Lynn inviting her to the Dance Hall meant she wasn't writing her washed-up pilot friend off. Not tonight, anyway.

Lynn frowned. "Tell me you're not going to disappoint the birthday girl."

"I'll go," she said, hoping her smile didn't appear too sickly.

"Good." Lynn glanced at Jeannie. "We'll have to continue our chat another time."

Christine hoped it would be soon, because she wouldn't be able to think about anything else until then.

THE DANCE HALL in Lynn's sector was similar to those in every other sector. There were always minor variations from one Dance Hall to the next, more or fewer rooms, or a different colour scheme, but otherwise seeing one meant seeing them all.

On the way, Lynn had circulated, chatting to different friends and family. Whatever she wanted to say to Christine wouldn't happen on the way to the Dance Hall. It was obviously something she wanted to say in private.

What would Lynn find difficult to talk about? She was so open. But she was also empathetic. Kind. If she had to tell someone their behaviour had offended her or made her feel uncomfortable, that would be hard for her. Anything that would make someone feel bad would be hard for her.

Christine could think of nothing else. She'd gone over what Lynn had said and concluded it wasn't the gift, per se. Lynn had said, "For a while." Maybe the gift had pushed her over the edge. Maybe it was an accumulation of little things. Christine didn't believe she'd behaved inappropriately with Lynn, but perhaps she had, without realizing it. She couldn't recall ever touching her, but maybe she had. Maybe she'd rested her hand on Lynn's shoulder without thinking, or on her arm or leg. No, that wasn't possible. She was super diligent about her behaviour. Was it something she'd said? Had she flirted without realizing it?

Now Christine was glad she'd agreed to come here because all she'd do tonight was lie awake and wonder. Might as well spend some time at the Dance Hall before returning to 72.

Lynn's group claimed two tables near the dance floor, though only a few people sat down. Several couples, Chosens, Christine assumed, went right onto the dance floor. Everyone else milled around, chatting. Lynn was talking to her parents. Christine hovered near the tables and wondered what to do with herself.

"What would you like to drink?" Derek asked her.

"Are you in charge of the drinks again?" she said to him. She liked Derek. He was easy to talk to, and he'd never treated her dismissively, even though he worked on 72 and knew she wasn't popular there.

"I am for you. We're the two from 72. Hey, that rhymes."

Her mood lifted a bit. "I'll have an apple juice, please."

"Coming right up."

Still feeling as if she didn't belong here, she pulled out a chair and sat, then wished she hadn't. At least standing, she could wander. She'd wait for Derek to come back, sip her juice, then wander. When could she politely leave? Half an hour? An hour? She wanted to be here for Lynn, but Lynn had to circulate. An hour, then. A bit longer than Christine wanted to stay, but she wouldn't feel like she was running out on Lynn too early.

Lynn's parents crossed her field of vision. Christine searched for Lynn, but didn't see her. She looked toward the dance floor—her heart sank. Lynn and Jeannie were taking up position. They stepped, and whirled, and their dance took them away from where Christine could see them.

It felt as if someone had wrapped a thick belt around her chest and squeezed it tight. Seeing Lynn dance with Jeannie was more difficult than she'd thought it would be. She'd known Lynn would eventually meet someone and be less available, perhaps not at all. But Christine had believed she'd be able to handle it if Lynn made the effort to keep up their friendship, that she could be there for her and not resent her partner. Now she wasn't sure.

Derek set an apple juice on the table, breaking her attention away from the dance floor. He sat where she had to look past him to see the dancers, something she felt compelled to do. Lynn and Jeannie reappeared, appearing comfortable with each other, so comfortable in each other's arms.

Derek turned to see what she was staring at, then turned back to her. Their eyes met. She tried to read them. Was it her imagination, or did he want to say something again, but was thinking better of it? Perhaps that was the difficult thing Lynn wanted to tell her. That she and Jeannie were together. That her time would be more limited. That there wouldn't be much left over for friends. Christine needed to know. She steeled herself, plucked up her courage.

"Are Lynn and Jeannie dating?" she asked Derek.

He hesitated. "You should ask Lynn. She wouldn't be pleased if she knew I was talking about her dating life. Seriously. Ask her."

She wouldn't dare. She didn't want to give away her feelings because it might be impossible for them to remain friends, especially if Lynn *was* with Jeannie.

To force her mind onto other things, she asked Derek a question about his research again, a question related to something he'd said when they'd discussed it at the party. She hoped the answer would keep him talking for a while. Three musical pieces later, Christine had finished her apple juice, and Lynn wasn't dancing with Jeannie. Now she was dancing with someone else, a male friend.

Derek politely excused himself. Christine stood to stretch her legs. Pam, who'd been standing alone, joined her. They chatted for a while, then Lynn's parents came over and Pam left. Through it all, Lynn was on the dance floor.

At one point, Christine managed a glimpse at her comm unit. Over an hour had passed since they'd arrived. Derek had mentioned returning to 72 with her, but she wasn't sure how soon he wanted to leave. She searched for him, spotted him sipping a drink on his own. In contrast to his sister, he was a bit shy and he'd told her the Dance Hall wasn't one of his favourite places. She wondered if he was single because he had trouble asking women out.

She told Lynn's parents she wanted a word with Derek, and was on her way over to him when Lynn blocked her path.

"I think I've danced with just about everyone, with one exception." Lynn grinned. "Do you want to dance?"

Christine froze. "What?"

"You know. Dance. Go out there," Lynn made a walking motion with her fingers toward the dance floor, "and dance."

Her mouth felt dry. "I'll be a little rusty."

"It'll come back to you. I'll lead." She extended her hand. "Come on."

Her heart pounding, Christine accepted Lynn's hand and mutely followed her onto the dance floor.

They took up position, Christine's arm around Lynn's waist because she had a few centimetres on her, then fell into step with the music. For the first minute or so, she felt like the clumsiest oaf on Rymel. She didn't step on Lynn's toes, but anyone watching might have the impression Lynn was dragging a jerking doll around the floor. But she'd danced quite a bit before that Death Notification had arrived, and it did come back to her. By the time the musicians segued into the next piece, she and Lynn were moving as one, their bodies smoothly swaying and turning in unison, their feet working together.

Now that Christine didn't have to concentrate on her movements so much, the warmth of Lynn's body, her hand, her flushed face, the synergy between them, permeated her senses. She lost herself to the music, the motion, to Lynn, occasionally coming up for air, to reality, but happy to dive into the sea of sensation again, where nobody else existed except her, and Lynn, and the warmth, the trust, the connection between them.

It was a shock when the music stopped. She stared at Lynn in a daze, Lynn who was still in her arms, smiling at her. The musicians started in on the next piece.

"Should we?" Lynn said.

Confused, Christine scrambled to understand. The music pierced through the haze. A waltz. Lynn took her silence for consent and moved closer to her. A moment later, Lynn's cheek pressed against hers, and they moved in unison again. Christine could feel all of Lynn now, every muscle, every curve.

She'd waltzed before, many times. This was a close waltz. They weren't dancing like the couple she could see over Lynn's shoulder, who were swaying, but with centimetres separating them, both bodies and cheeks. There wasn't even the tiniest sliver of space between her and Lynn.

Part of her could sense every one of Lynn's movements and wanted to melt into her and forget where she was. The other part couldn't help but fret about it. Had she pulled Lynn this close? Had they stepped toward each other? Was Lynn okay with this? Well, she wasn't pulling away, but would she do that in front of everyone?

"Your feet need to move when we're dancing," Lynn said, her body vibrating, and her voice tickling Christine's ear.

"Sorry." Christine swallowed and forced her feet to move. "Are you okay dancing like this?"

"Like what?"

She was so glad Lynn couldn't see her face. "This close."

"I'm completely okay dancing this close." Lynn paused. "Are you?"

She nodded, then said, "I just nodded yes."

Lynn chuckled. "I know." She squeezed Christine. "Relax."

The squeeze had lasted half a second, but it had still surprised Christine, and made her want to tighten her hold on Lynn. Of course, she didn't, despite believing she understood what Lynn was trying to say by relax. That she wasn't stepping over a line. That Lynn wouldn't leave the dance floor and report her to one of the Interior officers always present at the Dance Hall. Or maybe that was just where Christine's mind couldn't help going.

Relax.

She'd do her best. She closed her eyes, focused on the woman in her arms, the softness of her, the scent of her hair, their bodies moving together.

It was over too quickly. They moved their heads to face each other. Christine let Lynn go and would have stepped away, but Lynn was still hanging on to her. Lynn uncurled one of her arms from around Christine's neck and pressed her hand above Christine's left breast. "Thank you." She sighed. "I'll have to circulate again now."

"As much as I'd like to stay longer, I should go," Christine said, aware that Lynn's hand was still lightly pressed against her. "It's a long ride back to 72."

"I figured. But I wasn't going to let you go without dancing with you at all." She grinned. "You're going back with Derek."

"Yes."

"If I wasn't the birthday girl, I'd walk with you to the train station."

"That's okay. I understand."

Someone brushed by her. She realized Lynn still had one arm looped around her neck as if they were going to dance, but they weren't, and the next piece was underway. Dancers were having to avoid the couple standing in the middle of the dance floor, talking. "We should get off the dance floor," she said.

They maneuvered their way back to the tables and turned to each other again. "When are you off next?" Lynn asked. "Not flying, I mean."

"This is the last day of the fourth part of the rotation. I fly for five days starting tomorrow and then I'm off for three."

"Figures. Five whole days." Her shoulders heaved. "Would you like to get together on your next day off? I said I want to talk to you about something, and I do, and I don't want to feel rushed, and I'd rather do it here than on 72, and that's why I'm wondering if you'll come down on your next day off. And I'm blabbing, and I'll shut up."

Despite her apprehension, Christine felt herself smile. "I'll come down, but it'll have to be on my second day off. I've already arranged to have supper with my parents on my first."

"Six days, then. It'll have to do. Okay. Good."

Because she was so comfortable with Lynn, she said what she'd normally keep to herself. "I'll worry about it."

Concern darkened Lynn's face. "There's no reason to worry. Trust me."

She'd try. They made arrangements to meet at a park Lynn loved. Trees, of course! They would meet there in the late afternoon, talk, then decide where to go from there.

"I'm so glad you came," Lynn said. "And the skirt you gave me was so thoughtful. My favourite gift."

Better than the bracelet, then. She chided herself. Was she really that petty? It was a nice bracelet. And Lynn might tell her she and Jeannie were together. Jeannie could get the last laugh.

They found Derek. Lynn stayed with them while they said goodbye to her parents and siblings, the others who were still there, and finally to her. As they strode from the main hall, Christine had to force herself not to glance over her shoulder to see if Lynn was going straight to Jeannie.

She didn't feel compelled to come up with something to say as she and Derek walked to the train station. The silence was a comfortable one for her, and she hoped it was for him too. They were about halfway to the station when he said, "Have you heard anything about the ship that will be docking in a couple of months."

"You mean the *Raptor*? Only rumours. Refurbished, I believe."

"That's two ships added to the fleet in the past year."

"Only one, really. The other one was out of service for a while."

"True, but there's that new ship coming in a while too. The, uh..."

"The *Harrier*."

Derek nodded. "I wonder why they're reinforcing the fleet all of a sudden." His mouth was set.

"Not because there's a conflict brewing," she said, wanting to reassure him.

"Are you sure?"

"Positive. Unless you've heard something."

"No. I just wondered."

"They took the opportunity to refurbish the two ships because it's so quiet. One's been sitting in dock for years." Since before she'd had her troubles with Interior, when she'd been in the loop and seen the documents about the refurbishment. "From what I've heard, the other one suffered a critical failure while on tour. Fortunately the backup system kicked in, but that meant no more backup, so they were forced to dock it and decided to give it a complete overhaul." Another ship had been recommissioned around the same time, making the personnel shuffling easier.

"Nothing to worry about then."

"No." She paused, then carried on. "I'm optimistic that when the *Raptor* is ready to undock, I'll be switched to days."

"No more eggs at noon."

"Exactly." And unless Lynn was too busy with Jeannie to see her, it would make seeing Lynn more convenient. They'd both eat lunch when they met in the eatery.

"Will flying days be better for you?" Derek asked.

"It'll put me on the same schedule as everyone important. Like my parents," she quickly added. "And the pilots on days are more experienced. Some even have tour experience."

He grunted. "I hope it happens for you, then."

So did she. Fervently. She was tired of flying with pilots half her age. She hadn't envisioned a career flying domestic day patrols, but at least it would be a step up from where she was now. Plus, the switch to days could mean the military and her former colleagues were beginning to forgive her. Maybe they'd even let her teach after she'd flown days for a couple of years.

She was feeling more optimistic about her life these days. Lynn was a big part of that, someone who'd given her a chance. Her throat tightened at the thought that Lynn might not be as available.

"Lynn said she wants to talk to me about something," she said to Derek. "Do you know what it might be about?"

He shook his head. "No idea."

She could tell he was lying.

THE NEXT SIX days crawled by. She and Lynn exchanged their usual morning dispatches and then some. Nothing felt different about them. No change in tone, no terseness, nothing that set off alarm beeps, nothing that felt fake. But then Lynn was about the furthest from fake anyone could get, something Christine appreciated about her.

By the time Christine stepped off the train near the park where they'd meet, she'd worried herself out. Almost. Now that she was here, her hands felt clammy, her mouth dry, her stomach was doing flip flops, and her heart raced, thudding against her chest. Lynn had said to trust her, and that had been after they'd danced, and rather closely at that, so she was certain, almost, that Lynn wasn't upset with her, wasn't going to tell her their friendship was over, or that she'd crossed some line, or offended her. If not for Lynn saying it would be a difficult conversation for her, and wanting to do it planetside, Christine wouldn't be so worried.

It must have something to do with Jeannie. Lynn telling her she and Jeannie were together and she wouldn't have as much time for friends for a while was the only possible thing Christine had come up with that made sense. But why would that be difficult for Lynn to say? And Lynn had said she'd been wanting to talk to her for a while. If Lynn and Jeannie were together—a big if—they hadn't been so for long.

She focused on following Lynn's directions and easily found the park. Her breath caught in her throat when she spotted Lynn waiting for her just inside the entrance. They hadn't even started talking yet and Christine was already a wreck. She took a moment to try to calm herself, then strode into the park and over to Lynn.

"Nice skirt," Christine said, after they'd greeted each other.

Lynn grabbed the skirt and swished it. "You like it? It fits me perfectly and has my favourite thing on it. Trees. A very thoughtful gift from a very thoughtful person."

Despite her apprehension, delight rose to the surface and coloured Christine's cheeks.

"Shall we walk?" Lynn said, sweeping her hand toward the dirt path. "There's a bench we can sit on in a little viewing area just up ahead."

They fell into step with each other, the trees swallowing them up. Lynn asked Christine how her day had been, how was the shuttle ride, wasn't the weather wonderful. She sounded all right, but Christine had come to know her and could feel the tension that wasn't normally there between them, hear it in the too-light tone Lynn was using.

They reached the bench. Lynn sank onto it and gazed up at Christine with too fixed a smile. Christine sat on the other end and twisted toward her. She swallowed, braced herself.

Lynn huffed a sigh. "I said I want to talk to you about something, and I do, but it's not easy, and normally I wouldn't be this blunt. But with you, I know it has to be me. And I know I need to be blunt." She moistened her lips. "Do you want to know what the highlight of my birthday supper and evening was? Apart from this lovely skirt?" she said, glancing down at it.

"What?"

"Dancing with you. Finally being in your arms, being able to touch you. I can't tell you what a relief that was."

Christine stared at her.

"I want more of that. I want more of you. I want our lives to intertwine. Remember I told you there are two types of Solitaries, one who wants as close to a Chosen relationship as they can get, and the other who doesn't?"

She numbly nodded, her mind in a whirl.

"I said I'm the first type, and I think you're the first type, and I don't know if you're the one I'll have that Chosen type relationship with, but I certainly want to give it a try. I have feelings for you, Chris, and I have no idea if you have any for me because you're so controlled, and I understand why you're so controlled. Completely understand. Which is why it has to be me, and why I'm being so blunt. Normally I'd flirt and drop hints and do the usual things, but with you, I have to whack you over the head with it. Otherwise you won't see it. You haven't seen it. I have tried. So I'm being blunt. Baring my heart. Asking."

Lynn gulped down air. "How do you see me? A friend? A close friend? Someone who could be more than a friend? Someone you've secretly wanted to ravish for months? Tell me. Please. Anything."

Christine felt as if she *had* been whacked over the head. Her mind reeled. She wanted to say, to shout, "I feel the same way. I want what you want. With you." So why wouldn't her mouth move? Why was she letting Lynn sit there? Why was she watching Lynn's mouth droop, her hands bundle her skirt, the light fade from her eyes? She had to do something, say something.

She lifted her hand, reached toward Lynn, gripped the hand Lynn extended to her and hung on to it. "I have feelings for you," she heard someone whisper.

Louder.

"I have feelings for you," she croaked. "I feel the same way. I want to try."

Lynn's shoulder slumped with relief. "Argamon, I thought I was going to have to slink away." Then she grinned.

They curled their fingers together. Christine's eyes closed as she savoured the sensation of Lynn's warm hand in hers. Then she opened them and gazed at her. "What about Jeannie?" she asked, wanting clarity.

Lynn's brows drew together. "What about her?"

"I got the impression...well, I don't know. That's why I'm asking."

"You think there's something going on between me and Jeannie?"

"No. Not now. But I think Jeannie wants something to go on."

Lynn nodded. "Let me tell you about Jeannie." Her fingers tightened around Christine's and she slid closer to her on the bench. Their knees touched. Lynn took Christine's other hand, squeezed it, held it. "Jeannie came to work at Sally's about fifteen years ago. She's the second type of Solitary, but she thinks she's the first type. She was with someone when I first met her. When they broke up—her relationships never last more than a year or two—she became interested in me. She wanted to date me. I said no. I don't date people at work. She tried to change my mind. I stood firm. She eventually found someone else. Then she broke up with them and wanted me again. That's been going on ever since I've known her. She can't stand to be single, and I'm her go-to potential partner whenever she has nobody. Except when I'm with someone. She's decent that way."

"I assume she's single now."

Lynn chuckled. "You assume correctly. We both know she'll forget about me as soon as someone else comes along, but she tries. Every time."

"She gave you a nice bracelet." A bracelet Lynn wasn't wearing.

"She did. But you might have noticed I don't wear jewelry. I wore the bracelet at my supper because she'd given it to me. As a polite gesture. And it's a nice bracelet. But Jeannie gave me something impersonal. Something quick. You, on the other hand, gave me this skirt." She looked down at it, a smile playing on her lips. "A gift that fits me, in more ways than one. I'm not saying every gift has to be so personalized. But a thoughtful gift is one you know the recipient will enjoy or use. That's not true of the bracelet. It will sit in its box until I feel an appropriate amount of time has passed and I can give to someone who'll appreciate it."

"Who do you think that will be?" Christine asked, genuinely curious.

Lynn pursed her lips. "Probably one of my nieces. Anyway, there's no need to worry about Jeannie." She squeezed Christine's hands again.

"Why didn't you mention her much? I hardly knew she existed before the party."

"I know this is going to sound silly, and there's nothing going on between me and Jeannie and never has been, but I thought maybe telling you about her would give away how I feel about you. I don't know why. Maybe I thought I'd slip and say I wasn't interested in her but I was interested in someone, or something like that, and you'd ask me who I was interested in, which I doubt you would have done. Like I said, silly."

"Not silly. Not wanting to talk about relationships. I can relate."

They beamed at each other. When their eyes met, Christine didn't look away, and neither did Lynn. For a moment, she wondered if she was dreaming, if she was actually in her bed on 72, making this whole thing up.

Lynn cleared her throat. "I'm glad I finally said something to you. I've wanted to tell you for a while, but I had no idea how you felt and I didn't want to ruin our friendship." She grimaced. "Now I wish I'd told you sooner. Hindsight and all that."

"I'm glad you told me too." Her cheeks were going to ache because she couldn't remember the last time she'd smiled this much.

"When I was in my twenties and Chosens were being notified and Solitaries were either pairing up or enjoying their freedom, I knew what I wanted. That Chosen type relationship. When I hit my thirties, I was still single. Sure, I'd had a few serious relationships, but none of them lasted more than a couple of years. Then I met Claire, my brother's friend, and thought, maybe this is it. Then she decided I wasn't good enough for her and had a list of reasons why." Lynn's eyes narrowed. "When I told you about it, you never asked me what was on the list."

"Maybe I have my own list," Christine said, her tone light.

Lynn pretended to be shocked.

"Or maybe I don't care what someone else thinks about you. Maybe you didn't judge me based on what others say, and I want to do the same with you."

"I'm glad. Because that last relationship almost had me giving up. I wasn't sure I'd ever want to be in a relationship again. I've had opportunities. I told you I've been on a few dates. A couple wanted second dates. I was the one who said no. I was starting to think, maybe I'm meant to be alone. That maybe that's not so bad. Then I met you. I'd say being friends with you for a while, getting to know you with no pressure for more, is what let my feelings grow, and my trust. But to be honest, I was smitten with you from the time I sat next to you on the shuttle."

Christine's mouth dropped open. "What?"

"You were kind. You didn't laugh at me because I was afraid. You listened to me, and not just politely. And you look great in uniform." She waggled her brows. "By the time we docked at 72, I knew I wanted to get to know you better. So, I did. And I've had feelings for a long time. But I value our friendship. And I know how important our friendship is to you. I didn't want to turn it into something awkward. I figured friends would be enough. Until it wasn't. Until my forty-fifth was approaching. Until I met with yet another grieving family who wanted articles for the Farewell Ceremony, or I listened to yet another regret, usually about something not said or done, rather than the other way around. And I wanted to tell you, to risk it, and if you'd said you didn't feel the same way, I would have tried to be a great friend to you."

"That would have been hard. I know, because I've had feelings for you for a while, but I didn't want to risk our friendship either. At the Dance Hall, seeing you dance with Jeannie and not being sure what was happening there, I realized it would be difficult, maybe too difficult, to listen to you talk about someone you were dating. I wasn't sure I could do it. But losing your friendship would have been a great loss to me, so I was determined to try."

"But losing our friendship wasn't why you didn't tell me about your feelings."

"Not completely."

"I understand the other reason."

A lump formed in Christine's throat. "I know. It's you understanding, not turning away from me because of what I did..."

Christine didn't protest when Lynn pulled her into a hug. She embraced Lynn tightly, held her for a long time, felt so calm, so content, in Lynn's arms.

They drew back, leaned in and kissed. Christine let herself go, let herself feel Lynn's soft lips and the longing, the raw desire, trusting not only Lynn, but herself. Then they were cupping each other's cheeks and smiling into each other's eyes.

"You'll be getting a lot more dispatches and seeing a lot more of me," Lynn said, her voice husky. "I hope that's okay."

Christine could feel the silly grin on her face. "More than okay."

"I'm getting hungry. We have two choices. We can go to an eatery, or we can go to mine and eat there. You haven't seen my place yet. It's about a fifteen-minute walk from here."

"I'd like to see your place."

"I was hoping you'd say that. You're not flying tonight, so there's no reason for you to go back to 72, right? You can stay until tomorrow."

Excitement and fear coursed through Christine. "Uh, I'm very rusty. In that area."

Lynn smirked. "That's what you said about your dancing, and it turned out wonderfully. And what did I say?" She waggled her eyebrows again. "I'll lead. If necessary." She leaped up from the bench and grabbed Christine's hand. "Come on."

Christine eagerly fell into step with her, still reeling from the revelation that Lynn had feelings too, that they were dating, that Lynn was taking a chance on her, that her own feelings for Lynn, now that they were allowed to surface, were strong. That she was elated, and afraid. But that it would be okay. Lynn was holding her hand, and Christine trusted her more than she'd ever believed she'd trust anyone.

HOPE

CHRISTINE LOOKED UP FROM THE LOVESEAT when Lynn entered the sunroom carrying two tzivas. Lynn set the mugs on the end table, peered down at Christine, and smiled. "That bathrobe looks wonderful on you. Blue is one of your colours. It's nice to see you in something other than your uniform. Let's see. I've now seen you in your military uniform, and out of your uniform, but not in regular old clothes. You do have some, right?" She pressed her finger to her chin. "Next time I'm in your quarters, I'm checking your closet."

She chuckled. "I have regular clothes. Not a lot, though."

"One of these days, when you know you won't be going outside, maybe you'll wear them so I can see what you look like." Lynn sank down next to Christine, pressed against her, and laid her head on her shoulder.

Christine wrapped her arm around Lynn.

"This is nice," Lynn said, tucking her legs underneath her. "I fit perfectly."

"You do." Christine gazed at the mountains in the distance, marvelling at the view from the sunroom at the rear of Lynn's cozy house. Last night, they'd somehow managed to have supper before they'd ended up in Lynn's bed. Lynn had joked it was because they weren't twenty, that they'd known it would be more fun if their stomachs weren't grumbling.

They'd fallen asleep tangled together, and when Lynn had stirred this morning, so had Christine, even though it was only 08:20. She was tired, but it was a good tired. Lynn had said she could sleep until her regular waking time, but Christine hadn't wanted to waste three hours. She'd have to leave for 72 soon enough. Right now, sitting here with Lynn nestled in the crook of her arm, gazing out at such a wonderful view, she wasn't in a hurry to go back.

"You said you've lived here for five years?"

"One of my grandparents left me credits almost ten years ago. I didn't rush out to look for a place right away. It took me some time after Claire to admit that maybe there wouldn't be anybody, so waiting for that person before trading for a house didn't make sense. I looked at quite a few places before taking this one. It's the view. And the nearest neighbour is a minute away by bike, longer on foot. And there's the garden, which you haven't seen yet but I'll show you later. Or another time. You'll be back soon. I hope."

Christine kissed the side of Lynn's head. "I hope so too." She felt Lynn's smile.

"You sure you don't feel like you need to sleep a little more? Or at least lie down. I could come with you. Keep you company."

"You know, maybe I should lie down for a bit. Especially if you'll keep me company."

Lynn reached for her mug and cradled it. "Let's finish these first," she murmured. "Somehow I think we'll be lying down for a while."

"Somehow I think you're right." Christine picked up her mug and sipped her tziva, half of her still wondering if this was a dream. If it was, she wouldn't mind staying in it forever.

WHEN CHRISTINE ARRIVED back on 72 later that day, everything felt weird. Nothing had changed. Same corridors, same sounds, same faces. But she felt an odd detachment from her surroundings.

It didn't last long.

Sub-lieutenant Channing, the green pilot she'd flown with for the past few weeks, was waiting impatiently near the launch area elevator. "I thought maybe you'd decided not to show up," Channing said.

Christine glanced at the digital clock next to the elevator. She was early, but not as early as usual. She never thought she'd be snapped at for not being early enough. She could point out the time to Channing. She could remind her that usually she was the one waiting or get uppity over the tone Channing was using with an officer who outranked her. But she murmured a sorry and stepped onto the elevator with Channing, making sure to stand some distance from her. One complaint to Interior and her life could be over. In a "she said, she said" situation, Christine hoped a commander wouldn't execute, but she didn't trust commanders as much as she used to. At one time, she'd thought them infallible.

Maybe most of them were. Maybe most of them were thoughtful and did want Rymellans to find a path back to the Way when they'd gotten lost. But not all of them were. The one who'd ruined her career, for example.

She chided herself. She'd ruined her career. She'd handled a situation badly. Morton had merely seized the opportunity to be cruel. The worst part was that she'd kept her mouth shut along with all the other instructors and officers at the academy about his bullying of cadets and his unreasonable expectations of his staff. Her silence, along with everyone else's, had allowed him to hold on to his position and ruin more lives. Now she was powerless. There was nothing she could do. If she was ever in a position of power again, she would not make the same mistake.

At least Channing was quiet while they flew. Back in her quarters, Christine checked her dispatches, even though she wasn't expecting one from Lynn. To her delight, Lynn had sent one, just before she'd gone to bed.

Wish you were with me. Can't wait to see you again.

Once again, she felt strange, as if part of her life was a dream. Lieutenant Christine Leeds lived and worked on 72, scorned by all, her career stalled. Chris Leeds spent time on the planet, with people who supported her. She'd say loved her, but she wasn't sure that applied to Lynn yet. She hoped it would one day.

Both her lives, that of Lieutenant Christine Leeds and Chris Leeds, were important to her. The military had been her life since she'd left the Learning Academy. She had to believe her career would get back on track if she continued to be reliable, to not rock the boat, to keep her record clean.

Patience. When she was switched to days along with the entire night roster, she'd be one step closer to reclaiming some of her dignity.

Lieutenant Christine Leeds couldn't wait for that day. Chris Leeds replied to Lynn's dispatch, the one Lynn would read when she got up.

I can't wait to see you, either. I hope you have a wonderful day. I'm sure I'm dreaming of you right now. Chris.

Four months later

"ARE YOU SURE you don't want more tziva?" Mama asked Lynn for the tenth time.

Chris wanted to tell her to stop fussing, but her parents had been wonderful, welcoming Lynn into their home, serving her a scrumptious supper, asking questions but not prying, and refraining from telling any embarrassing stories about Chris's childhood. It felt a bit surreal relaxing in the living room with them and Lynn, sipping tziva. Chris couldn't remember the last time she'd introduced them to someone she was dating.

Ugh. She didn't like that word when it came to Lynn. That and "girlfriend" felt inadequate. Over the past four months, their lives had indeed intertwined. Chris spent almost all her off days on the planet with Lynn and missed her terribly when she was back on 72. The 5-day part of her rotation was the worst. But that would change soon. Very soon.

"I think it's time for us to go," Chris said to Mama. "It's already almost 9:00." She didn't use military time with her parents and had stopped using it with Lynn.

"Is it?" Papa glanced at his comm unit. "You're right."

Chris rose, hoping Lynn would follow suit. She did, and beamed at Mama. "Thank you so much for the lovely supper and for being so welcoming. I'm glad I finally got to meet you."

"And we're so pleased to meet you. Chris talks about you all the time," Mama said.

Uh-oh.

"I've been asking her to invite you over for supper for months now."

She wanted to roll her eyes. They'd only been dating for four months, though in fairness to Mama, Chris had mentioned Lynn before they'd confessed their feelings for each other. She remembered telling them over one of their suppers that she'd made a friend, and how pleased they'd been for her. It had made her feel bad, that her life was so small and her social standing so negligible that her parents were pleased that their almost forty-year-old daughter had managed to make a friend. Now that woman was more than a friend. Much more. And Chris was bursting with joy and gratitude.

She thanked her parents, savoured their warm hugs, and stepped into the crisp evening air.

Lynn looped her arm through Chris's as they strolled to the train station. "They're lovely. Absolutely lovely."

"I hope my mama didn't annoy you with all her fussing."

"Not at all. It's nice to be treated like the Preeminent Ruler every once in a while," Lynn said. "And they clearly love you very much."

"They do." Despite everything. "I should have some good news to give them tomorrow."

Lynn's forehead creased with worry. "Are you sure you'll be switched to days?"

"Everything I've heard, every rumour, every snatch of conversation, says the same thing. The entire night roster is switching to days. New orders are coming tomorrow."

Lynn squeezed her arm. "You've always been left on nights in the past, though. I'm not saying that will happen this time, but it could, right?"

"I suppose, but the talk is different this time. They're short on pilots. They're allowing the graduating pilot class to fly nights, even though they haven't graduated yet."

"Still." Her eyes searched Chris's face. "Do you want me to come up with you to 72, just in case?"

"You have to work tomorrow."

"We're not terribly busy right now. Jeannie can manage without me."

Jeannie, who was now madly in love with some other woman. Her name had stopped setting Chris's teeth on edge. They'd even gone out for supper with Jeannie and Mona, her new love. Chris had learned Jeannie was really good at her job and a great support for Lynn at work. Chris also trusted Lynn. Completely. So she had put aside her unfounded jealousy and embraced Jeannie as much as she could.

"I'll be fine," she said. "The worst that can happen is they'll keep me on nights. Nothing new. I'm used to that."

"You're expecting to be switched to days. It'll be even more of a letdown than usual if you're not. I just want to make sure you'll be okay."

Lynn was right. She'd be terribly disappointed. She'd want to cry. But she'd be okay. She'd get over it, survive it. She had no choice. "I'll be okay."

"What time will you get your new orders?"

"They usually arrive around 1:00."

"Beep me. Don't send me a dispatch. Beep me as soon as you know. Whatever those orders are."

"I will." She wouldn't want Lynn to worry, and honestly, there was nothing for her to worry about. "Don't worry about me. I'll be fine."

Lynn smiled, but her eyes and the tenseness of her mouth revealed her true feelings.

Chris wished she could reassure her more. She'd overheard one of the schedulers say to another officer, "The entire night roster will change." Her patience was about to be rewarded. She would fly days. Best of all, her sleep schedule would align with Lynn's. But she could tell that nothing she'd say would lessen Lynn's worry for her. At least Lynn wouldn't have to worry for long.

Tomorrow, soon after eating her usual breakfast, Chris would receive her new orders. She'd beep Lynn right away and celebrate with her. It had taken eight years, but her life, her career, was finally turning around.

SHATTERED

THE NEXT MORNING, CHRISTINE ROLLED OUT of bed half an hour
earlier than usual. Her new orders should come through around
13:00. Normally she'd view them in a public place, which helped keep her
reaction in check when she saw she was still on nights. That wouldn't be
necessary today. She'd wait for them in her quarters, so she could beep
Lynn as soon as they were confirmed and celebrate with her.

Time felt as if it were moving at a different pace. By the time she was
eating her breakfast, it felt as if she'd woken up hours and hours ago.

After breakfast, she sat on the edge of her sofa, waiting. When her
comm unit beeped twice, it sounded unnaturally loud. She hesitated,
then checked her dispatches.

New Orders.

Finally. After all this time. She opened the dispatch and began
reading.

Lieutenant Leeds,

*The Raptor, a refurbished Rymellan ship, will be departing on tour within
the next month. Up to this time the Rymellan fleet has been operating below
capacity. With the addition of the Kite and Raptor, it will almost be back to
full strength once again. However, this means that many of Space Station
72's domestic pilots will be going on tour. As a result, we have reviewed both
the day and night rosters and made the necessary changes.*

You will no longer be stationed on Space Station 72.

What? Her chest tightened. Her hands trembled.

*Your new orders are to report to Space Station 65 to resume your admin-
istrative duties.*

No. It wasn't possible. She swallowed, tried to hold the comm unit
steady as she read the sentence again.

*Your new orders are to report to Space Station 65 to resume your admin-
istrative duties.*

Tears blurred her vision. Her hand clenched around the unit, mainly
to stop her from hurling it against the wall. How was this possible? After

pushing paper for six flaming years, and then flying nights for almost two flaming years, listening to the whispers, taking attitude from junior officers she could fly circles around, slinking around the station so her existence wouldn't offend anyone. How was this fair? What did they want her to do? Beg?

Reporting for every shift early, never talking back, never doing anything that had even a remote chance of earning her a strike, and this was her reward? To be removed from the cockpit again, while cadets who hadn't even graduated yet would be welcomed to 72 and assigned a night shift? What did they want from her? What would it take?

What was the point?

She imagined herself bursting from her quarters, marching down to the scheduling office, and telling them exactly what she thought of her new orders, and them, and their flaming refusal to acknowledge she'd made a mistake, a terrible, horrible mistake, all those years ago, but she'd done what was required of her, learned and grown from her experience, regained her strength in the Way. She wanted to serve it to her full potential, if only they'd let her. But no, she wouldn't give them the satisfaction of seeing her pain, her humiliation, her despair.

Maybe she should grab the first Chosen she saw instead, kiss her, grab another one, keep going until Interior officers wrestled her to the ground, hauled her off, and put her out of her misery.

A dangerous fantasy, and she'd never do it. She wasn't that person. She was not that person. She'd never been that person.

This would not, could not, get her down. She would make sure her uniform was impeccable. She would show up for her shift tonight. If anyone asked, she would smile and say, "Yes, I received new orders," and leave it at that. She would not show her pain.

Miller's face floated into her consciousness. Counsellor Miller, who'd helped save her life all those years ago. *Don't keep it bottled up. Talk to someone.* Otherwise, at some point, her grief, her pain, would explode, and in a way that could end her life and devastate everyone she loved.

This time she had someone, someone she could trust with her agony. Someone who was expecting to hear from her. Someone who would be terribly disappointed with her.

She beeped Lynn.

"I was wondering when I'd hear from you," Lynn said, without preamble. "Did you get your new orders?"

Christine tried to speak, but a sob escaped her throat.

"Chris?" Lynn's voice shot up. "Chris, what's going on? What's happened?"

"I'm being transferred back to 65," she managed to rasp.

"What do you mean?"

"Where I was before. Admin."

"You mean you won't be flying at all?"

Trying not to completely break down, she could only nod.

"Chris?"

"Yes," she croaked.

"Come down to the planet. Please."

"I can't. I'm flying tonight." And there was no way she would back out. She'd regret doing so for the rest of her life.

Silence, then, "I'll be on the next shuttle."

"You don't have—"

"I'll be on the next shuttle," Lynn said firmly. "Will you be okay on your own until I get there? Do you want me to beep Derek? He can sit with you."

"No, don't bother him. I'm not going to do anything stupid."

Lynn was honest enough not to deny she was worried about that. "I want to get up there, be with you, so I'm leaving now. We can keep talking. I can talk to you the entire way."

"I'll be okay. Especially knowing you're coming."

"Beep me if you need to. I mean it. I'm here."

"I'll be okay."

They disconnected. She glanced around her quarters, feeling just a smidgen lighter. Her quarters. Not for much longer.

She forced herself to read the rest of the dispatch. Her report date was in three weeks. They'd already assigned her quarters. She would be reporting to the same person she had before, going back to the same group. She'd lost touch with Joshua and wondered if he was still there. The thought made her sick. Not because of them. They weren't terrible people.

The dispatch shocked her for a second reason. They were giving her three weeks off. Her final shift was tonight. Tonight.

She wanted to puke up her eggs and hash browns because she couldn't process it, couldn't understand it. Did they hate her that much? So much that when they were short on pilots, they still wanted to keep her from days, to deny her that one tiny shred of approval, of acceptance? So much that they wanted her gone right now, that they wouldn't even let her fly another couple of weeks? There was no denying she'd done a terrible thing. She wished she could turn back the clock and handle the Death Notification differently. But she'd found her way back. Why were they still punishing her? Was it Morton? Was he really that powerful?

Wanting to move, she pushed herself up from the sofa. Her head felt fuzzy and her hands, her body, shook. She sat back down, hung her head, and waited for Lynn.

SHE WAS STILL sitting there when Lynn arrived and held out her arms. Christine fell into them and let it happen. The tears, the ugly sobbing, the wailing.

"Let it out," Lynn whispered. "Let it all out."

She clung to Lynn until she'd purged herself, until she had nothing left but dry heaves and a thumping headache. When they drew back from each other, Lynn's forehead creased. "I am so sorry. I can't believe it. I can't believe they'd do this to you."

Christine wearily sank onto the sofa again. "Staying on nights. I thought that would be the worst."

"Can I see your orders?"

The dispatch was still open on her comm unit. She handed it to Lynn, watched her pace as she read the dispatch.

"This makes me so angry," Lynn finally said. "It's cruel, pure and simple. You don't deserve this."

"There's nothing I can do about it."

"I thought the rosters were being shuffled because there aren't enough pilots."

Christine had thought more about that while she'd waited for Lynn to arrive. "Maybe they didn't want me on days, but moving everyone else and leaving just me on nights would make it too obvious they hate me."

"They've never worried about that before."

"That's why I figure they just want to get rid of me, and they took this opportunity to do it, when everyone's shifting around so it won't be blatantly obvious they hate me."

"Won't they be short of pilots?"

"Final year cadets will be flying, and they adjust the number of cadets they accept into the training program every year. I'm guessing they increased the number a few years ago to prepare for this." She was out of the loop when it came to anything related to the program. "Maybe they had another reason for moving me now. Maybe someone complained about me. Maybe they don't want me flying with pilots half my age anymore." She swallowed her bitterness. "Like I said, there's nothing I can do about it."

Lynn opened her mouth, then closed it. "It says you have to report in three weeks and your last shift is tonight."

She nodded.

"Come spend your time off with me. You'll want to see your parents and we'll go, but stay with me."

She wasn't about to argue. "I'd like to do that."

"Good. We'll have to come back here to pack your things, but otherwise, I want you planetside." Lynn sat next to her, enveloped Christine in her arms again and kissed her softly on the cheek. "Are you going to be able to fly tonight?"

"I can fly that patrol in my sleep. I'll be okay. I'm sure I look terrible, though."

"Nothing a shower won't help. And I had Derek pick up pain killers from the infirmary. He gave them to me when I arrived."

Christine managed a smile. "Thank you."

"You'll need to eat. I'll beep Derek, tell him to bring us food."

"I'll be okay if you go."

"I'm not going anywhere."

"I'm walking to the launch elevator by myself," she said. "I have to do that. I have to do it alone."

"Okay. But remember I'll be here when you come back."

She'd hang on to that thought, that promise. It would help her get through her shift without sniffling the whole time. She met Lynn's eyes, forced herself to admit what she dreaded the most at this moment. What made her feel small. "You'll be disappointed, but..."

"But?"

She blew out some air. "The day and night rosters will be posted tomorrow. Everyone will see my name's not there. I shouldn't care about what they think. I know that. But it'll be hard, really hard, going for breakfast tomorrow."

"What time will the rosters be posted?"

"Usually at 10:00."

"That's easy, then," Lynn said briskly. "Don't be here. We'll take the 8:00 shuttle and be long gone. I know you'll be tired, but you can sleep on the shuttle, sleep on the train, sleep at my place. I'll get you up at 7:30. I'll pack your bag while you're flying."

"It will feel like I'm hiding."

"You'll be doing what's best for you. Taking care of yourself. So we'll be on the 8:00 shuttle, okay?"

She laid her head on Lynn's shoulder. "Thank you for being here."

"You don't need to thank me. I will always be here for you because I am with you. Wait until the run up to the Festival of the Way when my stress level goes through the roof. When I'll need to lean on you."

"I'll be there."

She felt Lynn's smile. "I know you will. And I'm not comparing my stress to what's happened to you, which is way worse. Inexcusable, in my opinion. You're upset, shattered. Let me do the anger. Not that I can do anything. I'd better not run into anyone who had anything to do with this, though."

"What would you do?"

Lynn drew back. "Look at them like this." She bugged her eyes out and gave Christine a menacing glare, making her chuckle. "Good. You can still chuckle. Okay. Can you eat?"

Her stomach wasn't its usual steady self, but flying on an empty stomach wasn't advisable. "I can manage something light."

They discussed what to get, then Lynn beeped Derek and gave him his orders. Lynn was good at doing that. Taking control. Telling people what to do. Maybe it would bother some people. Maybe it had been on Claire's list. But Christine appreciated it. She needed someone to take control right now. It made her feel safe. Cared for. Loved.

"We'll eat, and then you'll take your shower. But first, pain killer." Lynn reached into the side pocket of her bag and handed Christine a transparent container holding several pills. "Not ideal, but I figured you wouldn't want to go to the infirmary."

The pills would take longer to assuage her physical pain, but they'd work. Her emotional pain, the anguish threatening to overwhelm her and cloud her vision, wouldn't be so easily managed. But she had Lynn. And she had Miller's advice. And she had her older and more experienced self. Somehow she'd recover from this. But right now, her career was a bleak wasteland that stretched out as far as she could see, making her want to curl up into a ball and give up on everything.

FEELING STEADIER, BUT wound tightly, Christine headed out for her shift, her last one for how long, she didn't know. Fortunately her flying partner didn't mention anything about new orders, because a smile would have been too difficult for Christine to muster. She hadn't been too worried about having to deflect any questions about her orders, anyway. None of her flying partners ever said anything beyond a "Hello."

In the cockpit, she tried to focus on the here and now, not on when she'd be up here again, but the question kept intruding. How many years would it be this time, and then how many years on nights? Would she be old enough to be her flying partner's grandmama? Not the career she'd envisioned for herself when she'd arrived for her first day at the Military Academy, bursting with her dream of flying fighters.

The teaching had been a happy accident. Two years after graduation, one of her former instructors had asked her to help out with practicums, because one of the other instructors would be away for an extended period of time. Now Christine wondered why. Then, she hadn't thought anything of it. She'd loved doing the practicums, so much that she'd expressed interest in continuing. A year later, she'd also taught in the classroom and had flown only supply from that point forward.

Her stupidity, her pride, her refusal to let others see her pain, had undone it all. At least she hadn't completely ruined her life. She had

Lynn. She'd done something right. But Lynn was a competent business-woman who was now saddled with a washed-up paper pusher, which was definitely a step down from a washed-up pilot. Christine was going backwards, not forwards. She wanted to make Lynn proud, but she didn't know how. For now, she forced her mind back to the present, to the cockpit.

About half an hour before her shift would end, she muted the music being fed through her earpiece and took the time to just be, to exist, in space, to appreciate the silence, the vastness, the awesomeness, the danger, the beauty. Then she was landing her craft in the launch area, stripping off her suit, returning to her quarters.

Her eyes were moist when she stepped into her sitting room. A packed bag sat near the door. Lynn was curled up in bed. Christine undressed, got into bed, pressed against Lynn. She doubted she'd fall asleep, and Lynn would wake her up soon. But eventually she nodded off, numb, humiliated, and wondering if she'd ever feel like a productive and useful person again.

CHRIS DROPPED HER bag inside Lynn's front door, her limbs heavy with fatigue. She'd slept a little on the shuttle but stayed awake on the train.

"Go lie down," Lynn said. "I'll wake you up around suppertime."

She shook her head. "I need to readjust to a daytime schedule."

"You don't have to do it today."

"True, but I don't feel like sleeping."

"Do you want tziva, then?"

"I'd love tziva." She wrapped her arms around Lynn's waist, hugged her. "Thank you."

Lynn drew back and kissed her. "Go sit in the sunroom. If you're asleep when I bring it in, I'll leave you be."

She did as she was told, once again grateful Lynn was taking charge. She felt adrift, even though she had orders and knew where she'd be in three weeks.

As she sat gazing at the mountains, her eyes welled up again. All the pilots she'd flown with for the last while would be slowly adjusting their sleep schedules. In a week, they'd excitedly fly days. They were moving up. Some would go on tour. A few might even end up teaching.

Most would be promoted to lieutenant, then some to lieutenant commander. She could think of two who might make it past that. The rest, probably not, but lieutenant commander was a respectable rank to reach. She was sure she would have attained it if she hadn't crippled herself.

She wondered again why she'd been released from the roster a mere day after she'd received her orders. Had they been that eager to get rid of her? Had someone actually considered her feelings for once and thought she might need an extra week to get over the shock? Or had it merely been a scheduling requirement, in that a pilot new to 72 was ready to fly and they wanted to get them started right away.

Either way, it was another blow, another way they'd treated her differently. She was brushing away a tear when Lynn carried in a tray containing a jug and two mugs.

"Sorry," she said, wiping away another tear. "I thought I was cried out."

"Why are you apologizing? Something terrible happened to you and you're crying about it. You have absolutely nothing to apologize for."

Her throat too thick to reply, she nodded, and tried not to suppress her pain.

Lynn poured the tzivas, but she didn't sit down. She folded her arms and stared down at Chris.

"What?" Chris said, apprehension making her voice quiver.

"I've been biting my tongue for so long now, keeping my mouth shut, telling myself it's your life. It's what's important to you and not to interfere. But I can't do that anymore. Not when I'm seeing you like this, in so much pain. So I'm going to have a really honest talk with you and you'll think I'm crazy. You might even get angry. But I have to say this now. I have to." Lynn drew a deep breath. "I'm going to ask you a question, and I want you to answer me honestly. Not what you think an upstanding Rymellan would say. Not what you think a loyal military officer would say. Honestly. Okay?"

"Okay."

"Do you want to do this admin work? Will it satisfy you?"

She didn't have to think about it. "No."

"Then don't do it."

Lynn was right. Chris did think she was crazy. "What do you mean? Those are my orders. I can't just say no."

          RYMELLAN 4

"Yes, you can. You can say no."

She was about to protest again when she understood what Lynn meant. "I can't. I can't do that."

"Why not?"

"Because it's my life."

"Do you want that to be your life, Chris?" Lynn shifted her weight and braced herself, as if she expected to be blown over. "I said you might get angry, so here we go. You are never going to get what you want from them. Forgiveness, to be welcomed back into the cozy colleague fold, whatever it is you think you need from them to rid you of that lingering shame you still have, even though you insist you don't. They are never going to treat you decently. They are never going to let you fly days. They might not ever let you fly nights again. Are you really going to keep giving them so much power over you? Don't you think it's time to let it all go? Time to move on?"

She shot to her feet. "I'm a great pilot. A good officer. The report said I can teach."

"All true. But they don't care. By them, I mean anyone who controls you on 72. I mean everyone who listens to the whispers. Anyone that Military Academy commander has poisoned. Frankly, 72 is a horrible, depressing place for you and the faster you can leave there, the better. I don't know if you've noticed, but you're different up there than you are down here. Down here, you're more relaxed. You smile more. You enjoy yourself. Up there, you're tense. Not as tall. Meek. Afraid, even."

Her vision blurred. "I'm sorry you see me like that."

"*I* don't see you like that. You do. You see yourself like that. You think they're punishing you, but at this point, you're punishing yourself. You're doing it to yourself by not moving on and letting it all go. Because here's the really tough talk. They're not punishing you. They don't even care about you. To them, you're not a person who deserves dignity. You don't have any feelings. You're an inconvenience, and nothing more. Look what they just did to you. Don't let them keep doing it. Take back control."

Lynn took a quick breath and kept going, pummeling Chris with her words. "You're not even forty yet. Still young. You have many productive years ahead of you. You can be doing something you enjoy, something that fulfills you, that others appreciate and recognize, or you can let those small-minded idiots on 72 and 65 and every other flaming military place keep treating you like you're nothing. You can keep letting them do that."

They stared at each other, Lynn's chest heaving, Chris's eyes moist and her fingernails digging into her palms.

After a tense few seconds, Lynn stepped toward her, unfolded her arms, pressed her hand against Chris's chest. "You still have shame. Deep in here," she whispered.

Tears ran down Chris's cheeks. She could feel herself trembling.

"Time to let it go, and part of that is not letting people treat you badly. You deserve love. You deserve respect, dignity. The first step is to give those things to yourself."

And give up? Give up on everything she'd ever wanted? All she needed was time. All they needed was time. Her colleagues would come around eventually.

She knocked Lynn's hand away. "You expect me to give up my career, just like that. And now I know how you really see me."

Chris whirled and marched toward the front door. Lynn's footsteps thudded behind her.

"Don't go," Lynn pleaded. "Stay. Let's talk."

Blood pounding in her ears, Chris yanked open the door and stormed down the path without a backward glance.

It was easy for Lynn to suggest she give up everything she'd worked so hard for. But why should she? She was strong in the Way. She was a wonderful instructor and a more-than-decent pilot. She hadn't caused her superiors or anyone else any problems since she'd left the Indoctrination Academy. And after waiting patiently for years, she was supposed to throw up her hands and walk away from everything? Really? How could Lynn, someone who supposedly cared about her, even voice such a suggestion?

Chris had no idea where she was going. All she could feel and see and taste and hear and smell was her rage.

SOMETHING KICKED IN deep inside her, that same survival instinct that had her acting out of character all those years ago. This time, it

   RYMELLAN 4

led her to her parents' house, as if she were blindly moving toward a homing beacon.

Mama looked up from her knitting when Chris walked into the living room. She put aside whatever sweater she was creating, stood, and held out her arms. "Come here."

Chris hugged her tightly, let a few tears fall, then clamped down on her inner turmoil. She needed to talk, not make a spectacle of herself. She drew back, took in Mama's concerned expression and the many lines creasing her face. How many of them had she caused? Probably most.

"Do you want tziva?" Mama asked.

Chris shook her head. She flopped into the chair usually occupied by Papa. Mama sat in her habitual chair and twisted toward her.

Force it out. "I received my new orders."

"I was wondering. I didn't hear from you, so I figured your orders were what you wanted and you were celebrating."

"No. They've transferred me back to 65, to do the same admin work I was doing before."

"Why?" Mama breathed. "You were so sure..."

"I guess they hate me that much." She continued before Mama had a chance to speak. "Lynn thinks I should resign my commission." There, she'd said it. "She says I have a lot of productive years ahead of me and it's time to stop giving them so much power over me."

Mama's expression didn't change. "What do you think?"

She should be surprised and angry that Mama was asking her a question rather than trying to talk her out of resigning, but she wasn't. "I don't know. I blew up when she suggested it, but...it's something to think about," she admitted. "But I don't know how to not be in the military, Mama."

"You haven't steered your own ship since you left the Learning Academy."

Normally Mama's use of a ship metaphor would make Chris smile.

"You'll learn, Chris. You're bright, and you have lots to offer."

But it would be surrendering.

"Don't cling to it," Mama said, as if reading her thoughts. "You've given it your best. That's all that anyone can do."

"I'll feel like I'm disappointing you all over again," she whispered.

Mama shook her head. "You won't be. Do you want to know what disappointed us the most about your...Interior affair?"

"What?"

"That you didn't talk to us back then. You didn't trust us. You kept it bottled up."

"It's not that I didn't trust you. I didn't want to be a problem."

"And that's a lack of trust in us. We love you. You could never be a problem."

They sat in heavy silence for a minute.

"If you resign, you won't be facing an uncertain future alone," Mama said.

"I hope I won't be."

"What do you mean?"

"I walked out on Lynn, said a few things I shouldn't have."

Mama tutted. "She knows you're upset, and she's made of stronger stuff than that. She loves you."

"I know." Something Chris was more grateful for than she would ever be able to express. "It sounds like you agree with her."

"I agree that it's time to think about whether continuing on your present course makes sense."

Fear quickened her breath and iced her spine. She didn't know how to not wear a uniform.

"You look tired," Mama said gently.

"I was on an early shuttle this morning. I've only had about three hours of sleep."

"Do you want to nap?"

"Actually, I'm kind of hungry." Which was making her a bit nauseous, or maybe it was the stress, the fear, the world shifting around her.

"Let me make you some soup. We can talk more over lunch."

"That sounds good." She forced herself off the chair. "I'm going to step outside and beep Lynn."

"Good idea." Mama headed toward the kitchen.

Chris wandered into the back garden and pulled out her comm unit.

"It's taken every shred of willpower I have not to beep you," Lynn said breathlessly. "But I thought it best to give you space."

It must have been hard for her, with all the scenarios running through her mind. "I'm at my parents'."

Lynn let out a relieved sigh. "Good."

"I'm sorry about what I said. You're right, we need to talk about my future. What you suggested, about me resigning. It's not outlandish." The words sounded odd, but nothing deep inside her rebelled at hearing them. Then she realized she'd made a huge mistake. "When I said *we* need to talk about my future, I mean, I didn't mean…"

"Chris Leeds, if you're about to say you shouldn't include me when thinking about your future, I will not be happy."

Chris smiled. Actually smiled. "I was going to say I shouldn't have presumed."

"It's time to presume. This is about *our* future."

She was so moved, she couldn't speak for a moment. Our future. She needed to keep her eyes on what mattered. "I'm dead on my feet here. Mama's making me some soup, and then I think I'll take a nap."

"That sounds sensible."

"I'll see you around suppertime. We can talk some more about everything."

"Okay. And don't forget, I love you."

"I love you, too."

She returned to the kitchen.

Mama studied her. "Everything okay?"

Chris nodded. "I don't deserve her."

"Because you had an argument?"

Not entirely.

"You're too hard on yourself." Mama wagged a finger, which instantly transported Chris back to her childhood. "You do deserve her. Don't dishonour her by saying you don't. She's chosen you to love. Never forget that."

A lump rose in her throat. Chosen. A different type of chosen. One she'd honour in return.

LATER THAT DAY, after a supper over which she and Lynn had stayed away from the one topic they both wanted to discuss, they sat outside on the bench, Lynn nestled in the crook of Chris's arm. "The military is all I've ever known. I entered the academy when I was seventeen."

Lynn continued to gaze at the mountains. "I'm not saying it'll be easy. But I think resigning would be the best thing you could do for yourself. Let me be clear. I'll support you, whatever you do. I love you. But I want you to love yourself." She leaned forward so she could reach the tziva on the nearby table and take a sip, then snuggled into Chris again. "You made a terrible mistake, years ago. You've more than paid for that mistake. Now it's time to move on and make a wonderful life for yourself. With me being part of that, of course," she added lightly.

Chris's chuckle sounded weird because she sort of sniffled at the same time. "I'd have to find somewhere to live."

She felt Lynn's laugh. "That's an easy one. And if you're uncomfortable because it's my house, we can find another place to live. But it can become our house. We'll figure it out."

She kissed the side of Lynn's head. "What would I do?"

"You'll have to figure that out on your own. And take your time. Don't rush it. Once you've resigned, I don't care if you want to sit here and sip tziva all day for weeks, or months, even. Finish that model you have going on in the shed. Ride around all day. Help in my garden. See me for lunch. Take long walks. Whatever. Take your time. Maybe the first thing you try won't be a good fit, so you'll try something else. You can do whatever you want."

"I love flying."

"There have to be other types of flying you can do."

"Only the military flies in space."

"Does it have to be in space? And what about teaching? You can't teach at anything military, but there are many other ways to teach. The Learning Academy. The Indoctrination Academy, even. College. Private classes."

Nope. Nothing private ever again. "I wouldn't do those."

"Okay, private group classes. Tutoring."

Her wheels started to turn. "What could I teach?" she mused aloud.

"Flying lessons. Not fighters, obviously. Aviacrafts. Cargo crafts. Or go back to college and learn something new that interests you. The college in B5 is great, and it's only three train stops away."

Go back to school? The prospect intrigued her. But so did teaching people to fly civilian craft, and she shouldn't be so quick to dismiss being a cargo or passenger pilot. Maybe she'd enjoy flying through the blue sky as much as she did through space. Maybe she shouldn't assume it would be a letdown.

"Or you might stumble on to something you've never considered. Maybe you'll love working in my garden and something will grow—ha ha—from there. Maybe on one of your leisurely bike rides you'll have a chance encounter with someone who'll say something that will make you think 'Aha! That's it!'"

Everything Lynn said sounded promising, but resigning from the military? Never wearing the uniform again? She wasn't sure she could do that. On the other hand, did she want to report to 65 and push paper again, with no idea of how long she'd do it? What if her next orders weren't to fly? What if they were something even worse than admin?

And Lynn was right. Chris was still hoping, desperately, that her colleagues from before she'd made that terrible mistake would see her as they had before she'd self destructed. Not as an officer who'd almost fallen from the Way, but as a dedicated teacher and a skilled pilot, strong in the Way. But would it ever happen? It had been eight years, eight years of accepting her orders without making a peep, always being on time, being ultra polite, enduring the whispers and the attitudes, having a spotless record. Never stepping one little toe out of line. Yet her new orders were to report to admin.

She turned to Lynn. "I'm giving it serious thought."

"Resigning?"

She nodded.

"When would you have to do it?"

"To be nice? Within the week, to give them time to find someone else for that admin position."

"I like the sounds of you doing that, but I'll support you either way."

But Lynn would be disappointed if she decided to remain in the military. Lynn would never say that, but she would be.

Chris had a lot to ponder, to wrap her mind around. Since receiving her new orders, she'd felt nothing but despair and dreaded her arrival on 65 and the humiliation she'd feel. Now she had options, but only if she gave up on the dream she'd clung to for all this time. Would that be loving herself? Or would it lead to another regret?

LIFE AND DEATH

IVE DAYS LATER, CHRIS REMOVED HER last uniform from the closet in her quarters and added it to the rack containing the others and her two military cloaks. She and Derek had carefully packed her models and other few personal items yesterday. They'd arrive planetside on a cargo ship and be delivered to Lynn's that afternoon. All that had remained were her uniforms and cloaks.

She'd slept here last night, her last night sleeping on 72 for who knew how long. She was more than willing to accompany Lynn on her visits to Derek, but Lynn had been adamant. No more 72 for Chris. They would see Derek whenever he came down to the planet, or Lynn would pop up on her own. Chris supposed she might find herself on 72 at some point for some other reason, though she couldn't imagine what that would be right now.

With a sigh, she ran her hand along the arm of one of the uniforms and straightened its collar. She wheeled the rack into the sitting room, where it would be seen as soon as someone came through the door.

It was time to go, to leave this life behind. She took one last look around her home for the past couple of years. Her eyes didn't well with tears. She didn't feel the urge to linger. Only her uniforms called to her, a pull she could still feel as she boarded the nearest elevator and rode it to Deck 19.

Even though she was early, a lieutenant she didn't recognize was waiting for her in the small conference room. "Please sit down," he said, motioning to the chair across from him at the rectangular table.

She did so, and reminded herself that Lynn was waiting for her, that she was to remain calm, that she was not to let any resentment, any bitterness, show.

"I'm Lieutenant Harris, and I'll be conducting your exit meeting. It's a standard meeting we always have when an officer has requested a discharge." He clasped his hands on the table. "I have to ask you, are you sure this is what you want to do?"

No. She wasn't sure. She was acting on instinct and the advice of those who loved her. She still wanted to believe that if she kept her head down, did everything she was told to do, didn't break any rules, didn't offend anyone, they would eventually see. They would see she was not that person, in fact, she had never been that person. She was dedicated to the Way, had served it for over twenty years, would die for it.

But inside, deep inside, where decisions were made with no rationale, she knew Lynn was right. Going to 65, doing the admin work, waking up every day wondering when she'd be able to fly, enduring the whispers, the attitudes, the insults, was remaining in an unhealthy holding pattern. It nurtured her shame and was being unkind to herself.

It was time to build a new life, rather than desperately trying to reclaim an old one. A new life with people who loved her, who saw her for who she was today, who believed she had something to offer to her fellow Rymellans. They knew she'd been ready for years to say the Words with pride.

"I'm sure," she said to Harris.

"Can I ask why?"

Her hands clenched and her jaw tightened. He needed to ask why? She didn't know him, but everyone on 72, from the highest ranked officer to the most green, knew all about Lieutenant Christine Leeds, knew she'd been marched from the Military Academy in disgrace and was stuck flying nights. He had the nerve to ask why she was resigning a commission that had defined her for years, why she was giving up her desire to fly days, to teach, to be treated like everyone else?

She should tell him she'd been treated unfairly by everyone on this station, that she'd suffered enough humiliation and didn't want to endure anymore. She should ask him if he was perfect, if he'd never said or done anything that even slightly pushed the Way, whether he thought it was fair something someone did or said five, ten, fifteen, twenty years ago was being used to keep them down, taint them, turn people against them. People grew. People changed. In her case, she'd left the Indoctrination Academy understanding why she'd behaved as she had and resolved never to repeat her mistake.

But she knew there would be no point, that even if what she said was true, anything but the most innocuous of answers would end up in her file, more proof that Lieutenant Christine Leeds was someone to be wary of, that sharing her air could turn someone weak in the Way.

Harris wouldn't care, anyway. He was an officer in the station's personnel department and couldn't care less about how Lieutenant Leeds, soon to be just Leeds, felt. They'd all be glad to see the back of her. And even if she were willing to tweak his nose a bit, she would not risk doing so. Not when Lynn must be thinking about her right now, hoping her soon to be ex-washed-up pilot wouldn't say anything stupid that would land her back in the Indoctrination Academy.

"I want a change. I'm not a good fit for administrative work." The words sounded hollow, but there, she'd put it all onto her. Not a good fit. Well, that was apparently true. What else could she have said that wouldn't indirectly harm her?

"I understand," Harris said, confirming her suspicion that everyone just wanted her gone. Pilots were valuable, even washed-up ones. If she were anyone else, this meeting would last hours and be conducted by someone with a higher rank.

"What are your plans?" he asked politely.

The fear that sometimes burst to the surface and grabbed her by the throat since she'd decided to resign reared within her. "I don't have any firm plans yet."

"Are your uniforms ready for pickup?"

"Yes."

"And you've removed your personal items from your quarters?"

"Yes."

"You understand the military has the right to call you back to service, for combat readiness exercises or combat missions, at any time."

"Yes, I understand."

"Then there's nothing left to say except good luck." He pulled out his comm unit and turned it toward her. "This is your discharge document, stating you are being honourably discharged at your request. Read it over and acknowledge it."

She read the short document that stated Lieutenant Christine Leeds had requested a discharge and it was being granted honourably, then pressed her thumb against the appropriate spot. The unit beeped. She handed it to Harris.

"I wish you success with whatever you decide to do."

"Thank you."

She rose when he did, glad the meeting was over. In the corridor, she took a moment to breathe before riding the elevator to the shuttle launch area. As she strode toward the boarding area, she felt surreal, as if she were moving through a dream.

On the way, she spotted Channing and another pilot lingering near the boarding area, chatting. She was vaguely aware of their faces turning toward her and wondered what they thought of seeing her in non-military clothing. They knew she'd no longer be flying. Part of her wanted to stop and tell them she'd resigned, not been dishonourably discharged. The other part of her, the mature part that kept its eye on what counted, didn't care about what they thought. She carried on past them without giving them a glance.

In the boarding area, she spotted Derek right away. Lynn had wanted to come up with her, but Chris had said no, that Lynn had already taken enough time away from her business to support her washed-up pilot person who was still a pilot, but perhaps no longer washed up, now she'd resigned. Or was it the other way around? She didn't know what she was anymore. That was what she had to find out, to discover. Fear stirred again, but so did excitement and a sense of optimism.

"I almost didn't recognize you in those clothes," Derek said, smiling. "How did it go?"

"I've been duly honourably discharged."

"You made the right decision, you know."

"I know," answered that deep and wise place within her.

They boarded the shuttle. As they waited to launch, two fighters burst from the fighter launch area and disappeared into space. Chris didn't repress the longing that rose within her and tightened her throat. It would subside, in time. She had to believe that.

She and Derek chatted about trivialities on the way down to the planet, where Lynn waited for her and had invited Derek for supper. Chris understood why. So she wouldn't be alone on the shuttle. So if she'd been despondent, Derek would have been there for her because she'd told Lynn to stay away. But Lynn needn't have worried. A couple of years ago, if someone had told her she'd make the decision to resign from the military, she would have imagined herself crying today, curled up in a ball, unable to think, eat, smile, function. It was amazing what love and support could do when one accepted and embraced it. Her parents, her family, had always been there for her. Why had it taken Lynn for her to see? Something to ponder as she puttered around Lynn's place—a place she needed to start thinking of as hers too—trying to figure out what to do with her life.

CHRIS FELT HERSELF smile when the train pulled into the station closest to Lynn's house, and there was Lynn, waiting for them on the platform. "You never listen to me," she said as they hugged each other tightly.

"You didn't really expect me to wait at the house, did you? The moment I got Derek's dispatch telling me what train you were on, I was on my way here."

Derek gave Chris a sheepish look. "I had my orders."

She grinned at him.

"Tell me what happened," Lynn said.

Chris recounted the short meeting as they walked arm-in-arm to the house, with Derek trailing behind them.

Lynn gave her a quick squeeze. "How do you feel?"

"Honestly? Terrified. But good. If it's possible to feel both those things at the same time."

"You can do anything you want now, Chris."

That was the terrifying part. No dispatch would arrive telling her where she was to be, when she was to report, and what she was to do. For the first time since she'd left the Learning Academy, her life stretched ahead of her, unplanned. An important part of it was already settled. Chris knew she always wanted to be with the woman next to her and she'd strive to always be there for Lynn, to love her and support her, to hurt her as little as possible. It was her professional life that was a blank slate now. It was up to her to write on that slate.

She'd decided, with Lynn, to spend the next few weeks working on that model she had going on in the shed, drinking tziva, tending Lynn's garden—the parts she was allowed to tend—and gazing at those mountains. Then she'd research the few possibilities she'd already thought about chalking onto that slate and see where they led her. The uncertainty frightened her, but she wasn't alone.

That she wouldn't be alone was made crystal clear when she heard voices drifting from the house as she and Lynn walked up the path.

"I might have invited a few more people to supper." Lynn opened the front door and motioned for Chris to enter.

She stepped into the living room, gaped at those who rose from the sofa, the chairs, pushed themselves away from the wall. Her parents, and Lynn's, their siblings, nieces and nephews, the people from Lynn's work they saw socially. "Welcome home," they shouted.

Tears filled her eyes, happy and grateful tears. Mama came over to her and grasped her shoulders. "That colour looks good on you," she said, her eyes also moist.

"I almost didn't recognize you," Papa said.

"That's the second time I've heard that today," Chris said, to laughter.

Then she was hugging everyone, including some Chosens, because chaste hugs were permitted between family, something she'd role-played many times during her stay at the Indoctrination Academy. She couldn't stop beaming, wrapped up in the warmth and humour that enveloped her.

Finally she snatched a moment alone with Lynn, who'd gone into the kitchen to check on the meal she'd ordered from her usual eatery.

Lynn searched Chris's face. "You're not angry with me, I hope."

"Why would I be angry?"

"Well, I wasn't sure whether I should invite everyone. But I kept seeing you walking in and," she waved her arm in a grandiose gesture, "everyone was here, and you looked happy, and I thought, okay, you might be angry, but I'm going to do it anyway."

She slipped her arms around Lynn's waist, gave her a lingering, tender kiss. "I'm not angry," she said when they drew back.

Lynn's face was flushed. "Obviously. Though now I wish we were alone. But I suppose there will be time for that later. And now you live here, which means we'll go to sleep together every night and wake up with each other every morning, which makes me happier than I can say." She pressed her hand against Chris's chest above her left breast, something she often did. "You'll be fine."

"Did I tell you I love you yet today?"

"Only via dispatch."

"I love you."

"I love you, too."

They embraced. Chris closed her eyes, focused on Lynn's warm cheek against hers.

Someone cleared his throat. "Do you want help serving supper?" Derek asked.

They reluctantly drew back. "Sure." Lynn pointed toward the living room. "Chris, you go mingle. This supper is in your honour."

"I can help."

"No, go mingle," Lynn said firmly.

Smiling from ear to ear, Chris returned to the living room. She'd still receive orders, orders she didn't mind taking from the most adorable person ever.

She surveyed the faces of those gathered and took a moment to process the realization they were all here for her, to celebrate the end of her military career, something that strangely didn't feel wrong. Lieutenant Christine Leeds no longer existed. She'd died a lingering, painful death, clinging to the hope that those who'd once respected her would welcome her back, absolving her of her shame.

Chris Leeds had been the one to put Lieutenant Leeds out of her misery, once and for all. Chris Leeds, who was determined to leave the past in the past and lead a wonderful and productive life with the woman she cherished.

As she sometimes did, she thought of the woman the Chosen Council had selected for her, the one who'd died before they could meet. "Goodbye," she whispered. It was time for Chris Leeds to live.

IDENTITY CRISIS

.....

CONCEPTION

JAYNE SIPPED HER JUICE AND SURVEYED the guests mingling in the living room. Despite knowing most of them, she felt more comfortable watching rather than socializing, though she no longer tensed when somebody headed her way. Of course, here in her own home, nobody looked down their nose at her. When she left the estate, most C3 residents treated her politely, but a few had made it clear that they'd prefer not to have an Adams in their midst. Well, she'd known that a name change wouldn't erase the past, and seeing Carol coming toward her reminded Jayne that a handful of disgruntled C3ers weren't the only ones who still held her responsible for her parents' crimes.

Carol grinned. "I just saw Susan. She's gorgeous, and good-natured. I wish my daughter was the same. If Rachel had so many visitors cooing at her, she'd be screaming her head off."

"You said you had new images."

"Right." Carol pulled out her comm unit. "Here."

Jayne peered at Carol and Ronald's daughter. "She has more hair," she said, keeping her voice even. It wasn't Carol's fault that Jayne could only snatch time with Rachel when Ronald's parents wouldn't find out. In fact, Carol was risking their wrath by letting Jayne see her.

"Mo said she'll fly you over next week, if you like," Carol said. "We should be able to find a time that will work."

"Is Mo upstairs with Susan?" Jayne asked as she handed back Carol's comm unit.

Carol nodded.

Susan wasn't Mo's first niece or nephew, but Mo was entranced by her. Was it the name? Worried that Mo might not be ready for another "Susan Middleton," Neil and Barbara had spoken to her before submitting the name to the Chosen Council.

"It's like a Learning Academy up there," Carol said. "Or a Level One Indoctrination Academy group." She gave Jayne a sly look. "Those empty bedrooms are filled right now, but when will they be permanently occupied?"

"I don't know," Jayne said casually.

"You've been Joined for a year. You must be considering a daughter by now."

A year. Jayne's eyes went to the "Happy First Joining Year" banner stretched across one of the living room's walls. She could hardly believe it, and yes, they were discussing having their first child. But she'd stayed out of it as much as possible, especially during the conversations about who would carry the baby. It wouldn't be her, and though she'd love Lesley and Mo's daughters and consider them her own—according to the Chosen Tradition, they *would* be hers—she felt uncomfortable offering them her opinion about anything related to having a child.

She hated to admit it, but a tiny part of her worried that a daughter would bond Lesley and Mo together in a way that would never happen with her. That was already true; they'd been together for years before the Chosen Council had forced another woman into their lives. But that was precisely her worry: would a daughter be a constant reminder of "that other Chosen" they could have done without? Would they resent her presence, her participation, her rights over their child? *Your child. You can't think that way. She'll be your child, too.* And knowing her Chosens, they'd do everything they could to ensure that Jayne felt like a third mama, not a third wheel.

It wasn't Lesley and Mo, it was her. The last year had been the best year of her life. Oh, she'd experienced ups and downs, especially as she and Lesley had grown into more than friends. For a couple of months, Jayne hadn't known from one day to another whether Mo was talking to her, and the triad had shared more tense suppers than she cared to remember. Would they ever live harmoniously with no jealousy, no envy, no tendency to interpret a kindness toward one Chosen as a slight to the other? They were getting better at it. In twenty years, they'd look back and laugh at themselves, or at least she hoped they would.

The prospect of a daughter shouldn't make her feel so insecure about her place in their lives, but Adams was still a part of her name. She'd been happy once before, until the military had burst into the house and destroyed her innocence. Life could change in an instant. Sometimes one didn't see it coming. Other times... She sighed.

"Sorry, are you getting asked about children all the time now?" Carol's brow crinkled. "I bet Lesley's parents keep bringing it up."

"Not to me." Adelaide occasionally hinted at the subject during the weekly family suppers, but that was all. If she was applying pressure, she was doing it to the two people who counted. "They know there's no point bugging me about it."

"Wait until it's your turn."

"I'm not having children—biological children."

Carol snorted. "You'll change your mind."

"No, I won't. And trust me, Lesley's parents won't be pressuring her to have a child with me."

"What about you and Mo? The Middletons aren't as uptight. Michael's fond of you."

"It doesn't matter. If Mo and I were to have a daughter, she'd still have the Thompson name."

Carol chortled. "I guess Adelaide wouldn't be too thrilled about that."

Jayne nodded, even though it wasn't Adelaide's reaction to the idea that would concern her—hypothetically speaking. It was Lesley's. She was as protective of the Thompson family's reputation as her mama and would balk at the notion of a child without Thompson blood bearing the name. Maybe she'd eventually come around to the idea, but it was moot anyway. Jayne had no intention of having a daughter who'd be vilified and shunned, corrupted by the Adams' taint before she could walk.

Maybe that was another reason Jayne felt ambivalent about Lesley and Mo having a child. Would their daughter be painted with the same ugly brush because of Jayne's presence in her life? Their daughter *would* be her daughter, and she'd love her, and cherish her, and feel guilty about being associated with her, and lie awake at night wondering whether her daughter would still love her when she realized that the Adamses stumbling around on the stage at the Festival of the Way were her third mama's parents.

At least she'd be able to defend herself by saying that no Adams blood ran through her veins. And that was why Jayne would never, ever have a biological child. She wouldn't blemish the Thompson line with Adams blood, and the Thompsons would never have to accept a child who had their name, but not their ancestry.

MO SANK INTO the chair with a tired sigh and relished the silence. She enjoyed parties, but after two celebratory family suppers, a surprise lunch on 72, and tonight's gathering for family and friends, she needed a break. "That needs taking down," she said, pointing to the banner hanging above the sofa.

Les gave her a look, then stood on the sofa and started to pull out the pushpins securing one end of the banner.

"I'll get the other end," Jayne said.

Watching them, Mo wanted to burst. She'd planned to wait until tomorrow, but since they were both here… "Let's have a daughter," she blurted. "Enough talk. Let's do it."

They stopped what they were doing and turned to her.

"I'll carry the baby."

"I thought you weren't sure," Les said, as Jayne turned back to the banner. "Last time we talked about it, you didn't like the idea of not flying for months."

She didn't. But demanding that Les carry the baby would be selfish; she'd become a commander less than a year ago. Getting pregnant shouldn't hamper Les's rise through the ranks, but why risk it? They didn't need two stalled military careers—not that Mo cared all that much about being grounded anymore, especially if they were going to have a daughter. The planet would be a better place for her than a ship like the *Falcon*, at least during her formative years. "It'll make more sense for me to do it, and I'm okay with that." She glanced at Jayne, hoping for support, but Jayne was focused on the banner.

"Why the sudden enthusiasm?" Les asked.

"Sudden enthusiasm? We've been discussing it for the last flaming month. Do you want a daughter, or not?"

"Of course I do." Les's eyes narrowed. "I'm just wondering if spending half the night with Susan and the rest of the children has anything to do with it. Maybe you won't be as enthusiastic about carrying the baby tomorrow."

Gently holding her newest niece's hand had chased away Mo's remaining doubts. What were they waiting for? She gestured toward the banner. "We've been Joined a year. Even if I were to get pregnant tomorrow—and I can't—it'll be nine months before we have a daughter. As my papa would say, it's time to get on with it. What do you think, Jayne?"

Jayne glanced over her shoulder. "Whatever you decide is fine with me."

Mo met Les's eyes and shook her head. "I'll set up an appointment at the Reproductive Technology Centre. For all three of us."

Jayne's end of the banner came free. Still hanging onto it, she dropped the last pushpin into the bowl holding the others, then handed her end of the banner to Les. "I'm tired. I think I'll go to bed."

Mo's hands involuntarily clenched as she watched Jayne kiss Les good night. But she was getting better. Her fingernails no longer made her palms bleed, and she knew she'd have her turn. When Jayne leaned in, Mo reached for her. "Good night," she murmured, after receiving her own soft kiss. She waited until a door closed upstairs, then lowered her voice and said, "Do you ever get the feeling that she doesn't want us to have a child?"

Les pulled the banner away from the wall, sat on the sofa, and motioned for Mo to sit next to her.

"I mean, every time we've talked about it, she says do whatever you want to do, or leaves," Mo said as she crossed to the sofa and plunked onto it.

Les rolled up the banner. "It's not unusual for her to defer to us."

"I know, but we're not talking about what to have for supper. We're talking about having a flaming baby."

"I don't think it's because she doesn't want us to have a daughter. I'm not sure what it is, but I don't think it's that." Les leaned forward and set the rolled up banner at her feet. "Maybe she's worried that she'll be left out."

"We're going to include her every step of the way. We'll all be having a daughter. She'll be as much Jayne's as ours." Didn't Jayne realize that she'd be the one caring for the baby when her two Chosens were on duty? She'd probably spend more time with their daughter than Les would.

"She'll be our biological daughter, though."

"Does she think that every time we look at her, we'll think, 'There's my biological daughter, but not Jayne's'?" Mo patted Les's knee. "It's not as if you'll have much more to do with her conception than Jayne will."

Les rounded on her, open-mouthed. "It'll be my DNA."

"Yeah, but you won't actually have to do anything. The Chosen Council already has your DNA. The Reproductive Technology Centre prepares it. Jayne can pick up and use the impregnators," Mo said, ticking off each point with her fingers.

"And it'll be my DNA," Les said, her eyes dancing. She tapped Mo's nose. "I know what you're saying, but we're not in her position. Give her time. Once we start the process, she'll see that she's going to be as much this baby's mama as we are."

Mo hoped so, because once she was pregnant, they'd be having a baby, whether Jayne liked it or not.

Around four months later

LESLEY LANDED HER aviacraft in the Reproductive Technology Centre's holding area and took a deep breath. While dealing with same-oriented female Chosens was routine for the physicians and scientists at the centre, Lesley couldn't help but cringe at what felt like an invasion of her privacy, and this was only her second visit to the facility. Mo was the one who'd undergone the physical examination, the psychological evaluation, and reported her menses for the past three months...all in preparation for today. It was time for Lesley to do her meagre part.

With a sigh, she swung open the door to the centre's waiting area and relaxed at the sight of all the empty chairs. The receptionist smiled.

"Right on time, Commander Thompson. Just go through to Room B. Physician Crawford is ready to see you."

"Thank you," Lesley murmured. She strode down the corridor and knocked on Room B's open door, then forced a smile when Crawford invited her into the office.

Crawford waited while Lesley shut the door and sank into one of the guest chairs. "This is the first impregnator," she said, placing her hand on the small box sitting on her desk. "I know it's inconvenient, having to come here four days in a row, but they're only good for twelve hours. The expiration time is stamped on the box and the impregnator itself. If you use it after that point, no harm done, but the possibility of conception will be minuscule. After today, you won't have to see me. Just ask at the desk and they'll fetch that day's impregnator. Did you watch the instructional video?"

Lesley crossed her legs. "Yes."

"Do you have any questions?"

"No."

"Instructions are inside the box, as a reminder." Crawford clasped her hands on the desk. "Now, don't be disappointed if conception doesn't occur during this first round. It's not uncommon to require several rounds. We don't worry about it until six rounds haven't resulted in a pregnancy. If it goes a year, Mo will have to come in for a thorough examination, but we won't worry about that yet."

"What do you do at six months?" Lesley asked, not wanting Crawford to think that she was being quiet because she was too embarrassed to ask anything.

"We'll have you and Mo, and Jayne, so she's included, come in, so we can review how you're using the impregnators, just to make sure you're following the instructions."

Lesley cringed at the thought. Mo was young and healthy; hopefully an awkward interrogation at the six-month mark wouldn't be required.

"Do you have any other questions?" Crawford asked.

"No."

Crawford picked up the box and leaned over her desk to hand it to Lesley. "In that case, I wish the three of you a positive outcome."

"Thank you," Lesley said, pleased that the centre was going out of its way to involve Jayne. Nobody had blinked when the triad had arrived for the initial consultation, and three guest chairs had sat in front of Crawford's desk, apparently not the usual arrangement, since there were only two now. When Lesley had mentioned to Laura that they had an appointment at the centre, Laura had sent its personnel a reminder about how triads were treated under the Chosen Tradition. Perhaps knowing that a commodore who also happened to be the sector's acting commander was watching had made a difference.

Half an hour later, Lesley strode into the triad's living room and held up the box. "Here it is."

Mo rested her violin on her lap. "I didn't expect you so soon."

"I was only in the physician's office for five minutes."

"Five minutes?" Mo squeaked. "Compared to what I've gone through…" She held out her hand.

Lesley gave her the box. "Where's Jayne?"

"In the kitchen," Mo said. "Jayne!" She peered at the box in her hand. "Jayne!" she yelled again.

Footsteps clattered down the hallway. Jayne stopped in the living room archway. "What?"

"I picked up the impregnator," Lesley said. "It's good for around twelve hours."

Mo handed the box back to Lesley. "There's four, right?" she said as she placed her violin into its case.

"Yes."

"Don't forget, I'm on 72 in three days."

"That's fine. We'll come to you."

"I don't have to be there for this," Jayne said. "I—I mean, it's up to you whether—"

Mo's face tightened; she drew breath. Lesley placed a warning hand on Mo's shoulder. "Of course we want you there," she said evenly. Why did Jayne keep begging them to exclude her? Lesley was certain that if they told Jayne to stay in her own room tonight, she'd be upset, and this morning, she'd seemed excited that the first impregnator would be ready today. What was she wrestling with that made her run hot and cold about having a daughter? "Why don't we go for a walk after supper and then have an early night?"

Mo blew out a sigh. "Why not?"

Lesley looked to Jayne, who nodded. Hopefully supper and the walk would soothe Mo's ruffled feathers. Lesley had imagined that using the impregnator, starting a family, would be a hopeful, joyous event, not one fraught with tension and hurt feelings. "Do you need help in the kitchen?" she asked Jayne.

"I already asked her and she said no," Mo said. Lesley could hear the irritation in Mo's voice. Jayne probably could, too.

"I'm fine." Jayne turned to leave.

"I'm going to get a drink," Lesley said to Mo. She set the box on an end table and hurried after Jayne. "Are you all right?" she murmured, putting her arm around Jayne and squeezing her.

Jayne smiled and said, "I'm fine," but she wasn't fooling Lesley.

Two weeks later

"I'M NOT PREGNANT," Mo said, her disappointment coming through the comm station loud and clear.

Lesley leaned over her desk. "We'll try again in a couple of weeks," she said, masking her own disappointment. "Remember what Crawford said. A few tries isn't unusual."

"I know. Oh well, I'd better go. I'm due on 72." Mo sighed. "I'll tell Jayne before I go, though."

"Mo."

"What?"

"I love you."

Mo's voice brightened. "I love you, too."

Around a month later

BENT OVER HER comm unit, Lesley pretended that she wasn't listening to the conversation taking place between Jayne and Joanna.

"We can include one and see how people react," Joanna was saying.

"I know how they'll react." Jayne paused. "I don't want to ruin it for the other artists."

"Oh, so it's the *other* artists you're worried about. Yes, I can imagine how traumatic it would be for them if everyone fawns over their paintings and turns up their noses at yours."

"They won't want their paintings in the same show as one of mine."

"Is that what they said when you beeped them all and asked?"

During the ensuing silence, Lesley fought the urge to lift her head. She imagined Joanna with her hands on her hips and Jayne with her arms folded. That was usually how it went when the two butted heads.

"It's fear, you know," Joanna finally said. "Everyone goes through it, but not everyone has a family history to hide behind."

"I'm not hiding behind my family history!"

"Yes you are. But I've pushed enough for tonight, and poor Lesley doesn't know where to look."

Lesley chuckled to herself. Joanna would have made a good Interior officer—if she could pass the psychological evaluation.

"Do think about it, though. The show's still a few months away, and despite the fuss around your Joining, I suspect most won't realize who Jayne Thompson is."

"I'll think about it," Jayne said; Lesley wondered if she would.

Footsteps approached her. "You can look up now, Lesley." Joanna said, sounding closer. "We've finished for tonight."

Lesley smoothed her expression and slipped her comm unit into its holder. She put on her cloak and waited for Jayne and Joanna to say their good-byes, then nodded to Joanna and followed Jayne from the studio. Jayne was walking faster than usual. Lesley had to increase her pace to keep up. "She only pushes because she cares and doesn't want to see your work languish."

Jayne kept her eyes on the path. "I know."

Her tone convinced Lesley to drop the subject. "Mo hasn't beeped. That's a good sign."

Jayne brushed a stray hair out of her eye.

"What's bothering you about having a daughter?" Lesley asked, hoping that Jayne might let something slip while she was still mulling over her conversation with Joanna.

"Nothing."

"You seem..." Conflicted was too loaded a word. "Unsure about it."

Jayne shoved her hands into her cloak's pockets. "I want us to have a daughter."

"But…"

"There is no but!" Jayne snapped, deepening Lesley's certainty that there was.

"Jayne…it might help to get it out in the open."

"I want us to have a daughter. I'm excited about it, most of the time. When I'm not, it's just me being…me. I worry about things nobody else worries about, and I don't need to burden you and Mo with it. I want you to enjoy the whole experience. I don't want to ruin it for you. I'll deal with it." She slipped her hand from her pocket and touched Lesley's arm. "You worry about Mo." Her hand was back in her pocket before Lesley could grasp it.

So she was keeping quiet for them, so they wouldn't worry about… what? *I don't want to ruin it for you.* Jayne had said something similar to Joanna. *I know how they'll react. I don't want to ruin it for the other artists.* Was Jayne worried that having a daughter would somehow turn everyone against them? That didn't make sense. C3 residents were growing used to having a triad and an Adams in the sector, and having a daughter would be the expected thing to do. By the time she was born, they would have been Joined for over two years. Neither achievement would cause Rymellans to turn their backs—quite the opposite.

As they walked on in silence, Lesley considered other possibilities. One interpretation of Jayne's words made terrible sense: perhaps Jayne thought the other artists would feel their paintings devalued, at least in the eyes of the critics, if they were shown along with hers. After all, the Adams taint was contagious.

They reached the aviacraft. Lesley slid into the pilot's seat and punched in the coordinates for the Thompson estate, but instead of lifting off, she turned to Jayne. "You're worried that everyone will look down on our daughter because of you," she stated.

Jayne stiffened, then slowly exhaled.

"She won't be in the same position that you were in," Lesley said gently. "Even if she has a hard time at the academies, she'll have us, aunts, uncles, cousins, children whose parents don't hold anything against you. She'll have sisters, too." Siblings who actually cared.

"That's all true, but if it weren't for me, she wouldn't have a hard time at the academies."

"We don't know that she will."

Jayne whipped toward Lesley. "You honestly don't think that some parents are going to say, stay away from—" Her breath caught in her throat. She squeezed her eyes shut.

"What is it?" Lesley reached for Jayne's hand. Her throat tightened when Jayne hung on.

"I'm going to love this daughter," Jayne said, her voice barely a whisper.

"I know you will." Lesley said, after waiting for more. "You said you don't want to ruin it for us. Don't let what might happen ruin it for you."

"I can't be naive. I can't pretend to myself that everything will be okay."

"If she has a hard time, it won't be your fault." Lesley bit back her frustration. It would be easy to say, "Don't let the narrow-minded mar everything for you," but expecting pithy advice to counteract Jayne's years of being ostracized would be unreasonable. Jayne had already braved so much since they'd met; she'd grown less fearful, but her past still cast a long shadow. Plus, her concerns were understandable, especially since some *did* consider her a threat to the Way. She wasn't being paranoid or overly sensitive. "She'll have her parents," Lesley said, to drive the point home. "We'll be there to support her. Especially you. You've been through it."

To her surprise, Jayne snorted. "I wish I could say that I'm completely concerned about her and want to protect her, but unfortunately I'm not that unselfish. Of course I'll want to protect her. But I also want to protect me. The problem is, I can't."

"What do you mean?" Lesley asked.

"I really am excited about this. Mo keeps saying I'll be taking care of her when you two aren't home. You'll think this is silly, but I imagine taking her with me to my favourite drawing spots, and when she's old enough, putting a pencil in her hand and guiding her through her first drawing." Jayne's tone grew mocking. "After we've had a sumptuous picnic lunch outside in the perfect weather with the birds twittering in harmony."

Lesley squeezed her hand. "That doesn't sound silly. I'm sure everyone imagines spending wonderful times with their children."

Jayne swallowed. "Except mine won't last. Because one day, she'll go to the Learning Academy, and that new friend she's been having lunch with every day won't want anything to do with her. When she asks why, her supposed friend will say, 'Because your mama is an Adams.' Now, maybe she'll brush it off the first time. Maybe she won't really understand what the girl meant, or maybe she won't care, but then it'll happen again, and again. And then she'll be eating lunch all alone, surrounded by hostile faces and whispers. Nobody will want to work with her on group projects. Nobody will want to be seen talking to her." Jayne's eyes glistened. "And nobody will be surprised when she comes home and blames me, and wants nothing to do with me anymore. The problem is, I can't protect myself. The moment I lay eyes on that baby, I'll love her. But every time I gaze at her, I'll know that it'll only be a matter of time before she turns on me. So I'm not only afraid for her. I'm afraid for myself."

Lesley wanted to say, "Your own daughter won't turn on you," but stopped herself. Jayne's parents had turned on her. So had her brother, and while her aunt and uncle had taken her in, their relationship with Jayne could hardly be described as warm. Only Carol had stuck by her. The triad would do its best to bring up their daughters to respect family and follow the spirit of the Way, but Jayne was right. Particularly during those adolescent years when fitting in was all-important for some, would their daughters have the strength to stand up for their mama in the face of losing their friends? Lesley believed that most parents in C3 wouldn't explicitly tell their children not to be friends with the Thompsons, but the way in which they explained to their children that Jayne was the Adamses' daughter would convey more than their words.

Lesley didn't want to warn her daughters that their friends might reject them because of Jayne's history; that would only lead to them having the same fear that Jayne was battling. But the triad would have to consider how to prepare them for the possibility that they might be unfairly judged. What Jayne feared might actually happen, and Lesley wouldn't belittle that fear. But it was beyond their control. All the triad could do was instill a deep sense of self-worth in their daughters, teach them about the spirit of the Way, and hope that their strong familial bonds would see them through any difficult times.

"As you said, you're going to love our daughter, no matter what," Lesley said. "I know this will be easier said than done, but try to assume that everything will be all right. After all, we'll be bringing her up."

"I know. And if she has to turn against me for a while to get through the academies, I'll deal with it. I'll understand." Jayne's voice dropped. "That doesn't mean it won't hurt, though."

"You won't face it alone."

"I know that, too." Jayne chuckled wryly. "Look at me, worrying about being rejected by someone who doesn't exist." She paused. "I can control what I do with my paintings. Joanna's pushing me to try one painting in a show, but I can say no. I can protect myself. But this baby..." She blew out a heartfelt sigh. "I can't do anything. I can't not love her, so I don't know why I'm wasting time struggling with it, because I don't have a choice. All it's doing is making you think I don't want a daughter."

"I thought something might be upsetting you about it, but I've never doubted that you want us to start a family." However, Mo had said a few things that indicated she might feel differently. "Are you going to talk to Mo about this?"

"I don't want to bother her with it, at least not until she's pregnant."

Lesley didn't have to ask why. "Speaking of Mo, we should head home, unless you want to talk some more."

Jayne shook her head. "Let's go home."

Lesley gave Jayne's hand another squeeze before letting it go. She lifted off and engaged the auto-navigation system. "Thanks for being honest with me." Suspecting that the prospect of having a daughter was tying Jayne up in knots hadn't tempered Lesley's anticipation and optimism, but it had always been at the back of her mind. She'd wondered if they were somehow hurting her. Now that she knew what worried Jayne, she could fully look forward to Mo becoming pregnant. If Jayne's fears came to pass, they'd deal with the situation then—together. For now, Lesley would do what she'd advised Jayne to do: assume that everything would be all right.

The moment they arrived home and stepped into the living room, her optimism fled. She didn't have to ask; the sight of Mo slumped on the sofa told her.

"Next time you pick up an impregnator, can you ask for an extra one, so I can kick it out the flaming window?" Mo muttered.

"You should have beeped," Lesley said, sinking onto the sofa. Since Mo's arms were folded, Lesley patted her leg.

"I figured I'd deliver the news in person." Mo looked up. "If you don't want a daughter, you're getting your wish," she said to Jayne.

"Mo!"

"It's okay." Jayne glanced around, then shoved her hands into her pockets. These days, she only took a sketchbook with her when she went out alone. "I'm sorry you're not pregnant, I really am."

"I'm sorry, too," Mo mumbled. "What did they say? Don't be concerned until six months have passed?"

Lesley nodded. They still had four months before they'd face a dreaded interview with the physician.

"What if there's something wrong with me?"

"There's nothing wrong with you. We've only tried twice." Lesley slipped her arm around Mo's shoulders. "It'll happen."

"I hope so." Mo unfolded her arms and reached for Lesley.

"It will." Lesley said, holding Mo tight and rubbing her back. "I'll go make tziva," she heard Jayne say.

When she was sure Jayne was gone, she kissed Mo's hair and whispered, "When you're feeling better, we need to have a talk about Jayne."

JAYNE FOLLOWED LESLEY and Mo into what would become their first daughter's bedroom and turned to them, wondering why they'd led her here.

"Do you remember telling me that you always wanted to paint a mural?" Mo said, her voice bouncing off the empty room's walls.

"Yes, I do." She didn't remember everything they'd said to each other since meeting, but she remembered that conversation. She'd surprised herself by trusting Mo with something she'd only ever told Carol, and wasn't at all upset that Mo had told Lesley. She'd assumed from the beginning that telling one would essentially tell both, that if she didn't want one of them to know something, she couldn't tell either of them. She was certain that Lesley had already told Mo about their conversation in the aviacraft.

"You said all you needed was a wall." Mo grinned and waved her arms toward the wall facing the door. "Here's your wall."

Now they were both smiling. It took Jayne a moment to understand. "You want me to paint a mural, here, on this wall?"

"Yes," they said in unison.

Excitement pushed through her worries and bubbled to the surface.

"Our daughter will wake up every morning and see the mural by one of her mamas," Lesley said.

"She'll have the best flaming mural on the planet," Mo added.

Jayne's natural tendency to find a dark cloud in every sky didn't stand a chance. A million possibilities, colours, shapes, and themes flew through her mind. Yes, their daughter would wake up to a glorious scene; it would be as close to perfection as possible. Wondrous. Breathtaking. Incredible. No matter what others whispered about her, no matter how much their daughter resented her, she wouldn't be able to deny that from her Adams mama could spring something beautiful and unblemished.

"Jayne?" she heard Mo say from a distance.

She shook herself. "I—I have to plan. I have to envision what—I need supplies. I have to make a list. I—" Her voice choked off. She reached for her Chosens and swallowed the lump in her throat when she felt their arms around her. "Thank you." *Thank you, thank you, thank you.* She pulled away from them and stared at the wall—her wall. "I need to think. I need to be alone."

Mo glanced at Lesley. "We're being kicked out so the artist can contemplate her creation."

Lesley nodded.

"When you know what you need, I'll fly you to the Trading Centre," Mo said to Jayne.

"It won't be today. I need time," Jayne said, feeling guilty because they'd just given her a wonderful gift, and she desperately wanted them to leave.

"Oh, excuse me," Mo drawled. "I'm not familiar with how you artists do, uh, whatever it is you do when you're trying to come up with an idea."

"She doesn't have the benefit of watching you work with Joanna," Lesley said, amusement in her eyes.

"If you don't mind, right now, I need to be alone," Jayne said, giving the wall her full attention. She bit her lip.

"Why don't you get your violin and meet me downstairs?" Lesley said. "We'll do some creating of our own."

"Sure," Mo replied.

"Can you shut the door behind you?" Jayne said without looking over her shoulder. She clenched her hands. She didn't turn around when one of them—it felt like Lesley—touched her back. The door clicked shut. She listened to Lesley descend the stairs. Mo traipsed along the hallway to fetch her violin and then returned. When Jayne could no longer hear Mo's elephant footsteps thumping down to the living room, she unclenched her hands, sat cross-legged on the floor, lowered her head, and wept.

Around a month later

JAYNE MIXED THE colour she'd use for three of the balloons and surveyed her creation thus far. Admittedly, it wasn't all that original. Balloons, clouds, teddy bears, cute animals…she hadn't mentioned this to Lesley and Mo, but she planned to paint a new mural every so often. Future murals would reflect this daughter's personality and interests. All Jayne had to work with for this first one was "baby girl." No personality, no likes and dislikes.

She dipped her paintbrush into the—

"No!"

The shout set Jayne's heart racing. As footsteps thumped up the hallway, she consciously calmed her trembling hand and turned around.

Mo stood in the doorway. "I'm so flaming tired of this. It's never going to happen."

Jayne swallowed. "It will happen," she said lamely.

"No, it won't!" Mo stepped into the room and thrust her arm toward the wall. "There's no point painting this mural. Argamon!" Her shoulders slumped. The frustration that had strained her voice turned to sorrow. "If I don't get pregnant soon, she'll want to have a baby with you," Mo moaned.

What? "No, she won't." Still clinging to the paintbrush, Jayne closed the distance between them. "I hope you're not worried about that, because there's no way Lesley will have a child with me." Not only would Lesley want Mo to be the other mama of her first child, but Jayne was not having any children, period. The Adams bloodline stopped with her. "Mo, it's early days. I know it's frustrating, but it *will* happen. Lesley knows that. She's not going to give up on you because you're not meeting some deadline."

"What if it goes six months? A year?" Mo looked up at her with moist eyes. "What if the Reproductive Technology Centre has to give us more help?"

"Then it will give you more help. But you're nowhere near that point yet." Jayne took Mo's hand. "And don't worry about Lesley. She's one hundred percent behind you." She gave Mo an encouraging smile, and felt it widen when Mo managed a small smile in return. "She'll be patient with you. She wants a baby with you because you're so," Jayne lifted her paintbrush, "flaming," she dabbed Mo's nose with the brush; laughter filled her voice at the sight of the red dot on Mo's nose, "cute!"

Mo's eyes crossed. "Did you just paint my nose?"

"Yes, I did."

"Oh." Mo's grip on Jayne's hand tightened. "I guess you thought that was funny," she said, walking toward the green paint Jayne had mixed earlier.

Uh-oh. "Well—"

In one motion, Mo snatched up a paintbrush, dipped it into the paint, and whirled. "Let's see how *you* like it." She lunged.

Jayne drew back. The brush caught her on the neck. "I have you at a disadvantage," she said, striping Mo's cheek. She laughed when Mo tried for her face again, missed, and followed up with a quick jab to her chin.

"I'll get your cheek!" Mo waved the paintbrush around, then decided it needed more paint.

As Mo refreshed her brush, Jayne quickly dabbed a matching stripe onto Mo's other cheek. "You're starting to look like you have whiskers."

"Hey, not fair." Mo touched her hand to her cheek and lowered her head.

Her brush almost dry, Jayne moved closer to Mo. "Sorry," she said, peering at her.

Mo's hand flashed up; Jayne felt the brush travel from her left cheek to her right. "Ha!" Mo barked.

"I think you got some on my lips." Jayne refreshed her brush and went for Mo's forehead.

"Hey, not my hair. You didn't get my hair, did you?"

Jayne leaned over to look. "No, I—" Her eyes instinctively closed when Mo's paintbrush headed in their direction. It flew across Jayne's forehead.

"Ha! This is too easy!" Mo cried.

"Really? Well, since you're worried about your hair." Jayne opened her eyes and waved her brush around Mo's head.

"Don't you dare," Mo said, raising her hands to protect herself. She groaned when her paintbrush hit her head. "Argamon!"

"The green streak in your hair suits you," Jayne managed to gasp out before doubling over. Her giggling intensified when she felt a paintbrush sweep across the top of her head. When she regained control of herself, she straightened. "I think you need more red." She lunged at Mo, who lunged at her. Paintbrushes flashed, paint flew, until they both collapsed into a heap, convulsing with laughter. They grew quiet, then looked at each other and burst into giggles again. If Jayne's face and hair looked anything like Mo's...at least the paint was water-based.

The front door thumped shut. They stared at each other wide-eyed, then scrambled to their feet. Footsteps pounded up the stairs. Lesley appeared in the doorway. "I can smell the paint. How's the—" Her brows shot up. She blinked at them.

"I, uh...Jayne's helping to cheer me up." Mo shifted her weight. "I'm not pregnant."

"I see," Lesley said, her eyes bright. "If...this," she gestured toward them, "helps, then who am I to argue? But if one speck of paint comes near this uniform, I won't be happy."

Jayne looked at the commander insignia sewn onto the uniform's left breast. The sight of one no longer made her want to run and hide.

Lesley smiled at them. "You both look ridiculous. And adorable. I'm going to change." She continued down the hallway.

"I don't think she's changing because she wants to come and paint," Mo said with a grin. "I have dibs on the upstairs shower."

Jayne could shower in one of the other bathrooms, but… "I'll shower later. I'm used to being covered in paint." Though on her hands and smock. "I want to finish up a couple of balloons."

Mo set her paintbrush down. "Thanks for cheering me up."

"Anytime." She watched Mo leave, then turned back to her work, rejuvenated. Another memory cleansed. Paint fights had always reminded her of Robert, but now she'd think of Mo. Little by little, she was reclaiming her life.

Around a month later

MO GRABBED HER head and stared at the closed bathroom door. She wished they weren't waiting for her. Why did she tell them her menses was late? She should have quietly done the test, rather than making a big deal out of it. Now she'd gotten them all excited for nothing, because the test—the one she refused to look at!—would be negative. She'd have to go out there and see the hope in their eyes, then watch them mask their disappointment when she told them she'd failed, yet again. Yes, *she'd* failed. She was the one who wasn't getting flaming pregnant.

How much time had it been? The test result must be ready to mock her by now. All she had to do was turn around and look. Oh well, they still had two months before the flaming Reproductive Technology Centre would try to figure out what they were doing wrong. What if they wanted Les to demonstrate how she was using the impregnator? Argamon, Les would love that! Yep, when Mo told her Chosens the bad news, she'd have to point out that they still had time. Maybe she could go to the centre and ask them to check her over and leave Les out of it. Yes, she'd give that a try. As for what she'd say to Les and Jayne when she left the bathroom… *Sorry, I'm not pregnant, but my menses was late, so we must be getting closer, right? I bet it'll happen next time. No need to worry. Why don't we go out for supper?*

Okay, she had a plan, and she'd warned them that it could be a false alarm. She should have said *very likely* a false alarm; in fact, she should have kept her mouth shut. But it was too late for that now. So it was time to turn around and get it over with.

Sighing, Mo wheeled and peered at the test. Her heart skipped a beat.

Green...didn't that mean... *Pregnant: green*. Her eyes moved back to the test result. Green. She read the legend again. *Pregnant: green.*

Argamon!

She screamed and pulled open the door. "I'm pregnant! I'm flaming pregnant!" she shouted, flying down the stairs. By the time she reached the bottom, Les and Jayne had rushed into the hall. "I'm pregnant!" She leaped into Les's arms, laughing and crying at the same time. Her throat tightened when she felt Les's tears mingle with hers. "I'm pregnant," she whispered again, and motioned for Jayne to join their hug. In the arms of the two women she loved and a new life inside her...for a moment, she couldn't fathom it. "We're going to be mamas."

We're going to be mamas.

DISCOVERY

One week before Mo's due date

CAPTAIN ROGER STANDISH'S EYES FLICKERED, THEN opened. He shot his hand out from under the blanket and hit the connect button on his comm unit. "Yes."

"I'm sorry to wake you, Captain, but we have a situation," Commander Hollins, who had command of the *Osprey* on the overnight shift, said.

"What's going on?"

"Patrol C has detected an alien ship."

Standish kept his voice even. "Contact Planetary Command and advise them of the situation. I'll be there shortly."

"Understood."

Standish's mind raced as he swung his legs off the bed and headed for the bathroom. The *Osprey* had left 72 only three days ago, and it had taken the customary detour to Argamon for the benefit of those on their first tour. They were still far within Rymellan space. What was a ship doing here, so close to Rymel?

After splashing water on his face, he quickly dressed and headed to the command centre. When the elevator doors swooshed open, Hollins, who stood in front of a viewing monitor, turned to Standish. "Situation report," Standish said, striding to Hollins' side.

"Patrol C is shadowing the vessel."

"Have the aliens engaged them or attempted communication?"

"No. Our lead fighter is transmitting the images onscreen."

Standish peered at the viewing monitor. Shock stabbed through him. He turned to Lieutenant Commander Higgs, one of the *Osprey*'s defence analysts. "If I'm remembering my alien technology course at the academy correctly, it appears to be Danlion."

Higgs nodded. "Based on our limited intelligence, it has a few more bells and whistles than the last time we ran across one, but it's definitely Danlion."

"Danlion?" Hollins frowned. "I thought they'd almost destroyed themselves."

"That was hundreds of years ago," Standish said. "They've had time to reproduce since then." Unfortunately. "According to diplomatic sources, they're well on their way to destroying another planet. You'd think they would have learned. But I don't care about their latest civil war. I care about what one of their ships is doing in our space." He punched a code into a nearby comm station.

"Yes?" said a fatigued voice.

"It's Standish. We need you in the command centre."

"I'll be right there."

"What more can you tell me about the vessel?" he asked Higgs.

"It's a cargo ship, pretty much the same design they've used for centuries. Primitive weaponry and defensive systems." She blinked at Standish. "It would be incapable of taking out a fighter, and one fighter missile—two at most—would destroy it."

That meant a strategically targeted laser shot from the *Osprey* would disintegrate it. "What are they doing here?" he said, more to himself than to his two colleagues. He suspected that the Danlions knew few details about Rymellans, but among those details would be the stories about travellers who strayed into Rymellan space and were never seen again. Considering that he hadn't been alive the last time an alien vessel had shown up uninvited, perhaps those stories were dying out or losing their power. Well, they might soon have a new story that would frighten their children. Rymellans weren't above helping ships in distress and turning them back in the direction from which they'd come, but those requiring aid usually requested it, especially when they ran into a warship that could squash them like a fly. Plus, Danlions weren't the diplomatic sort. They reacted violently to everything and everyone, including those who wanted to help them.

"It looks like it's taken some damage at its stern," Higgs said. "Without a closer examination, I can't say who inflicted it, except that it wasn't us."

"What is the ship's heading?" Standish asked her.

Higgs raised her brows. "On its present course, it's headed straight for Rymel."

He'd forgive the Danlions on board for not knowing that an

automated defence system would destroy their ship long before it reached the planet. The space stations and domestic fighter squadrons would obliterate any ship that managed to break through the initial onslaught. So far, that had never happened. No hostile ship had ever survived taking a run at the planet; in fact, none had attempted it for decades. So what was this? Were they stupid? Lost? Here on some ridiculous dare? Or was it a suicide mission? The latter possibility concerned him. He hit the button on the station that would connect him with all the pilots in Patrol C. "Standish here. Disable the vessel. Do not destroy it. I repeat. Do not destroy it."

"Understood," a voice crackled. Moments later, several flashes appeared on the viewing monitor. "Ship disabled."

"Stay with it." Standish cut the connection. He stared at the ship, now drifting in space. Something didn't feel right. No communication, no evasive maneuvers, no attempt to fight back. Yes, it was a cargo ship that wouldn't survive a skirmish, but...maybe they were hoping to be captured? Maybe they thought those who never returned from Rymellan space lived out their lives here. In that case, they could be on a mission to infiltrate Rymel, hoping to pass themselves off as innocent civilians on a cargo ship held together with elastic bands. No, without knowing what had happened to those who'd disappeared, the Danlions wouldn't risk it. To succeed, it would have to be their best people. Why send them on a ship that couldn't defend itself against the weakest of hostiles, let alone the Rymellan fleet?

The comm station beeped. He activated it. "Standish."

"Commander Richards at Planetary Command. What's your status?"

"We've disabled a Danlion vessel."

"Danlion?"

Standish almost chuckled. "I'll attempt contact, find out what they're doing here, and then decide on a course of action." His uneasiness made him add, "We have the situation under control, but I'd suggest raising station alert levels."

"Already done. Keep us apprised. Richards out."

The elevator doors opened. Translator Lieutenant Lloyd marched onto the deck and looked at Standish with bleary eyes. One more person, and the command centre would be filled to capacity. Standish hadn't sat down since he'd entered it, and Lloyd also remained on his feet. "How good is your Danlion?" Standish said to him.

Lloyd's brow crinkled. "I know the basics."

"We've been assuming that Danlions are on board, but we don't know that for sure," Hollins pointed out. "They could be Rymellans who ran into trouble and managed to get an old Danlion cargo ship off the ground."

"We haven't received any reports of missing military, but we'll start there." Standish motioned for Lloyd to move nearer to the comm station. "We've disabled an alien ship that appears to be Danlion. We need to make contact with whoever's on board. They might be in trouble, or they might be trouble. Start with Rymellan, then Danlion."

"Yes, Captain. Initiating communication over the common frequencies." Lloyd raised his voice. "This is the Rymellan ship *Osprey*. You are in Rymellan space. State your reason for entering our system."

Dead air.

"If you're in distress, we can assist."

Nothing.

Lloyd glanced at Standish. "I'll try Danlion." He straightened. "*This a Rymellan ship Osprey. You...in our...place, our...area. Say why.*"

No response.

"I'm not even sure I'm speaking a current dialect," Lloyd murmured. "*If you, uh...in help—no—need help, tell me.*"

The comm station remained silent.

"Try Jessimite," Standish suggested. "I don't know why they wouldn't respond, but to be thorough..."

Lloyd cleared his throat. "*This is the Rymellan ship Osprey. You are inside Rymellan space. What is your purpose here? Do you need assistance?*" When no one answered, Lloyd said, "I have a few other languages I can try."

"Go ahead." Standish waited while Lloyd spoke more gibberish, and wasn't surprised that Lloyd was still talking to himself. "That's all for now. You can return to your quarters," he said, not wanting Lloyd to be present for the conversation he'd have with Hollins and Higgs. "but don't go back to sleep. We might need you again."

"Yes, Captain." Lloyd nodded to everyone and left.

As soon as the elevator door closed, Standish said, "We'll have to board, but something's not right. Could this be some type of trap?"

"Do you think the vessel might be booby-trapped?" Higgs said.

"It could be a scout ship for a larger force," Hollins suggested. "Or perhaps they're hoping we board, so they can capture the strike team."

"But to what end?" Standish said. "If it's booby-trapped and we don't detect the trigger, we lose a team. Obviously we don't want that to happen, but if it does, what will they have gained? The same goes for capturing the team. Their ship is disabled. Even if it wasn't, they wouldn't make it very far. And I can't see using a cargo ship as a scout."

Higgs nodded in agreement. "If it's a scout, it's not a very good one. It flew right into a patrol and was making a beeline to the planet with no regard for being intercepted along the way."

"So it's not here to gather intelligence, either."

"It has to be on its own," Higgs said. "We'd detect any larger ships on the way long before they made it this close to the planet."

So what was it doing here? It didn't make sense, and that was precisely why Standish was uneasy. What were they missing? Maybe it was deserted, which would explain why nobody had responded. But if that was the case, why was it on a course for Rymel? It was normally sound to assume that someone was manning a ship that wasn't adrift. He blew out some air. "I want you to lead the boarding party," he said to Higgs.

She sprang to her feet. "I'll assemble the team."

"Higgs," he called when she reached the elevator. She turned. "Keep communication open and run a cam."

"Yes, Captain." She disappeared into the elevator.

Twenty minutes later, Hollins said, "Shuttle away. Fighter squadron escorting."

Standish watched the images streaming from Higgs's head cam as she briefed the team, while Hollins monitored the chatter from the escorting pilots. Standish couldn't make out the team's faces through their helmets, but he knew they'd be wary and determined.

"Approaching port hatch," Higgs said.

"External visual on monitor five," Hollins murmured. Standish watched the shuttle maneuver into position, then shifted his attention back to Higgs's cam.

"Extending boarding tunnel," crackled another voice.

"Expand to 2.5 times radius." Higgs again.

"Expanded and sealed."

Higgs's arm flashed across the image. "Sanders, secure the hatch and get us in. Martin, you're with me. The rest, remain at the head of the tunnel until you get the all clear. Moore, prepare to eject the tunnel and leave on my command."

"Are you sure?"

"Yes." Higgs said firmly, knowing that ejecting the tunnel would mean that she, Martin, and Sanders would drift in space until rescue shuttles could get to them.

"Understood."

Higgs entered the boarding tunnel; her cam followed Sanders as he approached the hatch and attached a sensor to it. Standish didn't know the details of how it worked; he'd dozed off during his countermeasure technology classes. Sanders backed away from the sensor and looked down at the instrument in his hand. Seconds stretched into minutes. "No suspicious readings," Sanders finally said. "Connecting to control system...calibrating...ready."

"Moore, extend side shielding and isolate the shuttle."

The shield that swung in front of Higgs obstructed the cam's view of Sanders.

"Prepare to engage," Hollins said to the pilots.

"Shuttle isolated," Moore said, indicating that the shuttle's end of the tunnel was now sealed. The cam briefly showed Martin across the tunnel taking cover behind a shield, then Sanders crouching behind the shield in front of him. The image went dark; Higgs had tucked her head behind her shield. "Ready?"

"Ready," Sanders and Martin said in unison.

The cam picked up the tip of Higgs's weapon. "Open it."

A muffled sound, then, "Done."

Silence, then the cam slowly revealed the image of the open hatch and the deck behind it. "Clear," Higgs said. "Unseal the shuttle. Everyone forward."

The image on the viewing monitor bobbed as Higgs slowly walked to the hatch and onto the Danlion ship. "Life support active. No life signs detected yet. Heading toward the command deck. We'll sweep along the way, in case they're somehow avoiding detection."

"Understood," Standish said.

The team slowly made its way up the lower deck's main corridor, checking rooms and decks as it went. "Clear."

"Clear."

"Clear!"

Was the ship deserted? Standish still couldn't relax. Life support active...something didn't add up. His jaw clenched. The images were starting to unnerve him. Eerie, seeing nobody in the corridors, storage bays, quarters...

"Proceeding to upper deck through maintenance shaft," Higgs said. Halfway up the ladder, she stopped climbing. "I have a faint life sign, approximately one hundred metres and fifteen degrees from my position, near the command deck."

"They could be waiting for us to emerge from the shaft," Martin said.

"No. We're not that far from the exit, but I'll be cautious." She continued her ascent, but stopped before popping the hatch. "Tossing neurolock grenade." The hatch opened; the cam caught Higgs's gloved hand as she tossed the grenade out and pulled the hatch closed. Fifteen seconds later, she opened the hatch again. The area outside the hatch slowly came into view. A yellowish haze prevented Standish from seeing whether she was in a corridor, a bay, a maintenance area...

"Clear," Higgs said a moment later. If there had been a welcoming party waiting outside the hatch, the grenade would have paralyzed it, but not the Rymellans, whose bio filters would have protected them from the toxin. "Now seventy-seven metres from life sign," she said, on the move again. "Will continue sweep."

"Clear."

"Clear," another voice rumbled.

"Clear."

"Lieutenant Commander! Over here."

The cam image showed a corridor, then two of the strike team's backs. They parted; Higgs stepped between them and stopped short. "Argamon," she breathed. "They're all dead." The cam swept the room. Danlions, Standish presumed, sat slumped over tables, or lay on the floor. The cam lingered on a couple locked in a macabre embrace.

"What is this?" Martin asked.

"They haven't been dead for long," Sanders said, his voice high.

"Stay focused," Higgs barked. "Our bio filters are active."

"I don't see any visible signs of injury," Edwards, the team's physician, said.

"How many are there?" Standish asked.

"I see ten."

The cam swung back to the door. "Let's keep moving," Higgs said. "Now twenty metres from life sign." The corridor came into view again. "Receiving more data. Heart rate of subject...140 beats per minute."

Good, whoever was in there was frightened.

"Ten metres. Five. Through that door. Readying another neurolock grenade. Martin, cover me." The door slid open. Higgs tossed a neurolock grenade into the room and quickly hit the Close button. Fifteen seconds later, she said, "Let's go."

The door slid open again. The yellowish haze left behind by the grenade dominated the cam's transmitted images.

"Edwards!" Higgs shouted. "To me. Administer neurolock antidote. Now!"

"Administering."

"Hurry!"

The haze began to dissipate. Standish could make out Edwards leaning over...then Edwards straightened...

Standish met Hollins' shocked eyes and contacted Planetary Command.

"Richards. Is the Danlion situation still under control?"

"Get me Admiral Jensen," Standish snapped.

"It's 03:30."

"Wake her up."

MO SWALLOWED A bite of oatmeal raisin cookie and continued her sentence. "They approved all but one."

"How many did you submit?" Ann asked.

She shifted in her seat and grabbed another cookie from the plate sitting next to the comm station. "Six."

"Which name did they reject?"

Should she tell her? No. Ann would ask why, and Mo didn't feel like reciting four generations of Les's family tree to get to the cousin a million times removed that already had the name they'd submitted and was still alive. "That's classified."

"Well, five out of six isn't bad. And, you know, Ann Thompson is all you really need."

Mo snorted. "Don't hold your breath."

"I was thinking the other day that you're the first person I've ever seen who's wider than you are tall."

"Excuse me. I'm not that short...or big. And after what I just did for you, I can't believe you're picking on me."

Ann groaned. "Come on, you're not going to hang that over my head now, are you? That won't be any fun."

Considering that allowing Andrew to build a house on her land was no skin off Mo's nose, she wouldn't keep reminding Ann of her generosity. Not every single time Ann cracked a joke at her expense, anyway. Maybe every second or third time. Andrew had his own small patch of land that he'd received on his eighteenth birthday, but in addition to a house, he wanted to build a workshop and have a decent-sized garden. Mo's land was located right next to his and she'd never use it, so... "I saw that the foundation is in. It won't be long now before you'll be living together—for real. Are you finally going to give up your room at the Military Academy?"

"Yeah."

Good.

"I can always get it back."

What did Andrew see in Ann again?

"So, any sign that the baby's coming?" Ann asked.

"No, but I'm only due in—" She jumped when a siren screeched from the comm station. It sounded like 72's evacuation alarm. "What's going on?" she shouted, not sure Ann could hear her.

"Wait!" Ann barked.

Mo could hear a muffled announcement in the background, but couldn't make out the words.

"They're telling us to evacuate this deck," Ann said. "Why do they always hold drills at the worst possible moment? I'm only halfway through my lunch."

"What deck are you on?"

"Fourteen." Ann paused. "They're evacuating ten, too, and they've pushed back all shuttle schedules by an hour. Maybe it's not a drill."

"Why do you say that?"

"Because when I was in the observation lounge earlier, I saw a shuttle with the *Osprey*'s number arrive. And now they're evacuating the shuttle deck..."

Now Mo's interest was really piqued. "I thought the *Osprey* just left. Why—oh, maybe someone's injured."

"Why would they have to bring them back? They could treat them on the *Osprey*. Plus, I just saw a bunch of physicians heading for the elevator with people on gurneys, so the infirmary is included in the evacuation."

Weird. The infirmary was usually exempt from routine drills. "What else do you see?"

"People moving, Mo, and that's what I have to do, or I'll get into trouble. My lunch had better be here when I get back."

"I wish I was up there!"

Ann snickered. "I can understand why you're barred at this point. They want the shuttles to be able to lift off, and 72 spiralling into the planet would be really bad. Anyway, I really have to go." She disconnected.

Figured! Something exciting was happening on 72 and she was stuck down here. Though it was probably just a drill. So the infirmary was evacuating...it had to practise its evacuation procedure every once in a while, right?

"Are you okay?"

Mo slowly turned her chair toward the anxious voice.

"I heard you shouting," Jayne said.

Mo bit her lip. "I'm not going into labour. I'm due in five days."

Jayne's shoulders sagged. "Oh. Okay. It could happen anytime now, though."

"It could, but it's not happening now."

"Do you need anything? A drink? Something to eat?"

"No, I'm okay, thanks," Mo said, trying really, really hard not to take advantage of Jayne and Les's attentiveness. Over the last few weeks, they'd waited on her hand and foot. It almost made up for her extra weight and the constant pressure on her bladder.

Jayne leaned against the doorframe and folded her arms. "What were you shouting about?"

"I had to shout so Ann could hear me above the evacuation alarm on 72."

Jayne's eyes widened. "They're evacuating 72?"

"Just a couple of decks, and it's probably a drill," Mo said, with a dismissive wave of her hand. Weird about the shuttle from the *Osprey*, though. Maybe a crew member's close relative had died, and since the ship had only been a couple of days out, they'd decided to leave the tour and return. Most wouldn't do that, though. When you went on tour, you understood that you'd have to miss important family events. "You know, I wouldn't mind a tziva," she said. "Do you want to play some cards?"

"Sure. I'll go prepare the tziva and get the cards." Jayne hurried away.

Mo turned her chair, put her feet up on the footstool Les had moved nearer to the comm station, and clasped her hands atop her round belly. She could get used to this. As for 72, whatever was going on up there, it didn't concern her.

LESLEY REVIEWED HER opinion of an upcoming case one last time and dispatched it to the assistant who'd present it to the overseer. She rubbed her eyes, flicked on her desk lamp, and opened the next case. It would be impossible for her to get through them all before Mo had the baby, but she wanted to finish as many as she could before her upcoming parental break. She'd only have a month, and she wanted to savour it, not worry about being too far behind when she returned. She glanced at the images of Mo and Jayne on her desk. It wasn't real yet—the baby. Lesley had felt her kick and peered at the ultrasound images, but it hadn't sunk in that her life was about to radically change.

At least this impending event wouldn't be like their notifications, when they'd received the shock of their lives. The baby was healthy. Mo was doing well. Jayne, while still fretting about their daughter's future, was anticipating her birth as much as her Chosens were. Mama and Papa were excited. The Middletons were eager to welcome the latest addition to their family. This break would be a joyous one. It wouldn't be fraught with the tension, disbelief, and agony their notifications had wrought.

Someone knocked on her open office door. She looked up—and straightened.

Admiral Hall nodded to her from the doorway. "Good, you're still here. I need someone with your unique skill set."

"What can I do for you?" Lesley asked.

"I'd like you to fly me somewhere in your aviacraft."

She masked her surprise with difficulty. "Of course. When?"

"Now."

Lesley turned off her monitor and lamp, and rolled back her chair. "Where would you like to go?" she asked as she reached for her cloak.

"72."

Lesley couldn't stop herself from turning toward him.

"You know how to fly a shuttle, as well." He met her eyes. "I did say I needed someone with your unique skill set. We'll pick up a few others on the way to the shuttle station."

Her mind racing, Lesley slipped into her cloak. "I'll have to let my Chosens know I'll be late."

"Meet me in the lobby in five minutes. Oh, and Commander...you're not to mention this to your Chosens. Just tell them you're working late."

"Yes, Admiral."

He strode away. Lesley waited until she could no longer hear his footsteps, then went to her comm station and beeped Mo. "I'm going to be working much later than I thought."

"How much later?"

She honestly had no idea. "I don't know. I could be really late. Don't wait up."

"You're not going to get through all your cases before I go into labour."

"I know, but Blair just threw a rush case into my lap. I said I'd do it." Her jaw tightened. She hated lying to Mo.

Mo tutted. "Well, if I go into labour tonight, too bad. Blair will have to find someone else to finish it."

"Look, I'm sorry about this. If it's not too late, I'll beep you when I'm done, okay?"

"Yeah, okay. But when you're off, make sure she knows you're off. No cases only you can do."

"I'll make sure. Anyway, I'd better get back to work." Lesley disconnected and blew out a sigh. What was so confidential that Hall had asked her to keep a secret from her Chosens? She didn't discuss case details with them, but she didn't outright lie, either.

Her curiosity was piqued further when she strode into the lobby and spotted Laura standing with Admiral Jensen and Commander Alex Fisher, who was Jensen's close advisor, as Laura was to Hall.

Laura broke away from the others and headed Lesley off several feet away from them. "Do you know what this is about?" she murmured.

Surprised that Laura would be asking *her*, Lesley shook her head. "Hall just told me he needed my flying skills, and my aviacraft."

Laura grunted. "Jensen knows, but she's not saying anything." She looked past Lesley.

Hall marched over to them. "Good, everyone's here. We'll follow you, Commander."

As Lesley led the way to her aviacraft, she tried to figure out why she'd fly four senior officers from Interior and Defence to 72, and who'd join them along the way. She listened to the conversation going on behind her. Neither Hall nor Jensen was giving anything away. They were making polite talk, discussing recent trivial military announcements.

When everyone was settled into their seats and the aviacraft was ready to lift off, Lesley said, "Where would you like me to go, Admiral?"

In the passenger seat, he twisted toward her. "The Chosen House in Sector A6. We're picking up two of the Chosen Council Heads."

What? It took all her self-control not to gape. She entered the coordinates and kept her eyes forward. Now she knew two things for certain: first, that the Way was threatened, and second, that she'd better not crash the aviacraft or shuttle. The only person they were missing was the Preeminent Ruler.

One of the Chosen Council Heads echoed that thought when he climbed aboard. "Commander Thompson," he exclaimed, to Lesley's surprise. "Your notifications caused quite a stir. I'm Humphrey Stevens. I consulted on your case."

She glanced over her shoulder. "Pleased to meet you."

"And you. This is Margaret Ellis." Lesley and Ellis nodded to each other. Stevens glanced around. "I don't see the Preeminent Ruler."

"We've decided not to involve the government," Jensen said. "This involves the Way, not civil regulations, and the fewer who know about it, the better."

"You said it was urgent. What is it about?" Ellis asked.

"Wait until we're on 72," Jensen said tersely.

"We'll proceed to the shuttle station now," Hall said to Lesley.

She lifted the craft off again, hoping to glean more clues as they flew to the station, but those in the know remained tight-lipped. They didn't encounter anyone when they transferred to the shuttle, making Lesley wonder if the area had been cleared before their arrival. The sight of this particular group would set tongues wagging.

Her suspicion was confirmed as the shuttle approached 72. "I'll deal with station control," Jensen said. She directed her next words to her comm unit. "This is Admiral Jensen. We should be cleared for docking."

"Bay 7 is clear," came the reply. "We've been advised that you'll be using the maintenance elevator."

"Correct. Is the conference area on Deck 14 still secure?"

"Yes."

"Good. Jensen out."

Not having docked a shuttle outside of a simulator in years, Lesley concentrated on ensuring that her important passengers would enjoy a smooth arrival. Mo could do this in her sleep. *Mo…if she goes into labour tonight…* A beep indicated that the shuttle had docked. Lesley opened the bay door and turned in her seat. "It's safe to exit."

Everyone else rose. "Wait here," Jensen said to her. "We shouldn't be more than an hour or so."

"No, come with us," Hall said.

Jensen's lips thinned. "This meeting is strictly need to—"

"Since Commander Thompson knows we're all here, she might as well know why."

Jensen stared at him for a moment, then said, "As you wish."

"*I'd* like to know why we're here," Laura said quietly to Lesley as they trailed after the others. "What's so important that the Chosen Council Heads have been kept in the dark?"

They reached the elevator before Lesley could respond. Nobody spoke as they rode up to Deck 14. The corridors leading to the conferencing area were eerily deserted. When the group strode into Conference Room

3, an officer sitting near the head of the oblong table rose and stood at attention. According to her insignia, she was a lieutenant commander in the Defence Division.

"At ease." Jensen pulled out a chair next to the officer's and sat. Lesley chose a place toward the other end of the table. She was only here as a courtesy, and decided to remain silent and observe. Someone closed the door behind her. When everyone was seated, Jensen gestured toward the officer, who was still standing. "This is Lieutenant Commander Higgs from the *Osprey*. I'll let her fill everyone in. Lieutenant Commander, you have the floor."

Higgs moved to the panel that controlled the large monitor hanging at the front of the room and pressed a button. The monitor flickered to life. An image of an unfamiliar ship drifting in space filled the screen. "Approximately forty-two hours ago, the *Osprey* encountered a Danlion cargo ship on a course to Rymel," Higgs said, her voice quavering slightly. Lesley wasn't sure whether it was the shocking knowledge that a Danlion ship was so close to the planet that was unnerving her, or addressing two admirals and two Chosen Heads. A Danlion ship, so close to Rymel? As alarming as that was, there had to be more. The *Osprey* wouldn't have any trouble destroying a cargo ship, or turning it around. A fighter could do it.

"After we had repeatedly attempted to make contact without success, we boarded the ship. I led the reconnaissance team." The monitor displayed silent images of what Lesley assumed to be the interior of the cargo ship. The cam-wearer, likely Higgs, was moving down a corridor. "At first we wondered whether the vessel was abandoned, but then we picked up a faint life sign. As we moved toward the source of the life sign, we cleared each area. Not far from our destination, we found this."

Gasps filled the air when the two strike team members on the monitor parted.

"They were all dead," Higgs said quietly.

"What killed them?" Hall asked.

"We'll get to that in a moment," Jensen, relishing being in the know, said. "Go on, Lieutenant Commander."

"We continued toward the life sign. We suspected that a Danlion was hiding in one of the rooms near the command centre." Higgs moistened her lips. "I tossed in a neurolock grenade," she said, sounding apologetic. Lesley, who would have done the same, wondered why Higgs regretted the action.

"What's that?" Stevens asked.

"I'm sorry." Higgs turned to him. "A neurolock grenade releases a paralyzing agent into the air."

Stevens grunted.

"We waited for the agent to take effect, then rushed inside." Higgs pointed toward the monitor. "The haze is due to the paralyzing agent."

The image bobbed as Higgs moved toward the life sign. Suddenly another team member was pushing in front of Higgs. The haze began to clear. The team member straightened. Lesley sucked in her breath. Others gasped again.

A baby.

"Did it survive?" Ellis asked.

"Yes. Our team's physician administered the antidote. Neurolock grenades aren't normally lethal, but they're not meant to be used against children, and certainly not against infants. If I'd known..." Higgs lifted her hands, then dropped them.

"It looks small."

"The physicians believe that she was less than a day old when we found her," Higgs said.

"Was it the only survivor?"

"Yes."

"Where is it now?"

"Down the hall, in the infirmary," Jensen said. "And now you all know why we're here, and why this information is of the strictest confidence."

Stevens cleared his throat. "Perhaps I'm being thick, but I don't understand why we're here. The baby's Danlion. We give it back. Case closed."

Lesley murmured agreement along with a couple of others at the table.

"I'm afraid it's not that straightforward," Jensen said.

"Why not?" Hall asked. "Why is the...subject here, rather than on the *Osprey*, or the cargo ship? What is there to discuss? I'm sure the Jessimites would be willing to take the subject from us and hand it over to the Danlions. Does it need medical treatment? Is that why it's here? What can 72's infirmary do for it that the *Osprey*'s can't?"

"It's a girl," Higgs said softly. "She's—"

Jensen cut across her. "The Danlion ship was on a direct course to Rymel. We wondered why, so we put feelers out over the diplomatic channels and reviewed diplomatic communiqués and intelligence, to see if we could find any clues as to why a Danlion cargo ship would make a beeline for our planet."

"There was nothing in the ship's records?" Laura asked.

Jensen shook her head. "We found the following Danlion communiqué, which had been passed on to us by the Jessimites." She read from her comm unit. "'Dangerous political prisoners escaped our custody and are on a cargo ship with the following identifier.'" Jensen looked up. "Which matches the ship adrift in our space." Her head went down again. "'We advise destroying the ship on sight.'"

"Why wasn't the *Osprey* aware of this?" Hall asked.

Jensen's mouth pinched. "We don't take orders from the Danlions, and the suspected location provided in the communiqué is nowhere near our coordinates, and certainly not deep within our space."

"I don't see how this changes anything," Stevens said. "The subject isn't dangerous. We can give it back."

"Oh, but she is dangerous—to them." Jensen clasped her hands on the table. "We asked the Jessimites to share with us everything they have on the Danlion political situation. The Danlions don't select their... rulers. Their leader is born into it. They've had the same ruling family for years now. But we all know how they love to fight each other, and this family is no exception, especially when so much power is at stake. Cousins kill cousins, brothers kill sisters, and vice versa. There have even been cases of patricide and matricide. I doubt any of them lead their people for more than five minutes."

"What does this have to do with anything?" Ellis asked.

"Two branches of this ruling family have been fighting for dominance. The balance of power constantly tips between them. One branch has pulled ahead and was well on its way to eliminating the other branch. It captured the one remaining son and his, uh, mate. They were to be publicly put to death, and the eradication of that branch of the family celebrated." Jensen raised her finger. "But a few supporters broke them out of confinement and escaped on a cargo ship. Those who participated in the plan and remained behind were executed."

"Why would anyone help the losing side, knowing they'd face certain death?" Hall murmured.

"Because they knew the mate was pregnant. Sometimes you run from one battle so you can return another day and claim victory."

"So this baby down the corridor is the last surviving member of that branch of the family?" Laura asked.

"Correct. As long as that child is alive, the Danlion ruler and his heirs can't sit easy."

Stevens' brow furrowed. "The subject isn't in a position to kill anyone."

Jensen curtly shook her head. "They'll kill *her*. The moment she's handed over and the Jessimites turn their backs, she'll be dead."

Several around the table spoke at once. "They wouldn't!"

"That doesn't change anything."

"It's a baby."

"Are you sure? That sounds incredible to me."

Lesley wondered if Hall would have called her in to be his pilot if she hadn't still been in her office, because this was a no-win situation. She wouldn't decide the child's fate, but that didn't matter. She would have preferred to be blissfully unaware of the dilemma. If they sent the child back...at the same time, the child couldn't remain here...

"I said I'd explain the deaths of the Danlions on board the ship," Jensen said loudly, effectively silencing everyone. "They committed suicide. We estimate that they died approximately two hours before we boarded it. They did it for the child."

"That doesn't make any sense," Hall said. "Why would they enter Rymellan territory, set course for the planet, and then kill themselves when they came into range of one of our ships?"

"Because they hoped we wouldn't be as barbaric as their own people are."

Stevens blew out a sigh. "We're not barbarians. At the same time, this baby isn't our responsibility."

"Permission to speak freely," Fisher, Jensen's aide, said.

"Please do. And that goes for everyone," Jensen said, scanning the faces at the table. "I'm sure Admiral Hall would agree."

"I do. But there's only one course of action, here." Hall paused. "As unfortunate as it will be, we should contact the Jessimites and arrange to give the child to them, so they can hand it over to the Danlions."

"Maybe they'll keep it," Stevens said.

Jensen shook her head. "They won't. The Jessimites strive to maintain friendly relations with everyone, and they're much more vulnerable to hostile action from the Danlions than we are. If we hand the child over to them, they'll give her to the Danlions, which is why we haven't informed them of our encounter with the Danlion ship."

"So only Rymellans know about this?" Hall said.

"Yes."

"How many know about the baby?"

"Those of us in this room. A handful of medical personnel, both here and on the *Osprey*. The team that boarded the Danlion ship. Captain Standish and Lieutenant Commander Hollins of the *Osprey*. That's all." Jensen peered at Fisher. "You wanted to say something?"

"Yes, Admiral." Fisher cleared his throat. "I agree with Admiral Hall. We have to hand the baby back to the Danlions. We shouldn't interfere with the culture or politics of other, uh, human civilizations."

"Civilizations?" Jensen snorted. "I'll sum up Danlion civilization for you." She pointed her finger at him. "You're dead. I'm taking over. There, that took all of five seconds."

Fisher's nostrils flared. "Be that as it may, it's not our place to interfere. We wouldn't appreciate it if the Danlions sheltered a Rymellan who'd committed a capital violation."

"That could never happen."

"Hypothetically speaking, we wouldn't appreciate it. In fact, we'd likely consider it an act of war."

"The baby in the infirmary isn't a criminal," Laura said.

"They might not consider someone who's committed a Chosen Violation a criminal."

"In our case, the Rymellan would be at least sixteen years of age and have committed an act that we consider criminal. The baby down the corridor is a child and is completely innocent. She's done nothing.

She hasn't violated whatever rules they have. Her existence threatens someone through no fault of her own." Laura jabbed her finger onto the tabletop. "By not handing her over, we wouldn't be interfering with their culture. We'd merely not be pandering to someone's paranoia."

"If we don't hand her over, what do you propose we do with her, Commodore Finney?" Ellis asked. "She's not Rymellan."

Laura didn't reply. Neither did anyone else. Lesley certainly couldn't answer the question. What *would* they do with her? Nobody would want her. Look at Jayne. Despite being Rymellan, her parents' crimes had tainted her. When she was twelve, Rymellans had petitioned for her execution, and the announcement of the triad had demonstrated that even though she'd followed the Way since her parents' deaths, she was still regarded with suspicion. Two Rymellans had almost killed her... Nobody would trust this baby. Nobody would want this child in their home, around their children, in the classroom, at the Indoctrination Academy. She wasn't Rymellan. She couldn't remain here.

Still, returning her to the Danlions, knowing that they'd kill her... Maybe Rymellans could somehow shelter her without exposing her to other Rymellans. How they'd do that eluded Lesley, but she felt compelled to explore other avenues. "Can we determine her potential strength in the Way?"

Everyone turned to her.

"I know that's usually determined by the Chosen Council when selecting Chosens, but—"

"The fact that they might kill the child is proof of this child's barbaric nature," Hall said.

"No, the commander has a point." Jensen said. "If we were to determine that this child's potential strength in the Way exceeds an acceptable threshold, that might provide us with more options than giving her back."

Stevens' face flushed. "No, it wouldn't! The child isn't Rymellan. Being Rymellan isn't about plucking random humans from the universe and evaluating them. It's tracing one's ancestry through generations of Rymellans who've lived, and sometimes died, for the Way. It's bloodlines, heritage, history...I'm surprised the commander doesn't understand that."

Blood rushed to Lesley's cheeks. Of course she understood it! At the same time, condemning an innocent child to be slaughtered because she wasn't Rymellan didn't sit well.

"I'd like to know the child's potential strength in the Way," Laura said quietly.

"To what end?" Stevens said, his expression pained.

"I agree with the admiral. The more information we have, the better. We're deciding the fate of a human being, a life."

"But a decision implies options. We don't have any. The child isn't Rymellan. We have to hand her over," Ellis said.

Laura gave a curt shake of her head. "It seems to me that we're forgetting the spirit of the Way."

"The Way is for Rymellans. If we protect this child, then why shouldn't we protect everyone who's running from trouble?" Ellis pointed toward the door. "What if an entire ship of Danlions arrived, running from their ridiculous wars? Would we protect them, too?"

"Can we stick to actualities, not hypotheticals?" Jensen said.

"What's the difference between one child and hundreds of Danlions fleeing from certain death?" Stevens pressed.

"The difference is that the child is innocent, real, and in our custody while we sit here going around in circles!" Jensen snapped. "Can you measure her potential strength in the Way, or not?"

"Of course we can. We'll need help, though," Stevens mumbled.

Hall ran his hand through is hair. "How many more?"

Stevens glanced at Ellis. "Two scientists?" She nodded.

"Make sure it's people you trust."

His face tightened. "I trust all my people."

With that settled, Hall turned to Jensen. "Why is the baby here? Why couldn't it have remained on the *Osprey*?"

"It's more difficult to keep a secret on a ship. We had to evacuate here, but everyone assumed it was a drill. The *Osprey* is maintaining its position, waiting for orders."

"I'm willing to allow the Chosen Council to evaluate strength in the Way, but I haven't heard anything that's swayed me from my original position." Hall looked at the Chosen Council Heads. "How long do you need?"

"A full evaluation will take the usual five days."

"I want your results tomorrow."

Stevens' eyes bulged. "You'll get our best guess, then," he sputtered.

"We don't need specifics, just a general idea. I doubt she'll be a border-line case." He nodded to Higgs. "Thank you for your report, Lieutenant Commander. We can take it from here. Dismissed."

Irritation flashed across Jensen's face, but she nodded at Higgs and said, "Good work. I'll update you as necessary."

Higgs returned Jensen's nod and left the room.

Hall rose. "We'll meet at headquarters at 17:00 tomorrow. Stevens and Ellis, be ready for pickup at 16:15. We don't want the baby on this station any longer than it has to be, so I want a decision by the time the meeting adjourns tomorrow night."

Jensen rolled back her chair and stood. "With all due respect, I—"

"This became an Interior matter the moment you brought the baby onto this station. We now have a Danlion a stone's throw away from the planet. I'm going along with the evaluation, but we all know where this is going." He strode toward the door.

Lesley scrambled to her feet. Nobody spoke on the way back to the shuttle bay. The majority were clearly at odds with Jensen. Laura seemed to be leaning toward not giving the baby back. As for herself, she could understand both sides. Rymellans wouldn't welcome interference in their affairs. At the same time, could they really give the baby back without hesitation? Would they go home that night and sleep? On the other hand, nobody had answered the question of what they'd do with her if they didn't return her to the Danlions. Lesley couldn't see a pleasant resolution to the situation.

Fortunately, she wouldn't decide the baby's fate, but she'd know. She'd know. Perhaps she shouldn't aspire to be an admiral, after all.

HER EYES ADJUSTING to the dimness, Lesley climbed the stairs and crept into the bedroom. As she reached for the pyjamas folded on top of the dresser, she glimpsed the still form lying on her side of the bed. Jayne, fully clothed. She must have fallen asleep while keeping Mo company. Lesley carefully pulled the blanket over her and used the connecting door to Jayne's bedroom. She was in the mood to be alone, anyway.

After changing into her pyjamas, she slipped into Jayne's bed and closed her eyes, but the meeting on 72 kept running through her mind. Fortunately, she was out of it. Her only involvement tomorrow would be to fly the Chosen Council Heads to headquarters. But that didn't matter. Next door, the triad's daughter floated in her sanctuary. Her arrival would bring joy and optimism to those who'd welcome her. She'd be loved, cherished, Rymellan. On 72 lay someone else's daughter. In a final act of desperation, her parents had brought her into Rymellan space and hoped that a people alien to them would keep her safe. But she was unwanted, inconvenient, and wouldn't see her first birthday. There was nothing Lesley could do. She wished she didn't know. She hoped she'd be able to look at her own daughter without thinking of that other baby. With a sigh, she groped for her comm unit on the nightstand. *01:12.*

She rolled over and shut her eyes again. Regardless of whether Mo went into labour, Lesley had a long, difficult day ahead of her. Four days remained until Mo's due date, but the baby would be fine if she arrived tomorrow. Lesley might be holding Mo's hand as she delivered their daughter when Hall forced a decision and the Danlion child began her journey to those who hated her. *Sleep!*

When it felt like half an hour had passed, she rolled back toward the nightstand. *01:23.* She fluffed the pillow, lay back and consciously relaxed her muscles, and tried to think about something else. Tomorrow she'd focus on getting through more cases. She'd just fly everyone to headquarters; she wouldn't decide the baby's fate— If she completed the two cases for Overseer Munroc, that should satisfy Blair. After that, she'd prioritize the cases she'd work on when she returned. She'd have forgotten about the Danlion child—how could she forget? What type of person would she be if she forgot? Once the decision was made, was everyone supposed to carry on with their lives as if they hadn't condemned a baby to death?

It was a Danlion child, not a Rymellan. The Danlions would kill a Rymellan without hesitation. Argamon, the Danlions killed anyone without hesitation, or would, if their technology wasn't so far behind everyone else's. They spent all their time and research figuring out how to most efficiently murder each other, and elegance wasn't required. What would they do to the baby? Smother her? Shoot her? Suck her out an airlock?

Lesley threw aside the blanket and sat up. 01:35. She stared at the comm unit's display, watched the time change to 01:36. When it suddenly beeped, it sounded surreal. She shook herself and snatched it up. *Cdre. L. Finney.* "Thompson. I guess I'm not the only one who's not sleeping."

"I haven't even been home," Laura said. "Neither has Jensen. Can you meet with us in her office?"

"Now?"

"Yes, now. We don't have much time. You don't want to hand over the child to the Danlions, do you?"

"I don't want to see her killed, but Ellis had a point. If we don't give her back, what will we do with her?"

"That's what we have to figure out. Are you coming? We could use another mind."

She might as well. At least she'd be able to tell herself that she'd done everything she could. "Yes. I'll be there as soon as I can." She disconnected, changed back into her uniform, and sent Mo and Jayne a quick dispatch, in case she was still out when they woke.

As she cycled to the aviacraft and flew to headquarters, she turned the problem of what to do with the child over in her mind, but nothing new surfaced that would resolve the dilemma. The child wasn't Rymellan. Why had the baby's parents believed that Rymellans wouldn't turn around and do what the Danlions would do? Had they irrationally hoped that a society they knew little about would stay its hand? Had they considered that Rymel was only for Rymellans, that Rymellan society was closed to outsiders? Had they thought about the issue of Rymellans subverting the wishes—some would say rights—of another culture? Had they expected Rymellans to risk war with the Danlions to save a single life? Since they'd all committed suicide, had they suspected that their desperate act wouldn't make a difference in the end? Had they hoped that only their own culture was cruel enough to murder a defenceless child, directly or as an accessory? If it were her child, wouldn't she grasp at the same straws?

Her head still swirling with all the different angles, Lesley strode into Jensen's empty reception area and knocked on her closed office door. Laura swung it open and beckoned her inside.

A weary Jensen looked up from her desk. "Good, you're here."

"Yes, Admiral," Lesley said, confused. She held Jensen in polite professional regard, nodding to her when they passed each other in the corridor. Jensen had grounded Mo, because she hadn't wanted a "threat to the Way" on one of her ships.

"Take off your cloak and sit down." As Lesley complied, Jensen said, "I'd like both of you to speak freely. Understood?"

Sure that Jensen's words were for her benefit and not Laura's, Lesley nodded.

"Good. The situation has grown more dire. Just over an hour ago, we received a message from the Jessimites. The Danlions suspect that their dangerous political prisoners are heading into our space and have warned us to be on the lookout. We don't want Danlions heading our way, looking for a war." She rubbed one of her eyes. "We'd handily beat them, but they'd keep coming back. We'd have to constantly patrol our borders and swat flies."

"So you've decided to give the baby back?" Lesley said, figuring Jensen must have found out about the message after Laura had beeped.

"Meaning that Hall is right. We don't have the luxury of time. Whatever we decide to do, we need to do it quickly."

"What are our options?" Lesley said, not seeing any. "If we don't want to risk war with the Danlions, we have to give the baby back."

"Not necessarily," Laura said. "They don't *know* that we have the child. We could keep it that way. In fact, they don't even know what's happened to the ship and its crew."

"That's true, but we haven't solved the problem of what to do with her, if we don't give her back."

"We'll integrate her into Rymellan society."

"How?" And how freely should she speak? Since a child's life and future was at stake, she decided to be honest. "Jayne—my Chosen," she added, on the minuscule chance that Jensen wouldn't know who she was talking about, "is Rymellan. Her parents were Rymellan. She's never committed a serious violation, but she's considered a threat to the Way, regardless. Two Rymellans almost killed her. When she was twelve, some Rymellans petitioned for her execution. Her own family saw her as an obligation. What chance would this child have? Who would take her? And should we take her? She's not Rymellan."

Laura and Jensen exchanged glances. Lesley wasn't telling them anything new or that they hadn't already discussed. "The primary difference between this child and a Rymellan child is her ancestry." Laura raised her hand before Lesley could protest. "I know, that's a huge difference, but she'd be raised by Rymellans, and she'd attend the Learning and Indoctrination Academies along with Rymellans. She's already lived more than half her life among us, if you don't count the time she spent in her mother's womb."

"That doesn't change the fact that she isn't Rymellan, and that nobody will see her as Rymellan. And that's just the internal problems. What about the diplomatic nightmare?"

"Forget the Danlions for now," Jensen said. "We'll deal with them once we've settled on a course of action."

"But the child isn't Rymellan," Lesley said. "I don't want them to kill her, but what else can we do?"

"If the child was raised by Rymellans, believed that those Rymellans were her parents, and believed that she was Rymellan, would you still believe she isn't Rymellan?" Laura asked.

"I'd *know* she isn't Rymellan, and so would everyone else." Lesley took a moment to quell her rising frustration. "We can't change her ancestry."

"No, but we can raise her to follow the Way. Isn't that the most important part of what it means to be Rymellan?"

Considering that Rymellans no longer viewed those with acceptable ancestry who fell from the Way as Rymellan, perhaps it *was* the most important factor. But there were others.

"All right, she isn't sanctioned by the Chosen Council," Laura admitted, "but the Chosen Council's primary purpose relates to strength in the Way. Rather than leaving it up to nature, it ensures that every child is predisposed to follow the Way. This child might not have the predisposition, but that doesn't mean she can't grow up to be strong in the Way."

"If she were older, it would be too late," Jensen said. "But she's what, three days old? And she's been with us for two of those days."

"Even if we agreed that we could try to raise her to be strong in the Way, many Rymellans would never accept or trust her," Lesley said. "They wouldn't see her as Rymellan. They'd see her as a threat." She, herself, wouldn't be comfortable with a Danlion living with

Rymellans and coming into contact with Rymellan children who were still impressionable.

"Not if they don't know that she isn't Rymellan, or rather, wasn't born to Rymellan parents," Laura said.

Perhaps Laura was tired, because she wasn't making sense. "How would we accomplish that? Where would everyone think she came from? Who would raise her? In the unfortunate circumstance that both parents die, relatives raise the children, but everyone knows who they are and who their parents were. How would we explain this child?"

"Everyone would have to believe that the child had been born to the Rymellan parents."

"How?" Lesley turned to Jensen, who didn't appear perplexed. "You've discussed a plan."

Jensen grimaced. "We did throw around an idea." She leaned forward and clasped her hands on the desktop. "The child would have to go to a family that's due to have a baby—imminently. That family would agree to take the child, raise her as their own, and keep her true origin a secret."

That still didn't make sense. "What about the child they were actually having?"

"They'd have twins. Fraternal twins," Laura said. "A week or so would actually separate them in age, but if anyone were to comment that one looked a little older than the other, they can say that one twin was smaller, or weaker, or something. Most probably wouldn't say anything, and it'll only be a potential problem when the twins are first born. They might look the same age."

"What about the physician who's been monitoring the pregnancy, and those present at the birth?"

"Obviously the circle of knowledge would have to be widened." Jensen unclasped her hands and ticked off several other points on her fingers. "The birth would have to take place in the infirmary, the Chosen Council would record the birth as usual, those involved would vow to keep the secret or be executed, and the child would be raised as a Rymellan."

"The Chosen Council will probably demand that the child be designated a Solitary," Laura added. "Considering it's that, or a probable death within the next week, we'll all agree."

"Fisher is ambitious. When I outline the plan for him and make it clear that I believe it's the best solution to our predicament, I'm certain he'll go along with it," Jensen said. "It's Hall we'll have to convince."

"But you'll still have the problem of finding a family," Lesley said, not saying "we'd" because it was their plan, not hers. "You don't have much time to find—and persuade—a family to..." She trailed off. Jensen was staring intently at her. She could feel Laura's eyes boring into her, too. Both were still. Too still. Holding their breath still.

A family, expecting a child any day now. With horror, Lesley suddenly understood why they'd summoned her here in the middle of the night. "No. You can't ask—no." She vigorously shook her head. "No."

"If we don't find a way to embrace this child, she'll die," Laura said quietly.

Mortified, Lesley struggled to organize the myriad of thoughts running through her mind. "Don't do this to me. The child isn't my responsibility. It's not fair to reduce it to 'if you don't take the child, you've killed her.' We're not the only Rymellan family expecting a child."

Jensen pointed at her. "You're the only one with someone who already knows about the situation."

It took all her self-control not to say something she'd regret to the admiral who'd grounded Mo and declared her other Chosen a threat to the Way. Was that why Jensen wanted the triad to take the child? To limit those she viewed as weak in the Way to one family?

"I'd take her, if I could," Laura said.

"Would you?" Lesley studied Laura's face. "Do you both understand what you're asking me—us—to do? Bring a Danlion child into our home. Lie to our families, our daughters, our friends. For a lifetime. Not for a few hours, or days, or weeks. A lifetime."

"It'll become second nature for you to view her as your daughter."

"I don't want it to become second nature!" Frustration made it difficult for Lesley to get her words out. "It doesn't—she's not...I can't believe you're asking me to do this."

Laura frowned. "Do you want this child to die?"

"No, of course I don't! Just because she's not Rymellan doesn't mean I'm comfortable with handing her over to a bunch of barbarians who will turn around and kill her. But there has to be another way to save her."

"The only way to save her is to not give her back," Laura said evenly.

"Unless we want her to be treated ten times worse than Jayne was, we have to hide her ancestry."

"We haven't told anyone we're having twins, because we're not. Don't you think they'll wonder?"

"You can say that the survival of one twin was in doubt, so you decided not to tell anyone about her."

"They might not believe me."

"They'll believe you," Jensen said. "If someone told you that they didn't want to tell everyone they were expecting twins because one might not survive, would you instantly think that one of the twins isn't their biological child? Nobody is going to suspect that your Chosen didn't give birth to her. Nobody is going to question where the child came from."

"In fact, to do so would be a capital violation," Laura said.

"What about medical records? Ultrasounds? They'll clearly show that we weren't having twins."

"We can either seal the records, or alter them." Jensen looked at Laura.

"Alter, I think," Laura said. "Sealing them would only raise questions if anyone ever wants to view them. But why would they? Once your daughters are born healthy and happy, nobody will have a reason to look at those records. If they do, they'll see that you were expecting twins. Your physician will agree to write up a medical history for the other twin."

Panic drove Lesley to her feet. She wandered toward the door. To give herself a chance to breathe, she turned to face it and tried to calm her conflicting emotions. Sympathy battled indignation. Compassion warred with fear. She wanted to save the child, but why them? Why did they have to take the child? It wasn't fair. If she refused to consider the possibility of bringing the Danlion up as her own, she'd feel as if she'd killed the child herself. But what they were asking of her...this could destroy her family.

She couldn't run from the decision forever. She forced herself to turn around. Laura and Jensen gazed at her. She could see the question in their eyes, but her throat felt paralyzed.

Jensen squared her shoulders. "As someone who's about to have a daughter yourself, you can appreciate—"

Blood pounded in Lesley's ears. "I already *know* that I'll think about the Danlion child when mine arrives. I already *know* that my child's birth—maybe her entire life—will always be linked in my mind with this child. I was lying awake thinking about that when you beeped me. Admiral." Argamon, she needed to get herself under control. How could a well-intended, compassionate request be so terrible? But it was! And so were the consequences, no matter what she decided. Had they understood that by speaking the request they were springing a trap? Despite the protests and doubts shrieking through her mind, she couldn't leave this office knowing that she'd condemned a child to death. Turning her back would leave her with a life tinged with sorrow—and shame. "I can't decide this alone," she said, hardly recognizing her tremulous and soft voice.

"Of course not. You have to discuss it with your Chosens," Jensen said.

Yes, she was going to share this horrible burden with them. Would they thank her? To protect them, perhaps she should say no; after all, she should think of them more than the Danlion child. But it was too late. If she made the decision without them, she'd have to live with it for the rest of her life, and so would they, except they wouldn't understand why their Chosen sometimes had trouble sleeping, and why a shadow always hung over the birthday celebrations of their oldest daughter— perhaps all their daughters. She needed to tell them. That made her feel weak and selfish, but it was the truth. However... "Yes, I do. I have a request in return."

"What do you want?" Laura asked.

Good, she wanted to talk to Laura. She was trying not to think about what Jensen thought of Jayne, who wasn't good enough to board a Defence ship, but was apparently strong enough in the Way to bring up a Danlion as a Rymellan. "Actually, I have two requests. I want to tell my parents."

"No," Laura and Jensen said in unison.

Lesley stifled the protest that sprang to her lips, sat down, and took a moment to calm herself. "You're asking me to give this child the Thompson name. I can't do that without talking to my parents. It's bad enough that I'm going to have to lie to my sister and brother, my cousins, grandparents, aunts, uncles...and that's just my family. I can't look my mama in the eye and lie to her about this."

Laura's expression didn't change. "What's your other request?"

"I want you to lift your grounding of my Chosen," Lesley said, turning to Jensen. "I'm not saying that she wants to go on a tour. We might never go on a tour. She seems to enjoy working with Commander Ross on 72. But if she ever decides that she wants to go on a tour, that would mean you'd have my other Chosen and a Danlion on one of your ships."

"I'd have your other Chosen and a *Rymellan* on one of my ships," Jensen snapped. "If this is going to work, you'll have to stop thinking of the child as Danlion." She leaned back in her chair and scowled. "Fine. I always intended to lift the grounding once the triad began to," she waved her hand around, "prove itself."

Lesley didn't believe that for a second. "What about my parents?"

"If you bring them into this, they'll have to carry the same burden you'll carry," Laura pointed out. "They'll have to tell the same lie. Everyone who knows about the true origin of the child will sign an agreement that will make it a capital violation under Article 522 to even hint that the child isn't Rymellan. Are you sure you want to tell them?"

"I want the option to tell them. Perhaps after speaking to Mo and Jayne, I'll change my mind. But right now, I don't feel that I can lie to them about this. I can't present the child to them as their granddaughter."

"You're her commanding officer, and the Thompsons live in your sector," Jensen said to Laura. "Use your judgment. You might be the one who has to clean up the mess."

Only Lesley could see Laura roll her eyes. "If you must tell them, go ahead. But let me know what you intend to do by 06:00. We won't send them the agreements until we've heard from you."

"Understood."

"Given how much time we don't have, the admiral and I will assume that you'll agree to take the child. We'll start working out the logistics of how to stage a rebirth."

"You've been up all night."

Laura nodded wearily. "I'll grab a nap at some point."

"Go speak to your Chosens, "Jensen barked. "Get them out of bed. We don't have much time."

Lesley nodded and grabbed her cloak. Military headquarters never slept, and it wasn't unusual to see a commander striding through the corridors at any hour. But nobody would ever suspect what had just taken place behind Jensen's closed door. Lesley could hardly believe it herself. Laura and Jensen were right. If they weren't going to return the child to the Danlions, she would live as an outcast and constantly under suspicion—unless their plan succeeded. Lesley understood why she, Mo, and Jayne were the ideal choice in Jensen and Laura's eyes. She wanted the child to survive, but a part of her hoped that Mo or Jayne would refuse to take her. She pulled out her comm unit to beep them.

DILEMMA

Yawning, Mo lowered herself into a kitchen chair and smiled gratefully when Jayne set a mug of tziva in front of her. "I wonder if it has anything to do with the evacuation on 72," she said, rubbing her swollen belly.

Jayne sat opposite her and threw her a quizzical look.

"It seems coincidental that on the same day there's an evacuation, Les doesn't come home, and now she wants to talk to us in the middle of the night."

"She did come home. Then she went out again. Didn't you read her dispatch? She ate the last piece of cake."

"Yeah, I read it. I was, uh..." Being dramatic. "She didn't say anything about the cake in her dispatch."

Jayne jerked her thumb over her shoulder. "I noticed the empty plate in the dishwasher."

Mo waggled her eyebrows. "How did you know I didn't eat the last piece of cake?"

Jayne's eyes narrowed. "If it was you, the plate would have been on the counter." She blew on her tziva. "What do you think she wants to talk to us about?"

"She's been working pretty hard. Hopefully she's not coming home to tell us that she's taking one day off for the birth and then going back on duty. Because if she says that, I'm going to beep Laura, or Blair, or whoever else thinks it's okay to—"

The front door thumped shut. Mo quickly picked up her tziva and tried to appear casual. Yep, she and Jayne always hung out in the kitchen at flaming 04:00.

Les strode in and heaved a sigh. Still in her cloak, she pulled out a chair, sank into it, and rubbed her eyes. She looked terrible.

"What's going on?" Mo said. "Does it have anything to do with the evacuation on 72?" Her worry that Les would go back on duty the day after the birth fled her mind. It had been a stupid thought, anyway. Les wouldn't wake them up for that.

"Do you want tziva?" Jayne asked.

"No." Les looked at Jayne, then met Mo's eyes. She swallowed. "Yes, it's related to the evacuation. Before I tell you anything, you have to know that you'll be required to sign a document that will make it a capital violation to ever tell anyone about this conversation or anything related to it. We should receive the documents within the next hour."

Mo gripped her mug and exchanged a glance with Jayne. They were both wide awake now. "Do we have a choice?"

"No. I have to talk to you about this."

Jayne pushed her mug aside. "We won't tell anyone."

"It started a couple of days ago, on the *Osprey*." Les paused. "They ran across a Danlion cargo ship."

Mo listened as Les described the boarding operation, the roomful of deceased Danlions, the baby they'd discovered that now lay in 72's infirmary, and what would likely happen if that baby was returned to its people.

"So we didn't make a decision during the meeting on 72, but the wind seemed to be blowing in the direction of giving the child back."

Mo forgave her for lying about working late; she'd had to obey Hall. "Why did you go out again? You said Hall wants you to pick up the Chosen Heads, and that's it. You won't be involved in making the final decision."

"I'm getting to that," Les said. "Laura and Jensen didn't go home. They've been wracking their brains for a way to keep the child without making her an outcast for the rest of her life. Laura asked me to join them. I thought they wanted me to brainstorm with them, but…"

Mo leaned forward. "But…"

"They already had a plan. They want to hide the baby's origin by having a Rymellan family take her as if she's their own."

"And how do they propose to do that?" Mo asked.

Les moistened her lips. "They want us to take her."

Mo's mind did a double-take. She searched for a sign that Les was joking or being sarcastic. Of course, she wasn't—why would she—she wouldn't. "Us." She gestured at Jayne, then at Les, then at herself. "They want us to take the baby."

"Yes."

"Are they out of their flaming minds?" Mo shrieked. "Even if the baby wasn't a flaming alien, we're about to have our own daughter!"

"That's the point," Les said levelly. "You'd have twins. Everyone would assume she's ours, that she's Rymellan."

Mo gaped. "Are you serious? That's the plan they've come up with? What about my physician? What about everyone at the Reproductive Technology Centre? What about the fact that we're talking about a Danlion here? They seriously think we would consider this? Why are you even talking to us about it?"

"Don't worry about anyone who knows that you're not expecting twins. Laura and Jensen will handle that."

Did Les want them to do this? Mo studied Les's face but couldn't tell. "You're avoiding the basic problem, Les. Okay, they ordered you to talk to us. You've talked to us. Tell them to go back to the drawing board."

"So you don't think we should do it," Les said.

"Look, I understand the position this child is in, but we didn't put her there. It won't be our fault if the Danlions...if they..." Kill her? *Argamon.* "Are you sure they'll, uh, that they won't want her?"

"We have to take her," Jayne said softly.

Mo pulled her eyes away from Les's face and gazed across the table at Jayne. "Why?"

"If we take her, she lives. If we don't, she dies."

"But why us?"

"I asked the same thing," Les said. "We fit what they're looking for and I already know about the situation." Her forehead puckered. "It doesn't hurt that I'm a commander in Interior and you're military, too."

Mo slowly exhaled. "Do you want to do this?" she asked Les.

"As Jayne said, if we don't—"

"Do you *want* to do this?" Mo roared.

Les lifted her hands, then dropped them to her lap. "I don't know. I understand the consequences if we don't." She glanced at Jayne. "But we'd be taking a Danlion child under our roof and pretending she's Rymellan."

"She would be Rymellan, wouldn't she?" Jayne said.

"You sound like Laura."

Laura? Flaming Laura? For Les's sake, Mo had forgiven Laura for sticking her nose into their lives and encouraging them to separate, but here she was, stirring everything up for them again. "Laura would consider the child Rymellan?"

"We'd bring her up to follow the Way. She'd go to the Indoctrination Academy. She'd be a Solitary."

Well, that went without saying.

"Laura's an expert on the history of the Chosen Tradition. The child won't have Rymellan ancestry, but Laura believes that following the Way is paramount when it comes to defining what it means to be Rymellan."

Mo studied Les's face again. "What do you think?"

"That does seem to be the point."

"But?"

"I'm not sure." Les shrugged apologetically. "I don't know."

"Are we willing to throw an innocent child's life away because of her bloodlines?" Jayne asked.

"Bloodlines are important!" Mo snapped as Les straightened in her chair.

"I know that. But..." Jayne turned to Les. "What about the spirit of the Way? The Way as a whole? It feels wrong to conclude that handing a baby over to be murdered is following the Way. I—I don't think that's what the founders of the Way had in mind. Maybe that's what..." Jayne cleared her throat. "Maybe that's what Laura's trying to say."

Mo looked from Jayne to Les, to Jayne, to Les. The silence stretched out. "You may have a point," Les finally conceded. "At the same time, I feel trapped. We've been put into a position in which they want us to feel responsible for something we're not responsible for."

"That's because it's true. That's exactly what's going on," Mo said.

"They're trying to save her." Jayne sat on her hands. "Regardless of how we came into the conversation, it's the reality now. We take her, or she's—she won't survive."

"And that's only if the others will go along with the plan," Les said.

Jayne nodded. "If they don't, that'll be on their consciences, not ours."

Mo wrapped a protective arm around her daughter. If anyone tried to hurt her... Les had said the Danlion's parents had sacrificed themselves for their child. That was a good sign, right? Her parents had a shred of decency. If the triad ever had to entrust their daughter's life to strangers, they wouldn't want those strangers to turn their backs. Mo looked down at her abdomen. "So what are we saying here?"

"There's still a lot that can go wrong, so we don't have to make a decision right this minute. Laura and Jensen are working on the assumption that we'll take the child, so they're working out the logistics. I'd like to hear what the Chosen Council says about the child's potential strength in the Way before we make a final decision." Les paused. "And I want to talk to my parents."

Mo drew back. "Why?"

"Because we'd be giving her their name. Because I don't want to have to lie to them."

"What about my papa?"

"I didn't ask about him."

Mo snorted. "Great. Thanks a lot."

"She won't have your name," Les snapped. "If the worst happens and she ends up at an execution site, it'll be Thompson that goes on the Wall, not Middleton. We won't be able to turn around and say to everyone, 'Well, she wasn't really a Thompson.'"

"Execution site?" Jayne cried. "Try not to be so pessimistic."

"I have to consider all the angles."

Jayne drew breath, then paused and said, "Okay."

"I don't want to worry Papa right now, anyway. He's happy, you know?" Mo hadn't been too thrilled when Peggy had moved into the family home a couple of months ago, but they'd been together for a while and she made him happy. That was all that mattered. "Plus, we don't know if we're taking her, right? You said you want more information."

Les nodded. "The first step was to find out if either of you are vehemently opposed to the idea. If you are, the time to speak up is now." She looked from one to the other.

Mo gulped. Jayne obviously wasn't opposed to the idea. As for herself... "I want to think about it."

"You don't have much time."

"I know. But I want it to sink in a little bit. You're going to see your parents, anyway."

"Can I go with you?" Jayne asked.

Les's brow furrowed. "You sure you want to go?"

"Yes, I am."

"You sure you don't want to go?" Les said to Mo.

"You don't want me waddling along with you, slowing you down, and there's no way I'm getting on a bike. And I want some time on my own to think about it." Part of her wanted to be there to see what Adelaide and Alan would say, though, and whether Jayne would make a case for taking the child—because Mo predicted a big fat no from both of them. If Adelaide could have scuttled the triad, she would have. But she hadn't had a choice. This time, Les would hand her the choice, and the answer would be no. Right now, Mo didn't know whether she'd support or oppose Adelaide, so she'd stay here and figure out where she stood. Let Jayne go stick her neck out.

Les pushed back her chair. "Perhaps you should stay with Mo," she said when Jayne did the same.

"Les, I'll be fine. If I go into labour, I can use a comm unit." Wait. "I guess if I do go into labour, that'll ruin the plan, right?"

They both stared at her.

Mo chuckled. "I'd say that I won't, but it'll be up to her." She rubbed her belly again. "You better go."

Given the urgency of the matter, they both pecked her on the cheek and strode from the kitchen. Mo listened as Jayne pulled on her cloak. The front door thumped shut. She sighed, rested her arms on the table, lay her head down, and tried to imagine what it would be like to accept the Danlion baby as her own.

The kitchen clock ticked away. Soon the sun would rise. A new day was arriving—one that might bring the birth of her daughter, and one that would decide whether a perfectly healthy baby girl on 72 would live or die.

JAYNE FLICKED ON the flashlight she'd taken from the hall closet and illuminated the path that led to the main Thompson home. "I wonder if we'll need this on the way back."

"I guess it depends on how long the conversation is," Lesley said.

Adelaide and Alan could say no and refuse to discuss it further, and Jayne would have to find the courage to press them. If it wasn't a child's life hanging in the balance, she wouldn't risk upsetting her Chosen parents, but—

"You didn't hesitate to say let's take the child." Lesley peered at her. "Why? Why are you so eager to bring an alien child into our home?" She sounded more curious than angry.

Jayne bit back the question, "Why are you considering sending the child back to be murdered?" Lesley didn't want that; she'd meant it when she'd said that she was considering all the angles. How to best serve the Way, how much of a threat the child would pose to the family, the Thompson name, their other children... Lesley had to weigh all that. Jayne swallowed. Maybe she should too, but as she'd listened to Lesley explain the situation, the Incident had come hurtling back. "This is a child nobody wants," she said quietly. "I know what it feels like to be that child. I was the child nobody wanted, the one some Rymellans wanted to execute." Carol had saved her. How could she not try to save this child? "She's a baby. She doesn't have Rymellan ancestry, but that doesn't mean she can't follow the Way."

"It might be more difficult for her."

"And it might not be."

"It'll mean having two daughters in a matter of days."

"We'll manage." Jayne gave Lesley a small smile. "At least we're a triad."

Lesley's face remained sombre. "Lying to everyone will be difficult. What if one of them suspects?"

"They won't. Why would they even think that one of our daughters isn't biologically yours?" Jayne winced at the frustration in her voice, but she couldn't help it. If Lesley sent the child back to the Danlions, she wasn't the woman Jayne thought she was. She wasn't upset with Lesley for having doubts, but some of her concerns were trivial.

"I forgot to ask whether her hair and eye colour will make sense."

"I'm sure Laura and the admiral checked that before they spoke to you about their plan." Jayne quietly sighed, then stopped and aimed the flashlight in Lesley's direction. "What's the real issue?"

Lesley blinked at her. "What do you mean?"

"You keep coming up with reasons for why we can't take the child." Jayne raised her free hand. "I know you have concerns and doubts. I'm not saying I don't. But you usually take the time to think things through."

"We don't have time."

No, that wasn't it. Lesley should be silently walking next to her, trying to figure out the ideal solution that would please all sides—not raising every possible detail that could go wrong, no matter how improbable. "What's really bothering you? What are you worried about?"

Lesley took her time answering. "There are so many ways the plan can fall apart. Someone will talk."

Jayne shook her head. "No. Interior will silence anyone who says a word about it. The person would have no proof. They'd be painted as a delusional liar and executed. You know that, and so will they." Time to take another tack. She wished she could be gentler, but Lesley was right about time running out. "Why are we going to talk to your parents? Are you hoping they'll say no, so *you* can say no without feeling guilty?" Lesley's jaw tightened, but Jayne kept going. "Maybe we shouldn't take her, because I don't want her to feel the way I felt. Like someone's duty, an obligation, a trial to endure until she turns old enough that we can find her an apartment, wash our hands of her, and tell ourselves she should be grateful that we'd cared for her." She paused to draw a breath, then softened her voice. "If we take her, we'll have to treat her as our own, to the point that if anyone ever found out, they'd be flabbergasted, because we love her and treat her as we do all our daughters."

Lesley grimaced. "I don't know if I can do that."

"What?"

She hesitated. "Love her."

Jayne blinked back tears of relief. The fear compelling her to push Lesley—the fear that she'd misjudged her Chosen, that her Chosen was cold-hearted and would turn her back on the baby...love eclipsed it. Because she deeply loved Lesley, and the woman she loved wouldn't turn over the child to those who'd harm her. Lesley was afraid! "Why don't you think you can love her? Is it because you won't see her as Rymellan?"

"No. I see what Laura is saying. If she was older...but she's not."

"Then why?"

Lesley's forehead creased. "She won't be my biological child, but she'll have my name."

"This won't happen, but if Mo and I had a child, the same would apply."

"That would be different. I know you'll love our child, but that's because she's our," Lesley made an embracing motion, "child. You love us, and you've been there right from the beginning. The same would be true for me if you and Mo had a child."

"All right, I agree that it's different, but that doesn't mean we can't love this other baby. We're the only parents she'll know, and we'll only have missed the first few days of her life."

"Our children...they'll be strong in the Way."

"We'll bring her up to be strong in the Way."

"But she doesn't have Rymellan ancestry. What if we love her, and then she grows up and," Lesley's voice dropped, "ends up at an execution site? I don't know if I can take that risk, to raise her and take care of her and potentially watch her ignore everything we've taught her."

Jayne pressed her hand to her chest. "If we take her, we'll all be taking that risk. You won't be doing it alone. All we can do is raise her as best we can. There are never any guarantees. I know that." When Lesley gently pulled Jayne's hand away from her chest and kissed it, Jayne fought a fresh set of tears.

"I know you do."

Jayne squeezed Lesley's hand and held onto it. "Have you seen the baby?"

"No."

So they'd all sat in a room discussing the child's fate while she lay in the infirmary a short walk away, and none of them had bothered to go see her? Pragmatism displaced Jayne's dismay. She could understand why they couldn't allow emotion to cloud their judgment—if that was the reason behind it. Maybe some of them suspected that once they'd laid eyes on her, they could no longer contemplate handing her back to the Danlions.

Lesley was studying her. "If you think I would have fallen in love with her on sight, I doubt that would have happened."

No, but it would have driven home the point that they were discussing a baby—a real, live, helpless baby. Something Lesley's parents could easily ignore. "Do you really think it's a good idea to talk to your parents?"

"I don't want to lie to them."

"Then why make them have to lie to everyone else? Not that they'll agree with the plan. You know they'll say no."

"I don't—"

"Yes, you do." Jayne braced herself. "Are you sure you're not asking them to put the responsibility of deciding onto them?"

Lesley shrugged and shook her head. "I don't know."

Jayne gave her a point for honesty. "If we take her, she'll have the best chance if they don't know."

Lesley's face darkened. "Why? What do you think they'll do?"

"Nothing intentional. But the fewer people who know, the more everyone will treat her the same. If your parents don't know, they won't treat her any differently. They won't have to worry about slipping up. They won't have to lie to everyone." She quickly reconsidered her words. "Not that we'll have to keep lying to everyone. We'll have to lie about her birth, but after that, she *will* be our daughter. She *will* be their grand-daughter, or niece."

"Or sister." Lesley said pointedly. "They'll think they're twins."

"Even more reason to keep it to the three of us. Do we really want the situation where your parents are favouring one over the other? Children notice things like that." And so would others. "Unless we're going to let your parents decide for us, telling them could be a huge mistake. If they're opposed to the plan, going ahead with it will cause a rift. They might refuse to see any of their granddaughters because they don't want to see...that one. On the other hand, if they agree to it, we'll be asking them to keep this secret for the rest of their lives. This is our decision, yours, mine, and Mo's. I think it would be better if we didn't bring them into it." She didn't backtrack when Lesley let go of her hand and looked past her. *Let her think it over.*

The minutes stretched out. Jayne wanted to check her comm unit, but she didn't want to rush Lesley. Fortunately it was a warm night, or standing here would make her shiver.

"Perhaps you're right," Lesley finally said. "I hate the thought of lying to everyone, so why make them do it? Your other point is valid, too. Once we've told them, there would be consequences if we were to ignore their wishes. Let's go back to Mo."

"Are you sure?"

"Yes."

Lesley looked exhausted. Jayne reached for her and pulled her close.

"They're asking a lot from us." She closed her eyes when Lesley's arms tightened around her.

"They don't have much choice, not if they want to save the baby." Lesley's breath tickled Jayne's ear. "So you think I'll be able to love her."

Jayne brushed Lesley's cheek with her lips. "I *know* you'll be able to love her." *Because you love me.*

LESLEY YAWNED INTO her hand and swung open the door to Jensen's reception area.

"You can go right in," the receptionist said.

"Thank you." She knocked on Jensen's closed office door, then opened it at the muffled invitation. When two bleary-eyed faces peered at her, Lesley wondered if Laura and Jensen had managed to snatch any sleep.

"So?" Jensen said.

Lesley remained standing. "None of us are opposed to the idea, but I'd like to hear what the Chosen Heads have to say about the baby's potential strength in the Way. My Chosens will trust me to make a decision after that." Mo was torn. Similar to Lesley, her doubts were giving her pause, but her fear that the alternative would haunt her for the rest of her life had won out. "Have you spoken to anyone else about the plan?"

"We've been very busy," Laura said. "Hall is thinking about it. Fisher supports the plan. We're going to tell Stevens and Ellis in the meeting."

"They'll initially oppose the idea." Jensen wearily shrugged. "But I think we'll be able to talk them around."

"We've also arranged everything at the infirmary and put a plan into place to transport the child."

"We received the signed agreements from you and your Chosens," Jensen said. "You made the right decision about not telling your parents."

Lesley wanted to smile. "Jayne talked me out of it."

"I see." Jensen cleared her throat.

"What's the next step?"

"I'm going home to get some sleep," Jensen said.

"I'll do the same." Laura jutted her chin toward Lesley. "You go about your business. Work on your cases. It's a normal day."

"Understood." Lesley nodded to Jensen and turned to leave.

"I'll walk out with you," Laura said. She didn't speak again until they'd left Jensen's reception area. Then she said, "Why don't you walk with me to the train station?"

"Do you want me to fly you home?"

"No. You're already in late. Let's not invite questions."

"Will Hall go along with it?" Lesley asked, when they were strolling down the path that led to the station.

Laura's lips compressed into a thin line. "We're all choosing between an unpalatable option and an uncomfortable one. Some of us are more uncomfortable than others, but none of us wants to see the child murdered." She turned to Lesley. "I know Jensen and I put you into a terrible position, but there's no other alternative. We need a Rymellan family in your situation to take her. Since you already knew, you were the obvious choice." She ran a hand through her hair. "Don't take that to mean you were convenient. If I didn't know that the three of you were so strong in the Way, I wouldn't have suggested it as a possibility."

Lesley wasn't surprised that Laura had raised the idea. The triad wouldn't have been Jensen's first choice. "Did you mean it when you said you'd take her, if you could?"

"Yes, I did," Laura said firmly. "And I'll help with...the twins, as much as I can, if you'll let me." Her voice dropped. "You won't be the only ones having to lie to everyone."

"That's true, and of course we'll appreciate any help we can get. Having twins has come as a bit of a shock to all of us." She chuckled along with Laura, though she wondered whether Laura wanted to help because she felt guilty about thrusting the baby on the triad, or to be super-vigilant and keep her eye on a potential threat. With Laura, Lesley could never quite tell, but she'd take any support she could get, and so would Mo and Jayne—if they took the baby. She hadn't made a firm decision yet. "Has everyone signed the agreements?"

"The key players have—Mo's physician, the assistants at the Reproductive Technology Centre, anyone who'll be involved at the infirmary..."

Yes, if they took the child, Mo would deliver their daughter in the infirmary, not at home. That would tip off the families that the physician expected complications during the birth, further bolstering the sickly twin story. "We haven't agreed to take her yet," she reminded Laura, who seemed to consider it a foregone conclusion.

"I know, but we don't know how much time we'll have if you do agree. Mo isn't due for a few days, but realistically, the baby could come anytime now. Plus, if you agree to take her, we'll want to move her to the infirmary as soon as possible." She gave Lesley a sidelong glance. "That way it'll be more difficult for them to change their minds."

Lesley knew she meant Hall and any others who had misgivings about the plan, though Lesley would include herself in that group, too. She'd be surprised if Laura and Jensen didn't have doubts. As Laura had said, it wasn't a matter of whether one was uncomfortable with the idea, but to what degree. "How did everyone react when they heard?"

"We pulled them out of bed, had them sign the agreement, then told them what might happen. They understood that we weren't asking them for their opinion. All they have to do is keep their mouths shut."

True. They didn't have to bring a Danlion into their home and raise her. "You know, the ones saying that we wouldn't like it if the Danlions refused to hand over a Rymellan who'd committed a violation had a good point. Hypothetically speaking," she quickly added, to head off Laura's reply that a Rymellan wouldn't stand a chance of getting away and making it out of Rymellan space.

"I agree, we wouldn't like it. Fisher was right. We'd go to war over it."

"Why?" Lesley held up her hand. "Hear me out. Wouldn't a Rymellan leaving our space lead to the same result as executing them? They'd no longer be Rymellan, and they wouldn't be here to corrupt the Way or others any further. I'm not saying I'd be happy about it. I'd prefer to see them punished. But they'd be gone, and they'd never be allowed to return."

Laura's face brightened, and her voice took on a new vigour. "The founders of the Way considered exile when they first drafted the Law and the Chosen Tradition. But they concluded that the risk was too high. Revenge, open wounds...better to kill the disease, than let it fester. Exiled Rymellans could form colonies, spread lies, rally others against us. Not only that, depending on who they were, they might have sensitive knowledge of our operations and technology." She peered at Lesley. "And why inflict our failures on other cultures? We contain our problems. We clean up our messes."

"That's what the Danlions want to do, I suppose," Lesley said. "The baby is a loose end."

"They don't have to kill her to contain the situation. The ruling family could raise her as its own. But no, she must be eliminated." Laura shook her head.

"As long as she's alive and Danlions know who she is, she could serve as a rallying point for those loyal to her family."

"We didn't kill rallying points when the advocates for the Way won the War of Social Reform."

At the Learning Academy, Lesley had received an overview of the last civil war Rymellans had fought. She didn't know the details. "Perhaps I should have taken the Ancient History course when I was at the Military Academy."

Laura quirked a brow. "Maybe you should have, especially given your family's heritage. I could have advised it, but I wanted you prepared for an eventual move to Interior. That didn't leave much room for electives." She stopped outside the station's entrance. "I'm surprised your mama didn't teach you anything about it."

"She did. But she limited herself to our family's role in the war and its aftermath. If we weren't directly involved in something, she left it out."

"Trust your mama," Laura murmured. "Do you think she opposed you going into the military because of the losses your family suffered?"

"I don't think so." Mama had told her the story about how if the one Thompson who'd survived hadn't had children, there wouldn't be a Thompson family, but it had happened so long ago. Plus, the Thompsons who'd fought and died hadn't belonged to the military. Neighbour had taken up arms against neighbour, and the military, which would have roughly corresponded to today's Defence Division because there hadn't been an Interior until the establishment of the Way, had split. Officer had battled and killed officer. It was amazing that any Rymellans had survived. "I think she was disappointed that I wasn't following in her and Papa's footsteps, though I guess I sort of ended up doing so, after all."

Laura nodded. "And you do it well." She pulled open the station's glass door. "I'll see you later. If any problems crop up regarding our, uh, situation, don't hesitate to beep me and wake me up."

"I won't." She watched Laura enter the station, then turned and strode back to headquarters, looking more relaxed than she felt. The Thompsons had given so much for the Way. Now the family, *her* family, was being asked to perform yet another service, one that could ultimately harm the Way and sully the Thompson name.

LESLEY CHECKED THE time on her comm station, reluctantly rolled back her chair, and turned off the monitor. A couple of hours ago, she'd strolled outside and met with Mo and Jayne to make sure neither had changed their mind—not that their minds were firmly made up. It was absurd to be rushed into a decision of this magnitude, to have only mere hours to make a choice that would have lifelong consequences. They needed more time to mull over the possible outcomes, to imagine the reality of lying to their families and friends, to consider the impact on their other daughters and themselves. As it was, nobody wanted to say no, but nobody wanted to say yes—not decisively.

Since the result of saying no would be violent, stark, and horrible, everyone was mumbling, "All right, perhaps, if we must." Jayne seemed to be the most decided, but she'd admitted that she had doubts. Mo felt they had no choice if they wanted to live with themselves, and Lesley had accepted the responsibility of making the decision, of sitting in a stuffy room and pronouncing whether a Danlion infant would live or die. If she knew for certain that the Danlions wouldn't kill the child, it would be a no, and Mo, especially, would agree with her. Should they bring the child into a family that wasn't sure it wanted her? Would a swift death be more compassionate? Should Lesley hope that those at the meeting ultimately rejected the plan, or would that be cowardly?

As she escorted the Chosen Council Heads to the conference room an hour later, fatigue wasn't responsible for her heavy heart and stiff gait. She wasn't nervous, just...perhaps this was how one felt as they were escorted to an execution site. There was no escape, no way to bow out until one felt up to it.

Only Jensen was missing when Lesley strode into the room, nodded to everyone, and sat next to Laura. Nobody questioned her presence. Hall had told her she wouldn't be required at the follow-up meeting after they'd dropped off the Chosen Council Heads the previous evening, and everyone else had since been briefed about her potential role

in saving the Danlion child. Jensen would introduce the plan, Laura
and Fisher would support her, and Lesley would do her best to appear
as if the Thompson triad would be delighted to raise the Danlion child,
provided nobody objected, and Stevens and Ellis didn't inform them
that the child had more of a chance of spontaneously morphing into
an elephant than she did of following the Way.

Jensen marched into the room and quickly seized control of the
meeting. "Good to see everyone," she said, settling into her chair. "Since
our meeting yesterday, several of us have drawn up an action plan to
save the Danlion child's life." She launched into a description of the
plan; Laura threw in the odd word. Lesley managed to maintain a neu-
tral expression until Jensen revealed that the Thompson triad, whose
present circumstances made them the ideal choice to take the baby,
were amenable to the idea.

"I don't care. It's not happening," Stevens thundered, as Lesley self-
consciously scratched her nose.

Jensen's brows drew together. "You won't consider saving this child's
life?"

"Stop framing me as a murderer because I don't want a Danlion mix-
ing with Rymellans," Stevens snapped. "You asked us to perform a quick
analysis of the child. We've done so." He tapped the sheet of paper in
front of him. "The results are poor."

Lesley's heart sank. While everyone digested his news, Ellis briefly
met each person's eyes, then gazed at Jensen. "We would never consider Joining Rymellans together who'd produce offspring with these
disappointing numbers. And you want to bring this child to the planet?"

"How accurate are the results?" Hall asked.

"As accurate as they can be, given that we know next to nothing
about the parents, especially the mother. We have autopsy results and
the genetic material from both parents, but that's simply not enough
to give us the complete picture. We told you we'd do our best, given
the time frame and what we have to work with. Based on these results,
I don't see any option except to send the Danlion back to her people."

A chair rolled back. Laura stood. Lesley glanced up at her determined face.

"If you would allow me, Chosen Council Heads, to speak my mind,

I'd like to remind everyone of our history. Most of those who fought for and established the Way would have failed your test. You know as well as I do that we've raised the bar over time. We've refined the acceptable criteria over many, many generations. The Way itself evolves, albeit more slowly now. But my point is that those who fought for the Law and Chosen Tradition, which only existed on paper at the time, were not sanctioned by the Chosen Council, because it didn't exist." She held up her hand. "I'm obviously not suggesting that the Chosen Council isn't necessary. It's one of the pillars of the Way, established precisely because our way of life before it was unacceptable. Without the Chosen Tradition and the Law, what would have become of us? Perhaps we wouldn't exist. Perhaps we'd have destroyed ourselves by now."

"Perhaps we'd be like the Danlions, which would obviously be undesirable, so why bring one into our midst?" Stevens said.

"Because the spirit of the Way demands it." Laura pulled out her comm unit. "Let me quote Mary Conley, the leader of the reformists." She cleared her throat. "'We are not animals. We can choose to regulate our behaviour, or we can continue to grapple with social instability, unions that fail, frightened and lost children, and a society that revolves around the individual and diminishes the community. The price of utter and complete freedom is too high. We've seen that. We're destroying ourselves.

"'I want to live in a society in which every child is loved. I want to live in a society in which everyone considers how their behaviour affects others. I want to live in a society in which we're all secure in the knowledge that our family was there yesterday, is here today, and will be there tomorrow. I want to live in a society in which we spend our intelligence, time, and resources on improving our lives, not on killing each other. I want my children, my grandchildren, my great-grandchildren, and all the Rymellans who come after them to be proud to be Rymellan.

"'I want to live in a society in which nobody will ever have to make a speech like this again. If I have to die fighting for that society, I will.'"

Laura looked up. "She was assassinated five days after making that speech, an event that galvanized the advocates for the Way and turned the tide in the War of Social Reform. Four million Rymellans died in that war. It pitted those who wanted to continue along our destructive path against those who valued social stability and community. When the advocates for the Way won the war, those on the other side didn't disappear, nor were they slaughtered. They accepted defeat and strove to follow the Way. Were there more violations back then? Oh, yes. The numbers were horrific. As I said, we've become much better at determining who will be predisposed to following the Way, and we've refined articles in both the Law and the Chosen Tradition."

Lesley nodded. In the early days, they'd Joined Rymellans when both Chosens were at least 21, and discovered that many weren't prepared to be Joined at that age. They'd tried 28, but Rymellans had complained that their lives were on hold for too long, and too many prime child-bearing years were wasted. Eventually they'd settled on 25.

"But the majority didn't end up at execution sites," Laura continued. "They followed the Way, even though they weren't sanctioned by the Chosen Council, and because they weren't, it would have been more difficult for many of them, including the founders of the Way. I'm sure some of them would have failed your test. They also weren't surrounded by Rymellans who were strong in the Way. This child will be. She'll grow up in the society that Mary Conley and her colleagues envisioned. Do you think they'd want us to stand on the letter of the Law and Chosen Tradition and hand over a child to be murdered in cold blood? Do you think that's what they had in mind when they were among the first Rymellans to give their lives for the Way?"

"Why don't we invite everyone in the galaxy to come to Rymel, then?" Stevens said sullenly.

"Argamon, we're talking about a child that fell into our lap when she was less than a day old, not about opening our doors to everyone!" Jensen glared at him. "Can you not take this personally? Every one of us in this room has the utmost respect for what you do. You are the foundation of the Way. *I* defend the Way. All of us here would give our lives for the Way. But we have to keep this in perspective." She leaned forward and gazed at the Chosen Council Heads. "We're talking about a baby. Do you honestly want to give a baby back to the Danlions, knowing that they'll kill her? Do you honestly believe that's what being Rymellan means, that Mary Conley fought and sacrificed her life so we could refuse to offer sanctuary to an innocent child? So we could hand a defenceless infant over to her murderers with a clear conscience?"

Stevens and Ellis glanced at each other.

"You'll designate her a Solitary, of course," Fisher said.

"No!" Stevens shook his head for emphasis. "It would be a capital violation to tinker with the Solitary list. I don't care that you'd look the other way in this case. If she's going to be Rymellan, she'll be evaluated and matched—or not, as the case may be—like everyone else."

Ellis nodded in agreement. "If we decide that this is the appropriate course of action, the only thing we'll have to do is add a fetal verification record, which will indicate that we confirmed the fetus's parentage. Apart from that, we only get involved when a child is born. We would also have Joined the parents, of course." Her mouth pinched. "Usually."

"If anyone compares her DNA to that of her...parents, they'll know that the Thompsons aren't the biological parents," Hall pointed out.

"Why would anyone?" Laura asked.

"The commodore is correct," Stevens said. "We would already have examined her parentage. The infirmary would have no reason to do such a comparison. They may request her genetic material for a procedure, but they'd never have a reason to compare it to the Thompsons'."

A loud beep pierced the air, making everyone jump. "Emergency communication for Commander Thompson," said the voice crackling from Lesley's comm unit.

"Excuse me," Lesley mumbled. She stepped outside the conference room and pulled the door shut. "Yes?" she said to Communications Control, which had remotely turned on her comm unit.

"I'm connecting you to Jayne Thompson."

Lesley's heart thumped.

"Lesley? It's time. Mo's in labour," Jayne said calmly. "Should we beep for a neonatal unit, or are we going to the infirmary?"

"I—I don't know. They're still discussing it."

Shuffling, then, "Les. Take their, uh, offer," Mo said, following Lesley's instructions that nobody was to explicitly refer to the Danlion baby over a comm unit.

"But—"

"Look, if we...accept it and there are problems, we'll work through them. If we don't take it and we regret it, it'll be too late. We won't be able to change our minds. We'll never be able to fix it."

"I don't know if there's time."

"It'll be a few hours yet, at least. Oh!"

Lesley's heart thumped again. "Mo?"

"I'm okay, just another contraction."

"They haven't decided yet whether to extend the offer." *She* hadn't decided yet.

"Well, go in and tell them they've just run out of time. We'll wait for your beep, but Argamon, make it quick. Based on how far apart the contractions are, I'm guessing we have time. I could be wrong."

"Remember when we talked about my worries for our daughters, and you said it would work out, that we'd be bringing them up?" Jayne said. "The same is applicable to the offer."

No! They'd been discussing *their* daughters, not someone else's.

"Do you honestly think we'll be able to live with ourselves if we don't take it?" Mo added. "Will you be able to come home and fully celebrate?"

No. But she wasn't sure about taking the Danlion child. She wasn't sure! They weren't deciding whether to mind someone else's child for a week. This would be for life, and the Danlion would take her name.

"Lesley, you need to go. We'll wait to hear from you, but as Mo said, we can't wait long."

"Jayne, I..." Her eyes filled with tears.

"We want you with us. So don't dawdle. Whatever you decide, we'll support you."

They would, but if she refused the Danlion, every time her Chosens looked at her, she'd know that she'd lost a little of their respect. Every time they cradled their daughter, she'd know they were thinking of that other baby. "Take care of Mo. I'll get back to you as soon as I can."

Blinking back tears, Lesley disconnected and stared at her comm unit. Risk ruining her life, her Chosens' lives, their daughters' lives, and the family's reputation, or look the other way and let a child be murdered. She took a moment to regain her composure and wipe her eyes, then forced herself to step back into the meeting room. Faces swam before her. "Are you all right, Commander?" Hall asked.

She steeled herself. "My Chosen has gone into labour."

Jensen gaped. "What?"

"We need to decide our course of action, then." Laura frowned at Lesley. "Assuming we have time."

Still standing near the door, Lesley nodded. "A few hours, at least."

"Admiral, I understand that you'll support our plan," Jensen said to Hall.

"I have my doubts," Hall said, "but...if she wasn't so young...if they weren't going to kill her..." He heaved his shoulders. "We'll keep an eye on her."

"And you?" Jensen said to Stevens and Ellis. "If we go ahead with this, you'll play a key role. We can't do it without you."

Stevens' chest puffed out. "We need more time, but...well, you all appear certain that we won't be making a terrible mistake, and I have to admit that Mary Conley's words have made me more open to the idea." He turned to Ellis.

She swallowed. "I suppose I'd like to sleep tonight, and it matters that the girl will be raised within one of our oldest and strongest families."

"That's assuming Commander Thompson and her Chosens have agreed to raise the child as their own." Hall raised his brows at Lesley.

She shifted her weight. "If we don't accept her into our family, the Danlions will kill her."

"Is that a yes, Commander Thompson?" he said lightly.

Her throat tightened. She had to force the word out. "Yes."

A frisson of excitement ran through the room. Laura and Jensen were instantly on their feet. "Fisher, get to the infirmary and prepare a secured route to the delivery room," Jensen barked. "Stevens, Ellis, create that verification record. Commodore, you know what to do. Admiral—"

Lesley didn't hear what role, if any, Hall would play. She strode into the corridor and beeped Jayne. "You're going to the infirmary."

Jayne's voice shot up. "Okay. We'll see you soon." A pause. "It'll be all right."

Would it?

"Mo's physician just beeped her. Hold on."

Lesley waited.

"They're sending a medical aviacraft for us." Her voice dropped. "In case the twins are born on the way."

The web of deception was already being spun. "Is Mo okay?"

"She's fine. Hurry up and come see for yourself."

"I'm on my way." Lesley disconnected, leaned against the corridor's wall, and closed her eyes. Her life felt out of control. *What have I done?*

"Are you okay?"

Lesley snapped her eyes open. "Not really. I don't know if we're doing the right thing."

"Yes, you do," Laura said quietly. "But that doesn't mean you won't have doubts. Come on. We need to get to your aviacraft."

"You're coming to the infirmary with me?" Lesley asked, surprised.

"No. You have a daughter to pick up."

"What? No, I need to be with Mo."

"Mo has hours to go yet. You and I are going to meet your daughter at the shuttle facility. We'll take her to the infirmary," Laura said, her tone making it clear that there was no room for argument.

Feeling as if she were in a dream that could be described as a nightmare, Lesley pushed away from the wall and mutely fell into step with Laura.

LESLEY'S BOOTS RANG on tile as she paced in the unusually quiet waiting area. What excuse had they used this time to evacuate the facility? "Are you still awake?" she asked Laura, who was relaxing on a nearby bench.

"I might have dozed off a couple of times," Laura admitted.

"It shouldn't be long now." Since it didn't take as long to travel from headquarters to the shuttle facility as it did from 72, they'd already waited for over half an hour. Lesley desperately wanted to be with Mo. Her Chosens were keeping her updated, but still.

Her comm unit beeped. "Is everything okay?" Lesley barked.

"Fine," Mo said. "I'm beeping be—" Her voice cut off.

"Mo?"

Silence, then, "I'm okay. My contractions are a little more severe, but the physician says it'll be a while yet." She paused. "Jayne and I were talking. We can discuss this when you get here, but in case things move quickly...I know we held off on naming the, uh, second twin, because we didn't want our hopes up. But now that they're certain she'll be okay, we were thinking we should give her the second name on our list."

Lesley's grip tightened on her comm unit. That name was supposed to be for their second daughter. The rest of the names on the list were meant for their other daughters, but it was too late to submit another name to the Chosen Council. "I suppose that makes sense. Just to be clear, the twin that we *intended* to get the first name on the list will get it, right?"

"Yes. The one who might not have survived *if everyone hadn't stepped in*," Mo said, conveying her message loud and clear, "will be Katherine."

"All right." Lesley sighed.

"You okay?"

"I wish I was there, instead of waiting for this…" Argamon, it would be easier if they could speak freely, "dignitary."

"If only Commodore Finney wasn't being so unreasonable," Mo said fervently. "She drives you into the ground."

Lesley glanced at Laura, whose eyes were closed again. "She's not listening."

"Oh. Too bad. So, you excited? We're going to be mamas today."

"It hasn't sunk in yet." She released another sigh. "Any of it."

"That's because you're not the one in labour," Mo said with a chuckle.

Lesley caught movement in her peripheral vision and turned to look. Laura was motioning toward the arrivals tunnel. "I have to go. The shuttle is arriving." Her stomach knotted. "I wish I was with you."

"Me too. See you soon."

Fortunately Mo disconnected, because Lesley wanted to hang on, keep her talking, delay what was coming next. Laura wandered over to the tunnel entrance. Lesley went to her side. They stood smartly, as if they *were* meeting a dignitary. She swallowed when a solitary figure appeared at the other end of the tunnel, cradling a bundle in her arms. With every step Lieutenant Commander Higgs took, Lesley grew tenser.

Higgs nodded to Laura as she approached. "Commodore." And to Lesley, "Commander." Then she frowned and glanced around. "I was told that the family who's taking her would be here, Commodore."

"That would be me," Lesley said, her eyes flicking to the tiny face and hand peeking out from underneath the blue blanket.

"The triad is taking her?" Higgs breathed.

"Yes. My Chosen's about to give birth."

"I see." She stepped toward Lesley and smiled down at the baby in her arms. "You'd better take her, then."

"Uh, no, the commodore will take her. I have to fly the aviacraft to the infirmary." In her peripheral vision, she could see Laura giving her a look.

"Give her to me." Laura scooped the baby from Higgs's arms and peered down at her. "Hello, there," she cooed. "Look at you. Look at you." She swung the infant toward Lesley. "There's your mama."

Lesley's jaw clenched. She looked down and idly noted that the baby had a healthy head of brown hair. "We should go. I need to be with Mo."

"I'm so glad you've agreed to have her," Higgs said to Lesley. "I hope I'm not speaking out of turn, but to give her back to the Danlions..." She shook her head. "That would have been wrong."

"We agree," Laura said.

"She's a good baby. Very quiet," Higgs said.

"Thank you for bringing her to us." Laura elbowed Lesley. "Let's go."

"Bye-bye," Higgs said, wiggling her fingers at the baby. She bit her lip.

Lesley nodded to her and turned to leave.

"Commander!"

She and Laura turned back.

"I...don't suppose I might visit her sometime. I feel like I found her." Higgs's shoulders sagged. "No, I—sorry, I'm being presumptuous. Forgive me. It would be dangerous, anyway. I don't want to give her away. Why would I visit you?"

Lesley studied Higgs's long face and glistening eyes. "My Chosen, Lieutenant Commander Thompson...she's in Defence and often on 72. I don't see any reason why you two wouldn't know each other."

Higgs brightened. "No, none at all."

"I'm sure you'll see each other next time the *Osprey* docks. When it's getting closer, send her a dispatch and arrange to meet her for lunch on 72. She'll invite you to visit during your leave."

"I'll do that. Thank you. And good luck. Oh, and congratulations!"

Lesley managed a small smile and resumed walking.

"Are you sure you don't want to carry her?" Laura said. "You don't want a closer look?"

"Laura, I'll be able to look at her for the rest of my life." She still wasn't sure how she felt about that.

REFLECTION

WHEN LESLEY STRODE INTO THE DELIVERY room, Jayne looked away from Mo and frowned.

"Where is she?" Mo said, voicing the question on Jayne's mind.

"She's outside with Laura." Lesley gazed at Jayne. "Would you mind getting her? I want to stay with Mo." She leaned over and kissed Mo's cheek.

Puzzled, Jayne let go of Mo's hand. She'd bring the baby in here, so why hadn't Lesley? She paused at the doorway and took a deep breath, then stepped into the corridor. Laura gave her a tired smile. "Say hello to your daughter."

Jayne ever so carefully took the baby from Laura and blinked at the infant staring up at her. Awe—she looked so innocent; fear—Argamon, this baby's life was in their hands!; love—this was her *daughter*; Jayne couldn't speak. The enormity of it...they'd done the right thing, and now they were responsible for this child. The baby—Katherine—she'd ended up with a triad for parents, and she might be horrified when she learned that her Mama Jayne was *their* daughter. But right now, none of that mattered. Jayne gently held one of Katherine's tiny hands. "You're safe now," she whispered, her throat tight. "And you're so cute."

"Her hair and eyes won't arouse suspicion," Laura murmured. Jayne had forgotten she was there. "A comparison of her DNA to Lesley and Mo's wouldn't pass muster, but we're past the stage where one would be performed."

Mesmerized by the child in her arms, Jayne only half-listened. Katherine's mouth opened, and...a loud wail filled the corridor. Was she frightened? Hungry? Did she need changing? Could anyone hear her? Mo hadn't given birth yet! She looked into Laura's amused eyes.

"She was dry when I gave her to you, so it's not that. Try rocking her."

Jayne did as she was told and made a face at her. Argamon, Katherine had quite the pair of lungs. Jayne hadn't thought she could cry any louder. No more faces.

"She's probably hungry," Laura said.

"I'll beep the physician. She said something about feeding her, and she wants to examine her, too."

"I'll leave you to it." Laura pointed down the corridor. "Once you've taken her in, don't bring her out again, because we're going to reopen the area."

Jayne had to lean in to hear Laura over Katherine's crying. "I'd better go." She winced at another loud wail.

Laura raised her brows. "You'll get used to it. It's a good thing there's three of you."

With a nod, Jayne carried Katherine into the delivery room.

Mo beckoned for Jayne to show her the baby. "Don't give her to me, I might drop her. The contractions are coming—" She gritted her teeth, then studied Katherine and winced at her screeching. "Sounds like she's ready for the screaming competition with me," Mo said wryly. "I wish I could hold her, but..."

"I think she's hungry," Jayne said. "The physician said—"

"Yeah, you better beep her. I think I might need her, too."

"I'll beep the physician," Lesley said when Jayne looked her way.

Jayne peered at her wailing daughter, then pressed her lips against Katherine's cheek and held her tighter. She didn't care about her ringing ears; she already loved Katherine to bits.

The slick infant was suddenly sliding into Physician Crawford's hands. "Got her." She placed the baby on the towel her assistant had laid on Mo's abdomen and clamped the umbilical cord. The assistant leaned in to suction the baby's nose and mouth. Crawford grinned. "Congratulations! You have a daughter."

A pitiful cry reached Lesley's ears, then a stronger, louder one. Still gripping Mo's hand, Lesley gazed down at her daughter. A lump rose in her throat. All those years they'd loved each other and hadn't allowed themselves to imagine being Joined, let alone having a daughter. She wanted to laugh and dance and weep, especially when she locked eyes with Mo, who looked exhausted, relieved—and happy. Lesley turned to Jayne and squeezed her hand.

"I can see both of you in her," Jayne said, peering at the new arrival.

"Hello, Eleanor. Hello." Fortunately they'd kept their list of names secret. Nobody would wonder why their oldest daughter had the second name on the list, and not the first.

"Would you like to cut the cord?" Crawford said, her gaze taking in Lesley and Jayne. "I suppose you could try doing it together."

"She'll do it," Jayne said, letting go of Lesley's hand.

"You'll do the next one," Lesley said, vowing to thank Jayne more thoroughly later. Under Crawford's watchful eye, she severed the baby's remaining tangible connection with her mama.

Mo lifted her head and shoulders and smiled at her daughter. Her forehead creased. "I want to hold her."

"Not just yet," Crawford said. "I want to examine her, and there's still the placenta to come." She scooped Eleanor into her arms and took her away. The assistant trailed after her.

Lesley cringed. Every image she'd seen of a placenta had turned her stomach. She focused on Mo and stroked her damp hair. "You did great."

Mo let out a long groan. "I want a couple of years' break before I go through that again." She looked in the direction Crawford had gone. "I can't wait to see her—to see them." She threw her arm across her forehead. "You should tell whoever's here."

"In a minute." Lesley wasn't eager to go and lie to everyone.

"Interesting." Crawford waved Lesley and Jayne over to her. Lesley's heart thumped. Was something wrong with Eleanor?

"They're about the same weight."

"There's nothing wrong with Katherine, is there?" Jayne asked.

Crawford shook her head. "She weighed less at birth, that's all. You have two healthy daughters."

Lesley read the name on the hospital crib. "Eleanor Thompson." Her eyes moved to the other crib. "Katherine Thompson." She took a closer look at Katherine. Her heart didn't burst. She was responsible for her, she would protect her, but she didn't feel the same way. Just glancing at Eleanor brought a smile to Lesley's lips. Looking at Katherine was like looking at someone else's child. Well, she *was* looking at someone else's child.

She caught motion in her peripheral vision. "Uh, I think something's happening," Mo said, waving her hand.

Crawford bustled over to her. "Why don't you go and inform your family?" she said over her shoulder. "Your Chosen and daughters are in good hands."

Lesley sighed. "I guess I should." She felt Jayne's hand on her arm.

"I'll go with you," Jayne said.

"Good."

When they entered the corridor, Jayne slipped her arm through Lesley's. "We won't be lying, you know. The twins part won't be true, but everything else will be."

"I don't see it that way."

"You will."

Lesley wished she shared Jayne's confidence in her.

They turned a corner, strolled past a desk, and entered the waiting area. Everyone leaped to their feet. She scanned the anxious faces, noting that even Jason was here. Well, he was fond of Mo. Of course, only two families were represented. As usual, nobody was here for Jayne, and Lesley wouldn't let her down by forcing her to tell everyone their contrived story. She was the Principal. The child was taking her name. She'd do it.

Michael's frightened eyes met hers. "What's happened? Why did Mo have to come to the infirmary? She didn't say much when she beeped."

"What's the matter?" Mama said, searching Lesley's face.

She forced a smile. She was supposed to be happy, and she was—for the most part. "Everything's all right," she said, motioning for everyone to remain calm. "Mo's fine. Our daughters are fine."

Several brows furrowed. "Did you say daughters?" Papa said.

She nodded. "We have twins."

"Twins?" everyone said in unison. Then, "Why didn't you tell us?"

"Why did they have to be born in the infirmary?"

"Are you sure everything's okay?"

"You look exhausted."

"As Lesley said, everyone's fine," Jayne said, squeezing Lesley's arm.

"You never mentioned twins." Now that Mama had been reassured, she sounded accusatory. "Not once did you mention twins."

Lesley took a deep breath. "We weren't sure one was going to survive. Earlier in the pregnancy, there was a problem. The physicians corrected it, and they were optimistic, but we didn't want to worry you. That's why we didn't tell you when it happened, and then we decided we'd keep it to ourselves and surprise you."

"How long have you known?" Michael asked.

Lesley was tempted to check the time on her comm unit. "Since the first ultrasound."

Karen asked the question that must have been on everyone's mind. "What was the problem?"

"Some medical condition with a long name." Even though Karen was a physician, she couldn't demand to see Katherine's file since she wasn't Mo's physician. Even if she could, Crawford had already created Katherine's medical history, including fabricated ultrasound images and test results. After all, she'd been pulled out of bed in the middle of the night. Lesley cleared her throat. "You can ask the physician. She said she'd answer any questions." Another Rymellan who'd have to lie through her teeth.

Jayne's touch on her arm reminded Lesley of the reason for the deception: so Katherine could lead a life free of the suspicion that had dogged Jayne since her parents' executions. That didn't make Lesley feel any better, though, and she'd lie to those in this room, the people she loved, for the rest of her life. At least she'd live in honesty with Mo and Jayne.

"But everyone's all right," Peggy said.

"Yes."

A palpable sense of relief rose from those gathered. "Twins," Andrew said, his voice filled with awe. Then everyone was grinning and hugging and slapping each other on the back. Lesley embraced Mama, then Papa. *I'm sorry.* Would she be able to bear watching them fawn over Katherine, or sit quietly as Mama regaled the "twins" with family stories and reminded them of their strong, proud ancestry? "When can we see everyone?" Mama asked.

Those around them echoed her question and waited for Lesley to answer. "It's late, so the physician said tomorrow would be best."

"Mo's tired," Jayne added.

"No wonder! She just gave birth to two daughters," Michael boomed. "What are their names?"

"Eleanor and Katherine. They both have dark hair," Jayne said. "Eleanor's hair is a little lighter than Katherine's."

"They're not identical twins?" Papa asked.

"No, fraternal twins."

"Twins. Two proud new Thompsons," Mama intoned, making Lesley's heart sink. "I can't wait to see them."

Footsteps thumped behind them. Physician Crawford beamed at everyone. "From your faces, I can tell you've heard the news," she said. "If anyone has questions, I'll be happy to answer them."

"We'll go back to Mo," Lesley said. "We'll see you all tomorrow." She nodded to Crawford and left the waiting area with Jayne.

"We've left behind some very happy people." Jayne's voice softened. "We've done the right thing. I know it's difficult to gloss over the truth, but we would have felt worse if we'd decided differently. Either way, Katherine would have been with us when Eleanor was born. I'm glad she was actually there, rather than on our minds, condemning us."

Lesley had to agree, but representing a child to her family as her own—their own—would never feel right. Katherine still condemned her. She always would.

CAPTAIN STANDISH ENTERED the *Osprey*'s command centre and nodded to Hollins and Martin, who was filling in until Higgs returned. Normally he wouldn't be here at this hour, but the operation had begun during the early morning hours, and it would end while the majority of the crew slept. Most didn't know about the child, or the bodies. The official story: the *Osprey* had intercepted a Danlion cargo ship and was awaiting orders from Planetary Command. Everyone had assumed that Higgs had travelled to the planet with confidential information gleaned from the Danlion vessel that the *Osprey* hadn't wanted to send over a communications channel.

He sank into the command chair. "Are we ready to proceed?" he asked Hollins.

"Yes, Captain. Target acquired. Disintegration protocol set."

"All bodies have been returned to the Danlion ship?"

"Yes."

He couldn't help but feel sorry for the Danlions who'd sacrificed their lives, particularly the parents. At least their child wouldn't be subject to the same madness that plagued her people. "Visual." An image of the cargo ship drifting in space appeared on the monitor to the right of his chair. "Ready."

Martin pressed a button on his control panel. "Ready, Captain."

"Fire."

A transparent beam travelled toward the Danlion craft. One second the cargo ship was there, the next it was gone.

"Direct hit. Target disintegrated," Martin said.

"Very good." Standish turned to Hollins. "We'll maintain this position until Higgs returns."

"Understood." Hollins paused. "I'm glad we saved the baby."

Standish gazed at him. "What baby?"

GLAD TO BE out of the infirmary, Mo strolled home with Les and Jayne and wished they wouldn't be greeted by a houseful of people—especially since those same people had packed her room that morning. What was it about babies that made everyone's brains fall out of their head? It was worse than when people were in love. At least lovers did all their baby-talking in private. Even Les had turned to jelly—with Eleanor. Mo had noticed her aloofness with Katherine and was sure that Jayne had, too. Even now, Les carried Eleanor while Jayne carried Katherine. Mo wouldn't have minded carrying one of them, but they'd insisted. After all, she'd done all the hard work yesterday. Well, yeah, she had, so maybe she could hold one of her flaming daughters!

As for Katherine, was she thrilled that they'd bring up someone else's child? She'd asked herself how she'd feel if it was a niece or nephew, or a friend's child, and knew that she'd agree to do it without hesitation. So she'd decided to do the same here. Did she feel the same way about Katherine as she did about Eleanor? Almost. Though Katherine had arrived at the same time as Eleanor, it was hard not to think of them as different.

But Mo was confident that would change. She'd warmed up to Katherine the first time she'd nursed her. Katherine's eyes were as innocent as Eleanor's, and her trust as pure. Give it a few days, and Mo would forget that Katherine wasn't hers—biologically speaking.

Asking Adelaide whether they should accept the baby would have been a disaster. Les would have lapped up every word about the Thompson family's reputation and sterling bloodline. Not that Mo was knocking it; the Thompson name *was* an honourable one with a long history. But Les would never have forgiven herself if she'd denied Katherine life by returning her to the Danlions. Mo wasn't sure what exactly was preventing Les from embracing Katherine—the dishonesty with her family, worry about Katherine's future strength in the Way, or something else—but she was positive that Les would come around. The part of her that had known she couldn't turn her back on Katherine would eventually prevail, with Mo and Jayne's gentle help, if necessary. Pushing her wouldn't do it. They couldn't force Les to love Katherine, but they could encourage it.

A baby's cry snapped her back to her surroundings. "We're almost there," she said to Eleanor as Les rocked her. "You can't be hungry yet, can you?" Argamon, she was a twenty-four hour feeding station. "Look. We're home." Mo pointed. "This is where you live." She could see Nathan and Andrew through the living room window. Both had volunteered to escort the family of five home from the infirmary, but the triad had wanted some quiet time to themselves.

"Can you get the door?" Jayne said.

Mo swung the door open and led the way into the noisy living room. She smiled when everyone rushed forward...and ignored her.

"Isn't she cute?"

"Which one is Eleanor again?"

"Can I hold her?"

Someone squealed. "She's looking at me!"

Mo sighed and waded through the commotion. *I'm fine, everyone. A little tired, maybe, but I guess I'll feel that way now for a while. Yes, I wouldn't mind a drink. Thank you for offering.* Argamon, the brains were already splattering onto the floor.

She broke free of the chaos and sank onto the sofa, then noticed that not everyone had lost their minds. Ann raised her brows from a chair across the room, then came over and sat next to Mo.

"I wasn't sure you'd be here," Mo said.

"I persuaded Barry to cover my shift, with Archer's approval." She gazed at those crowding around the babies and scrunched up her face. "Babies have to be cute, to offset all the screaming and puking and burping and smelly diapers, and you have two of them to deal with." Her eyes went to Mo's stomach. "Now I know why you're so big."

"Excuse me—"

"It must have been a shock when you found out you were having twins. Imagine when people didn't find out until they were born."

Yeah, at least she'd had a few hours' notice.

"Are you going to bring them up to 72 with you? I'm not babysitting."

Mo stifled a snort. "I wouldn't expect you to. I wouldn't bring them up by myself. Jayne or Les would be with me—maybe both."

"That's good. Oh, look who's coming." Ann leaped to her feet. "Talk to you later." She moved over to the group clustered around Jayne.

Adelaide plunked down where Ann had sat five seconds earlier. "This is the first set of twins for us. Are there any in your family?"

"I don't know. I haven't checked."

"I should have known you were having twins. You'd put on so much weight."

"I'm not that big," Mo said through clenched teeth. "And it's all coming off. I start seeing a trainer next week. I have to get my weight down before I can fly again."

Adelaide patted Mo's knee. "I'm glad you'll be getting help. Do you want something to drink?"

"Sure." Anything to put an end to this annoying conversation with her Chosen Mama. "I wouldn't mind a glass of grape juice, please."

"I'll be back in a minute." Adelaide bustled away. Uh-oh, one of the babies was crying. Mo struggled to her feet and went to the Chosen who looked the most uncomfortable. Les smiled sheepishly. "She might be hungry."

"I'll take her upstairs." Mo held out her arms, but Les said, "I'll carry her up."

A chorus of groans ensued. "We won't be gone for long." Mo glanced at Jayne. "Bring her, too," she mouthed; otherwise poor Katherine would be surrounded by even more people cooing and making faces and grasping her tiny hands.

She looked around in confusion when they entered the nursery. There'd only been one crib in here yesterday.

"Laura brought it over and set it up," Les said, correctly guessing at the reason for Mo's puzzled expression. Mo reached behind her to push the door shut. Someone in the hallway pushed against it from the other side.

Adelaide poked her head into the room. "I have Mo's drink."

"Thanks," Mo said, taking it from her. "Tell everyone we'll be down soon." She shut the door, and after drinking some juice, she set it on the changing table and sat on one of the rocking chairs. A smile sprang to her lips at the sight of Jayne holding Katherine in front of the mural. "I don't think she really sees it yet."

"I know, but I'm showing it to her, anyway."

See? Brains gone.

Les peered at Eleanor. "She seems to have calmed down."

"I'll try her, anyway." Maybe Eleanor had just wanted five minutes of peace. Mo couldn't blame her. She reached for her, then pulled her arms back when her comm unit beeped twice. "Since she's not starving, let me just check my dispatches. My comm unit's been beeping non-stop since last night, and I haven't had a chance to read any." She was curious to see who'd sent congratulatory messages. She read down the names. *Cmdr. T. Baker?* The subject read, *Congratulations!* News of the births had already reached the *Falcon*? "Did you send a dispatch about the twins to anyone on the *Falcon*?" she asked Les.

"No, I haven't told anyone except family yet."

Baffled, Mo read Baker's message. *It's great to hear that you're eligible for tours again. I guess the next Falcon tour will be too soon, but maybe the one after that? Make sure you let us know when you've welcomed your daughter.* Okay, maybe fatigue was finally catching up with her, because she had no idea what he was talking about. Maybe he'd mixed her up with someone else.

"What is it?" Les said.

Mo looked up. "I'm not sure." She continued to scan names; another one jumped out at her. Jensen, or rather, her assistant. *Lieutenant Commander Thompson, the admiral is pleased to inform you that she has completed the evaluation of your suitability to serve on Defence ships...* Mo's mouth dropped open. Evaluation? Is that what she called it? *...and has* *concluded that the restrictions on your permitted duties can be lifted. You are welcome to apply for a slot on any Defence tour. The admiral apologizes for any inconvenience.*

She lifted her head again. "You won't believe this."

"What?" her Chosens said in unison.

"Jensen has cleared me for tours again. I'm no longer grounded."

"Really?" Les said.

"Maybe now that we have daughters, we're acceptable to her," Jayne said.

Mo nodded. "She does seem to have a soft spot for Katherine, or maybe babies in general. Then again, when she grounded me, she did say that she'd reconsider my grounding when we have some time behind us." It seemed coincidental that Jensen would choose now to change her mind, though. Too coincidental. She searched Les's face. "Did you…"

Les peered down at Eleanor. "I might have asked for something in return for your willingness to go along with Jensen's plan. I didn't want it to influence your decision about Katherine, though."

"I wouldn't have taken her just so I could go on tour again." Argamon, raising a child as her own in exchange for Jensen righting a wrong would hardly have been a fair exchange. "But thanks for getting her to agree to it."

Jayne's forehead creased with worry. "Does that mean we'll be going on a tour?"

Mo glanced at Les. "Not for a few years yet. Maybe never. It's nice to have the option again, though." She slid her comm unit back into its holder and held out her arms. "Okay, who am I feeding first?" Her triumphant return to being a hot shot tour pilot would have to wait. She had more important things to do.

DOUGLAS TIBBS, A senior translator in Communications Control, reviewed his colleague's translation of a short communiqué. He didn't often see a document written in both Jessimite and Danlion, but given the document's contents, the need for both languages was perfectly understandable:

To: the Jessimite ambassador to the Danlion colonies
From: Rymellan Communications Control

Thank you for agreeing to transmit the following communication to the Danlion leadership:

In regard to your recent communiqué about escaped political prisoners, we intercepted and destroyed a Danlion cargo ship that matches the description you provided. We assure you that the ship was disintegrated. There were no survivors. While we consider this matter closed, we remind you that incursions into Rymellan space will not be tolerated and will be considered an act of war.

Tibbs couldn't help but feel proud as he approved the translation. He'd sleep better at night knowing that Defence was patrolling Rymellan space and protecting the Way. Imagine if the cargo ship had approached the planet—with Danlions aboard! He abhorred violence, but between having a Danlion near the planet and a Danlion blasted into a billion microscopic particles, he definitely preferred the latter. With a shudder, he flicked off his monitor, slid open his drawer, and lifted out his bagged lunch.

LESLEY PEERED INTO the nursery and smiled at Mo, who was sitting in one of the rocking chairs with Eleanor in her arms. It was easy to tell the two girls apart; Eleanor's hair was lighter than Katherine's, so glimpsing the baby's head was all Lesley needed. She stepped into the room and waved her hand to catch Mo's attention.

"You can talk," Mo said. "She's not sleeping."

Lesley glanced in the direction of Katherine's crib.

"Why don't you get her and join me?" Mo suggested, looking at the empty rocking chair next to her.

"I don't want to disturb her."

"Last time I looked, she was awake."

"Then why are you holding Eleanor?"

"Because I only have one pair of hands and Eleanor was fussing," Mo snapped. "I'd really appreciate it if you could bring Kat over so she doesn't feel neglected."

Lesley wouldn't ask where Jayne was; Mo would bite her head off. She reluctantly went to Katherine's crib and lifted the baby into her arms. Disappointment made her frown. She should feel something when she held Katherine, but nothing stirred. She'd tried to see Katherine as her daughter, but every time she looked at her, she saw a rescued Danlion child and felt the now-familiar sting of inadequacy.

How did Mo and Jayne do it? Since bringing the babies home two weeks ago, Lesley had watched her Chosens coo at and play with them, and she couldn't see a difference between how they treated Eleanor and Katherine. Could she not get past Katherine's ancestry because she'd sat in the meetings, viewed the images of the reconnaissance team discovering her, and listened to the arguments against saving her? She'd always protect Katherine—or Kat, as Mo and Jayne called her—and she'd take good care of her, but she felt as if there was a stranger in the house, that she lived with her Chosens, her daughter…and someone else.

With a sigh, she sank into the rocking chair and gazed into the two baby brown eyes blinking at her. Nothing. Perhaps it was easy for Mo because she nursed Katherine, and perhaps Jayne didn't wonder when Katherine's parents were going to arrive and take her home because she saw herself in Katherine's situation. Lesley futilely tapped Katherine's nose. Why couldn't she feel anything for the child in her arms?

Mo smiled down at Eleanor. "I see Mama in her." Her voice quavered. "I like that."

Lesley made sure that Katherine was securely nestled in her left arm, then reached out with her other hand and patted Mo's arm.

Mo cleared her throat. "These two have a commodore wrapped around their pinkies."

Lesley nodded. Laura hadn't been lying when she'd said she'd drop by more often.

"Just before she left, she was telling me more about how the Danlion family ruler thing works. She's done some research." Mo's face grew animated. "Can you believe they're born into it? I mean, what happens if the oldest child is an idiot? What happens if it's a family of idiots that keeps having idiots?"

Lesley chuckled. "Perhaps that's why they're always fighting each other. You can't blame Katherine's family for wanting to save her from it."

Mo groaned. "We're her family. You have to start seeing it that way."

Easier said than done.

"But don't force it. It'll happen in its own time," Mo said, more confidently than Lesley felt. "Oh, Ross beeped me about a planning meeting on 72. She knows I won't be back for a couple of months, but since they're considering some new training exercises, she wants me to go. I said I would."

"When is it?"

"Well, that's the problem. We'd already scheduled the twins' checkup for that day, but I don't have to be here, do I? You and Jayne will be here. I'll leave bottles."

"Go. You've hardly left the house since we brought them home."

"It'll be a busy week. First the supper with your parents, then 72, then the presentation to the Chosen Council." Mo paused. "Seems odd that I did all the work, but you get to present them."

Lesley could tell she was teasing. "I don't make the rules."

"Everything will go okay at the presentation, right?"

Now she heard anxiety. "Her birth has been recorded like any other child's. So don't worry. Everything will be fine." For once, Lesley wished she wasn't the Principal. She'd have to present the child in her arms to the Chosen Council and declare Katherine as her own. That wasn't fine. Not fine at all.

JAYNE HELD THE tray steady while Alan lifted two mugs of tziva from it. "Thank you," he murmured. "I wouldn't have minded preparing the tziva."

"That's okay. I wanted to do it," she said, meaning it. By the time the triad had moved out of this house, she'd no longer felt like an intruder, and Lesley's parents didn't intimidate her. But she still liked to make herself useful. After Lesley and Mo had taken their tzivas, she set the tray on an end table and sank into a chair. Adelaide smiled down at Kat, who lay contentedly in her grandmama's arms.

"She's a quiet one, isn't she?" Adelaide lifted her head. "I can't believe they'll be presented to the Chosen Council this week." Kat's face suddenly grew scarlet. She started to cry. "Oh, I spoke too soon, didn't I?" Adelaide said, pitching her voice high.

"Do you want to switch?" Mo asked, sitting on the other end of the sofa with Eleanor.

"No, that's all right." Adelaide rocked Kat. "Have you been keeping your mamas up at night?"

Mo nodded. "Yes, they have."

"Is that why your Mama Lesley has had such a long face all night? Is she tired?" Adelaide said to Kat.

"I haven't had a long face all night," Lesley said from the other chair.

"Yes, you have. Here." She rose and carried a still wailing Kat over to Lesley. "You might have better luck."

"Give her to Jayne," Lesley said.

"Why?" Adelaide roared. Kat's cries grew louder.

"Because she's better with her when she's fussing."

Adelaide tutted. Wanting to avert an argument, Jayne held out her arms. "I'll see if I can quiet her down." Adelaide handed Kat to Jayne, then whirled to Lesley. "What's the matter with you?"

"Nothing," Lesley said, as Jayne held Kat against her and rubbed her back.

"You've been surly all night. I'm sure they're tired too, but at least they're making an effort. You'd better not be in this mood at the Chosen House." Adelaide sat down and let out an exasperated sigh. "I understand that you're not getting enough sleep, but you have two beautiful girls about to take their first real step as Rymellans. Don't spoil it for everyone."

Jayne gave Lesley a sidelong glance. That was the problem. Lesley didn't believe Kat was Rymellan, and Jayne didn't know what to do about it. She'd thought Lesley would have come around by now, but while Lesley fed and changed Kat and made sure she was all right, there was no spark between them. Lesley played with Eleanor, talked to her, carried her around the house. With Kat, it was all duty and obligation. When they were with others, as they were now, Lesley pretty much ignored both babies. It was the only way she could come across as treating them the same, and both their daughters were poorer for it.

Her ears were ringing. She felt Kat's diaper—ah. "She needs to be changed," she said, rising. "I'll go do it." As she passed Lesley, her throat tightened, and she wished she could reach out and touch her. Lesley was hurting; the situation was tying her in knots. Did she regret taking Kat? Did she want to love her, but couldn't? Was she afraid to love her? Jayne vowed to find out. Lesley should be enjoying this time in her life, not sitting in an armchair in her parents' house, hiding her tension and misery.

Jayne didn't want Lesley to feel outnumbered, so she'd broach the subject when Mo was on 72. They'd have some time together before the physician arrived. She couldn't make Lesley love Kat, but if she could get to the root of the barrier Lesley had erected, maybe she could break it down, or at least help Lesley disassemble it piece by piece.

JAYNE REACHED THE bottom of the stairs and walked into the living room. "They're sleeping," she said.

Focused on her comm unit, Lesley grunted.

"Are you looking forward to going back?"

"Yes and no." Lesley slid her comm unit into its holder. "I wish I had more time, but I know you and Mo will be here, and I have a pile of work waiting for me."

Jayne sank onto the sofa next to her. How could she open the conversation about Kat without sounding accusatory? She took Lesley's hand. "You've been quiet since the supper with your parents."

"I'm just tired."

"Your mama wasn't too pleased with you."

Lesley's face tightened. "She'd be even less pleased with me, if she knew I was lying through my teeth."

"You're not lying through your teeth," Jayne said.

"Yes, I am. So are you."

"What's the lie?"

Lesley yanked her hand from Jayne's and stood. "Don't play games, Jayne. I'm not in the mood."

"I'm not playing games. I don't think we lied to your parents. You do. So tell me why. What's the lie?"

Lesley plunked into a chair and pointed toward the archway. "They think they have twin granddaughters."

"They do have twin granddaughters."

"They're going to stand in the Chosen House and grin from ear to ear as they watch their daughter present two more Thompsons to the Chosen Council."

"But you won't see it that way. You'll see it as a lie."

"It *is* a lie. She isn't my daughter. She isn't even Rymellan."

Jayne listened to the anguish in Lesley's voice, torn between shouting at her and wanting to comfort her. "We went through this already. The only difference between Kat and Eleanor is that Kat isn't your biological child and wasn't sanctioned by the Chosen Council."

Lesley gave her an incredulous look. "The only difference?"

"She might be weaker in the Way than you. But she'll grow up on Rymel, belong to a strong Rymellan family, and attend the Indoctrination Academy like everyone else does. She'll learn the Law, the Chosen Tradition, recite the Words with pride, know all the important articles. She'll see herself as Rymellan, because she will be. Why can't you accept that?"

"I understand what you're saying. I've heard Jensen say it. I've heard Laura say it." Lesley lowered her head and studied her hands. "I understand that the Chosen Council gives everyone the best head start possible. Katherine—Kat—won't have that head start, but that doesn't mean she'll fall from the Way."

"Then what's the problem?" Jayne asked quietly. "Are you afraid that she *will* fall from the Way? Is that what's keeping you from warming up to her?"

"I don't know."

"Being a Rymellan sanctioned by the Chosen Council isn't a guarantee. I know that from experience."

"I know you do." Lesley lifted her head. "And I know I'm using Katherine's ancestry as a way to justify why I don't feel anything for her. Maybe it happened too fast. Maybe if we'd had more time."

Despite fearing the answer, Jayne forced out the question on her mind. "If we had, do you think you'd have preferred to give her back to the Danlions?"

Lesley shook her head. "No. I know we did the right thing. Perhaps I'm just not the right person for this."

"I don't believe that." Jayne wanted to go to her, but she'd learned that when Lesley was upset, she preferred space. When she was ready for a hug, she'd make the first move.

"Well, it's too late now, isn't it?" Lesley said softly. "At least she'll have you and Mo."

"And you! She *is* your daughter. I wish you'd see it that way. You knew about her before we did. You flew her to the infirmary, you were with her when she came home. You feed her, change her, look in on her to make sure she's all right." A lump rose in her throat when Lesley's eyes reddened. "You need more time, that's all. Spend time with her, when you're not doing mama duty."

Lesley's voice quavered. "I want her to see loving faces, not a cold one."

Jayne wanted to cry with relief. "That sounds like someone who cares about her."

"It does, doesn't it?" Lesley said flatly. "Now if I could only feel it, rather than just sounding like it."

You already do. If she'd only give herself permission. "You will."

"You think so?"

"Yes. Why don't you forget about trying to be her mama? Take the pressure off."

"I don't know if—"

A cry, from the baby monitor sitting on the end table. Jayne inwardly sighed. "I'll go." She went to Lesley and gave her a quick hug and kiss, then went upstairs, feeling better about Lesley and Kat. In whatever internal battle Lesley was waging, the side for love and compassion and fairness would prevail. With Lesley, it always did.

AN HOUR LATER, Lesley sat glumly in front of her comm station and thought about the conversation with Jayne. She didn't need anyone to tell her that she was failing at being a parent to Katherine—not that Jayne had said that. She'd been her usual sensitive self but couldn't sugar-coat reality. Katherine had two mamas and a minder.

The doorbell rang. "I'll go down," Lesley shouted, knowing that Jayne was in the nursery. She went downstairs, and quickly masked her shock when she swung the door open expecting Physician Crawford but found a stranger standing on the doorstep. "Can I help you?"

The woman smiled. "Good afternoon, Commander. I'm Physician Russell. Physician Crawford was unexpectedly called into a meeting, so she asked me to come and see the twins."

What? Crawford knew about Katherine. This woman didn't. What if—

Russell's brow furrowed. "I *am* a qualified pediatric physician."

"I'm sorry," Lesley said, mortified by her rudeness. "I had something else on my mind. Come in."

"I'm used to dealing with frazzled parents." Russell stepped into the entranceway and glanced around. "I should have beeped."

"No, don't worry about it. The twins are upstairs. This way." Lesley led Russell up the winding staircase and into the nursery.

Russell's brows shot up. "What a delightful mural! Who did it?"

Lesley looked to Jayne, who was bent over Eleanor's crib, but Jayne didn't lift her head. "Jayne did."

Russell followed Lesley's gaze. "You did it?"

Jayne straightened. "Uh, yes," she said, her face scarlet.

"It's wonderful. You're very talented. We could use something like this in the infirmary's pediatric waiting area."

"Thank you," Jayne mumbled.

"I'll examine your girls on the changing table," Russell said, dropping her bag to the floor. She approached the nearest crib. "Who's this?"

Lesley tensed. "Katherine."

"Hello, Katherine. Why don't I have a look at you first?" She reached into the crib.

Wanting to give them space, Lesley returned to the doorway and leaned against the doorframe. She folded her arms and tried not to appear stressed, but every time Russell grunted, Lesley almost hit the ceiling. Jayne hovered near Russell and Katherine for a while, then came over to Lesley and touched her arm. "I have to go to the bathroom," she whispered.

Lesley stepped into the room so Jayne could pass. A moment later, Russell turned to her. "She's doing well, aren't you?" she said, tickling Katherine's belly. Uh-oh. Katherine's eyes squeezed shut. Her mouth opened. She wailed. "Oh, dear, she didn't like that." Russell picked her up and smiled down at her. "I've upset you, haven't I?" She hugged Katherine and rubbed her back, but Katherine continued to cry—loudly. "Oh, you want your mama, don't you? Come, Mama, come get Katherine."

Lesley looked over her shoulder for Jayne.

"Come on, Mama, Katherine wants you."

She froze when she realized that Russell was referring to her. Apparently deciding to carry the baby over to Lesley, Russell approached her and lifted Katherine into her arms. "Here's your mama."

Lesley stared down at Katherine, who blinked up at her. Katherine's cries grew weaker. She calmed down.

Russell's face scrunched up. "Aw. Giving them to Mama or Papa doesn't always work, but this time, it did." She pinched Katherine's toes and jiggled her foot. "You just wanted to see a familiar face, didn't you? You love your mama. You wanted someone you trust." Her voice returned to its normal pitch. "I'll have a look at Eleanor now."

Katherine loved and trusted her? No. Mo and Jayne, perhaps, but not her.

"Are you all right, Commander?"

"Yes, fine. Call me Lesley."

As Russell nodded and went to fetch Eleanor, Lesley laid Katherine back into her crib. Katherine wailed again. "Oh, dear, she wasn't ready to be put down," Russell said. Lesley leaned over the crib and gently took Katherine's hand. To her surprise, Katherine grabbed her index finger—and quieted down.

"She wants you to stay with her, Mama," Russell said, carrying Eleanor over to the change table.

"Yes, she does," came a voice from the doorway.

Lesley looked up. Jayne raised her brows, then went over to Russell. Lesley watched Jayne and Russell over her shoulder, aware of the little hand grasping her finger, and noticing the instant Katherine let go.

CERTAIN THAT JAYNE was busy drawing in the living room and Mo wouldn't be home for at least half an hour, Lesley climbed the stairs and crept into the nursery. She smiled at a slumbering Eleanor, then turned her attention to Katherine, who also lay fast asleep. Russell's words came back to her: *You just wanted to see a familiar face, didn't you? You love your mama. You wanted someone you trust.*

Too busy spinning her wheels over how she viewed Katherine, Lesley had given little thought to how Katherine viewed—or perhaps would view—her, and how Katherine would see herself. She wouldn't know, would never suspect, that her biological parents were Danlion. She'd grow up believing she was Rymellan, identify as such, and the three women she lived with would be to her exactly what they were to Eleanor—her mamas. There would be no angst over her ancestry, no identity crisis. She wouldn't pretend to be Rymellan; she would *be* Rymellan, in her mind and in her heart, and Lesley, Mo, and Jayne Thompson would be her parents.

Parents did more than feed, clothe, and shelter their children. If Lesley was to be a good role model, she needed to start right now. Someone strong in the Way should see bringing up a rescued infant as Rymellan as a privilege, and do so with love. Lesley would teach Katherine what it meant to be the Rymellan Katherine Thompson. Katherine wouldn't grow up wondering why, no matter how hard she tried and how often she reached out, her mama Lesley remained distant. She wouldn't ask herself what was wrong with her, what she'd done to disappoint her Mama Lesley, why only two of her three mamas truly cared.

Tears prickled at Lesley's eyelashes. Wrapped up in herself, she'd approached the situation from the wrong direction. While she'd struggled not to condemn Katherine based on her lineage, Katherine—her daughter—had condemned her. Fortunately, she was too young to understand how her Mama Lesley had failed her. Lesley was bound to let her daughters down at various times throughout their lives, but she vowed never to do it on this scale again.

She wanted to place her hand atop Katherine's warm head, but that would only wake her up. *I'm sorry. I'll do better from now on.* She turned to Eleanor's crib. *I let you down, too.* She'd let them both down. But her step was lighter as she left the nursery, and the joy that had battled for freedom ever since Eleanor had slipped into Physician Crawford's hands finally burst to the surface. She had twins! Two daughters! She'd love and nurture them both.

MO SNICKERED AS Les described her reaction when she'd opened the door to Physician Russell. "What did you think would happen? Did you think an alarm would sound when Russell examined her?"

Les smiled. "I'll admit, panicking was silly."

Mo grinned, not only at Les's words, but at her mood. Les had smiled more in the past ten minutes than she had since she'd first told them about Kat.

Les patted Mo's knee. "So everything went okay on 72?"

"Yeah. But I felt torn."

"Why?"

"It was good to be back in the hustle and bustle, but I kept thinking about Eleanor and Kat. I figure my schedule will be perfect, though." She brushed a stray hair out of her eye. "I'll be here, and then just when I'm starting to get sick of them, it'll be time for me to go up to 72 for a couple of days. By the time I get back, Jayne will be sick of them and I can take over."

"Aren't you missing someone?"

She quirked a brow. "You're the evening shift." Les would soon return to duty, so she wouldn't be much help during the day. Unless Mo had an early report time on 72, she and Jayne would answer the twins' cries during the night. "You'll be getting off easy."

Les drew breath, then frowned when Jayne walked into the living room.

"What is it?" Mo asked, her heart thumping at the concern on Jayne's face. "Are the twins okay?"

"Fine." Jayne lifted the comm unit Mo hadn't noticed. "I just received a dispatch from Physician Russell. At her next department meeting, she's going to suggest that the infirmary commission me to paint a mural in the pediatric waiting area."

"That's great!"

Jayne shook her head. "No, it isn't. I can't paint a mural in the waiting area."

"Why not?" Mo and Les said in unison.

"Because...I can't."

Mo held out her hand. "Can I read the dispatch?"

Jayne handed her the comm unit, then turned to Les. "Don't mention this to Joanna. She'll start in at me again about putting my work into a show."

"She hasn't talked about it since you told her no last year," Mo heard Les say as she scanned the dispatch from Russell.

"That doesn't mean she's happy about it. If I tell her about this, she'll probably stop tutoring me."

"Are you sure you don't want to show even one painting?"

Silence, then, "I didn't want to be an artist. I didn't want to be like my papa, so I had to fight for my drawings and paintings. I'm not ready to put that on the line yet. I know Joanna wants me to display a painting, but I can't, not yet. I hope she'll continue to work with me."

"Tell her what you just told me. I'm sure she'll understand."

A sigh. "Maybe."

"She will." Les paused. "I don't know if you've noticed, but Joanna doesn't really tutor you anymore. She enjoys painting with you. You're friends."

Mo was only half-listening as she typed a reply to the dispatch. Jayne seriously needed to get over her aversion to showing her work. Everyone who visited the nursery gushed about the mural. If Jayne would just—

"What are you doing?" Jayne asked. "Why are you typing?"

"Don't worry, I haven't sent it." Mo quickly finished typing her sentence. "But this is what I think you should say."

Jayne snatched the comm unit from Mo's hand and read her handiwork. Her eyes widened. "If the department agrees, please contact me about my fee? Thank you for your interest." She stared at Mo. "I can't send this."

Why not? Mo had thought it an appropriate way to end the missive. "Come on, Jayne. She's suggesting you paint a bright, happy mural, not a flaming masterpiece. Not that it *wouldn't* be a masterpiece," Mo hastily added when Jayne's brows knitted together and her free hand went to her hip. "But it would be a different audience. It wouldn't be Rymellans who care about art."

"I thought you were trying to talk her into it," Les murmured.

"They won't care about the details of the, uh..." Mo flailed around, "technique, and the...uh, brushwork. They'll either like it or they won't. They won't write a flaming critique."

Les's mouth twitched. "What Mo's trying to say is that your mural could brighten an otherwise trying day for children and their parents."

Mo nodded. "Yeah, that's what I'm trying to say."

Jayne didn't budge.

"Sending the dispatch doesn't mean the mural will go forward," Les said. "The department might not approve it."

"It might not be able to afford your fee," Mo said mischievously, then she stifled a yelp when Les elbowed her.

"Do you think Russell knows who I am?" Jayne asked softly.

Les's eyes lit up with amusement. "Yes, I'm pretty sure she knows who you are. You're becoming respectable."

Concern flitted across Jayne's face. "I don't know what that's like."

Mo grinned at her. "It's past time you found out."

JAYNE SMILED DOWN at Eleanor and tickled her tummy. "You ready? You ready?"

Standing next to her, Mo said, "The next few days are going to feel weird."

Jayne nodded. She was looking forward to the nights of uninterrupted sleep, but she'd worry about the twins, hoping they weren't frightened and crying for their mamas. A surge of anger took her by surprise. She would do anything to protect Eleanor and Kat. How could her parents have been so selfish? Had their son and daughter given them even a second's pause? Did they think Rymellans would embrace the children of two monsters? Where had they thought it would lead?

No, she wouldn't let them ruin today. Here she was, among family and friends, with a daughter in her arms and two Chosens standing nearby. She still wanted to pinch herself every time she glimpsed her Chosen ring as she painted. She'd expected to endure a loveless Joining, but had ended up with a life so filled with love that she sometimes had to stop what she was doing and convince herself that she wasn't making it up. She'd worried that Eleanor's arrival would place her on the outside again. Instead, her bond with her Chosens had grown stronger and she adored the two daughters who made her smile, got her up in the middle of the night, and sometimes had her wanting to hug them and groan with frustration at the same time. Her heart had room for more. When Lesley and Mo decided they were ready for a third daughter, Jayne wouldn't fret. She wouldn't have time!

Things had certainly changed since her notification meeting, when she'd wondered how many days she had left until the Thompsons and Middletons had her dragged to an execution site.

When she'd climbed the steps to the Chosen House today, she hadn't cringed, hadn't immediately flashed back to that horrible day when she was twelve, hadn't wondered if those inside would sneer at her.

You're becoming respectable. Argamon, she was starting to see herself as respectable. Jayne Thompson, Joined for over two years, in love with two Chosens, mama to two daughters, and discussing the possibility of painting a mural at the infirmary. Her personal and outward identities were changing, but she'd never forget the desert she'd wandered alone for all those years, or stop being grateful for the women at her side.

The Chosen Tradition was precious. Her parents had deserved their fate. She'd tell Eleanor and Kat as much, when they asked. As if reading her mind, Eleanor squirmed and yawned. Jayne gazed down at her.

"I hope she stays that quiet for the ceremony," Mo said.

Jayne nodded, then smiled when Lesley broke away from a conversation with Karen and joined them. "I'm glad they'll only be gone for a few days," Lesley said.

"Wait until they go to the Indoctrination Academy," Karen murmured as she passed by them on her way to William.

"We might not mind as much by then," Mo said, to chuckles.

Jayne watched Lesley make a face at Eleanor. Last week, she'd expected Lesley to be on edge today, but Lesley's attitude and mood had changed since Russell's visit. It had taken a stranger's observation to drive home what those closest to Lesley had told her for weeks. Jayne couldn't be cross with her. Carol and her Chosens had always complimented her drawings, but she hadn't truly believed she had talent until Joanna had reached out to her. She still had her doubts, but a tiny part of her was hoping that she'd find herself in the infirmary's pediatric waiting area, painting balloons.

"Time to take your daughter back," Michael bellowed, carrying over a crying Kat. Clucks of sympathy mingled with cooing voices as Michael transferred Kat into Lesley's arms.

Adelaide leaned over Kat and shook a rattle. "You're going first, aren't you? Because you're older. Yes, you're older."

Officially, Kat was sixteen minutes older. Unofficially, it didn't matter. Jayne had already stopped thinking about Kat's origins. The screaming daughter in Lesley's arms was Kat Thompson, and about to be introduced to the Chosen Council.

When the Chosen Council member who'd receive the twins strode into the room, Kat was still crying. "Don't worry about it," Council

Member Jessica Roberts said to Lesley. "I'm used to crying babies." Roberts strode to the front of the room. Everyone—except Kat—quieted down as two assistants carried in a pair of basinets and placed them on the wooden table behind Roberts. "Shall we begin?" Roberts said.

With her Chosens and daughters, Jayne moved to the centre of the room and self-consciously watched everyone form a circle around them. Her vision blurred. Being surrounded by familiar and friendly faces was still a novelty. It wasn't only Carol and Ronald anymore. Jayne looked for Carol and bit her lip when she spotted her. She felt Mo's hand on her arm. Kat's cries faltered.

"Let us say the Words," Roberts said.

Jayne looked down at Eleanor. "Disobedience means death," everyone intoned. "Death to those who commit a Chosen Violation. Death to those who disobey. Death to those who violate the Way. Death to those who violate the Way. Death to those who violate the Way!" Only Mo was able to clap along with the others. Oh dear, now Eleanor was crying.

Roberts grinned. "I never know which way it's going to go after saying the Words. Some babies cry, others quiet down. I see we have both cases here." She let go of her neighbours' hands to break the circle. Everyone else remained in place. "It is my pleasure and privilege to welcome two new Rymellans to the Chosen House and to receive them on behalf of the Chosen Council. Let us witness the daughters of Lesley, Ramona, and Jayne Thompson taking their first step toward following the Way." Roberts beamed at Lesley. "Will you introduce me to your oldest daughter?"

"I will." Lesley stepped forward and carefully handed Kat to Roberts.

Roberts smiled down at her. "Who am I holding?"

"You are holding Katherine Thompson," Lesley said.

"And who are you?" Roberts asked.

With moist eyes and a lump in her throat, Jayne listened as Lesley replied, sounding both proud and humbled, "I am Katherine's mama."

FAMILY COMES FIRST

.....

JAYNE COULDN'T BELIEVE IT WHEN ANDREW'S workshop came into view up ahead, with the home he shared with Ann just behind it. Usually the walk here took and felt much longer, because Ellie or Kat would be trying to drag her away to play, or would stop to look at an insect or a flower or grass or a bird or dirt or whatever else caught their attention.

Every time Jayne passed by the twins' bedroom, she had to will herself to look forward, to not stop and linger in the doorway, the longing to see them pressing against her heart. As it was, she still looked behind her whenever she needed to step backwards, to make sure she wasn't going to trip over a toy. For at least a week after they'd gone, she'd leaped out of bed in the morning and rushed to their room in a panic, sure that the silence meant something terrible had happened to them.

She'd sometimes grumbled when they interrupted her drawing. Now she'd give anything for them to toddle toward her, holding out something to show her or wanting something to eat or crying because they'd hurt themselves. All right, maybe not that last one, but she missed them so much she wouldn't mind dealing with a scraped knee.

She'd visited them a week ago at the Indoctrination Academy, but it felt as if she hadn't seen them in months. As their entry day for Level One had approached, she'd told herself it would be wonderful to not have them pleading with her to play with them when she'd just finished playing with them, and to not be woken up five minutes after she fell asleep by the patter of little footsteps coming toward her bedroom door, or Lesley and Mo's.

The peace, the quiet, the ability to focus without interruption was wonderful, but she'd rather have Ellie and Kat here. She'd take the irritations. The pleasures, the bursts of joy, far outweighed them. At least she'd see them again soon, the reason she and her Chosens were strolling hand in hand toward Andrew's workshop. When they entered the workshop, Jayne squeezed Lesley's hand and let it go.

Andrew looked up from the pair of blue trousers he was hemming and smiled. "Everything is right over here." He moved to another table and the rack sitting next to it. "Blouses, pants, dresses…" He spread his arm toward the folded clothes sitting on the table, then removed a blouse from the rack and held it up for them to see. Jayne knew he'd made it for Kat, who always gravitated toward purple. Ellie's clothes would be shades of blue.

"They're growing up too fast," Lesley murmured.

Jayne nodded, even though Lesley wasn't looking at her. She glanced at Mo, who'd plunked into a chair and pulled out her comm unit. Mo always tuned out when it came to clothes. Trading for toys was a different matter. Jayne always had to practically drag her from the Trading Centre.

A light touch on her arm made her look back in Lesley's direction.

"What do you think?" Lesley asked.

Jayne studied the blouse Andrew was holding. "It's purple." She felt the material, rolled the cotton between her fingers. "As for size, hard to say. They're growing so fast."

"Even if it's a little big now, it won't be soon."

"I doubt it will be too big," Andrew said, a hint of indignation in his voice. He hung the blouse back up. "I measured them and accounted for the typical growth rate at their age."

Lesley didn't contradict him. She shifted her gaze to the blue blouse he'd lifted from the rack.

"Where's Ann?" Mo had lifted her head from her comm unit and was gazing at Andrew. "She usually pokes her nose in when we're doing this."

"She had to fly tonight," Andrew said as he lifted a mauve pair of pants from the table.

Mo's forehead furrowed. "Really? I just came down from 72 and didn't see her there."

"It was a last-minute thing. One of the pilots wasn't feeling well."

Mo still appeared surprised, but her eyes went to her comm unit again. Jayne inwardly chuckled. They could take home the most garish clothing ever created and Mo wouldn't care. At least they didn't have to go to the Trading Centre and keep trading for clothes. Having two tailors in the family was handy, though Michael spent more time on his government duties, leaving the business in the capable hands of his son.

Her comm unit beeped. *Carol.* Now wasn't a good time. Expecting that Carol would leave a message, she silenced the unit and smiled at the adorable teddy bears Andrew had sewn onto the legs of the pants he showed them.

More beeps pierced the air. Jayne's jaw tightened when she checked her comm unit's display. "I'll be back in a minute," she said to nobody in particular. It was unusual for Carol to be persistent. Jayne stepped outside the workshop and pressed the connect button. "I was going to beep you later," she said tersely to Carol. "We're with Andrew. He's showing us new clothes for the twins."

"I know you would have beeped me back, but I...I don't know."

Jayne immediately regretted her irritated tone. She could hear the tears in Carol's voice. "What's wrong?"

"It's your grandmama Hutchins. She, uh, she passed away this afternoon. She's gone."

She stiffened with surprise, but otherwise felt nothing. Her mama's mama had abandoned her along with just about every other relative, but the woman had meant something to Carol. "I'm sorry."

Carol was too upset to pretend she thought Jayne would care. "I just wanted you to know and hear it from me.

Jayne didn't know who else would have told her. "Thank you. I appreciate it. What happened?" she asked, out of curiosity, not concern.

"She was closing in on her late nineties."

Her late nineties? A vague memory entered her consciousness, one in which Mama had mentioned that her mama had been in her late thirties when she'd had her last child.

"She went peacefully."

"That's good." Jayne pondered what else to say. The family wouldn't want her at the Farewell Ceremony, which was fine because she didn't want to go. "Is there anything I can do?" she asked, for Carol's sake.

"No," Carol said with a sigh. "I just wanted you to know."

She hated that she thought of him, but… "You've told Robert?"

"He's next."

They lapsed into silence.

"I won't keep you," Jayne said, not wanting to abandon Carol, but not knowing what else she could do at this moment. "Beep me if you need to. I'll be thinking of you."

"Thanks," Carol murmured.

They disconnected. Jayne took a deep breath and went back into the workshop.

Lesley frowned at her. "Everything all right?"

For an instant, she thought of saying yes, everything was fine, but at some point she'd have to tell them her grandmama had died. Even though she'd been estranged from her for many years, and her Chosens would understand that, given that they'd never met her, they might still be surprised if she downplayed her death to the extent that she glossed over it now.

"My grandmama died."

"I'm so sorry," Lesley said, at the same time Andrew murmured a platitude.

"It's fine, really. We weren't close. But Carol's really upset." Jayne pointed to an adorably tiny purple dress Andrew was holding. "Kat will love the birds."

She could feel Lesley's eyes on her, could sense that Lesley wanted to hug her. But Jayne didn't want a fuss. There was no reason for it. She was fine. Concerned for Carol, but otherwise fine.

"Yes, she'll love the birds," Lesley finally said.

Jayne mentally thanked her. Then she felt Mo's arm slip around her waist. She wrapped her arm around Mo's shoulders, like she had many times before. She pulled Mo close, felt Mo lean into her. A quick squeeze, and then she let Mo go and moved closer to the table to examine another pair of pants.

She did not want a fuss. Her grandmama was a stranger to her. If she felt anything, it was disappointment. She'd always wondered what, if anything, her grandparents knew about the Incident. She'd asked them each once, and they'd insisted they'd known nothing until that horrible day. Carol had occasionally brought it up, but they'd never budged from that position. Now her grandmama was gone, along with any answers she might have offered to her granddaughter to explain how her daughter had fallen from the Way, and why that daughter left her children behind to live with the consequences.

BACK AT HOME, Mo went into the kitchen for a glass of water. For some reason, the workshop always made her thirsty. Maybe it was due to the environmental controls that maintained the work area's constant temperature and low humidity, or maybe it was the many rolls of fabric clogging up the place, or maybe pretending to care about clothes just taxed her physically. She was happy to leave all the cooing and praise to her Chosens, trusting them to not accept anything that would result in the twins being teased.

She'd just filled a glass when her comm unit beeped.

"Thompson."

"Sorry to bother you so late, but can you fly a shift tomorrow at noon?" Archer asked.

She wanted to tut. She'd just finished a supply rotation and wouldn't supervise a practicum on 72 until next week. She'd looked forward to a few days' downtime.

"One of the pilots isn't feeling well."

Archer must have sensed her reluctance. "That's two pilots. There must be something going around."

"No, only the one."

"And the one on nights. The reason Ann had to fill in tonight."

"Ann isn't filling in for anyone. None of the night pilots are ill."

Mo frowned at her comm unit. "Are you sure?"

"Mo, I know who's flying and who isn't," he said tersely.

She mumbled a sorry. Maybe she'd heard Andrew wrong.

"Can you fly the shift tomorrow?"

"Yeah, sure."

His voice lifted. "Thank you."

She disconnected and carried her glass into the living room. "Did either of you hear Andrew say that Ann's flying tonight, or did I imagine it?" she asked her Chosens, who were on the sofa discussing the clothing they'd approved, the second reason Mo had escaped to the kitchen.

Les met her eyes. "He said one of the pilots is sick."

So she hadn't misheard.

"Why?" Les asked.

"Uh, no reason," Mo said, not sure what she was dealing with. Had Ann lied to Andrew, or had he misunderstood something she'd said? Either way, it was none of her business. She'd learned to stay out of their relationship. When they were mad at each other and one of them was telling her about it, she'd nod, and murmur, and grunt, and not choose sides. She had her own life to worry about, not that she was worried about anything right now except the twins. And she wasn't really worried about Ann and Andrew. They'd seemed okay last time she'd seen them together.

She sank into the armchair across from Les and Jayne and sipped her water. "Okay, so are we going to talk about it, or not?"

Neither one of them asked what she meant. Les's eyes grew wary. Jayne stood, went over to the archway that led to the hallway, and leaned against its frame.

Great. She'd figured this was the way it would go.

"It is the ideal time," Les said, repeating what she always said when they started this discussion, the one that never went anywhere. They all agreed that yes, it was the right time, that lots of Rymellans planned their pregnancies to coincide with when at least one child was away at the Indoctrination Academy. They all agreed they didn't want the twins to come home at the end of their Level One to a new baby, so they'd try to plan it so the baby was due a few months after that. They'd not agreed on the most important part of the plan. Who was going to carry said baby.

"I have a new supervisor at work," Les said.

Here we go. Mo looked to Jayne, who was wound so tightly that if she moved at all, she'd snap.

"I'm not doing it," Jayne stated flatly.

Mo wasn't surprised. "Ever, or right now?" she asked, suspecting the answer.

Jayne hesitated, hugged herself. "Ever."

Mo glanced at Les. It had been a while since Jayne had said it out loud.

"It won't look good if you don't have children," Les said.

Jayne snorted. "I don't care. It's not happening. And yes, it wouldn't look good—if I were anyone else. Trust me, nobody's going to be upset that the Adams line isn't perpetuated. They'll be pleased."

"We won't be," Mo said, then wished she'd phrased it differently. "I mean, we won't be mad, but don't you want children?" Jayne was fantastic with the twins, and because she was home more than her Chosens, she spent the most time with them. "You're a wonderful mama."

Les nodded her agreement.

"It's not a matter of wanting or not wanting children," Jayne said.

"We know your children will be strong in the Way," Les said. "The Chosen Council wouldn't have Joined you if they thought otherwise."

"That's only part of it." Jayne blew out some air, then rubbed her forehead. "Any children I have...I know Ellie and Kat are my children. I love them dearly. But they're not Adamses. Which is a good thing. They can use that when—if they run into problems because of me. Any children I were to have wouldn't be able to. They wouldn't be able to distance themselves like that."

"According to the Chosen Tradition, the twins *are* Adamses," Les pointed out.

"You know what I mean. Officially, yes. In the way Rymellans see them, no. Maybe the twins will still run into trouble when their peers understand who one of their mamas is, but they can say, 'We aren't of the Adams line'."

Mo hoped they wouldn't. It would hurt Jayne. It would deny the reality that Jayne was their mama in every sense of the word, especially when it came to Kat, though the thought was fleeting. Mo rarely thought of Kat's origins. In fact, she couldn't remember the last time she'd remembered that Kat wasn't related to any of them.

"Any daughter I carry won't have that luxury," Jayne said.

"But they'll have us," Mo said. "They'll have their sisters."

"Why deliberately put anyone into that situation at all?"

Les leaned forward. "If you want children, you should have them. Why deny yourself that?"

"It would be selfish." Jayne's tone was firm, almost defiant.

With a sinking feeling, Mo mentally crossed Jayne off the list for the next baby. "Okay, we can wait and see what happens when Ellie and Kat's peers understand who they are. You'll still be young enough."

"You're not listening to me. Ellie and Kat will have an out. Any children I have won't." Jayne folded her arms. "You can't talk me into this. I hope you won't force me to have a child."

Les drew breath. Mo quickly jumped in. "Fine. I'll carry the baby again, but there's a condition."

They both turned toward her.

"I'm not setting foot inside the Reproductive Technology Centre until one of you has committed to carrying the one after this one. So talk amongst yourselves." Mo pointed her two index fingers at each other. "Talk. And tell me who it's going to be."

Jayne nodded. "Thanks, Mo."

Les did not look happy, maybe because it seemed that Jayne had assumed Les would do it. Well, they could sort it out themselves. Until one of them came to her and said that she'd carry the next-next baby, and at least pretend to be happy about it, Mo would stand her ground. No pregnancy.

"Tziva, anyone?" Jayne asked, glancing up the hallway, her means of escape.

"Sure," Mo said.

As soon as Jayne had gone, Mo left the chair and sat next to Les. "She's not ready," she said, keeping her voice low. She laid her hand on Les's leg and was surprised by how tense Les felt.

"Remember that conversation I had with Jayne in my aviacraft a few years ago? She was essentially worried about the same thing. I thought she'd come around after we were Joined. Things are going well."

"She was ostracized for years, Les. Still is, to some degree. That's hard to go around." She forced a smile. "Let's see what happens with the other children as they get older. She might change her mind. Oh, and I meant what I said. I'm not carrying the one after this, and I'm not getting pregnant until I know who will." She gave Les's arm a playful nudge. "Start thinking ahead."

She would have chuckled at Les's expression, if Les didn't look so stressed.

THE NEXT MORNING, Lesley sat at her desk at Military Headquarters, her mind still on the conversation she'd had with her Chosens the previous evening. She knew it was selfish, but she was desperately hoping Jayne would agree to carry their fourth daughter. At the same time, she knew the chances of that happening soon, in time for Mo to get pregnant before Ellie and Kat came home from the Indoctrination Academy, were slim. Still, she'd have to talk to Jayne, see if she could encourage her to have a biological child. Jayne was a wonderful mama! And she wouldn't be alone. But Lesley understood Jayne's hesitation. The question was whether Jayne would overcome it, and soon.

A triad stopping at three children would be seen as a failure, and Mama wouldn't stand for it. Lesley could already hear Mama's voice in her head, chiding them for letting the family down. As it was, she'd been agitating for them to have a baby for months, to the point that they'd made excuses the last two times Mama had invited them for supper. Lesley couldn't imagine telling her the next baby would be the last, and there would be a next baby, because Mo would eventually agree even if neither of them committed to the next one. It might take her months, though, and Lesley couldn't expect Mo to carry every child. So hopefully Jayne would come around. Otherwise the duty would fall to Lesley, a thought that made her stomach clench. She did not want to carry their fourth daughter, or their fifth, or any after that, and she did not want to have to explain why to her Chosens.

Her sour mood overshadowed the usual anticipation she felt when she checked her dispatches for any new assignments. She'd finished her last opinion for Blair just a few days ago, even though Blair had already moved to another position by then. A promotion, and well deserved. Now Commander Trenton oversaw the opinions and divvied out the assignments, an officer who had only moved to the Military Headquarters in B2 last month. Lesley expected her first assignment from Trenton today and was determined to make a good impression, so she had to clear her mind of babies, Mama, and anything else that could distract her.

Ah, a dispatch from Trenton. Lesley read it, then read it again. The assignment wasn't at all what she'd expected. She'd been writing opinions for a number of years now and was viewed as quite good at it. So why had Trenton assigned her something so easy that a junior officer who'd never written an opinion before could do it? This was the sort of assignment they'd give when training someone, the sort of opinion Lesley would finish by lunch.

Perhaps Trenton wanted to start everyone with something easy, to see what they could do. Well, Lesley would show her, and now she was feeling grateful that the assignment wouldn't require much heavy thought, because her mind was still filled with her Chosens, babies, and Mama's disappointed face and raised voice.

A COUPLE OF days later, Jayne viewed the partially completed mural of fluffy animals and flowers in the twins' bedroom. She was refreshing their wall while they were away. She'd had a conversation with them, or at least tried to have one, about what they might want in their mural, but given they were still using two-word sentences and had a limited vocabulary, she'd ended up paying attention to what grabbed theirs. So far, they loved hearing stories about fluffy animals and cooed over any flowers they came across while playing outside or walking with their mamas, so fluffy animals and flowers it was.

When they went into the Indoctrination Academy for their Level Two, they'd be able to tell her what they wanted, or even if they wanted a mural. She'd be disappointed, and sad, if they didn't. They might even want their own bedrooms by then. But she doubted it. They were close, did everything together, and seemed to like each other.

Her comm unit beeped. She wiped her hands on a rag. "Hi, Carol. How are you?" she said, mentally scolding herself at the same time. She should have beeped Carol and asked her how she was feeling, but the conversation about their next daughter, and who would carry the one after that, had pushed her grandmama's death to the back of her mind.

"I'm all right," Carol said, not really sounding it. "Listen, we're going through Grandmama's things, and we found something. A letter, addressed to you."

"To me?" Why would a grandmama who hadn't spoken to her granddaughter for years leave a letter for her?

"I was going to drop by and give it to you, but then I figured that would be rude."

And strange. Carol always beeped first. "You want to come over now?" Jayne asked, suspecting that Carol wanted to get away from everyone. "How long will it take you to get here?" Had grandmama still lived in the same sector, or had she moved? Jayne didn't know.

"A couple of hours."

"You could stay for supper, and Ronald, Rachel, and Anthony, too. It's just me and Lesley tonight. Mo is up on 72."

"I'll come, but alone. We didn't want Rachel getting underfoot while we were at Grandmama's, and I need my hands free and didn't want to be holding Anthony all the time, so Ronald's at home with them."

"They can still come."

Carol paused. "Honestly, I just want to get away for a bit and not have to worry about them. Sorry, I know you haven't seen them for a while..."

Jayne swallowed her disappointment. "No, it's okay. I'll see them soon. And you sooner."

They said their goodbyes and disconnected.

A letter. Jayne couldn't imagine what would be in it. She tried to push down the hope that sprang within her, but it managed to escape anyway. Had Grandmama left behind what she knew her granddaughter wanted the most? Would the letter answer some of her questions about the Incident?

WHEN JAYNE OPENED the door to Carol a few hours later and ushered her into the living room, she could hardly contain herself. She asked how everyone was, then couldn't stop herself from bringing it up, even though they were still standing and she hadn't offered Carol anything to drink. "You said you have a letter?"

"I don't know if it's a letter, but I assume it is." Carol dipped into the bag slung over her shoulder and pulled out a small white envelope.

She handed it to Jayne. "I found it when I was sorting through Grandmama's things."

Jayne accepted it and looked at the flowery script—shocked recognition made her stiffen. She stared at her name on the envelope. *Jayne.* "Where did you find it?" she asked, her voice sounding far away.

"In Grandmama's things."

"But where specifically?"

"In a box she had tucked away. In the attic." A pause. "Are you all right? You look pale."

Jayne tore her eyes away from the envelope. "I don't think this is from Grandmama."

Carol appeared even more confused. "Who's it from?"

Her mouth dry, she forced out the word. "Mama."

Carol froze. "Why do you think that?" she whispered.

Because Jayne had seen her name written this way many times, on gifts and letters she'd received while at the Indoctrination Academy, and the few other times Mama had handwritten it.

"Why would Grandmama have a letter from your mama? Are you sure it's from her? It looks like Grandmama's handwriting."

Jayne nodded. "They wrote similarly. But Mama's *J*'s always had a flair to them that Grandmama's didn't." In her hand, in front of her eyes, she held what she hoped was a letter from Mama. Her heart raced. Almost dizzy with shock and anticipation, she stumbled over to the nearest chair and sank into it. But she didn't rip open the envelope. She was still thinking clearly.

Interior had destroyed everything related to her parents. This envelope and its contents had survived because they either hadn't found it, or they hadn't known who'd written the name. Had Grandmama known? She must have known, unless Mama had slipped it into the box Carol had found.

"You said you found it in a box tucked away in the attic."

Carol nodded. "From the dust, it looked like it hadn't been disturbed in years."

In years. She looked down at the envelope again, at her name. She could feel the envelope wasn't empty. It must be a letter. "I'm going to have to think about what to do."

Carol knew what she meant without needing Jayne to explain. "If I were you, I'd talk to Lesley."

Yes, she had ready access to an Interior officer who wouldn't presume the worst. "I'll put it away for now. Don't bring this up at supper. Please."

"Okay. Whatever you want." Carol swallowed. "A letter from your mama. Argamon."

Yes, Argamon, fifteen times over. She bounded up the stairs and into her bedroom. With trembling fingers, she slipped the envelope into a drawer, one she wished had a lock.

WHEN LESLEY ARRIVED home a few hours later and heard the voices in the living room, she reminded herself to be sociable. She wasn't in the greatest mood and would have preferred a quiet supper with Jayne, with no pressure to engage in conversation.

That afternoon, not long after she'd sent Trenton the uncomplicated opinion she'd written, she hadn't been surprised to receive a dispatch from her. She'd hoped that Trenton's reply would contain a juicier assignment. But as she'd read the missive, she'd grown confused and irritated. The opinion she'd submitted was "satisfactory," and her next assignment was on a similar level to her last one. Easy. Straightforward. One they would give to someone new, who'd never written an opinion before.

Some overseers requested that Commander Thompson submit the military's opinion, and those opinions often took weeks, even months, to ponder, investigate, and write. Were those overseers not busy? Lesley found that hard to believe. Perhaps Trenton was using these easier opinions to get an idea of the competence of each member of her group. It was the only explanation Lesley could think of, but it didn't really make sense. Such easy assignments would make it difficult for Trenton to gauge anyone's skill.

At least she was home now, and after Carol had left, she'd try to relax. She took a moment to rally herself, then went into the living room.

JAYNE HAD NEVER thought she'd be so eager to be rid of Carol, but she couldn't wait to bid her good night. The letter in the drawer upstairs kept calling to her. The sooner she spoke to Lesley, the sooner she could stop obsessing about it.

Unfortunately, something was bothering her Chosen. Carol hadn't noticed because Lesley had participated in their conversation over supper, but to Jayne it had been clear that Lesley's heart hadn't been in it, that her mind had been occupied with something else. She wouldn't have noticed a few years ago, when she didn't know Lesley well, but now she knew how to read her—most of the time.

If she wasn't in possession of what would probably be considered by Interior as prohibited material, she'd wait until Lesley had dealt with whatever was bothering her. But Jayne wouldn't be able to sleep, concentrate, draw, paint, do anything, while that letter's existence beckoned to her.

"You know you can beep me anytime, right?" she said to Carol as they strolled to the front door.

"Are you sure you don't want me to fly you home?" Lesley added.

"I'll relish the time on the train," Carol insisted. "Seriously, I want to be alone for a bit."

They took her at her word and said their goodbyes. Jayne closed the front door. Not wanting to jump on Lesley right away, she smiled at her, followed her into the living room, waited until Lesley had sunk into a chair and brushed a stray hair from her face.

Then she jumped on her.

"I have to talk to you," she said, hoping anxiety wasn't making her sound terse.

Lesley's lips thinned. "I know we have to talk, but can we do it another time? Mo can wait another few days."

"It's not about who's going to carry the baby." Jayne hoped that if she stood her ground, Lesley would agree to carry her daughter with Mo. "It's something else, and it's urgent. The reason Carol came over."

"I thought she wanted to get away for a while, to escape everyone else's grief."

"That too, but it wasn't the only reason."

Lesley looked at her expectantly.

Just spit it out. There was no easy way to tell her this. "When she was going through my grandmama's things, she found a letter addressed to me. She brought it over."

She could almost read Lesley's mind. She was wondering why a letter from her Chosen's grandmama would require an urgent conversation. Her words confirmed Jayne's impression. "What did she say that would..." She trailed off.

"It's not about what she said, because it turns out that it's not from her." Jayne swallowed. "It's from my mama."

Lesley's eyes widened and she looked like she was about to bolt off the couch. She recovered herself quickly. The mask came down. "Did you read it?" Her voice was steady, but Jayne could hear the hint of alarm.

"No. Interior destroyed everything related to them. I know...it's not something that should exist. The letter."

"Do you want to read it?"

The question hung in the air. Of course she wanted to read it! Maybe it was only motherly advice, but why would her mama have written to her rather than just speaking to her? Maybe this was wishful thinking, but she must have written it because she knew she was going to be executed. Jayne hoped the letter contained an explanation, or at least more details about what had happened.

But what would Lesley think if she admitted that yes, yes, she wanted to read it? Would she be disappointed, expecting her Chosen to not want to lay eyes on anything related to one of the most notorious criminals in Rymellan history? Maybe, but Jayne wouldn't lie to her.

"I do want to read it," she admitted, but she wasn't going to leave it at that. "Maybe it has some of the answers I've craved. Maybe even an apology. She probably wrote it because she knew what was going to happen to her."

Lesley's clear blue eyes that weren't giving anything away, met hers. "Let's say she did know she was going to be executed, and she wrote a letter to you during that time. Then she'd fallen from the Way when she wrote it."

Jayne nodded. She knew this. She hated thinking about it, but she knew it, and she knew what Lesley would say next, and she'd expected it.

"Which means what she wrote could be contrary to the Way." Lesley's voice was still even, controlled.

"Which means nobody should lay eyes on it? What if it isn't? What if it's just—" Her throat tightened, choking off her voice. What if it said, *I'm sorry. I'm sorry that what I've done is going to have terrible consequences for you*. What if it said, *I regret what I've done but it's done now and I have to take responsibility*, which would show that her mama had returned to the Way. What if it said, *I love you*. What if it said *I didn't do it. Don't believe what you're told*. That last one was a childish fantasy, one she'd clung to during the worst times. After receiving more details about her father's crime from Kevin Stewart, she knew for sure her papa had fallen, but the child within her could still hope that her mama had been innocent.

Maybe she shouldn't read the letter. Maybe she didn't want to sever that wafer thin thread still tying her to that hope. No. She was an adult, not a child.

"I need to know," she said, her voice trembling. "Try not to judge me for this, but if Interior takes the letter and destroys it without even opening it, I'm not sure I'd ever get over that, knowing I could have found out more about why it happened."

When Lesley's hand grasped hers, she almost jumped. She hung on to it, squeezed it, felt tears spring to her eyes when Lesley didn't let go.

"I can understand why you feel the way you do," Lesley said gently. "I'm not judging you. I'm warning you. Opening the letter, reading it, could lead to you knowing something you wished you didn't. You won't be able to unknow it."

Dread, anticipation, fear, swirled through her. "Are you saying we're going to open it and read it?"

"No. I'm not."

It took her a second to register the words. She almost pulled her hand away, but she needed to lean on her Chosen right now, her Chosen, who was also an Interior officer. She searched Lesley's face, saw nothing but concern. It must be difficult for her. If she wasn't in Interior, would they be upstairs already, ripping open the envelope? Or would she still be saying no.

"You're going to just take it, then? And do what with it?" she asked her.

"I'm going to speak to Laura. Privately."

"About reading it?"

"Yes." Lesley's fingers tightened around hers. "She might tell me to hand it over to Interior, and we'll never see it again. But if we go up there and open it ourselves and whatever it contains is contrary to the Way, we'll have violated multiple articles."

"And if it's all innocent, we won't have violated any."

"I'm not quite sure that's true. Article 81 might apply."

Knowingly reading material that violated the Way. A serious strike. "The problem is, we won't know until we open it."

"Exactly. But given the writer of the letter, an argument could be made that we should have assumed and never opened the letter, regardless of what it says."

Jayne conceded the point with her silence. It was why the letter was sitting upstairs unopened, why she'd instantly known that she should talk to Lesley before doing anything, why she'd resisted tearing open the envelope even though she could think of nothing else.

"I want you to give me the letter," Lesley said.

Surprise harshened her tone. "Why?" she barked.

"So I can lock it away."

"You don't trust me." Jayne wanted to back away from her, even though her more rational, wise self reminded her that Lesley loved her.

"I want it in a safe place, that's all. And I want to be able to tell Laura it's locked away."

Once again, she thought about how difficult this must be for her Chosen, whose instincts were probably screaming at her to get the letter and burn it right now. "Okay."

"I'll talk to Laura as soon as I can."

Which meant not over a comm unit. Why did everything to do with her parents have to be like this? Feel dirty, and wrong? Maybe she should burn the letter herself. What were the chances it contained anything but filth?

But then she'd wonder, and regret, for the rest of her life. Laura might say they must destroy the letter without opening it, and Jayne would obey her without question, but at least she wouldn't have denied herself the chance to get some answers.

Still holding Lesley's hand, she led her upstairs into her bedroom and stopped in front of her dresser. She slid the drawer open. There it was, just an envelope, but the air felt ominous, and her heart thumped in her chest. She lifted it from the drawer, offered it to Lesley.

Her Chosen took it, then let go of her hand and strode away. Jayne didn't follow her. She imagined Lesley holding it away from her and flinging it into the lockbox where she kept confidential Interior papers she brought home with her. She'd probably feel like disinfecting her hand afterwards.

Jayne inwardly snorted. And her Chosens wanted her to have a biological child? Maybe they'd reconsider after this, because the writer of the letter Lesley was so eager to lock away would be that child's grandmama.

IN THE CANTEEN on Deck 15, Mo finished off her after-shift tziva and was about to leave when her comm unit beeped twice. Andrew. Mo skimmed the dispatch. *Can you ask Ann when she expects to be home? I've tried beeping her but she's not answering. Same with dispatches. I thought she was only flying until noon but she's not back.*

Weird, given that Ann wasn't on 72 and hadn't flown since yesterday. Something was going on with her. Mo hoped it wasn't what she suspected, but why else would Ann lie and spend so much time away from home without Andrew?

She beeped Ann, but Ann didn't respond. She tried again. No response. Okay, now her temples were pulsing. She tried a dispatch instead. *I'm trying to beep you. So's Andrew. Are you okay? If you don't respond with something, I'll wonder if you're lying unconscious somewhere.*

Ann responded a minute later. *I'm fine.*

Mo stared at the two words. That was it? *Where are you?*

Who are you, my mama?

Hmm. She could ask again, but come to think of it, she hadn't seen Ann much lately. Just how long had Ann been lying to Andrew? *Let's get together. Haven't seen you in a while. I'm planetside for the next few days and not teaching.*

The minutes ticked by with no reply. Mo was carrying her mug to the dirty dishes rack when Ann's response arrived.

Okay. I have some time tomorrow afternoon. 14:00? Your place?

Sure. See you then.

On her comm unit, Mo pulled up the patrols roster for the previous two weeks. Ann had flown fewer shifts than usual, another concerning piece of information. Before she'd met Andrew, Ann's pattern had been to meet some guy, go gaga over him, spend as much time as possible with him for a few weeks, then dump him. Was that happening now?

Had she grown bored with Andrew and was out with someone new and exciting? Why else would she lie to him and ask Archer to reduce her shifts? Mo could try talking to Archer, but he wouldn't tell her anything.

She'd have to think about how she wanted to approach this tomorrow. Ask Ann outright, try to catch her in a lie and then accuse her, or dance around it, hoping to get more information before she revealed her hand? She wished she'd be playing cards with Ann tomorrow afternoon, rather than trying to figure out if she was betraying Andrew.

Her comm unit beeped twice again. Les, this time. Mo read Les's dispatch, then read it again. *Come home when you can.* Translation: don't hang out on 72 longer than necessary. *Need to talk.* About what? The baby thing again? She'd told Les and Jayne to figure it out. Oh, maybe they had. Maybe Mo would find out who would carry Les's third biological daughter, because it would be Les's baby, even if it was Jayne. Les was the Principal. Jayne's first child would be with her.

No, that wasn't it, either. Les would just say, "We figured out who'll carry the baby. Come home and we'll tell you." It must be something else, something she didn't want to say over a comm unit.

Mo wasn't flying tomorrow, but since her last shift had finished at 21:00, she'd planned to remain on 72 and take a shuttle home tomorrow morning. Now she headed to her quarters to pick up her bag. A cryptic dispatch usually meant something serious was happening. She'd get home late and would try not to wake up Les when she crawled into bed, but she didn't want to have to wait all day tomorrow for Les to come home before she found out what was going on.

AT HER DESK the next morning, Lesley stared at the most recent assignment Trenton had given her. Another easy one. Surely overseers had requested more complex opinions since Trenton had taken over from Blair. Who was writing them? Trenton? Perhaps she was the type of superior who had problems delegating. Whatever the reason, Lesley was bored out of her skull. She'd gone from being satisfied with her work and looking forward to it, to wanting to periodically slam her forehead against her desk to keep herself awake.

She'd only met Trenton once and didn't know the best way to approach her about the assignments. She could drop hints that she'd prefer more challenging work along the lines of what she'd done for Blair. She could also ask if Trenton was dissatisfied with her work, though that couldn't possibly be the reason. It wasn't as if Lesley was new at this. She had a track record, and Trenton hadn't complained about the work she'd done for her so far.

Fortunately, she had something else on her mind this morning that would prevent her from stewing about it. A glance at her comm station told her it was an appropriate time to drop by Laura's office.

A few minutes later, she knocked on Laura's open office door and accepted her invitation to enter. She closed the door and didn't waste time.

"I was wondering if you'd like to go for a walk."

Laura cocked her head. "Now?"

"No, later. Somewhere other than here."

When Laura glanced past her, Lesley knew what she was thinking. *And you closed the door.*

Lesley rocked on her heels. "We haven't gone for a walk for a while. I miss discussing complex situations with you, ones that sometimes arise when we're investigating tips."

Laura's brows rose. "What time and where?"

"Whatever time is convenient for you. I can fly to you."

"How about 19:30? We can walk in the park near me."

"Sure."

"Is there a specific situation on your mind?" Laura's eyes were bright with curiosity. "Just wondering in case I need to give it some thought before we meet."

"I'd rather tell you about it all at once."

Laura's brows really shot up this time. "See you later, then."

On the way back to her office, Lesley ran into another member of the opinions writing team. "I'm glad I ran into you," Lieutenant Crofton gushed. "I wanted to thank you."

"For what?" Lesley said.

"Giving me a chance. Letting me show Commander Trenton what I can do. When I joined the team, I was told you normally handle opinions for Overseer Ferguson, so I was surprised, and grateful, when I was assigned the last one."

Lesley quickly masked the shock that jolted her, hoping Crofton hadn't noticed. "Have you finished yet?" she asked, wanting some idea of when Trenton had given Crofton the assignment.

"Not yet. I figure it'll take me at least another month. Trenton's helping me a bit. She knows it's my first tough one." Crofton's voice lowered. "She's great, isn't she?"

Lesley grunted.

"Anyway, just wanted to say thank you." Crofton bustled up the corridor.

Perplexed, Lesley returned to her office and sank into her chair. Why would Trenton give Crofton what would usually be Lesley's assignment, and why did she appear to be limiting Lesley to those given to junior writers? Lesley would like to think that Trenton initially rotated assignments around her group to get a sense of what each writer could do, but if that were true, Lesley should have received a mix of assignments, not only the easy ones.

But the other possible explanation that sprang to mind, that Trenton didn't like her or wasn't satisfied with her work, didn't make sense. They'd barely interacted with each other in person, all of Lesley's dispatches were professional and polite, and Trenton wouldn't get a sense of her competence with the easy assignments she was handing her. Also, reviewing Lesley's past opinions would tell her all she needed to know.

What did Overseer Ferguson think? Had he assumed she'd write the opinion, even requested that Commander Thompson write it?

Lesley had never run into a situation like this and didn't know how to handle it. She could talk to Trenton, but she didn't want to come across as entitled or whiny. She could wait to see what her next few assignments were like, hoping a complex opinion would come through, but what if none did?

Her comm station beeped, pulling her out of her thoughts. "Thompson."

"Why do things always come up a minute after someone has left my office?" Laura said.

"You can't make it tonight."

"No, I can, but we've just received a tip that requires investigation, and you're up."

If Lesley didn't know she'd be investigating a possible Chosen

Violation, she'd punch her fist into the air. Finally she'd feel useful. She jotted down the details. "I seem to be less busy than usual, lately," she said, when she'd recorded everything. "Trenton's not keeping me as busy as Blair did."

"I'd say I wish there were more tips I could send you to investigate, but I don't."

Lesley chuckled. "I haven't been out on patrol for a while."

"I'll mention it to Bradley."

"Thanks."

They disconnected. Lesley grabbed her cloak and headed out. She could investigate tips. She could go out on patrol. But if Trenton continued to treat her like a junior writer, eventually Lesley would have to speak to her about it, a prospect she did not look forward to.

MO TRIED TO calm herself as she went to the door to let Ann in. Les had filled her in on the letter from Jayne's mama, but that wasn't what had upset her. Yes, it was disconcerting, and yes, she wondered what was in it, but what had really made her jaw tighten was finding out that her two Chosens hadn't talked about who would carry a flaming baby. Mo had suspected, but she'd asked anyway. They'd both mumbled that they hadn't decided yet. Part of Mo wished she hadn't issued her ultimatum, because she'd feel like an idiot if they didn't come to a decision. The other part still hoped they'd talk, and soon, but nothing would happen now until they dealt with the letter.

Les would speak to Laura about it tonight. Hopefully Laura would tell Jayne to open it, Jayne would read it and have all her questions answered, and her Chosens would sit down and have an adult conversation about carrying a baby. Mo snorted to herself. Yeah, and she was about to find out she'd been promoted several ranks at once to admiral. She was delusional. About them having an adult conversation, not the letter. She hoped it would offer Jayne some answers. In the meantime, Jayne had gone to the Trading Centre to trade for paints, saying she needed to be doing something.

Mo swung the front door open and motioned for Ann to come inside.

As usual, Ann strode into the living room and flopped into a chair without waiting to be asked. "I've only got about an hour," she said.

Mo shrugged. "That's fine." She still wasn't sure how she was going to approach this conversation. She started reasonably. "How've you been lately? I haven't seen you the last couple of times I've been on 72."

Then her concern about the letter, and her worry about her ultimatum and what Ann was up to, chased away her determination to remain calm and reasonable. "You know, when Andrew thinks you're flying." She glared at Ann, then wanted to smack her when Ann didn't seem perturbed.

"Watch my mouth and listen to my words," Ann said slowly. "Mind. Your. Own. Business."

"He's my brother."

Ann straightened in the chair. "What do you think I'm doing? No, don't tell me. You think I'm carrying on with someone else."

"The thought had crossed my mind."

"You honestly think I'd do that? Lie to Andrew while I'm out gallivanting?"

"All I know is you're lying to him. And lame lies, by the way. All he has to do is beep someone on 72 to find out you're not there."

"I'll take that under consideration."

Mo blew out some air. "Argamon, Ann, what are you flaming doing? And don't tell me to mind my own business. Why can't you just answer a simple question."

"Maybe there are things I don't want you to know."

"Like what?"

"If I told you, you'd know them."

Mo's hands went to her hips. "I don't need to know whatever it is. But why are you lying to him? You must be doing something you can't tell him."

Ann raised her finger. "Something I don't want to tell him. Big difference."

"That doesn't excuse the lying. You're lying to him. Repeatedly. And what's so bad that you don't want to tell him? You're spending a lot of time doing whatever that thing is."

To her surprise, Ann's shoulders sagged and her voice dipped. "I know."

Ann's changed demeanor sucked Mo's irritation away. She lowered herself onto the sofa. "Why can't you tell him?"

   RYMELLAN 4

Ann lowered her head. "If he knows, he might not want to be with me anymore," she mumbled.

Mo gaped. "What could be so bad that he wouldn't want to be with you? If you're not betraying him..."

"I'm not, honestly."

"Then what could you possibly not be able to tell him? You must trust him."

"I do."

"If he finds out you're lying..."

"I'd tell him, then. But I really would prefer not to. Can you just leave this alone?" Ann raised her head. "Please?"

Mo was momentarily nonplussed. She believed Ann wasn't betraying Andrew with someone else, but... "If you're involved with something, doing something, that might make him break up with you if he knew, then don't you think he needs to know?"

"I'm asking you to stay out of this and not ruin my life." Ann added something under her breath that included the word "already," but that's all Mo could make out.

Mo's mind raced. Did she tell Les and Jayne everything? Not every little thing, but she certainly told them the important things. The significant things. Anything that might disappoint them? Well, yes, if it was major. Minor stuff, usually glossed over. But whatever Ann was up to wasn't minor. "Are you violating the Way?"

"No! Argamon, can you give me some credit and not think the worst, for once? I love Andrew. I'm not doing anything that can hurt him."

Then why wouldn't she just tell him? Mo knew there was no point in asking her, so she needed to decide what to do. Normally her loyalty would lie with Andrew, but she did not want to aim a missile at his relationship and blow it up. If Ann wasn't seeing someone behind his back and wasn't violating the Way, she'd let it be, for now.

"Okay," she said to Ann. "I'll leave it alone."

Ann's shoulders heaved and she rubbed her eyes. "Thank you."

Mo suddenly noticed the dark smudges under those eyes, and maybe she was making things up now, but Ann's shirt didn't fit as snugly as it usually did. "If there's something wrong...if you need help..."

"Leave it."

"Okay." But she didn't want Ann to leave. She'd gone from seeing Ann as someone who would devastate Andrew to someone who needed support. "You want tziva?"

"Sure." Ann almost smiled. "I never thought I'd say this, but it seems weird without the twins around. Too quiet."

Mo barked a laugh. "You hated it when they wanted to show you something."

"I didn't hate it. I'll just prefer them when they can form coherent sentences and wash their hands without being told." She pointed at her right sleeve. "Do you know how many times I've gone home covered in paint?"

Mo could relate, but she missed them dearly and couldn't wait to visit them. "When I see them, I'll tell them Auntie Ann misses them."

She waited for one of Ann's acerbic comebacks, but it didn't come. "I'll go make the tziva." She left for the kitchen. She'd begun the day worried about Andrew. Now she was worried about Ann.

AT THE PARK near Laura's house, Lesley strolled on the dirt path beside Laura, trying to come up with a way to ease into the subject of the letter. Laura was silent, waiting, and probably growing impatient. Just saying it would be best.

She kept her voice low. "You know that after the Adams Incident, Interior destroyed everything related to them. Their house, all the paintings Peter Adams had done, his studio. I don't know much about Joan Adams, but I assume anything external to their home that was hers was also destroyed."

"I know," Laura murmured.

Say it. "They missed something."

Lesley's words hung in the air. They kept walking, with only the sound of their breath, their footfalls, and the rustling of tree leaves from the light breeze breaking the silence.

"What did they miss?" Laura finally said.

"A letter. To Jayne, from her mama."

"How do you know this?"

"Jayne's grandmama—her mama's mama—died not too long ago. When Carol was cleaning out her things, she came across the letter. She didn't realize it was from Jayne's mama. She thought it was from her grandmama. But Jayne recognized the handwriting on the envelope."

"Where is this letter now?" Laura's tone was level, but Lesley knew she was shocked.

"At home, locked in my safe box. Unopened," she added, to answer the obvious question. "When Jayne realized who it was from, she came to me. And I came to you."

"What about her brother? Was there one for him?"

"Carol didn't mention one."

"Find out."

"I will." Lesley forged ahead. "Jayne wants to read it. She's hoping it will answer some questions."

"If it answers questions about the Incident, I'm willing to stake my career on the certainty that whatever it says will be against the Way."

"That's why she brought it to me. As much as she would like to read it, she hasn't. But she wants to. I'd feel the same in her shoes."

Laura didn't speak right away. They continued to stroll, Laura lost in her thoughts, Lesley's turn to wait.

"Let's do this," Laura said. "Let's meet here again, tomorrow, same time. Bring the letter. We'll open it and read it and decide where to go from there."

"What about Jayne? Shouldn't she be with us too?"

"If it's against the Way..." Laura scratched her cheek. "If you weren't Interior, her only choice would have been to hand the letter over to some anonymous Interior officer. She never would have seen it again."

"But I am, and I know her well. You know her quite well, too. We can still read the letter first and then decide whether she should too."

"What if it's against the Way?"

"Then we'll tell her that. If it does have answers, I can relay them as safely as I can. To both her and Mo. This is too big to not include Mo."

Laura softly snorted. "Why don't we invite the entire Thompson and Middleton families to read a letter from Joan Adams that might violate the Way on a level no Rymellan is accustomed to?" she said dryly.

Lesley didn't respond. On the one hand, she knew what she was asking for was outlandish. On the other, it was completely reasonable.

"Bring them too," Laura said with a sigh. "I can see it would be a burden on you to have to deny them what's in the letter. And there should never be secrets between Chosens. Not big ones, anyway."

"And if the letter does violate the Way?"

"We'll decide what to do with the letter once we've read it. I already have an inkling, but I want to sleep on it." Laura stopped walking and turned to look at Lesley. "Has Jayne considered how she'll feel if the letter confirms every terrible thing that's ever been said about her parents?"

"I'm not sure. Right now she's hoping there will be answers."

"How will she feel if there aren't?"

Lesley didn't have to think about it. "Disappointed. Crushed, probably. But not knowing, having a letter and not reading it, will haunt her. She'll always wonder. No matter what's in the letter, I think reading it will be the only way she'll ever be able to let it go."

Laura nodded. "I can understand that. And if it were anyone else, a parent leaving a letter for their child would be an insignificant event, except for the child. But this parent, and this child." She shook her head. "I hope there isn't anything else waiting to be discovered."

Lesley half agreed. She understood Jayne's need for answers. But she'd prefer they came from sealed Interior files, not from the mouths of the criminals themselves.

LATER, IN BED, Lesley rolled over for the tenth time, then fluffed her pillow and rolled over again.

"What time is it?" Mo murmured.

It was too dark to see Mo's face. "I don't know."

"Have you fallen asleep yet?"

She hesitated. "No. You?"

"Almost. After the sixth time you rolled over, maybe."

"Sorry."

Mo turned on the bedside lamp and propped herself up on her elbow. "Is it the letter, or the baby?"

The letter, the baby, her confusion over why her new supervisor wasn't giving her challenging assignments... She went with the safest and obvious choice. She did not want to discuss carrying the baby, and she tried not to bring home any problems at work. "The letter."

"What's in it, or how Jayne will react?"

Lesley chuckled. "How many questions are you going to ask me?"

"Enough to hopefully make you sleepy." Mo lowered her head to her pillow, so they were lying face to face.

"I'm more concerned about how Jayne will react," Lesley said.

"Really? You're not concerned about what's in the letter?"

"I said *more* concerned. I don't want to read something that's against the Way, but it won't be surprising if it is. But Jayne's got her hopes up again."

"Yeah. I can't imagine what it's like loving your parents and hating them at the same time. Like, really hating them, and having everyone else hate them, and not knowing how it all happened. Not that I'd want to know," Mo added quickly. "Who would want those details?"

"Jayne."

"Yeah." Mo fell silent.

Lesley intellectually grasped how Jayne must feel, but she agreed with Mo. She couldn't imagine it. She'd want to know more too, but because she was more objective, she could see that it probably wouldn't help. "It's impossible, for her, to reconcile the parents she knew right up until Interior apprehended them, with the people who were executed. Even if the letter gives her answers, I don't think she'll ever be able to reconcile it all. I think she needs to let it go."

"Easier said than done, Les."

"I know."

"She could have been with us tonight, but she wanted to be alone."

To fret. Lesley doubted Jayne was asleep and wondered if they should get up and go talk to her, but then decided it would be a bad idea. If she wanted to be with them, she would be.

"She's obviously having trouble putting it behind her. That's why she doesn't want to have a child," Mo said.

This was not a conversation Lesley wanted to have. She already felt guilty for desperately hoping that somehow Jayne would agree to carry their fourth daughter. How petty was that? But the alternative would be telling her Chosens why she didn't want to do it, and she didn't think she could. Even if she did, Jayne wasn't likely to change her mind.

She fluttered her eyelids a few times. "I think I'm feeling sleepy, finally."

Mo gave her a skeptical look. "You'll need to decide soon. The twins won't be at the Indoctrination Academy forever, and I want to be pregnant before they come home."

"One thing at a time. I can't talk to Jayne about it until she's dealt with whatever's in that letter."

Mo frowned. Lesley could read her mind. After the letter, what excuse would she use next? The letter wasn't an excuse, though. As she'd said to Mo, one thing at a time. She wished she could delay the baby conversation forever, but instead she'd talk to Jayne, repeat what she and Mo had said in the past about how Jayne's biological children would be born into a loving family, and know it wasn't going to make a difference.

"We'll talk about it, I promise," she said to Mo.

Mo turned out the light and snuggled into her, pinning Lesley's left arm to the bed. At least she wouldn't be able to toss and turn now. She lay awake for a while, content to be there with Mo and doing her best to focus on her breathing, to calm the thoughts that kept intruding, until she eventually dozed off.

THE NEXT MORNING, Mo slammed her bike into the bike rack outside Andrew's workshop and went inside. Andrew was busy measuring some fabric and didn't look up from the worktable that dominated this part of the workshop. If Mo was a client, she would have entered through another door that led into an office and a fitting room. The workshop also contained a second workroom, where Andrew's two apprentices must be, because they weren't in this one. She'd given him permission to build on her land so he'd have room for all this. Otherwise, her land would have sat empty, and her brother wouldn't be as content. The brother she loved, the love that had compelled her to ride here.

"Is this a bad time?" she asked.

When he looked up, she sucked in her breath. He knew. He knew something was going on with Ann. The dark circles under Ann's eyes were also there, under his. His mouth was pinched, his cheeks pale. He didn't grin at her, or tell her off because she could have shocked him and made his hand jerk. He just mumbled hello.

She pretended not to notice that he wasn't himself. Until she knew more about what was going on, she didn't want to say the wrong thing and cause more problems. Maybe being Joined in a triad and having two children had matured her somewhat. Ten years ago she would have bumbled in without giving any thought to the consequences.

"I was just riding by and thought I'd drop in."

"I'm fine," Andrew said, even though she hadn't asked. Then he set his tape measure down and scratched his cheek. "Have you seen Ann lately?"

"Yeah. Yesterday. Why?" She waited with bated breath.

He shrugged, in an exaggerated way that told her he had a reason for asking but wasn't going to tell her. "Did she seem okay to you?" He didn't wait for an answer. "She just flies a lot lately at night."

Nope, she didn't, but Mo held her tongue.

"I hardly see her," Andrew said. "And when she's home, she seems tired."

Flying too many shifts might have explained why Ann had looked so washed out—if it were true. "Maybe you should talk to her about passing on some shifts." Mo wondered what Ann would say. "When Archer beeps in a panic, she can say no. He'll just move on to the next pilot."

"I don't think she likes to do that."

Mo bit her tongue again. "If it bothers you, talk to her." Advising that they talk was okay, right? How else would whatever was going on with Ann be resolved? Mo couldn't shake the feeling that if it didn't come out into the open, it would eventually hurt their relationship, maybe even scuttle it. That ten years ago, her more immature self wouldn't have cared, but now, she didn't want that, for either of them. They'd proven they were serious. Okay, Ann had proven she was serious. Mo knew Ann loved him.

He shrugged again. "It's not really a big deal. I just miss her."

She didn't call him on his obvious lie. "It's good that you miss her." She mentally added, "Keep that in mind when you find out what's going on with her. You do love her."

Out loud, she said, "I'll let you get back to work. I just wanted to drop in and say hi." And see if he'd talk, but he clearly wasn't ready, and this stilted conversation was awkward.

Back on her bike, she headed in the direction of the Trading Centre in case he was watching her. After all, she'd claimed she was "just riding by." When she figured it was safe, she reversed course and sped down the path that led home, pondering what else she could do and deciding there wasn't anything that wouldn't cross the line into interfering with their relationship. So she'd leave it. For now. And be there if either of them needed her. Fortunately the amount of time she'd been spending on 72 would soon decrease.

After the twins had entered the Indoctrination Academy, she'd relished the lack of guilt she'd felt when she was away from home on 72 and taken advantage of that to fly more supply patrols. But she missed Les and Jayne when she was away so often, and she would soon be pregnant—she hoped—so she'd agreed to teach two classes at the Military Academy. If Andrew and Ann hit a nasty bump, she'd be around.

Her mind moved on to her next worry. The letter, and what it said, and how Jayne would react. After that, Mo moved on to concern number three, and hoped her Chosens would move on as well and come to a decision. She wasn't getting any younger, and the twins wouldn't be at the Indoctrination Academy forever.

OUT ON PATROL with Lieutenant Fiddian, Lesley quickened her pace when she rounded the curve on the path and could see the train station's bike rack up ahead. Command Control had beeped them a few minutes ago with a report of a bike having potentially been taken without permission, a serious strike if it was true. Not only were Lesley and Fiddian in the area, but the bike had been taken from where she and Fiddian had left their bikes.

As she approached the rack, shock stopped her dead in her tracks. It was gone. Her bike, gone.

"My bike is gone," she breathed.

Fiddian gaped.

Someone had taken her bike, just taken it. She glanced around, vainly hoping the criminal had just left, but the only cyclist she could see was riding toward them, and there were too many tire tracks leading to and from the rack to distinguish in which direction the criminal had gone.

"That way," a voice said.

She and Fiddian turned toward it.

A young man standing near the top of the steps leading down to the train station pointed up the eastern path. "You should go that way."

"You're the one who beeped Interior?" Lesley asked him.

He nodded.

"You saw someone take my bike?"

The man grew solemn, perhaps thinking about the consequences of not only stealing a bike, but a commander's bike. "I saw a boy run up and grab it. I knew it wasn't his as soon as he got on it. Too tall for his legs, but he was in a state, crying, and he rode off best he could. I was over there." He pointed up the northern path. "I ran after him, but couldn't catch him, and I thought it best left to Interior. I doubt he got far, though."

Fiddian pulled his bike from the rack.

The cyclist Lesley had spotted had arrived and was observing them, wondering what to do. "Do you mind if I borrow your bike?" Lesley asked her. "Someone has taken mine."

Her eyes widened. She dismounted and rolled her bike to Lesley.

"Thank you. I'll return it here and leave it in the rack."

She and Fiddian rode down the eastern path. It didn't take long for them to spot a figure wobbling along up ahead, and as they rode closer, they could hear him wailing. Lesley rode up alongside the rider, intending to tell him to stop, but when he noticed her, he lost his balance. The boy and the bike crashed to the ground.

Fiddian hopped off his bike, letting it fall on its side. Taking more care with someone else's bike, Lesley dismounted and placed it gently on the ground.

The boy was sitting on the path, crying. "He's going to die," he wailed.

Lesley crouched in front of him. The boy looked to be about nine. "Who's going to die?"

"Timmy. My friend. He fell into the river."

She looked at Fiddian. The boy must mean the river about a quarter of a kilometre to the north. It ran quick in places. Someone could easily be swept away. "What's your name?" she asked the boy.

"Steven."

"Can you show us where, Steven?"

He nodded, and accepted her hand when she offered it.

Once on his feet, Steven ran to the north. Lesley would ask him why he was riding east later, and about her bike. Right now, the priority was saving anyone who'd fallen into the river.

When they reached it, Steven led them to the top of a rock overhang. "He's down there," he said, sobbing. "I can't look."

Lesley and Fiddian carefully approached the edge of the overhang and peered down at the river. At first she didn't see anything, but then a flash of black caught her eye. There was Timmy, standing on a rock a couple of metres from the nearest bank, the river's water rushing by on both sides.

Fiddian's lips thinned. Lesley pulled out her comm unit and called for a rescue team, and a vet. Timmy was a black, shaggy dog.

While they waited for the team to arrive, Steven told them that Timmy hadn't fallen in from the overhang, but further up the river. Hoping to help him out, Steven had run along the riverbank until Timmy had somehow ended up on the rock. Then he'd panicked, raced to the train station, and grabbed a bike. He'd been riding to get his mama when Lesley and Fiddian had caught up to him. Rymellans were not assigned comm units until they were twelve years old.

"Why didn't you ask someone at the train station for help?" Lesley asked.

"I wasn't thinking. I just wanted to save Timmy. Will he be okay?"

"The rescue team will do everything they can to get him out safely."

A minute later, the team arrived. Wanting to keep Steven out of the way, she remained with him at the overhang while Fiddian joined the team down at the river. It didn't take them long to remove Timmy from the rock and bring him to the vet waiting to examine him.

As Lesley was taking Steven to where the team was now gathered, a woman rode toward them. Lesley could guess who it was. She'd beeped Steven's mama while they were waiting for the rescue team to arrive. Lesley watched Steven and his mama hug, then they all went over to Timmy, who was now wrapped in a blanket.

"He's fine," the vet said. "A few scratches here and there but nothing broken."

"Can I hug him?" Steven asked.

The vet smiled. "You can."

Now that the crisis was over, Lesley's thoughts returned to her bike. When Steven had finished assuring himself that Timmy was fine, she motioned for him and his mama to join her and Fiddian. They walked out of earshot of the vet and rescue team, who were packing up their gear.

"We have to talk about my bike," Lesley said to Steven. "The one you took without permission from the train station's bike rack."

The blood drained from his mama's face. "You took the commander's bike," she said, her voice hushed. "Why?"

"I didn't think it was wrong," Steven said. "There are exemptions to Article 368. There's one about Rymellans needing help."

"You think Timmy is Rymellan?" his mama asked.

He nodded. "When Cindy asked if animals can violate the Way, Indoctrinator Cane said no because they naturally do what they do so they can't violate the Way. That means they're Rymellan. They always live according to the Way."

His mama looked at Lesley and Fiddian, her eyes hopeful and pleading at the same time.

Lesley could see the logic in Steven's interpretation, and if there was ever a time to broadly interpret a section of an article, this was it. The Way would certainly not expect a Rymellan to stand by and do nothing while an animal was in trouble. Quite the opposite.

"That makes sense to me," she said to Steven. "What would you have done if you had a comm unit?"

"Beeped Mama," Steven instantly said.

She couldn't help but smile. "You could beep your mama, but you could also beep the help code. You'll learn all about that when you get your comm unit."

"I wouldn't have taken your bike if there'd been someone at the rack. I would have asked to take theirs."

"That's good. Well, you should go back to Timmy and take him home."

"That's all?" his mama said.

"That's all." Lesley could see no reason to strike Steven.

"Thank you. I'm terribly sorry about your bike." She put her arm around Steven's shoulders and steered him in the direction of the rescue team.

Fiddian, who'd stayed silent and let his superior officer handle it, chuckled. "You never know what's going to happen when you're on patrol."

They returned to the bikes and rolled all three back to the bike rack, then Lesley and Fiddian peddled over to the next train station, where Lesley would catch a train and return to headquarters.

BACK IN HER office, Lesley hung her cloak on the rack in the corner and sank into her chair. Patrolling had distracted her for a while, especially what had happened with Steven and his dog, but now her mind returned to what would happen that evening. Jayne would find out if the letter answered any of her questions. Lesley wasn't sure what would be worse: if the letter did, or if it didn't. Either way, it would be a difficult evening, to cap off another day without a challenging opinion to write. She'd never been so happy when she'd been asked if she could cover someone's patrol at short notice.

This couldn't go on, but she still didn't know what to do about the assignments she was receiving from Trenton. Buckle down and see if anything changed, or talk to Trenton. She'd have no choice but to do the latter if nothing changed, but she'd rather—

Someone rapped sharply at her open door. Trenton marched in and swung the door shut. "Where have you been?" she barked. "This is the fourth time I've come by your office."

Surprise slowed Lesley's response. "On patrol."

"I sent you a dispatch three hours ago."

"I don't check my dispatches on patrol." She stopped herself just in time from adding that if an officer needed to speak to her urgently, they usually beeped.

"Why were you on patrol?" Trenton snapped.

"I'm on the supply list," Lesley said, her voice even, despite her thumping heart. These weren't the types of conversations she was accustomed to having at headquarters, and surely Trenton knew about her other responsibilities. Blair would have told her, and everything was in Lesley's file. "If I'm not busy, I fill in when someone's required."

"Why didn't you tell me you'd be on patrol?"

"My name was added to the patrol roster." Lesley resisted the urge to add that Blair had known to check the roster when she wasn't around.

"You report to me," Trenton said, enunciating every word. "If you are not going to be available, make sure you let me know."

Lesley clenched her hands on her lap, where Trenton couldn't see them. "I will."

"You're not busy?"

"I dispatched my last assignment this morning."

"I didn't see it."

"I sent it directly to the overseer."

Trenton's eyes blazed. "All your assignments must go through me."

She bit back the obvious question. "I'll be sure to send them to you from now on."

"Is there anything else I should know about? Any other reason you won't be in your office when I'm looking for you?"

"I might be out investigating a tip. I—"

"Ah, yes, Commodore Finney's group." Trenton's lip curled. "You're stretched thin, Commander. I'll speak to the commodore about replacing you."

Shock chased away Lesley's determination to remain calm. "I'm not stretched thin." And this would be the perfect time to bring up the easy assignments she was receiving. "I could do with more assignments, especially of the nature I used to write."

"I will decide what opinions you write. I came by to find out why I hadn't received the one I assigned to you yesterday. Now that I know you've completed it, I'll dispatch your next one."

Lesley wanted to suggest that she send two or three, but she didn't want to irritate Trenton further, and she wanted time to think, to try to understand why Trenton seemed to dislike her for no reason, to the point that she was making her work life difficult. "I'll look out for it."

Trenton whirled, yanked open the door, and left. In the ensuing silence, Lesley realized she was shaking. What was going on? If she'd sent Trenton a sloppy opinion or offended her in any way, she'd understand, but she hadn't. In fact, the conversation they'd just had was the longest they'd ever spoken to each other.

She considered talking to Laura about it tonight, but rejected the idea. She didn't want to run to her with every little problem, and if Trenton spoke to her about dropping Commander Thompson from the Chosen Tradition group, Laura would become aware of the tension soon enough.

She could feel a headache coming on. Trenton, the letter, the looming conversation she had to have with Jayne about who would carry their fourth child... She had to figure out what to do about Trenton's attitude toward her, but she'd never been faced with a supervisor who'd taken an instant dislike to her and apparently didn't trust her competence.

EVERY FOOTFALL SOUNDED like someone had struck a gong as Jayne walked down the dirt path in the park near Laura's house, flanked by her Chosens, her hands in theirs. A small part of her wanted to tell them to forget it, to rip up the letter, that she'd be better off not knowing. But it was drowned out by the part of her that would regret not knowing for the rest of her life. Mama must have written the letter because she knew Interior would come for her. Why else would she have left a letter with her grandmama, a grandmama who'd kept the letter secret all these years, even though she must have realized it could contain information her granddaughter craved.

On the other hand, maybe that was why she'd never handed it over. Maybe she'd been afraid of its contents. Maybe when she'd realized that she had a letter that could get her into trouble with Interior, she'd placed it in the box in the attic and pretended it didn't exist. Given her own apprehension, Jayne couldn't blame her. If she wasn't Joined to an Interior officer, one she trusted with her life, she might have done the same when the letter had finally been placed into her hands.

Poor Carol. She'd had no idea what she was handing over. Robert hadn't received one. Lesley had beeped him, probably shocking him, and asked him if his grandmama had left anything behind for him. If he'd received a letter, he would have known what she was talking about, but no. Lesley had also asked Carol about Robert and received the same answer.

When they stopped among a group of trees that blocked the moonlight, the sudden silence felt ominous. Anyone who managed to see them, despite the darkness, would wonder what the small group was up to, until they approached and saw the three military cloaks, and if they got close enough, the insignia and rank on two of them. They'd quickly move along at that point.

"All right," Laura said. "Lesley and I will open the letter and read it, and if we think it's safe, we'll give it to you."

Both of Jayne's hands were squeezed at the same time, then Lesley let go and stepped to Laura's side. Mo hung on and leaned into Jayne.

Lesley and Laura walked away from them and stopped about five metres away. Light filtered from the gap between them, from a flashlight, no doubt. Their heads ducked. Jayne consciously slowed her breathing.

A minute went by. She couldn't tell from the posture of the two Interior officers whether they were repelled. Horrified. Confused. None of the above. They appeared frozen, to the point that she jumped when they started murmuring to each other. Lesley turned around and strode toward her. Jayne stiffened when Lesley offered her a piece of paper.

The letter.

"It doesn't violate the Way," Lesley murmured. "But it's not what you hoped for. I'm sorry."

Jayne took the letter, braced herself, and read.

Dear Jayne,

I'm sorry your papa and I couldn't visit with you today, but your papa has a very important exhibit and he needs me to be with him. I wish it wasn't happening on the same day as today, but sometimes we can't get what we want.

I hope your grandmamas and grandpapas told you how much we miss you. We told them over and over to tell you. I'm glad the next visiting day won't be too far away.

How many sketches have you done since we saw you last? Did you finish that one of the tree outside your bedroom window? I can't wait to see it. What about your clarinet? I hope you've been practicing every day. The concert isn't too far away.

I'll be thinking of you and your brother all day today. Show him this letter and tell him not to be upset that I didn't write him one. He's older than you, and you need to practice your reading.

Be good for the indoctrinators, Jayne. We'll see you soon.

Love,
Mama.

She blinked back the tears that had welled and read the letter again, trying to commit every word to memory. Because she knew, so she wasn't surprised when Laura returned to her and gave her an apologetic look.

"I know," Jayne said. "I just want to read it one more time."

Laura didn't protest or hurry Jayne along.

Not wanting to deal with her conflicting emotions here, Jayne distanced herself from the writer of the words as she finished her fourth pass over the letter. She handed it to Laura, knowing she'd never see it again, then searched for her Chosens. Her awareness of Mo returned, and she realized that Mo had never let go of her hand. Lesley was close by, her eyes on Jayne.

"What are you going to do with it?" Mo asked.

Lesley moved to Jayne's side and took her hand again.

"Strictly speaking, I should log this in and report it to someone," Laura said.

"But…"

"It's harmless, but still. If anyone else finds out about it, someone will hit the panic button. There will be questions and searches, and with a wide net." Laura slipped the letter back into the envelope. "Fortunately it's a bit of a chilly evening. I'll throw it into the fire later." She raised her finger. "It never existed, understood?"

Jayne nodded along with her Chosens' affirmative murmurs.

"The matter is closed then." Laura's gaze fell on Jayne's face. "I'd say I wish it had answers for you, but given what that would have meant, I'm relieved it didn't. But I understand your desire to know."

"Do you think the Interior records will ever be unsealed?" Jayne didn't want to lose this opportunity to ask Laura, the commodore. It wasn't that they pretended the Incident had never happened, but it wasn't the sort of topic people discussed around a supper table, even when the daughter of two of the criminals was present.

"No," Laura said flatly.

The finality, the starkness and hopelessness of it, brought her mood lower than it already was. Afraid that she'd lose the battle here, howl, sob heaving sobs and ask herself for the millionth time why, she squeezed her Chosens' hands. "Shall we go?"

They seemed to understand, and after thanking Laura, they headed to the nearest holding area, where Lesley's aviacraft waited. Nobody spoke. Her Chosens did exactly what she needed them to do. They held her hands. Anything more would have had her weeping in their arms, and she didn't want that. Not now. Not for the parents she'd never understand.

AFTER WAITING FOR what she believed to be a respectful amount of time, Lesley knocked on Jayne's closed bedroom door and was relieved when a muffled invitation to enter reached her ears. Jayne was sitting in the comfy armchair in the corner, her legs tucked under her.

"I wanted to make sure you're okay," Lesley said, noting Jayne's dry eyes, but worried regardless. Jayne tended to be stoic when it came to her parents and the Incident, but she'd allowed hope to soar once again, only to have it crash against the rocks.

"I'm all right. Disappointed, but all right." Jayne barked a laugh. "Can you believe it? A letter to me when I was at the Indoctrination Academy. My grandparents obviously forgot to bring it with them and I guess thought it would be best not to tell my mama."

"Do you remember anything about that time?"

"I've thought about it. I have a vague memory of them not coming on one of the family visiting days. But I was in my Level Two. There are a lot of visiting days for the first two levels, so she was right. It wasn't long before I saw them." Jayne shot Lesley a quick smile. "I wouldn't need to practice my reading in Level Three, and she was dead by the time I was in Level Four."

"I didn't know you played the clarinet," Lesley said, not wanting Jayne to dwell on her Level Four experiences at the Indoctrination Academy.

"I don't. I mean, I did. But after the Incident, I stopped playing."

Lesley was about to ask if she'd ever thought of taking it up again, but Jayne continued on.

"See, this is why I don't want to have children," she said. "Look at the fuss the letter caused. Just finding it had to involve Interior. Fortunately I know an Interior officer I can trust. Two, actually. But the existence of anything my parents breathed on is enough for Interior to get involved. How do you think it will be for any biological children I have? How do you think they'll feel when they find out who they are? I don't want to give life to a daughter, knowing what she'll face."

Lesley took a moment to choose her words. "I know how difficult it was for you, and what you sometimes face now. But any children we have will be in a different situation. In addition to us, they'll have three families who love them."

"Two families," Jayne murmured.

"Three. Carol and Ronald will be in their lives. They'll have parents who'll love and cherish and protect them. They'll have sisters who love them."

"They shouldn't have to worry about who loves them and who hates them," Jayne said, anguish creeping into her voice. "But they will. And they will face harassment because of their line. There's only one way to prevent anyone else from being ostracized because they have Adams blood, and that's not to perpetuate the direct line. So that's what I have to do."

Lesley could tell from Jayne's tone and posture that she wasn't going to budge, and tonight wasn't the right time to have this conversation, anyway. Jayne had brought it up, not her. But Lesley would bring it up again, because she hoped Jayne would change her mind, and Mo was waiting for a decision.

She went to Jayne, leaned over and embraced her tightly. When she drew back, she cupped Jayne's face in her hands and studied her, to reassure herself that Jayne would be okay. She'd always admired Jayne's strength, and she'd come to understand that Jayne was used to working through things alone, to the point that she preferred it. They were alike in that respect.

"I have to let it go, don't I?" Jayne said, surprising Lesley.

"You have to do what's best for you."

"What's best for me is to focus on what I have."

Lesley hugged her again, and felt herself smile when Jayne hugged her back.

"Give me a bit more time and I'll come down," Jayne said.

"Take all the time you need." Lesley gently kissed Jayne's forehead, then left, closing the door behind her. She couldn't imagine what it would be like to be in Jayne's situation, reading a letter that any loving mama would have written, but knowing the terrible things that mama had done, including abandoning the child who was meant to receive that letter. How could anyone reconcile the two? How would it ever make sense?

She was still thinking about it when she went into the living room. Mo looked up from the sofa. "How is she?"

"She'll be down soon." Lesley plunked next to her. "Did you read the letter?"

"I might have peeked." Mo's voice grew more animated. "She wanted me to read it. She was holding it so I could see."

Lesley had noticed. "She said she's going to let it go."

"She might be able to let it go, but will it let go of her?"

That was a question Lesley hoped time and love would answer in the affirmative.

THE NEXT AFTERNOON, Mo practiced her violin in the recreation room tucked at the back of the house, trying hard not to smash the instrument against the wall when she kept botching the same four bars. Her comm unit beeped, giving her an excuse to lay her violin down, carefully.

"I need a favour," Ann said, before Mo could get a word out. "But you have to promise me not to tell anyone, not even Lesley and Jayne."

Normally Mo would have snorted and told her to forget it, but Ann's voice lacked vigour. It was barely a whisper. "What do you need me to do?" she asked, figuring if she didn't explicitly agree to Ann's terms, she didn't have to keep them.

"You're planctside, right?"

"Yep."

"Can you come to the coordinates I send you and fly me home?"

Mo's curiosity shot up several notches. "Sure. Now?"

"Yeah."

"Okay, I'm leaving." Her violin and ears were relieved.

An aviacraft ride later, she landed at the coordinates Ann had given her, a holding area in B9. She didn't have to search for Ann because she could see her approaching the craft. Ann slid the door open and crawled into the passenger seat. Mo didn't want to pry, but she couldn't help it. Ann was as pale as a sheet. "What's going on?"

"What do you mean?"

"Come on. You look like you're about to collapse, and I can count on one finger how many times you've beeped me out of the blue to pick you up."

Ann leaned back in her seat and closed her eyes.

"I'm worried about you," Mo said. "Tell me something. Please."

Ann huffed a sigh. "If I don't tell you, you'll never shut up. So I guess I will, just so I don't have to listen to you the entire way home. I'm here because of my mama. She's in the infirmary here."

"Okay."

"She's dying."

Sympathy dampened Mo's voice. "I'm sorry."

"Some disease with a long name that they can slow down but can't cure. They've been slowing it down for years, but even when you slow something down, it gets there eventually, right?"

A question popped into Mo's mind, but she held her tongue. It would be insensitive to ask.

"The Chosen Council can't screen for it," Ann said, answering Mo's question. Perhaps other people hadn't been so sensitive. "I've been helping out, visiting. Not sure she cares." Ann gave Mo a wry smile, her eyes still closed. "I've also been donating blood. They can manufacture it, but at this stage, they need all they can get. Only one of my brothers and I are matches."

That explained the fatigue Mo had noticed before and could see now.

"They've been giving us something, but it's still tiring. Usually I take the train home, but I just couldn't face it today."

"So you beeped me."

"Yeah," Ann whispered.

"You could lie across the passenger seats in back," Mo suggested.

"No, I'm okay here." Her brow furrowed. "So are we flying home, or are we going to sit here chatting all day?"

Usually Mo would come up with some lame retort, but now wasn't the time. On the way to C3, Ann didn't say a word. Mo wasn't sure whether she was asleep. Dozing, maybe? She thought she'd have to nudge her awake when they landed, but as she approached the holding area nearest to the home Ann shared with Andrew, Ann's eyes opened. Mo smiled to herself. Ann had sound pilot instincts.

She brought the craft down and cut the flow to the energy cells. "So why don't you want Andrew to know?" she asked, not wanting to let Ann go without finding out.

"He doesn't need to know."

"Uh, if he's home, he's going to know right away that something's going on. Why are you lying to him? You're not doing anything wrong."

Ann stared out the aviacraft's window. "If I tell him about this, he'll find someone else."

"What do you mean?"

"He doesn't need this. It's not his problem."

"Of course it's his problem. Seriously?"

"My mama could survive for another month or two. He doesn't have to worry about me and my mama's flaming health. He can have anyone."

Mo couldn't believe her ears. "Wait, you think if he knew about this, he'd break up with you?"

"We're Solitaries, Mo. We don't have to stick around if we don't want to."

"You honestly think Andrew would break up with you because you're helping your mama and you're tired? If the situation was reversed, would you break up with him?"

Ann hesitated a beat. "No, but he has less to lose than I do. If I broke up with him, he'd be okay."

"And you wouldn't?"

Ann closed her eyes again.

"He wouldn't break up with you over this."

"But what if he does?"

"He won't."

"But if he does, I'll lose everyone," Ann whispered. "Losing him would be bad enough. I'd also lose you three. The twins. All the brothers and sisters and nieces and nephews." She swallowed. "I see myself as part of the family." Her eyes opened. She lifted her chin, in a display of defiance Mo was familiar with. "I know you don't, but I do."

Mo stared at her. "Of course you're part of the family. And as part of the family, you should have told us what was going on, so we could help you. And no matter what happens between you and Andrew, we'll still be friends. We were friends before you two even met." She'd introduced them, an act she'd once regretted but no longer did. "Sometimes you make me wonder about you. I know you don't have a good relationship with your family and maybe you think everyone wants to get away at the first sign of trouble, but Argamon, you're talking about a family that has a triad and embraced an Adams. Use your flaming head."

Ann's mouth turned up at the corners. "You're mad at me."

"Yeah, I'm mad, because you think we're that shallow, and I'm mad about Andrew because you're not trusting him. Tell him. Stop lying to him."

"I'll think about it."

"He's probably home. I'm sure he's noticed something and is agonizing over whether to ask or wait for you to smarten up. But if you don't want to tell him now, we can fly to my place and you can nap in the guest room."

"Can we do that?"

"Sure."

The aviacraft lifted off again. Mo glanced at Ann, torn between wanting to reassure her that everything would be okay and telling her off some more. She'd never explicitly acknowledged, to herself, or Ann, that Ann was part of the family, but she obviously was, and Mo was okay with that. At this point, Ann was one of her oldest friends, and someone she trusted, something she never would have believed would be true when they were at the Military Academy. Another way her life had turned out to be very different than she would have expected, but she wasn't complaining.

THE CACOPHONY OF voices emanating from the Indoctrination Academy's playroom quickened Lesley's pace, and she knew her Chosens were eager to see the twins too. She tuned out the shrieks and laughs and excited conversations and searched for them.

She spotted Ellie first, then Kat, who was never far away from her sister. "Mama Lesley is so happy to see you," she said, scooping Ellie into her arms and watching Mo do the same with Kat. She quickly did the once over. Ellie's cheeks were rosy and her eyes were sparkling.

"Show drawing," Ellie said.

Lesley knew what that meant, and that Jayne was waiting patiently to embrace her daughters. Ellie and Kat's feet touched the floor at the same time. Jayne crouched and stretched out her arms. The twins tumbled into her, shrieking with delight.

Mo caught Lesley's eye.

"She's such a good mama," Lesley murmured.

"But she's not ready. She might never be."

"What's that?"

Ah, Mama and Papa had arrived. Lesley turned to them. "We were just saying how well they look. We just got here," she added.

"Your papa and I have been wondering if you'll be making an announcement soon."

Mo chuckled. "I'm just finishing a class."

Mama frowned. "You'll carry the baby again."

"Yes, Adelaide, I'll carry the baby again. I want to do it. I'm looking forward to it."

Lesley appreciated Mo's overstated enthusiasm over what would be her second pregnancy, and her tiny lie about a class. What she really meant was she was refusing to get pregnant until she knew who would do it the next time. Fortunately Mama wouldn't be concerned about their fourth daughter until they'd had their third.

She watched the twins present the drawings they must have had nearby to their Mama Jayne, who was now sitting on one of the play mats covering the tiled floor. Lesley knew Jayne wasn't hearing anything but Ellie and Kat's voices, wasn't seeing anyone but them. When she was with the twins, they had her full attention. If only she could get past her fear about how others would react to daughters of her bloodline. If Jayne didn't have biological children, Lesley was sure she'd regret it. But she wouldn't force Jayne to have children, wouldn't bully or cajole or shame her into it.

Kat ambled over to her, a drawing flapping in her hand. Happy to think about something else, Lesley crouched to peer at it. As she praised Kat's creation, part of her mind remained on the decision Mo was waiting for. If Lesley were anyone else, she was sure the matter would be settled by now. She'd agree to carry their fourth daughter and that would be that.

But she was her, and she did not want to do it. Between the impasse over the triad's third pregnancy and her supervisor at work who seemed to have taken a dislike to her, she couldn't fully focus on the twins. She tried, but her worries kept intruding, and that saddened her and made her want to hug her daughters tight.

THE NEXT DAY, Jayne strolled next to Mo on the path that led to the estate's holding area. It was a blustery morning, with a breeze that stung and coloured Jayne's cheeks. She shoved her hands into her pockets.

"I wish I wasn't going up to 72 today," Mo said,

Surprised, Jayne glanced at her. "Why?"

"Two reasons, really. I'm getting tired of it."

Jayne wanted to say good. It wasn't as if she wanted Mo to be on the planet all the time, but when the twins had entered the Indoctrination Academy, Mo had made herself more available for supply patrols, and she'd volunteered to teach a course on the space station. Over the past month especially, she'd spent more time on 72 than off it. Jayne missed her, and knew Lesley did too. But she appreciated that Mo had passed on quite a few opportunities on 72 after the twins were born, and she'd soon get pregnant again.

"What's the second reason?" she said to Mo.

"Hoping you're okay."

This conversation was full of surprises. "You're worried about me?"

"The letter must have been a real letdown. I know you were hoping it would give you some answers."

She inwardly sighed. "I've got to stop hoping because it never works out."

"It did with Kevin Stewart. You found out more about the Incident."

But had it helped? Had it stilled any questions, or increased her understanding of why her papa had committed a Chosen Violation? No. If anything, it had made her angrier at him. She'd managed to get past it, but the knowledge had raised even more questions.

"Maybe it's time to stop hoping you'll get answers," Mo said. "Maybe it's time to accept that you'll never understand it and move on."

Jayne nodded. "It is. It's long past time. I even said so to Lesley, that I should move on. But saying it and doing it are two different things. I understand what's best for me up here." She tapped her right temple. "But I can't stop wondering. I want to let it go, though. I really want to."

"What about your counsellor? I know you never tell counsellors anything because you think they're useless, and in your case, I'll give you that some of what you've faced is beyond them, but moving on from it might not be."

"We don't discuss anything related to the Incident."

Mo snorted. "Of course you don't."

Jayne wasn't offended. She knew she could be stubborn. In this case, it wasn't the counsellor's fault. Counsellor Curious, as Jayne thought of her, was okay. She must have been horrified when she'd been assigned Jayne, the newest resident of C3 at the time, but Curious had always treated her kindly and fairly. "It's me who doesn't want to discuss it. I already know what I have to do."

"Then why haven't you done it?"

Sometimes she thought it was habit, that her brain was wired to wonder about her parents because she'd done so endlessly. Other times she couldn't help but ask how and why, often when she looked at Ellie and Kat and knew she could never, ever, do anything that would cause them to be ostracized for the rest of their lives. Those were the real questions she wanted answered. Details about the Incident would satisfy her curiosity, but she really wanted to know how they could have done that to her. Didn't they know what her life would be like afterward? Had they given her and Robert any thought at all, or had they been carried away by lust or whatever madness had gripped them. She'd gone through a phase where she'd told herself that perhaps they'd been ill, which might have worked for one Rymellan, but not four, and two of them Joined.

"I'm trying," she murmured. "When I overhear something about the Incident, or someone gives me the side eye, I've become good at reminding myself that I'm not them."

To counteract her instinctive reaction, she told herself that she was unique, that the Adams bloodline wasn't tainted because she wasn't weak in the Way.

"I know myself, or at least I think I do," she told Mo. "I've never committed a serious violation. The Chosen Council Joined me." She swallowed when Mo took her hand and squeezed it. "I'm winning the battle. I think. But I'm not sure my doubts about myself will ever completely go away. Lose their edge, maybe. Not surface as often. But still be there."

"Is that why you don't want to have children?"

"It's part of it." If she were honest, a small part. "I'm more worried about how any biological daughters of mine would be viewed and treated. Maybe I'll get past that. But I haven't yet."

"That's okay. Fortunately, you're in a triad."

"That's true."

Mo chuckled. "Bet you never thought you'd agree to that. Me, either."

Jayne smiled.

"But in this case, it works out. Les will get pregnant after me, and that will give you time to get ready."

Time might completely persuade her that her bloodline wasn't corrupted, that her daughters wouldn't be weak in the Way, that she wouldn't be tweaking her nose at the Way by having them, that they would handle any scorn directed at them because they'd be surrounded by love. But right now, the prospect felt scary. The moment she gave birth, she'd be asking herself if she'd done the right thing or had guaranteed heartbreak and pain in the future. It didn't help that the decision would be irreversible. There would be no way to go back, no way to fix any mess.

They reached the holding area. Mo let go of Jayne's hand and slid her aviacraft's door open, then turned back to Jayne. They embraced, and shared a tender kiss before drawing back and gazing at each other.

"I miss you two too much," Mo said with a sigh. "Oh well, only another couple of weeks and I'll be teaching at the Military Academy."

She brushed a hair out of Mo's left eye. "I'll miss you too."

Mo climbed onto the craft, then turned around. "Tell Les to hurry up and tell me she'll be carrying the next baby. I don't want to feel pressured. You know what happened last time."

Jayne didn't want Mo fretting, either. Maybe she'd get pregnant right away, or maybe it would take months again. "I'll talk to her," she promised.

She returned Mo's wave, then watched the craft lift off. Mo would be home in a few days, so Jayne didn't have much time. She was perplexed as to why Lesley hadn't already said she'd carry their fourth daughter. Normally she stepped in immediately when duty—and Mo—were involved. Carrying a daughter wouldn't stall her path to admiral, and it would make both her Chosens happy. It didn't make sense that she hadn't volunteered already. Jayne hadn't wanted to push her, but time was running out. She would have to force the conversation neither of them wanted to have.

TWO DAYS LATER, Lesley was writing another opinion she could do in her sleep when her comm station beeped. "The admiral would like to see you," said his assistant. "Can you come to conference room 12B in ten minutes?"

She agreed, wondering why Hall would want to speak to her personally.

When she entered the conference room, she swiftly quashed her alarm. Hall wasn't alone at the rectangular table. With him were Finney and Trenton. When Hall invited her to sit across from them, she surveyed their sober faces with dismay. Laura hadn't warned her.

Hall cleared his throat. "Thank you for coming, Commander. I wanted to speak with you and Commander Trenton because I've received complaints from Overseers Ferguson and Sanford about you."

Blood rushed to her cheeks. It didn't make sense. She hadn't written an opinion for them since Trenton had taken over, and they hadn't expressed dissatisfaction with her work prior to then.

"When overseers complain to me personally, I want to understand why they're upset." Hall clasped his hands on the conference table. "Commander Trenton, are you satisfied with Commander Thompson's work?"

Lesley didn't know where to look. She glanced at Laura, but Laura was looking at Trenton. Why was Laura even here? The overseers had complained to Hall, and Trenton was Lesley's supervisor. There was no reason for Laura to be included, though Lesley did belong to Laura's Chosen Tradition group. Hopefully Laura was there as a friend, but there had to be a reason Hall wanted her there. Had Trenton spoken to her about removing Commander Thompson from the Chosen Tradition group, or had someone in the group also complained about Lesley's work? Nothing made sense.

"The opinions she's written were satisfactory," Trenton said, in answer to Hall's question.

Hall's eyes narrowed. "But?"

Lesley swallowed.

"The commander isn't a good fit for my group."

"Why not?" Hall asked, his tone mild.

Hoping she appeared calm, Lesley gazed at Trenton. If Trenton was going to criticize her, she could at least look her in the eye, but Trenton was focused on Hall.

"May I speak freely?" Trenton said.

"Of course."

"While I understand that Commander Thompson has a sound record of service, I believe her circumstances mean she should be strictly supervised and not privy to anything that could be considered sensitive. That includes your Chosen Tradition group," Trenton said, glancing at Laura. "And certainly not patrols."

"What do you suggest she do?" Hall asked. "Run errands for officers?"

Lesley felt a glimmer of hope. Trenton smiled, as if Hall had told a joke.

"What did you mean by her circumstances?" Laura asked.

Trenton's brows rose. "Surely you know what I mean."

"I don't like to presume."

"Her constant contact with one of the Adams children."

Lesley quickly masked her surprise. Perhaps she should have anticipated Trenton's response, but she hadn't. The memory of standing huddled with Laura and her Chosens in a park, reading a letter written by Joan Adams by the light of a flashlight, burst into her consciousness. She wondered if Laura was thinking about the same thing. Even if she were, they had not violated the Way. Their intention had been to protect it.

"Even Rymellans strong in the Way aren't incorruptible," Trenton continued. "I'm not suggesting the commander has been corrupted, but that any prudent officer would be wary of the possibility."

"You're worried that her opinions might violate the Way," Hall stated.

"Not overtly, which is why I've been limiting her to straightforward ones. There's less of a possibility of weak ideas slipping into them unnoticed."

"I'm sure the overseers would notice anything that violated the Way," Laura said.

"Why let it get that far?"

Lesley might have spoken up for herself, if a suspicion hadn't formed in her mind about what she was doing here, listening to Hall question Trenton. Not her. Trenton.

"One of her Chosens isn't the only worrisome circumstance," Trenton said.

"What else is there?" Hall asked.

"My statement contains the answer. *One* of her Chosens. While triads aren't against the Way, they're an anomaly."

Lesley couldn't help but glance at Laura, who appeared unfazed.

"A triad, and close, sustained contact with one of the Adams children, warrants concern."

"Why do you think I've received complaints from the overseers?" Hall asked Trenton.

Trenton didn't hesitate. "I can't say for sure, but I'd imagine they share my concerns."

"Even though Commander Thompson wrote many opinions for them before you became her supervising officer? Why do you think they're only complaining now?"

"Perhaps they complained to Commander Blair but she didn't address their concerns, and out of deference to her, they didn't pursue it with you. Now that there's been a change in leadership, they've decided to come forward."

"That might make sense if they were concerned about Commander Thompson." Hall paused. "But they're not. They're upset because Commander Thompson is no longer writing opinions for them."

Trenton flushed but remained silent.

"They say they've asked you to **assign** projects to her, but you've ignored their requests. It has also come to my attention that you spoke to the patrol logistics officer about dropping the commander from the supply list. You haven't spoken to Commodore Finney about removing the commander from her Chosen Tradition group, but I'm sure you would have gotten to her eventually."

"I am merely trying to protect the Way," Trenton said indignantly.

"I can understand that, but we're all Interior officers. We all want to protect the Way. Is it your assessment that we're all too weak in the Way to do so?"

Trenton drew breath, then thought better of it.

"Would you like to say anything, Commander Thompson?" Hall asked Lesley.

Having grasped the purpose of the meeting, Lesley kept her words brief. "I'll let my record, both before and after I was notified, speak for itself."

Hall grunted. "I understand the situation now. Thank you all for meeting with me. Dismissed."

Lesley didn't glance at Trenton or linger in the corridor and wait for Laura. She returned to her office, and only allowed herself to think about what had just happened when she was safely inside it. She sank into her chair and slowly exhaled.

If she'd read the room correctly, her work life was about to improve. She hoped nothing terrible would happen to Trenton. Despite the commander's negative assessment of Lesley's capabilities and strength in the Way, Lesley appreciated that if the situation was reversed, she'd probably have her reservations too. But she'd handle it differently. Quietly double check opinions, speak privately to her superior officer about her concerns, and treat the officer in question courteously.

She wondered if there were others who secretly felt the same way as Trenton, who smiled at her in the corridor and said hello, but felt as if they'd just rubbed elbows with someone under the influence of a weak Chosen.

Her understanding around Jayne's reluctance to have biological children deepened, but her hope that Jayne would change her mind wasn't swayed. Lesley did not want to get pregnant, but she was coming to the terrible realization that she'd have no choice.

LATER THAT DAY, after a quiet supper, Jayne straightened when Lesley joined her on the swinging bench on the triad's front porch. Mo's frequent stays on 72 meant Jayne and Lesley were spending a lot of time alone together, which Jayne didn't mind. She'd enjoy it even more once the conversation she knew was about to happen was over. As she'd sort of promised to Mo, she'd suggested over supper that they sit outside for a while before having tziva, so they could talk, and Lesley had known exactly what she'd meant. Jayne didn't want to have to worry about a mug of hot liquid while having the discussion they both knew they had to have.

"We need to come to a decision," Lesley said, relieving Jayne of having to bring it up.

Jayne pushed the swing into motion. "I can explain again why I really don't want to do it."

"You're worried about any children you'll have."

"And about me. Selfish, I know, but I'm worried they'll hate me for having them."

Lesley's hand slipped into hers. "I doubt that will happen."

"I'm not so sure." Jayne moistened her lips. "Look, we can have the same conversation we've had many times now, and go around in circles, or you can accept that I don't want to do it. I know it places a burden on you, and Mo, but you two will be the only ones upset about me not carrying a child."

"That's not true."

"I think it is. The families would never say it out loud, but they'll be relieved."

Lesley shook her head. "I'm not so sure. In the beginning, yes. Now that they know and love you, no. They'll expect all of us to have biological children."

Jayne didn't agree with her. Whether they realized it or not, the Thompsons and Middletons wouldn't mind if she didn't reproduce. The Chosen Council would likely rejoice, too. The Adams line was their spectacular failure. If it wouldn't violate the Chosen Tradition, they would have changed her from a Chosen to a Solitary. She was surprised they hadn't done it anyway, given how the Way seemed to fade into the background where she was concerned.

"It's not as if we won't have more children after Mo carries the next one," Jayne said. "I won't get pregnant, but you will." When Lesley didn't respond, Jayne turned to look at her. "You'll get pregnant. Right?"

She frowned. She'd learned how to read her Chosen, maybe not as accurately as Mo, but close. Lesley's face, her posture, and her body language no longer made Jayne feel like she was trying to read a book written in Jessimite. She'd learned that the more controlled Lesley seemed, the more indifferent, the more distant, the greater the chances she was struggling. And right now, she appeared stoic, her eyes distant, her expression giving nothing away, but her fingers wound a little too tightly around Jayne's.

"You won't get pregnant?" Jayne murmured, confused.

"Have you ever wondered why there's only me, Karen, and Jason?"

She hesitated, wondering where this was going. "Not really."

"Mama and Papa wanted more. Mama, especially, believes that strong families have lots of children. It's not true. It's more a societal expectation. But she believes it. You know she's always proclaiming how strong in the Way our family is, so why do you think they only had three of us?"

Jayne had honestly never thought about it before. She was used to others questioning her strength in the Way. She was rarely the one doing the questioning, and Adelaide was right. The Thompsons were strong in the Way. They'd certainly stepped up and followed the Way when other families might have taken the easy way out and exercised CT134.

"Mama was pregnant more than three times. She had more miscarriages than pregnancies that made it to term."

"I'm sorry she went through that." She wasn't surprised that Adelaide had never said anything. It was too personal, and Jayne couldn't think of a conversation they'd ever had where it would have made sense for Adelaide to reveal her heartbreaking experience. "Is that why you don't want to get pregnant? You're afraid the same will happen to you?"

Lesley pulled her hand from Jayne's and left her side. She leaned against the porch railing, folded her arms, and stared down at Jayne. "I could say that, use it to wiggle out of this conversation. But it wouldn't be true, and it wouldn't be fair to Mama."

Jayne's confusion grew. She felt like she was in a dark room, feeling her way through it for a light she could turn on that would illuminate everything. She waited for more, but Lesley appeared uncomfortable.

"You can tell me anything," Jayne said, wanting to go to her, but knowing it was best to stay where she was. "You know that. Just tell me. Get it off your chest."

Lesley shifted her weight. "I don't want to get pregnant," she said softly.

"I know that, but—"

"No, I *really* don't want to do it. I've thought about it, tried to imagine it, and it feels alien to me. My entire being balks at it. I know that makes me sound weak in the Way, and maybe I am for feeling this way, but if I do it, I'll feel like I'm not me the whole time."

Jayne stared at her. Not wanting to say something inadvertently insensitive or dumb, she considered what Lesley had just confided to her. She didn't feel the same way. She could see herself pregnant. She just didn't want to create daughters who would always be whispered about, and she already worried that Ellie and Kat wouldn't love their Mama Jayne as much when they understood her lineage. They might even resent her, blame her for any difficulties they faced due to their closeness to the Adams line and the possibility they'd been negatively influenced by her.

"You're disappointed with me," Lesley murmured.

Jayne jerked herself out of her head and focused on her Chosen. "No. Absolutely not. You can't help how you feel. I'm sure you're not the only woman who feels that way." She paused. "But that doesn't change how I feel, which means we're at an impasse."

Lesley's arms were still folded. Jayne wished Lesley felt more comfortable, trusted her more. Lesley could tell her anything and Jayne would still love her, still see her as strong in the Way. "I suppose three children won't be acceptable for a triad," she said to her.

"Even if everyone else accepted it, and they wouldn't, Mama would be beside herself. Papa and Michael wouldn't be happy, either." Lesley tapped her fingers against her arms. "I understand where you're coming from, being worried about how your biological children would be treated. Rymellans who don't know you, who don't know us, can be quick to judge."

"Exactly. I know my children will be one generation removed in the sense that they never breathed the same air as my parents, but it probably won't matter. I was brought up by my parents. They'll be brought up by me. I don't know if the chain of suspicion, of assumed weakness, will ever end."

Lesley nodded. They fell silent, the only sound the crickets chirping, the only sensation a tension between them, which Jayne hated. She'd be perfectly happy with three children. She hadn't expected to have any. If only everyone else wouldn't judge, they could end this conversation, go inside, and spend a cozy evening together. Instead, nothing felt right. Nothing.

She almost jumped off the bench when Lesley unfolded her arms and pushed herself away from the railing. "One of us has to get pregnant, and I'm the logical choice. I'll do it."

"But—"

"It's not as if I can't get pregnant. And it's only nine months, right?"

Yes, but Lesley's distaste, her revulsion at the idea of herself carrying a child, was plain on her face and in her voice. "Let's just stop at three. Who cares what everyone else thinks?"

"We can't do that. You know we can't do that."

Jayne fervently wished they could. She did not want Lesley to be miserable for months because she was living in a state that didn't feel natural to her.

"I have to do it," Lesley said. "If I don't, and we only have three children, everyone will blame you. They'll forget we're a triad. They'll forget that Mo and I also decided to stop at three. They'll blame you. I can't let that happen. I have to stop being selfish." Lesley pulled her comm unit from its holder. "I'll beep Mo and tell her we've come to a decision and will tell her when she gets home tomorrow."

Lesley waited a few seconds. Jayne wished she could say, "No, it's okay. I'll do it." But the words wouldn't come, and she knew that even if she tried to speak, her voice wouldn't cooperate.

"Hey," Mo said cheerfully.

"Are you still coming home tomorrow?" Lesley asked.

"Yep."

"Jayne and I have had the conversation, and we've reached a decision."

Mo's voice lifted. "Tell me."

"We will. Tomorrow night."

"Come on."

"Tomorrow night," Lesley said, managing a smile.

"Okay, maybe I shouldn't have said I wouldn't go to the Reproductive Technology Centre until one of you committed to the next one. But you can't blame me, right? Tell me."

"We will. Tomorrow."

Mo groaned. "Okay. Tomorrow. Is Jayne listening to this?"

"Yes."

"Good. You're both awful."

"We're going to disconnect now."

"Okay. I have an important card game to get to anyway."

They said their goodbyes. Lesley slid her comm unit back into its holder. "At least it's settled." She met Jayne's eyes. "What I told you… keep this between us. Mo doesn't know."

Jayne inhaled sharply. Lesley couldn't have said anything that would have relayed her disappointment with herself, perhaps her shame, more than the three words, "Mo doesn't' know." Jayne wanted to reassure her that Mo would not judge her, that she'd understand, that how Lesley felt wasn't wrong or weak in the Way. But now wasn't the time. Not when her Chosen felt so vulnerable.

"I have some papers to read. I'm playing catch up with an opinion an overseer is waiting for."

Jayne wondered if that was true, or if she just wanted to be alone. "Do you want to continue our book later?" When Mo was on 72, they'd taken to reading together. Sometimes they read out loud to each other, sometimes to themselves, waiting until both had finished to go to the next page. It meant they snuggled, with a blanket over their laps and steaming tziva nearby.

"Sure."

Jayne felt her shoulders relax. Lesley didn't hate her, then. She remained on the bench long after Lesley had left, listening to the crickets. It was settled. She would not give life to daughters who would face what she had. She also had a Chosen who wanted to protect her, who would do something terribly difficult to prevent others from whispering about her. Jayne was loved, truly loved.

She felt terrible.

MO DISCONNECTED FROM Lesley and hurried out of her temporary quarters on 72. She hadn't been kidding when she'd said she had a card game to get to. Bruce had won most hands last night. She and the others wanted to make up for it tonight.

She groaned aloud when her comm unit beeped twice in the elevator.

Fortunately it was a dispatch, and at first she was going to ignore it. But what if it was Les again? Or Jayne. Or Papa. Or her superior officer.

It was from Andrew.

Okay, family, and he rarely sent her dispatches, so when she stepped off the elevator, she stopped at the first lounge area and read it.

I was going to beep you until I remembered you're on 72 and probably busy. Ann told me about her mama, and she told me you already knew because you picked her up once. Thanks for doing that. I know you kept your mouth shut because she asked you to. I'm still a bit irritated about it, though.

She would be too in his place.

She's seeing her mama again on Friday. Will you be down here? We can go on the train, but it would be nicer if you flew us home, so Ann can put her head down right away. Can you do that? Can you?

He was more than a little irritated. She replied to him.

Sorry I didn't tell you, but she wanted to tell you herself. Yeah, I'll fly you home. And whenever she has to go, we'll figure something out. If I can't go, Les might be able to. If neither of us can, we might know someone who can do it. At the very least, Jayne will be able to go with her on the train.

His reply came when she was pumping her fist into the air after winning the second hand. She took the time to read it, and for the rest of the evening, they carried on their exchange between hands.

Thanks. I don't know why Ann didn't tell me. Why did she lie to me?

Because she loves you, which I know makes no sense, but she was afraid of how you'd react. She didn't want to be a burden.

She had nothing to worry about. I'd do anything for her.

Mo had stopped wondering what he saw in Ann. She still didn't get it, but there must be something, and he seemed happy. *She's told you now. She was pretty wiped when I picked her up. If you can't be with her, she can sleep it off at our place. She did that last time.*

I'll go with her whenever I can, but it's good to know she won't be alone when I can't make it.

Their conversation had run its course. Mo was glad Ann had told him the truth. She'd known Andrew wouldn't be angry with her, or break up with her for being too much trouble. She had the feeling Ann would be around for while, and that would be okay.

Most of the time.

* * *

THE NEXT MORNING, Lesley finished the straightforward opinion Trenton had assigned to her the previous day and wondered how she'd fill the hours between now and when it would be acceptable to go home. Unfortunately idle hands meant she was free to think about the appointment she'd make at the Reproductive Technology Centre. The thought turned her stomach, even though it wouldn't happen for two to three years.

She almost wished it was happening right now, so she could get it over with. Then again, Jayne could change her mind in those two to three years. Lesley would hope, but would not pressure her in any way, overtly or subtly. She understood Jayne's concerns. She'd always known it was unlikely that Jayne's biological children would escape the Learning and Indoctrination Academies unscathed.

But she'd also always believed their children would endure whatever was thrown their way, that they would thrive, because they were so loved. Their situation would not be the same as Jayne's had been. They would still have their families. They would not be lost and bewildered, and made to feel as if they were worthless and should have been executed.

Pregnant. She tried to imagine it, but the prospect seemed so alien to her, and so repulsive, that she gave up. Not repulsive when others were pregnant. Just her. Was Jayne right? Were there other women who felt the same way, who would rather do anything but carry a child and give birth? Only those same-oriented could pass the responsibility on to someone else. She felt for diff-oriented women who couldn't.

She'd have to do it, no matter how much her mind and body balked at the notion. And she'd have to do it at least twice, to be fair. Perhaps thinking about it until her time came would get her more used to the idea, or numb her to it. Or perhaps it would make things worse and fill her with dread.

A knock at her open door broke into her thoughts. Grateful, she motioned for the stranger to enter.

"Good morning, Commander," the male officer said. "I'm Commander Waters. I've taken over the opinions group."

"What happened to Commander Trenton?"

"The admiral determined she wasn't a good fit for the position. She's moved on to another post at the military headquarters in Sector A4."

Lesley hoped it wasn't a demotion. As much as Trenton's behaviour had been unfair, Lesley understood it. If she was honest, she and everyone else in this headquarters would have been wary of any officer Joined to an Adams, triad or no, if Lesley had not been the officer who was Joined to one, an officer they were already familiar with. The experience with Trenton had taught her that if she was ever moved to another location, something she didn't expect would ever happen, she would likely face suspicion from her peers.

"I'm pleased to meet you," she said to Waters.

"Likewise. I'm dropping in on everyone, but I came to you first. I just dispatched an urgent assignment to you from Overseer Ferguson." Waters smiled. "He wants it done yesterday, and done by you. Just so you know how I work, I will be reading everyone's first and second opinions, to get a feel for what you can each do."

"That's understandable." Lesley didn't want another officer to lose out, though. "I believe Lieutenant Crofton has been writing some opinions that would usually be given to me. If she did well, she'd likely appreciate more challenging assignments."

"That's good to know. Well, I'll let you get to that assignment. My door is always open."

He wheeled and left. The tension that had dogged her since it had become obvious that Trenton was treating her oddly drained from her body. Next time she saw Laura socially, she'd ask what had happened to Trenton. She assumed Waters had been asked if he'd have a problem working with her, and wondered if all her future superior officers would be asked the same question before being assigned to B2 Military Headquarters.

For now, she was happy to have a substantial assignment to sink her teeth into, though as she read the overseer's request, part of her mind lingered on an appointment that already loomed large, even though it was at least two years away. She and Jayne would tell Mo tonight, which would make it real. When the time came, Lesley wouldn't be able to back out, no matter how desperately she'd want to.

* * *

Lesley's improved mood over Trenton's departure dissipated as she flew home. By the time she strode into the living room, where she knew Mo would be waiting, she would have done anything to avoid the inevitable conversation and the commitment she would make.

Mo wasn't alone. Jayne was waiting too, and motioned for Lesley to sit next to her on the sofa. With Mo sitting across from them in an armchair, Lesley was reminded of the brief meeting she'd had with Hall, Laura, and Trenton, except this time she wasn't alone on her side of the imagined table.

"I figured we'd get this conversation out of the way and then have supper," Mo said.

Lesley suspected Mo was afraid that if she didn't make them tell her right away, they'd stall again. When Jayne took her hand, she absent-mindedly hung on to it as she willed herself to begin the conversation that would seal her fate.

"Jayne and I talked," she said, "and we—"

"I'm going to get pregnant," Jayne said.

Mo gaped. Not even trying to mask her surprise, Lesley looked at Jayne.

"Are you sure?" Mo said, her eyes on Jayne, to Lesley's relief. "You seemed so against it."

Lesley wanted to add, "Even in the conversation we had just last night," but she held her tongue. She wished she could look into Jayne's eyes, but Jayne hadn't so much as glanced at her.

"I thought about it, and I decided I shouldn't limit myself because of what my parents did. I'm not them."

Mo smiled. "No, you're not."

"Are you sure?" Lesley asked. "I know we, uh, talked about it, but are you sure?"

Finally Jayne looked at her, at the same time her fingers tightened around Lesley's. "I'm sure. I want to do it. And I'll be doing it at least twice, because I'll want one with each of you."

"When you say twice, do you mean one after the other?" Mo asked.

Family Comes First

Jayne nodded.

"And what about you, Les? You must want a chance."

"Well, um—"

"Let's worry about the next three pregnancies first," Jayne said.

"Three!" Mo clapped her hands. "That'll make five daughters."

Would it be enough? Lesley wasn't sure, and she wouldn't worry about it now. She was still reeling over Jayne's decision to have a biological daughter. If Jayne really didn't want to do it, Lesley didn't want her to. She wanted to ask Jayne if she was sure again, but she'd wait until they were alone, which wouldn't be for a while, because her two Chosens were already talking about going out to supper to celebrate three pregnancies that hadn't happened yet.

"I'll beep the Reproductive Technology Centre tomorrow." Mo leaped to her feet. "Let's go eat."

Lesley forced herself to let go of Jayne's hand. She wanted to thank her. She wanted to hug her. Most of all, she wanted to ask her why. One little word, and the word that remained on her mind throughout the evening.

JAYNE WASN'T SURPRISED when Lesley cornered her when she was getting ready for bed. She'd expected Lesley to catch her alone ever since she'd uttered the words, "I'm going to get pregnant." Since then, she'd alternated between believing she'd lost her mind, and trusting that it would be okay.

Lesley quietly shut Jayne's bedroom door. "I don't know what to say."

She met Lesley's eyes. "Say you're happy we're going to have a daughter." Saying it out loud like that made it real. Her fear burst to the surface. Suddenly her chest felt tight and she couldn't breathe.

Lesley grasped her shoulders and pulled her into a hug. "You don't have to do it. I'm willing to do it."

"But you don't want to. You really, really don't want to." Jayne slipped her arms around Lesley's waist and pressed her cheek against hers. "It'll be okay. Everything you and Mo have said is true. They'll have us, they'll have Kat and Ellie and our third daughter. We'll make sure they know they're loved. I have to believe it won't be as bad for them as it was for me. And I'll be able to help them through whatever they face."

"But you knew all that before," Lesley said.

"Intellectually, yes." She drew back just enough so she could gaze into Lesley's lovely blue eyes. "But do you know what finally got through to me and made me actually believe it?" She didn't wait for an answer. "You, willing to get pregnant to protect me, even though it's the last thing you want to do. So I wouldn't be blamed for a triad having so few children." Her eyes teared up, but she didn't care. "When I thought about that, I understood, believed, that it'll be okay. Because they'll be born into love, and raised with love, and told every day they're loved." And when she'd understood that and decided she would step up and have children, nothing inside her had rebelled. She was afraid, yes, for reasons no other Rymellan had to worry about.

But what she'd told her Chosens was true. She'd decided not to let Rymellans she didn't know make such a monumental decision for her, especially when Lesley had confided in her, told her the real reason why she didn't want to get pregnant. Lesley and Mo had stuck by her when many others would have cast her aside. She refused to ask more of Lesley, when all that had been stopping her from agreeing to have a child was fear. Her apprehension about things that might happen. It showed a lack of trust in not only herself, but in her Chosens. And that was wrong. Forget about what others thought. Jayne would not dishonour the two women she so dearly loved.

All their daughters would be born into love, into strength, into families who would always stand with them. And if—when—Rymellans whispered ugly things about them, or said those ugly things to their faces, Jayne would have a few things to teach them about how to weather the storm.

Still.

"I'll worry about it. I'll fret. But that doesn't mean it's not what I want."

"You'll have us. And I already know they'll be wonderful daughters."

Their arms tightened around each other. Jayne closed her eyes and laid her head on Lesley's shoulder. If only she could keep those daughters in a bubble and only expose them to those who loved them. But she knew that to rebuff those who scorned her without knowing her, she must be willing to have daughters who would face scorn too.

"Don't be alone tonight," Lesley said.

Jayne had already planned to spend the night with them. She did that most nights Mo wasn't on 72. They drew back from each other and went into the hallway. Jayne felt compelled to embrace Lesley again. She'd get used to the idea of perpetuating her line at some point. Tonight, she wanted to cling.

Mo bounded up the stairs and stopped. "Are we celebrating?" She grinned. "Triad hug."

As she had many times before, Jayne held out one of her arms while still holding Lesley with the other, and knew Lesley was doing the same. Mo tucked herself into the space they'd created. She fit perfectly.

"We're going to be mamas again," Mo said. "And have at least five daughters. But you know Jayne, our next one will make three for Les and me officially. Are you really going to stop at one each?"

Jayne chuckled. Maybe. She'd see how the first two went and then decide. For now, she wanted to stay right where she was, in this moment with Lesley and Mo.

The Adams line would go on. Time would determine whether her decision to throw caution to the wind and give birth to scorned daughters was the best or worst decision she'd ever made. Here, in her Chosens' arms, she believed historians, and Rymellans who would see her parents as criminals for years to come, would judge her kindly.

Author's Note

Thank you for reading Decisions.

Be the first to hear about upcoming releases. Join my mailing list and get a free story. You can unsubscribe at any time.

Subscribe here: http://sarahettritch.com/salbine

Books by Sarah Ettritch

The Salbine Sisters Series

Playing With Fire
The Salbine Sisters
Rose and Nora
Salbine's Embrace

The Rymellan Series

Disobedience Means Death
Shattered Lives
The Triad
Decisions

The Deiform Fellowship Series

The Atheist
The Cult
Unseen Bonds
Scarred Souls

The Daros Chronicles

Pawns and Puzzles
Fate or Folly

Standalone Titles

Love Me for Me
Threaded Through Time
The Missing Comatose Woman
Their Last Hope
The Voice in My Head
The Perfect Christmas Gift

Thanks for reading!

www.ingramcontent.com/pod-product-compliance
Lightning Source LLC
Chambersburg PA
CBHW060727190726
48285CB00001B/108